DATE			

The
Accidental
Bride

The
Accidental
Bride

a romantic comedy

Janice Harayda

St. Martin's Press ❧ New York

This book is a work of fiction. Names, characters, places, and incidents are a product of the author's imagination, except in the case of historical figures and events, which are used fictitiously.

All quotations from Jane Austen represent an attempt to preserve, as faithfully as possible, her original spelling, punctuation, and capitalization.

ISBN 0-312-20357-8

First Edition: June 1999

10 9 8 7 6 5 4 3 2 1

With love to
Hans and Phyllis Heilbronner,
for reasons that would
require another book to list

and

With special thanks to
Ned Samuelson,
who proves that being a great reader
is not incompatible with having
an eighty-nine-mile-an-hour tennis serve

"An engaged woman is always more agreeable than a disengaged. She is satisfied with herself. Her cares are over, and she feels she may exert all her powers of pleasing without suspicion. All is safe with a lady engaged; no harm can be done."

—Mansfield Park

The
Accidental
Bride

1

Place Cards

"If I were to marry, I must expect to repent it."

—Emma

O ne month before her wedding to the third richest man in the second largest city in Ohio, Lily Blair awoke in the middle of the night and realized that she did not want to get married. This turn of events did not faze her mother, who regarded brief lapses of sanity as inevitable among young women on the brink of matrimony.

Upon hearing the news the next day, Charlotte Blair scarcely looked up from her computer, which perched atop a table in the sunny yellow breakfast nook that she had converted into the war room for her daughter's wedding. The screen displayed a dozen circles, each of which held eight rectangles, representing tables and place cards at the reception.

"I'm afraid that canceling the wedding is quite impossible," she said. "The caterer's deposit is nonrefundable. If you and Mark had wanted to elope like Todd and Isabelle, you should have said so earlier."

Todd, Lily's older brother, lived in Paris and, a few years

earlier, had sent his parents a telegram announcing that he had married the woman who shared his apartment on the Avenue Victor Hugo. A photograph of the couple, holding hands in a field of lavender, stood on a shelf in the breakfast nook. Allowing her eye to rest on a row of white wicker baskets filled with fabric swatches and sample menus, Lily took a moment to steady herself.

"I don't want to elope," she replied calmly. "I don't want to get married at all. This is not about 350 veal medallions. This is about my life."

Charlotte Blair tapped a computer key, which caused a rectangle to dart from one circle to another. "Darling, don't be melodramatic. It's one of your least attractive characteristics."

"I'm not being melodramatic."

"Oh, yes, you are. You've always had a theatrical streak. I nearly died of embarrassment the year you insisted on dressing up as Ethel Rosenberg for Halloween. Every other child on the block was content to be something normal, like Cinderella or Little Red Riding Hood. But you had to parade up and down the street with a sign that said, I WAS FRAMED."

"That's how Mark and I got together, remember? When we met at the fund-raiser for the museum, he told me he had defended Julius Rosenberg in a mock trial in the fifth grade. He said he knew it was fate when he learned that I had gone trick-or-treating as Ethel."

Charlotte Blair ignored the comment and returned to her daughter's earlier point.

"Anyway, what makes you think life isn't about veal medallions?" she asked. "In your twenties you think life is about things like truth and beauty and the effects of acid rain on Micronesia. In your fifties you know it's about what's for dinner, should we renew the snow-removal contract, and do we still like the Hapwoods now that they're divorced?"

"That's exactly why I want to—"

"Now, tell me. Whom don't the Jensens speak to?"

Gwen and Ed Jensen were the favorite aunt and uncle of Lily's fiancé, Mark Slayton. They were also the most self-effacing members of a family that had attached its name to several streets, a shopping mall, and the head-injury wing of a distinguished teaching hospital. Lily knew no one who did not like them.

"The Jensens speak to everybody," she said, taken aback. "They might be the only people in Mark's family who do. They even like their sadistic seven-year-old grand-nephew who sets fire to the monogrammed cocktail nap-kins at every reunion."

"Nonsense. Everybody doesn't speak to somebody. So everybody can't sit next to somebody at a wedding recep-tion. Think, Lily. There must be somebody whom the Jen-sens have threatened to disinherit, or a former baby-sitter who claims that Ed played footsie with her under the ta-ble."

"I've told you," Lily said, "the wedding is off. The Jen-sens aren't going to be sitting next to anybody, because there isn't going to be any reception."

Her mother moved several more rectangles from one circle to another. Frowning, she studied the result as though she were Gary Kasparov contemplating an unset-tling variation on the Sicilian defense.

"This is absurd. All your life you've envied your Grand-mother Blair's Audubon silver pattern. Now you have your own service for forty-eight, and you want to send it back. And what about that dreadful bathroom shower Mark's sisters gave for you? It was bad enough that you had to spend an afternoon opening rolls of toilet paper embossed with the Ohio State University seal. Think how embarrassing it would be to have to write notes returning them all."

"It won't be embarrassing. I'll just send Penny and Fran notes saying, 'I'm sorry to inform you that, now that my wedding is behind me, your toilet paper will never be.'"

"Lily, I don't find this amusing. The final fitting for your dress was last weekend, the invitations have gone out and many of the guests have made their travel arrangements. This is nothing to joke about."

"I'm not joking."

Her mother closed her eyes the way Lily had seen her do when she had come across one of Hieronymus Bosch's paintings of hell in an art book.

"You know that I have been under a great deal of stress because of this wedding. Please don't add to it by telling me you are serious about calling the whole thing off."

"I'm not trying to add to your stress. I'm trying to end it by telling you that you will never again have to worry about whether you should have ordered the cassis instead of the Grand Marnier sorbet as a palate cleanser, because three hundred and fifty palates will no longer need cleansing."

Lily's mother turned away from her *World of Weddings* software program without rising from her chair.

"I knew I should have insisted that you get a Valium prescription from Dr. Burns," she said gloomily. "No bride in her right mind ever approached her wedding day without gaining a new appreciation of the contribution that tranquilizers have made to the human race. Tess Mahoney has been married three times and says she would never have made it through any of her engagements if she hadn't kept a Valium tucked into her bra for emergencies. Let me call Dr. Burns and see if he can prescribe one over the phone."

"My generation doesn't take Valium. We're the flag-bearers of Prozac Nation. But I don't need a tranquilizer."

"Then you need a drink. The trouble with your generation is that you've never come to terms with the value of a properly mixed martini."

Lily shook her head. Much as she disagreed with her mother, she envied her simple pietistic faith in the things she saw as the underpinnings of civilization, such as the sterling silver vermouth dropper.

"A drink won't help any more than a Valium will. And you'd be surprised at how many members of my generation drink martinis—they're back in style now."

Charlotte Blair looked out the window of the breakfast nook. She appeared to focus on the pink-and-white geraniums along a footpath from the terrace to the back-yard, where the reception was supposed to take place under a huge tent. Despite an underground sprinkler system and a gardener who came twice a week, the flowers were browning at the edges.

"This heat—" she began, then turned abruptly toward her daughter. "Wait! It's the heat, isn't it? The heat wave is making you act this way. Nobody likes living in an apartment without air-conditioning in weather like this. But if that's the problem you can move back into your old bedroom here until—"

"Mother, you don't call off a wedding because you live in an un-air-conditioned apartment."

"Then why do you call it off?"

"Because I don't want to get married."

"Nonsense. Every woman wants to get married."

"I'm not every woman, and I'm not ready to commit to settling down with Mark and spending the rest of my life in Colony Heights."

"What's wrong with Colony Heights? You didn't complain about it when you were playing tennis at the club every day, or giving parties in a backyard ten times the size of that overpriced garret you had in New York."

Lily knew that she would only enrage her mother by admitting that she found Colony Heights a stodgy and oppressive suburb of a dismal Rust Belt city that had never recovered from the collapse of its manufacturing base. She decided to tell the least disputable version of the truth.

"What's wrong with Colony Heights? The weather. You always said I don't look good in gray, and the only sunny days we seem to have in this part of Ohio come in the middle of droughts like the one we're having now."

"So you admit that the heat is getting to you."

"No, I don't. I'm only saying that, if bad weather were a federal offense, Colony Heights would be the Jimmy Hoffa of suburbs. Racketeering charges would follow it to the grave."

"In other words, you would rather live someplace like New York, where you have to take an elevator up to the roof to see the sky."

"I didn't say that."

"But you thought it."

Lily considered how to respond to this. She loved New York and had returned to Colony Heights only because her current employer, the *Daily Rectifier*, had recruited her when her New York paper was rumored to be about to fold. At that vulnerable moment, she convinced herself that unemployment might be worse than going back to a city in which a councilman's wife once turned down an invitation to the White House because it conflicted with her cha-cha lessons. So she had shelved her misgivings about working for a paper whose name reflected that bizarre form of Midwestern optimism that cast anything short of a nuclear holocaust as a temporary setback.

She had never intended to stay at the *Daily* forever and, until she became engaged to Mark, had been planning to look for a New York job after she had been at the paper for a year. But she could hardly say this without at once offending her mother and conceding her point.

"I didn't come here to talk about New York," she said evenly. "I came here to talk about my wedding."

Charlotte Blair toyed with a swatch of fabric from the gown of one of Lily's bridesmaids, then looked sharply at her daughter.

"Sally put you up to this, didn't she?"

Lily had chosen Sally Levin, a police reporter she had worked with in New York, as her maid-of-honor despite the vehement objections of her mother, who believed that respectable women did not earn their living interviewing convicted felons. Charlotte Blair tossed the fabric swatch back into its wicker basket.

"I must have been out of my mind to let you have a maid-of-honor who is probably going to come to the wedding on the arm of a serial killer."

"Mother, they don't let you out of Sing Sing so you can do the Bunny Hop at fancy weddings in Colony Heights. Besides, Sally doesn't date her sources. It's a journalistic conflict-of-interest." Lily glanced at a box of ecru envelopes lined with tissue paper. "Now, do you think we could have a sensible discussion about how to recall all the wedding invitations?"

"How can we have a sensible discussion about such a silly idea? Do you know how many women would love to marry someone who has just been ranked the third richest man in the city by its leading financial journal?"

"Are you saying I should marry Mark because he is rich? You didn't marry Daddy for his money."

Lily saw an odd look cross her mother's face, a strange

mix of guilt and regret. An alarming silence fell between them.

Charlotte Blair took a sip of Armagnac from the crystal snifter next to her computer—she viewed martinis as a predinner drink—and avoided Lily's gaze.

"Mark is more than rich," she said, choosing her words the way she picked over cherries for clafoutis. "It's true that his grandfather left him a fortune. But he is also handsome, charming, and a partner in the largest law firm in the city. Frankly, I think you should give serious thought to the likelihood that—if you don't marry Mark—you will be making the biggest mistake of your life."

"I have given serious thought to it, and I think I may be making the biggest mistake of my life if I do marry Mark. That's why I'm not going through with the wedding."

Her mother took another sip of Armagnac. She looked at Lily the way a doctor might examine a patient whose electrolyte levels had gone through the roof but who showed no outward symptoms of disease.

"All right," she said wearily. "Tell me what you want. Buffalo chicken wings instead of veal medallions at the wedding reception? You can have the chicken wings. I'd rather pay a little more to change the menu than lose the caterer's deposit altogether."

"I said, this is not about veal medallions."

"Your fat cousin Libby out of the bridesmaids' lineup? I'll talk to Aunt Grace. She'll be hurt, but she'll be over it by the time you and Mark have your first child."

Lily looked at her mother in disbelief. For someone who owned eight pairs of white gloves and a set of pearl-handled fish knives, the woman could be ruthless.

"Libby's not fat. She's just a muscular field hockey player. Besides, I like her. I wouldn't exclude somebody from my wedding party just to make the pictures look better."

"Your dress, then? I noticed that you looked a little queasy at the bridal salon the other day, but I thought the fitter might have stuck you with a pin."

In fact, Lily had not decided to call off the wedding because of her gown. She had not consciously decided to do anything but had simply awakened at 3 A.M. knowing that she could not go through with the ceremony. The idea had resembled a revelation more than a decision.

But her dress was so far from what she at first had wanted that she had come to see it as a symbol of all that she was trying to escape. Since becoming engaged she had felt that her life was rushing forward without her, driven by the self-propelled engine of her approaching marriage. She measured the distance lost in the yards of billowy white tulle gathered into the train of her wedding gown.

At the age of seven, she had been a flower girl at the wedding of her Aunt Grace, who had married in her mid-thirties in an intimate ceremony in a friend's rose garden. The bride had worn a wisp of a dress, in the palest of pinks instead of white, and carried a nosegay of violets. Lily was enchanted. If she married, she thought—*if*—she would want the kind of day her Aunt Grace had.

Instead her wedding had turned into a production number that might have been choreographed by Busby Berkeley, the Mormon Tabernacle choir, and a graduate school of restaurant management. Her parents could have sold ads for the gilt-edged booklets the ushers were to hand out at the church.

Worse, the more lavish the wedding had become, the bigger the dress it had seemed to require, until Lily found herself being fitted for a gown suitable for the bride of a Crown Prince of Luxembourg. Which, in turn, called for a cathedral-length veil and a bouquet so large, her father joked that the florist might have to lower it into her arms with a forklift.

Despite all this, Lily said that her dress was not an issue. This was more or less true, now that it would never leave the bridal salon.

"But if you're not upset about your reception or your bridesmaids, or your gown, this doesn't make any sense," her mother replied, getting up from her chair and beginning to pace. "Every time I talk to Isabelle, she tells me how much she wishes she'd had a big wedding like yours."

"Isabelle also votes Socialist, lets five-year-old Sylvie drink from her wineglass, and thinks that all of America's problems could be solved by the establishment of topless beaches up and down the East Coast. Would you want me to take her advice on those things, too?"

Her mother dismissed the comment with a wave of the hand that did not hold her Armagnac snifter. "Isabelle can't help it if she's a Trotskyite exhibitionist who views Château Latour as a health food. The French have these things in their blood. You had the best American upbringing that money could buy. And yet you've been saying since you were a girl that you didn't want to get married—"

"And I still—"

"You wouldn't even play with bride dolls. It broke my heart when you showed no interest in that beautiful porcelain bride your father and I bought you in Copenhagen, with its own rhinestone tiara. But I said nothing, because I knew you'd get over it when you met the right man. Now you've met the right man, and you're still acting like a child."

"Walking away from the wedding might be the most mature thing I've ever done."

"How can you do this to me?"

"I'm not doing it *to* you. I'm doing it *for* me."

"You may think that now, but you'll regret it later."

"If I regret it later, I can marry Mark later."

Her mother acted as though she said she could buy the Astrodome later. "Do you think you can expect a man like Mark to wait around until you recover from whatever has come over you?"

"Why not? Isn't that what women do all the time for men?"

"Don't bring Gloria Steinem into this," her mother snapped. "She puts ideas in people's heads."

Lily did not know how to respond to this.

"Even if you don't care what I think, have you no respect for your grandmother?" her mother continued. "She will never get over this. The whole time she was recovering from her hip-replacement surgery, she kept saying she wanted to be able to walk down the aisle at your wedding. Now that she's back on her feet again, I have to hit her with this."

"You don't have to hit her with anything," Lily said. "I'll talk to her." She paused. "Where is Gran, anyway?"

"She's in Maine with Mr. Brooks."

Lily's paternal grandmother lived in a mother-in-law wing of the Blairs' stately neo-Georgian home when she was not traveling. She had met Austin Brooks several years after becoming widowed and, since then, had taken almost all of her vacations with him. Much as she envied her grandmother's energy and independence, Lily wished that she had not chosen such a moment to spend on a weather-beaten island accessible only by ferry. She had always found her grandmother to be her fearless champion in her battles with her mother.

"I don't think you're giving Gran enough credit," Lily

said. "An anthropologist who did fieldwork in New Guinea isn't likely to be undone by my violating the mating rituals of a tribe that wears belts with spinnakers on them."

Lily instantly regretted the unkindness of the remark about the spinnakers and tried to soften its impact.

"Remember when I was eleven and polled everybody in the family about how old a girl she should be before she started dating?" she asked. "Most people said, 'Thirteen.' Gran said, 'Thirty.' "

Ignoring the comment, her mother looked across the room toward the Regency carriage clock on the breakfront.

"None of this would have happened if your father hadn't gone to his club tonight. He would tell you how selfishly you are behaving."

"He can't change my mind on this one. This doesn't involve him."

"But it does involve Mark. May I ask what he thinks of all this?"

Lily felt slightly flustered. "Well, actually, he doesn't know yet. He's in California trying that big age-discrimination case he's been working on. I plan to tell him as soon as he returns. But it just didn't seem right to break the news to him over the telephone and in the middle of a trial that's so important to his firm."

"You came all the way over here to tell me about something that Mark is only going to talk you out of anyway?"

"He isn't going to talk me out of this."

"You always say that Mark can talk anybody into anything, and it's true. That man could talk the double-glazing off a storm window. That's why he's such a successful lawyer."

"Might I have some credit for being able to resist his extraordinary powers?"

"You didn't resist when he gave you a diamond the size of a sweet potato."

Lily blinked. "I didn't ask for a diamond the size of a sweet potato. A five-carat ring was Mark's idea."

"But you didn't reject it any more than you're going to reject the wedding."

The two women's eyes met. Lily sat very still as an idea took shape in her mind.

"Would you like to see me reject this ring?" she asked. "All right, I'll show you I can do it."

Lily walked into the kitchen, took a dish towel off a hook near the Aga, and hung her ring in its place.

"I'm going to leave this here as a reminder that you are not going to see me walk down the aisle of Holy Family Cathedral a month from now. I'm sorry, but I can't do it."

Charlotte Blair shut off her computer and walked to the window overlooking the yard in which her daughter's reception was to take place. She had just written a five-figure check to have the lawn resodded for the wedding.

"Oh, God," she said. "This is why I wanted only boys."

2

Red Light

". . . you are quite the Stranger at home."

—The Watsons

After leaving her parents' house, Lily drove to her health club, where she ran into Edie Vogel. Atop her exercise bicycle, Edie alternately read a book called *Men and Other Reptiles* and lamented the difficulty of meeting the sort of lizards who came up to her standards. She chided Lily for working out in gray sweat pants and no makeup.

"Honey, you're never going to land a husband that way," she said. "Trust me, no man wants to marry somebody who looks like the girl next door."

Lily almost regretted having left her engagement ring at her parents' house. Studying herself after her workout in the full-length mirror in the aerobics room, she realized that her chestnut hair had lost some of its gloss since she had returned to Ohio, and that she had grown so slender that she could count her ribs through the leotard she wore under her sweat pants.

As she changed into her street clothes, Lily was stung

by the criticism of her looks. In Manhattan she had a loyal circle of friends whom she could count on to admire every new haircut or Henry Lehr blouse; in Colony Heights no one except Mark praised her appearance. Her fiancé's older sisters, Penny and Fran, insisted that her wardrobe was "too New York" for Ohio—all her dresses were either too short or too black—and offered to take her to shops with more suitable clothes.

Still deflated by the markdown of her appearance, Lily left the club and returned to her apartment. There she saw the red light on her answering machine blinking six times and hit the Play button:

1. *"Hi, sweetheart. How are you holding up in the heat wave that I hear has hit the Midwest? Hope things out in Ohio are better than they are out here. We've drawn the worst judge possible for the case—an ex-litigator named Arch Ferguson, better known as Winks Ferguson for his habit of nodding off on the bench. Apparently part of the challenge of winning a case in his courtroom is getting him to stay awake long enough to hear your evidence. It looks as though the trial will last about a week. Hope your day went better. Love you."*

2. *"Hello, Ms. Blair? This is Jill at the Heart and Sole shoe salon. We have great news for you! Your bridal shoes are in. Can you stop by and pick them up tomorrow?"*

3. *"Hi, sweetheart, me again. We just got back from dinner and are about to settle down for a couple more hours' work. We hope to finish by midnight. In case you're at your parents', I'll try you there. Lots of love."*

4. "Lily, it's your father. Could we meet for lunch at the Commodore's Club tomorrow? My secretary will call you tomorrow morning to work out the details."

5. "Hi, sweetheart, where are you? I called your parents' house, and your mother said she didn't know. She just kept asking whom my Aunt Gwen and Uncle Ed don't speak to. Do you think the strain of the wedding is getting to her a little? I'm about to turn in, so I guess we'll miss each other tonight."

6. "Miss Blair? It's Jeremy Ryan, the new night copy intern at the *Daily.* Sorry to bother you at this hour. But, in your story for tomorrow's paper, you have a quote from somebody named Henry James. As you know, the *Daily* has a policy of identifying all sources by their age and place of residence. Could you call in as soon as possible and let me know how old this guy is and where he lives?"

After performing mental triage on her messages, Lily called the *Daily* and learned that the copy intern had gone home. That bothered her less than the news that Mark might not return for another week. To keep him from hearing about her decision secondhand, she would have to avoid talking about it with almost everyone but her parents, the risk of leaks being otherwise too high in a town in which both of their families were well known.

Replaying her messages, Lily felt the full weight of her engagement. Less than a year earlier, at twenty-six, she had returned to the Rust Belt with no romantic prospects and few hopes that any would emerge in a city in which most of her peers had married soon after high school or college.

Dating soon became redundant. The men who asked her out were nearly interchangeable, with a literal turn of mind and enough confidence in their own charms to ensure that they would remain charmless to all but the women who eventually would marry them. They had opinions she could have set her watch by, the chief among them that she had returned to town at the perfect time: The city was making a shining comeback that would at last show the world that it was, as its slogan proclaimed, "The best location in the nation."

After a while, Lily decided to build her social life on her office. But the office had a mind of its own that shut down at the end of the workday. Her coworkers declined her invitations to go out with all friendliness for which the Midwest was famous: They would love to join her, it was wonderful to have a new face in the office, but they had to go home to have dinner with their families.

Lily eventually realized that they had known something she hadn't: that there was little to do after work, anyway, in a city that, despite its much talked-about renaissance, looked like the site of an air-raid alert after 6 P.M. Within weeks, she had reread most of Jane Austen in the hours she used to spend in Third Avenue bars with other reporters, and she did not entirely mind this. For the first time, she realized that nothing was more relaxing than being completely ignored.

Like Jim Burden in *My Antonia*, Lily felt erased by the flat and characterless Midwestern landscape, just as she had felt thrown into relief by the saw-toothed Manhattan skyline. She had rationalized returning to the city of her birth by imagining that she might make a greater contribution there than in New York.

But its institutions had little desire for her contributions. In New York, volunteer organizations put her quickly to work. In her hometown, they put her on waiting lists drawn up by staunch civic boosters who had too much respect for their own friendliness to squander it on the unworthy.

One Sunday Lily slipped into Colony Heights Episcopal Church thinking that she was sure to feel at home in the church in which she had been baptized and confirmed. A few moments later, a man had tapped her on the shoulder and informed her that she had to move, because she was sitting in his family's pew. She had never gone back and, in defiance of her mother's wishes, insisted on getting married at Holy Family Cathedral—a church that, though larger, had a lower social status by dint of its having once been Catholic.

Then she had met Mark at a fund-raiser sponsored by the Young Friends of the Arts, the rare civic group that welcomed the unmarried, and she felt herself become visible again. For the first time since leaving New York, she knew what Jane Austen called "the happiness of being listened to" and encouraged by just appreciation and real taste.

Mark admired her work and quoted Byron: "There be none of Beauty's daughters/With a magic like thee." Almost as unexpectedly, he never insisted that the local theaters were as good as any in New York or that she would find that America had no finer citizens than lived in his hometown. Nor did he argue when she suggested that perhaps the Shakespeare Festival's feel-good *Hamlet* had been misconceived.

"That's the first honest thing I've heard about that production," he said, smiling. "That play could have been called, *The Beverly Hillbillies Go to Denmark*."

Lily had never met a man who spoke so truthfully of a city whose residents—like people keeping vigil beside a dying patient—tended to behave as though the least disparagement might finish it off for good, and inflated the smallest improvement into a sign that it would be running the triathalon in no time. The miracle was that he was also the kindest person she had ever met, someone who sent flowers to her grandmother on her birthday and took all the pro bono cases that his law partners shunned in favor of more lucrative corporate work.

With Mark, Lily had the sense of having been not reborn so much as restored to herself—an emotion for which she was so grateful that she did not hesitate to accept his proposal when it came three months after their first date. They agreed to hold the wedding three months later, on Labor Day Weekend, in order to avoid getting married in September, when snow often fell, signaling the start of eight months of cold, wet gloom.

It was not until weeks later that Lily realized she had not listened hard enough to a comment that Mark made at a barbecue at his widowed father's house. As the other guests boasted of a favorable write-up the city recently had received in *Forbes*, she asked him why after graduating near the top of his class at Harvard Law School he had remained in his hometown instead of joining a New York law firm.

She was unprepared for the long pause that followed, and even less so for the answer that finally came.

"Because," he said, "I knew that someday I would meet a woman who would make all this endurable."

3

D-Day

"You men have such restless curiosity! Talk of the curiosity of women, indeed! Tis nothing."

—Northanger Abbey

The morning after she told her mother that the wedding was off, Lily arrived at her office hoping nobody would notice her missing ring. This, she realized, was like walking into a French restaurant, picking up a yard-long baguette, stuffing it down the front of your shirt, and hoping nobody would notice the bulge.

Lily had longed to keep her engagement out of the office, if only to retain mental privacy in a cavernous newsroom that all but ruled out physical privacy. But this became impossible after her coworkers learned that she was marrying the only son of a brash real-estate developer whose dragnet of business interests led him to spar regularly with *Daily* reporters.

Buck Slayton was known in the newsroom as an example of the adage that you can tell a lot about God's sense of humor by the people he gives money to. One reporter suggested that Mark had been conceived by parthenogenesis: Buck Slayton could not have produced a son who seldom raised his voice and never swept into a room like an Ohio State linebacker barreling onto the field for the kickoff of the Michigan game.

Lily dreaded the questions she would face after her broken engagement became known and was grateful that she planned to spend most of the day out of the newsroom on assignment. If she was lucky, the air-conditioning at the fair might even work, unlike that of her office, which was chronically on the blink.

Hurrying into the newsroom, she picked up a copy of the day's paper from a stack near the entrance and, after settling into her desk, scanned the story that the copy intern had called about the night before. He had deleted the line by Henry James, with which she had ended her article, so that the piece she had crafted so painstakingly now sat on the page like a highboy with a missing leg.

Lily put aside the paper and listened to a voice mail message from her father's secretary, directing her to the Commodore's Club at noon. She had just called to confirm the lunch date when Jack O'Reilly approached her desk.

"How's the Operation Overlord of weddings going?" he asked. Jack, who covered veterans' affairs for the paper, had picked up the habit of linking the key events of his colleagues' lives to the military victories, defeats, or leaders that he thought they resembled. As a result, the *Daily* had the only newsroom in the country in which reporters routinely answered to "Verdun," "Manassas," and "Dienbienphu." Jack himself had become known as Waterloo Flannery in response to his often-repeated lament, "Women are my Waterloo."

In that spirit, he had pegged Lily's wedding as the Operation Overlord of marriages and drawn up an intricate chart that linked its participants with key figures in the Normandy invasion. Lily's mother became Dwight Eisenhower, the Supreme Allied Commander; Mark's father, Winston Churchill, the prime minister who wanted to run the show; the ushers and bridesmaids, the members of the 82d and 101st Airborne Divisions.

But Jack initially had maintained that he could find no counterparts for Lily and Mark. This, he said, was because the bride and groom in any wedding played minor strategic roles, resembling neither generals nor foot soldiers so much as the battlefields on which the other combatants fought for their own interests.

At last he conceded that he might compare Mark to the dashing Lord Lovat, striding into the surf at Sword Beach to the music of his private bagpiper. But he could find no match for Lily until she confessed to feeling sandbagged by complaints that, even with hundreds of names, her guest list left out too many of her mother's friends and her future father-in-law's business associates.

"I've got it!" Jack said. "You're Marianne, the symbol of France. You can't be liberated from the tyranny of lifelong spinsterhood without being partly destroyed."

At first the jokes had amused Lily. But, having mentally broken her engagement, she cringed at the thought of having to endure them until Mark returned. As she was trying to decide how to deflect the latest quip, Jack looked down at her hand.

"Hey, were you at a singles' bar last night?"

"No, why?"

"You have a white mark on your hand where your engagement ring used to be—the telltale sign of someone on the prowl for a secret fling. At least you don't have one of those green spots married men get when they take off wedding rings they've worn for twenty years."

At such moments, Lily yearned for a private office instead of a desk in an overcrowded newsroom. This was just the sort of conversation she wanted to avoid.

She tried to strike a note of lighthearted neutrality. "If I were looking for a fling, with your sources at City Hall, you'd probably hear about it before I did."

"So what happened to the rock? Get a stress fracture from trying to wear it and type at the same time?"

"Actually, it never quite fit. So it has to go back to the jeweler's."

Lily had worked out this reply, after much thought, while driving to work. On the one hand, she hated to lie. Journalists pounced so fiercely on the misrepresentations of others that she allowed herself no margin for hypocrisy. On the other hand, she couldn't allow Mark to hear of her decision from a reporter. So she had prepared a double-edged response to questions about the ring. If Jack picked up on the ambiguity, he didn't say so.

"Keeping that ring out of sight won't hurt you in this office," he said. "It probably cost more than some reporters make in a year."

"I know. But it was Mark's idea. He picked it out on his own and surprised me with it."

Jack began humming "Highland Laddie." It was a private joke: Lord Lovat had asked his bagpiper to play the tune as his men scrambled off their landing craft.

"So where is the dashing commando these days?"

"In Los Angeles, trying a big age-discrimination case. His client could have to pay millions if he doesn't win."

"Age discrimination? Didn't we have something on that case in the paper this week? There was a story in the business section about a high-tech company run by a group of newly minted MBAs who referred to employees over fifty-five as 'Geezers' and 'Geezerettes.'"

"Same case—and you can imagine the damages the company could be liable for if he doesn't win."

"I thought Mark only represented plaintiffs in discrimination cases. Somehow it doesn't sound like him to be representing a bunch of Neanderthal B-school graduates who have never heard of the Civil Rights Act. Didn't he once spend a summer doing volunteer work on some sort of voter-registration project in the Deep South?"

Lily turned to see if any other reporters could hear her and then, satisfied that none could, nodded.

"To tell you the truth, it isn't really like him. He usually does represent only plaintiffs. But his firm put a huge amount of pressure on him to take the case because it's so big, and he has more experience with civil-rights cases than anyone else in the litigation department."

"But, if I remember our article correctly, it didn't even mention Mark. I had the impression that Caroline Van Allen was trying the case."

"Mark is trying it with Caroline and a partner in his firm's office in Los Angeles. That's where TechnoCorp has its headquarters. But Mark likes to stay in the background and Caroline loves to talk to reporters, so she's handling the press on the case."

Jack looked at Lily's left hand again. "Well, I'm glad the absence of the ring doesn't mean that Caroline has spirited Mark away from you."

"Caroline? What does she have to do with my engagement?"

"Aren't she and Mark staying in the same hotel in L.A.?"

"Mark always stays in the same hotels with the other partners in his firm when he tries out-of-town cases. This one is no different."

"Has he ever tried a case with Caroline Van Allen?"

Lily, trying to remember, wondered if she was being

baited. It was hard to tell with a reporter like Jack, who was proud of his ability to read memos upside down on politicians' desks.

"It really doesn't matter whether he has or hasn't tried a case with Caroline," Lily said cautiously. "I trust Mark."

"I'd trust Mark, too. It's Caroline I'd be worried about." Jack paused. "Just a bit of friendly advice."

"What does that mean?"

"It means I covered the courts before I began writing about valiant Ohio soldiers who have been denied their combat medals by a heartless Pentagon."

Lily had met Caroline and knew her as an attractive partner in the litigation department of Mark's firm and the ex-wife of a well-known law professor. But it rankled that she was supposed to worry about any unattached woman who checked into the same hotel with her fiancé.

"Jack, why do men always assume that two women who have anything to do with the same man are in competition with each other? I thought that idea went out with the beehive hairdo."

"You're forgetting that the beehive hairdo never went out of style in this town." Jack nodded toward a Classified Department secretary standing near an elevator. A knitting needle stuck in her hair would have stood straight up.

Lily felt deflated but unwilling to concede the point. "Why don't you worry about what's going on at the AmVets Hall and let me worry about what's going on in California?" she asked.

"Okay, okay," Jack said. "I was only trying to help. You've been a little tense lately, and I wondered if anything was wrong."

"Jack, nothing is wrong. It's just that all your jokes about my wedding are getting to me a little."

"They are? I thought I'd eased up on the D-Day theme

lately. You may have noticed my amazing restraint in never having called you Frenchy."

Lily marveled at the ability of men to pat themselves on the back for declining to insult you. "Thanks, Jack."

Jack caught the edge in her voice.

"Honestly, Lily, once you're married, you won't remember a thing about all the ribbing you've had lately. Mark is a great guy, and even if he weren't, marriage is a wonderful invention."

Lily looked at him in amazement. "Jack, you've been married and divorced three times. And the last time you went to court, you said you wouldn't get married again if Princess Caroline of Monaco said that she wanted to see her face next to yours on a postage stamp."

"Why does everybody take me so literally?" he asked. "You know what Groucho Marx said: Marriage is the chief cause of divorce. But that doesn't mean people should avoid getting married. It just means they should avoid bad divorce lawyers."

"Maybe some people shouldn't get married."

"Lily, trust me, you're not one of them. No matter how much grief you might get from the reporters here, or from your mother's carriage-trade friends, you can't let it get to you. Because ten years from now, you're going to think getting married was the best thing you ever did."

"You didn't think getting married was the best thing you ever did."

"Yes, but that's because I never found a woman I could stay married to for ten years. My max was eight."

Lily began to say that this was hardly a resounding endorsement when Jack motioned to Craig "Dienbienphu" Solomon, an editor famous for driving reporters out of journalism the way General Giap drove the French out of Vietnam. Craig was talking to Art Felden, head of the grievance committee of the Reporters' Guild, who was known as Armageddon Felden for his belief in a last great battle between management and labor from which the union would emerge victorious despite a quarter century of humiliating defeats.

"Hey, guys, tell her I'm right," Jack said. "Tell Lily that getting married will be the best thing she ever did."

"He's right," Art said. "Everybody needs somebody to commiserate with in good times and bad."

Lily was about to ask why you would need to commiserate in good times when Craig put a hand on her shoulder, as if to restrain her from doing anything so rash as staying single.

"I'll second that," he said. "You might be getting married to the son of a man who never wants anything off the record, because he's convinced that everything he says ought to be broadcast from here to Sandusky. But he's still the man who owns the best skybox in town. You've got it made."

"See, Lil?" Jack said, grinning again. "Just what I was trying to tell you. You've got it made."

4

Hazards

". . . she had never felt so strongly as now, the disadvantages which must attend the children of so unsuitable a marriage . . ."

—Pride and Prejudice

Lily waited for her father in the lounge of the Commodore's Club, which did not allow unescorted women in the main dining room. She had never gotten used to the place, an immaculate white plantation-style building attended by a valet in heavy blue-and-gold nautical livery with a black half-moon-shaped hat. Chiseled into the architrave above its fluted columns was the legend: "We have met the enemy, and they are ours."

Far from the nearest body of water, the Commodore's Club struck Lily as an almost comical relic of another era—more than one era, given the mixed metaphors of its decor. The legend above its entrance reproduced the message sent by Oliver Hazard Perry at the Battle of Lake Erie even though Perry never attained the rank of commodore, a title held by his brother Matthew. Every so often, vandals obliterated the *o* and the *r* in *ours* with spray paint, so that for a few days afterward the club appeared to display a line by Pogo instead of a naval hero.

It was a bad sign, Lily thought, that her father had asked her to meet him at a spot that gave men the high ground. He had selected a place at which he could press every advantage, including that of his sex, as he always tried to do whenever he went head-to-head with an opponent.

But Lily wanted to accommodate her father. Like many kind-hearted men who had underestimated their wives' capacity for controlled fury, he had learned to take the path of least opposition in domestic affairs, which meant that he spent most of his time at his club or office.

On those occasions when he could not contrive a reason to visit one or the other, he tended either to defer completely to his wife or to oppose her so implacably that she retreated into a heavy silence that hung over the house like moss over a bayou. Lily knew that, if she could win her father over to her point, he would put an end to her mother's protests about the cancellation of the wedding.

"Would Madam like a drink?"

Looking up from a black Chesterfield sofa that came up to her armpits, Lily saw a waiter in a white jacket. Before she became engaged, the staff at the club called her "Miss."

But over the past two months, she seemed to devolve in the waiters' eyes into a matron. She was starting to feel like a flower she had seen bud and wither in seconds in a time-lapse film in a junior-high biology course.

Lily asked for mineral water with lime and took a goldfish-shaped cracker, which was stale, from a bowl that rested atop an eight-month-old golf magazine. Her father entered the lounge before the waiter could return with her drink.

"Sorry I'm late, darling," he said, kissing her on the cheek. "I stopped to buy you a little present."

After the maître d' had led them to a table, Lily opened a tiny aqua box tied with a white ribbon. After becoming engaged she had begun losing things, including an earring shaped like a dogwood blossom from a pair that her parents gave her when she graduated from Colony Heights Country Day School. The box held a set that matched the fugitive.

Lily was overjoyed to have the gift but alarmed by its expense, clearly her father's initial settlement offer in the dispute over her wedding. She recently had written a story about Ohio-based Political Action Committees, and she remembered a quote by Congressman Barney Frank that she had used in the piece: "The difference between a contribution and a bribe is timing." After thanking her father as warmly as possible under the circumstances, she asked about his friends at the club.

He nodded discreetly toward a man, who appeared to be in his eighties, eating alone at a table beside a bay window.

"Tom Rayburn was just named a Hazard," he said. "Poor fellow, he's waited so long for the honor, I hope he can still enjoy it."

At the Commodore's Club, the members were known as Olivers and the officers as Perrys. The trustees were called Hazards. *An apt label*, Lily thought, given their tireless opposition to the extension of equal privileges to women, who could hold only auxiliary memberships and had to resign on becoming divorced or widowed.

She wondered if Tom Rayburn had been invited to her wedding. Drawing up the guest list had resembled negotiating the North American Free Trade Agreement—a process so complicated that, in the end, she had forgotten exactly who had made the cut. Early on, the question had arisen whether to invite a few trustees for the sake of the family's future relations with the club; the word "sop" had been used. Lily could not recall how the issue had been resolved.

As she had expected, her father did not mention the reason for their meeting until their lunch had arrived: prime ribs for him, cold poached salmon for her.

"Well, Lily," her father said, spearing a pat of butter shaped like a scallop shell and mashing it into a steaming baked potato. "Your mother tells me you want to break your engagement, and I can't say I blame you for feeling a bit fed up. It must be exhausting to try to plan a wedding while holding down a full-time job. In your mother's day, women quit work a month or two before they married, just to deal with the preparations."

Lily could not tell whether her father was criticizing her for working or just stating a fact.

"If I didn't work, I might have bailed out sooner," she said. "My job is demanding enough that it may have distracted me from something I should have done much earlier."

"Even so, it must have been all the more difficult to have tried to plan your wedding with Mark off in Los Angeles." He paused. "I'm afraid it was rather insensitive of him to fly out there just now with Caroline Van Allen."

"How was it insensitive?" Lily asked. "It wasn't his fault that his case went to trial last week, and Caroline has been working on it as long as he has. She has as much right to be in Los Angeles as he does. It would have been insensitive for Mark to try to have her taken off the case at this point."

"Lily, your loyalty to your fiancé is as admirable as your defense of your sex. But it's an open secret in the legal community that Caroline has been after Mark for years."

Lily's father had spent his life in the trusts-and-estates department of a white-shoe law firm that, though not as large as Mark's, was older and therefore preferred by many members of the city's upper crust.

"So what? To hear Mark's sisters tell it, half the women in the Tri-County region have been after him." Fearing that this might sound self-congratulatory, Lily qualified her remark. "Of course, Mother always says that, on family matters, Penny and Fran have the credibility of the Pravda archives."

"She's right about those girls. But Caroline—" Lily's father hesitated. "Caroline is rather—tenacious."

"Every good litigator is tenacious."

"Caroline is also an extraordinarily beautiful woman."

"Beautiful?" The characterization took Lily aback. Though formidably well-groomed, Caroline had none of the natural candlepower of the models and actresses she had known in New York, who looked lovely even after rain had ravaged their makeup along with their collapsible umbrellas. That some men might consider Caroline beautiful had not occurred to her.

Uneasy with the idea, and uneasy with her uneasiness with it, Lily refused to allow herself to dwell on it. "At any rate, it doesn't matter whether Caroline has designs on Mark, because the engagement is off."

Her father seemed to debate whether to pursue the subject of Caroline before deciding against it. "I wonder if you haven't been a little hasty in making that decision."

"Not nearly as hasty as I was in getting engaged in the first place."

Lily watched her father stick his fork into an anemic nest of canned green beans. Looking at them took away her appetite.

"Darling, you know I'll support you if you are serious about calling off the wedding," he said. His tone, though gentle, was too smooth for comfort. "But I'd like to ask three favors of you first."

Lily braced herself for the silky bargaining that would follow. After years of resolving squabbles between the overprivileged children of the city's elite, her father rarely gave something away without getting something in return.

"Don't worry," he said. "My requests aren't difficult, and I know you'll understand the first. I'd like you not to tell your grandmother just yet, or Todd and Isabelle. You know how emotional Isabelle is, and I'm afraid that if she finds out she'll tell your grandmother even if you don't."

Lily felt as though a trap door had opened beneath their table. She did not mind keeping her news from her brother and sister-in-law; she spoke to them only once a week or so, and Mark might have returned by the next time they called. But she adored her seventy-six-year-old grandmother and had been counting on her support. By making such a request her father—had he done it consciously?—had moved to rob her of her most valuable potential ally.

"But I've never lied to Gran, ever," Lily said.

"I'm not asking you to lie. I'm just asking you not to tell her. She hasn't been well lately, and I'm afraid of the effect your news would have on her. Some days the only thing that keeps her going is looking forward to your wedding."

Lily was not sure she believed this remark, which she unhappily recognized as a variation on a point her mother had raised the night before. Despite her hip-replacement surgery, her grandmother had a mind as tough as a Brazil nut. But Lily could see no harm in waiting to talk to her until Mark had returned from California. After allowing as much, she asked about the other two favors.

Her father kept his eyes on a baked potato that, encased in aluminum foil, looked like a small bomb.

"I'd like you to see a psychiatrist before you make your final decision," he said.

"I've *made* my final decision, and you know you feel exactly as I do about psychiatry. Weren't you the one who always told me that psychiatry is the study of the id by the odd?"

The line had become a family joke after Johnny Carson delivered it on the *Tonight* show years earlier, though her father rarely seemed to be joking when he retold it. Several decades as a lawyer had left him deeply jaded about the forensic psychiatrists his partners used as expert witnesses; he often said that he had never heard of a case in which, if a lawyer hired a psychiatrist to say one thing, another lawyer could not find a psychiatrist willing to say the opposite for enough money. Her father looked embarrassed by the reminder of the *Tonight* show joke.

"I didn't mean that line seriously—"

"Well, I mean seriously that seeing a psychiatrist is out of the question."

"I'd be grateful if you could hear me out on this. I know I've had a lot to say about psychiatry—"

"I'll say."

"But I didn't mean to imply that psychiatrists never have anything to contribute. This might be a time when they could be of some benefit. You've had enough on your mind lately that it might be a good idea for you to talk to somebody before you do anything rash."

"Why is it rash to call off a wedding in a country with a fifty percent divorce rate? Why isn't it rash to go through with it instead?"

"Lily, you are being argumentative."

"We're not in court. Being argumentative is allowed."

Her father smiled, a bit regretfully. "Point well taken. But all I'm saying is, why not talk to somebody just to clear your head?"

"My head is perfectly clear. I don't want to get married."

"What harm could it do you to spent fifty minutes with someone who might have had similar experiences with other brides-to-be?"

"A lot of harm if, to quote another of your favorite expressions, psychiatry is a shoehorn to get you into a shoe that doesn't fit."

Her father concentrated on trying to detach a piece of overcooked prime rib from its bone. Lily gave up on her salmon, which was dry. For the first time, she wondered if her parents had argued about their wedding the night before.

"I said earlier that I wanted to ask you a favor, and I meant just that," her father said, at last. "Even if you don't want to see a psychiatrist for your sake, I'd like you to do it for your mother's and mine."

"But why? This is completely out of character for someone who once said that three things he never wanted his son to become a were gangster, a politician, or a psychiatrist."

"I'd just like to have every assurance that you are doing the right thing. Maybe talking to somebody wouldn't help you. But it would help your mother and me feel better about your decision. Your mother seems to think you are doing this"—he seemed to be suppressing a slight smile—"just to humiliate her in front of all of her friends."

Lily wished that her mother drove a harder bargain on the public-humiliation market, or at least held out for higher bidders than Tess Mahoney. Before she could say so, her father reached into an inner pocket of his suit and pulled out a list containing the phone numbers of three psychiatrists who would see her on short notice. Naturally, he said, anything she said to any of them would remain confidential. A psychiatrist would not report back to him, only help her to clarify her thoughts.

Looking at the sheet of white paper imprinted with the words "From the desk of . . . Ward Blair," Lily was too startled to ask where he had found the names on it. Their conversation had gone on longer than she had expected. She glanced at her watch and realized that she was supposed to have met a photographer from the *Daily* at the convention center twenty minutes ago. Continuing to argue with her father would cut into the time she had allocated for writing a story for the next day's paper.

For a while Lily said nothing, weighing the disadvantages of another hour lost over lunch against an hour lost after work later in the week. At last she reluctantly slipped the list of names into her purse.

"All right," she said. "You win. But I'm going to see a therapist for one session only, and that's it." She looked at her watch again. "Now, what was your third request?"

"Perhaps we should save it for another time?" Lily could not remember when she had seen her father look so uneasy.

"If you have the time, I'd like to hear it now," she said. Hoping to ease the tension, she decided to risk a small joke. "Who knows? Maybe it will be one of those things I'll want to discuss with my psychiatrist."

Her father looked almost sheepish. "If you don't mind, I'd still like to propose Mark for membership in the Commodore's Club. Even if he's not going to be my son-in-law, he'd still bring some young blood into this geriatric ward, and it would help if the membership committee didn't find out about your decision for as long as possible."

This request seemed so trivial after the other two that

Lily wondered why he had even mentioned it. Mark refused to join clubs that treated women, in his words, as "parties of the second part." And he had declined when Lily's father first offered to propose him for membership for in the Commodore's.

But after seeing how much the club meant to his future father-in-law, Mark agreed to allow his name to be proposed, only to have his nomination run into opposition from members who feared that if they accepted him they would also be asked to take his combative father. Lily knew that, afterward, her father had lobbied discreetly for weeks until he believed he had rallied the membership committee around his future son-in-law's cause. But she had stayed out of the matter—which she saw as Mark's decision alone—and saw no reason to involve herself in it at the eleventh hour.

"Believe me, I won't do anything to jeopardize the nomination," she said. She added, more lightly, "If Mark is losing a fiancée, why shouldn't he at least gain a club?"

Her father looked so relieved that Lily felt a twinge of unexpected regret. He clearly adored Mark, who helped to fill the void left by her brother's departure for France. Lily wished she had not raised her father's hopes so rashly and, for the rest of the meal, tried to lighten his mood by telling lively anecdotes about her job.

She told him that the *Daily* had received such a good response to its "meet cute" engagement announcements—which told amusing stories about how couples met—that it had taken to running "die cute" obituaries that gave entertaining accounts how people had died. The latest involved a man who had suffered a fatal heart attack while watching *Home Improvement*.

"That reminds me," her father said, just before they left

the dining room, "did you see in the paper that Thaddeus Payne became a Commodore last week?"

At the club, the Commodores were the members who were dead.

5

Vertigo

"Nothing ever fatigues me, but doing what I do not like."

—Mansfield Park

Not long after she entered the convention hall, Lily realized that she did not want to write about molded chicken-liver cruise ships. But by then it was too late.

Upon becoming engaged, Lily had proposed writing a series of articles for the *Daily* on marriage in the nineties. She had an absurdly short time to plan a wedding for 350 guests—one caterer had burst into nearly deranged laughter on hearing what she wanted to accomplish in three months—and thought she might be able to make up for her late start by doing some of her research on office time.

Luckily, or so she had thought, her editors had loved the idea. At the *Daily*, as at most newspapers, writing about weddings was seen as a notch above writing obituaries. To the Young Turks of the newsroom, it reeked of the dreary society coverage of yesteryear—of the days of bland photographs of club women who wore pearls and hats as they sat around tables planning charity benefits for the Symphony or Junior League.

To those to whom the beat did not represent a journalistic throwback, it was simply a dead end. Nobody won a Pulitzer for writing about weddings. To become a star you had to write about something sexy, like the mismanagement of industrial-waste disposal systems. And weddings—somewhat paradoxically it seemed to Lily—were considered about as sexy as bedbugs.

But, as much as reporters hated to write about weddings, readers loved to read about them. So Lily's editors were making the most of her idea: They were running her series on page one.

Weeks after suggesting the project, as she waited for the *Daily* photographer who was to meet her at the convention hall, Lily regretted the idea. Her ears hurt as she took in the clamorous scene: a vast room filled with rows of booths separated by white carpet runners. Each area of the hall had a theme such as china, lingerie, or flowers. Many people were walking around in pink and purple leis that travel agents were handing out in the honeymoon section.

Towering over the hall was an immense Ferris wheel, turning to the soundtrack from *Pretty Woman*. Each pair of seats held a bride and groom, who scattered rose petals on the crowd. It reminded Lily of a childhood trip to Disneyland; she half-expected Minnie Mouse to roam the hall in a wedding gown. At least the *Daily* photographer would get great pictures at the show.

"Have you seen our chicken-liver cruise ships?"

On hearing the voice, Lily turned. It belonged to a woman whose clip-on badge identified her as the co-owner of a firm that specialized in edible centerpieces of molded chopped chicken liver.

"Cruise ships?" Lily repeated.

Then she saw them: two ocean liners made of chicken liver with black olives for portholes.

"They come in varying lengths, up to a yard long, and we can spell the name of the honeymooners' cruise ship in pimiento strips," the woman said brightly. "I saw your badge saying that you were a member of the press and knew you wouldn't want to miss these."

She held out a pleated white paper cup containing a tiny spoon and a dab of chopped chicken liver. Lily took a bite. After she put down the cup, she pulled out her notebook.

"The cruise ships are the most popular of our molded specialty items," the woman went on. "But we have hundreds of others, too."

Lily knew the cruise ships would make good copy. But she wished she didn't have to write about them; they reminded her of all the paté her mother had ordered for her wedding reception. In planning their two-week honeymoon in France, she and Mark had kept up a running joke about the number of Alsatian geese that had died for their wedding. They fantasized about driving to a farm in Strasbourg and placing a wreath on the Tomb of the Unknown Foie Gras Donor.

Examining the cruise ships, Lily groped for a question she could ask with a measure of detachment. "What's your most unusual 'molded specialty item'?"

"Probably our Dead Heads," the woman said. On seeing Lily's baffled expression, she went on. "No, they're not refreshments for Grateful Dead concerts, although we recently did get a custom order for a chicken-liver bust of Jerry Garcia. It was a memorial tribute by two Grateful Dead fans who were getting married and wanted to remember Jerry at their wedding. That was very touching. But, usually, people ask us to make Dead Heads of the bride or groom or both."

The woman picked up a binder filled with color photographs. "Here's an example."

She showed Lily a photograph of the chicken-liver head of a groom on a silver tray edged by a ring of parsley. It looked like a scene from *Salome*.

The woman turned the page to reveal the disembodied head of a bride with edible nasturtiums on top. Lily felt her stomach do a back flip.

"Thank you," she said, turning swiftly away from the picture of the decapitated bride. "I'm sure I'll be able to use some of this in my story. This is just the sort of thing we like to write about."

"I knew it would be," the woman said, with a self-assurance that left little room for further questions.

Lily jotted down the price of the heads and moved on to a booth run by a company called Fit to Be Dyed. It sold bulk quantities of dyes used to tint mashed potatoes and other food to match bridesmaids' dresses.

At the booth a chef in a white toque was piping chartreuse rosettes onto rounds of bread in a coordinating shade of green.

Lily tried a canapé, which tasted better with her eyes closed, and asked about the range of colors.

"We can do just about anything a bride wants," the chef said, refilling his pastry tube. "Blue, green, pink, mauve, yellow. Rust is very big right now."

"Rust?" Lily asked. She tried to envision a serving of mashed potatoes that looked as though they had been made with a rusty egg beater.

"Sure," the chef said. "Let's say you're having a fall wedding. You have your bridesmaids in gold, your centerpieces of red and yellow leaves, and then your rust mashed potatoes. Perfect."

Lily made a note of the trend toward rust, then tried to think of how to phrase her next question tactfully.

"Are people ever squeamish about eating foods in colors that are—offbeat?"

"As far as potatoes are concerned, we've found that we can sell just about everything except black," the chef said. "For some reason, black mashed potatoes scare people. Remember when brides didn't want their bridesmaids to wear black because they thought it would be bad luck? Sadly, the same sort of prejudice still exists when it comes to potatoes."

The chef brightened. "But we've made a lot of progress with pasta. We've found that, if a bride is having a black-and-white wedding and we can't sell her on black mashed potatoes, we can often sell her on black pasta, which is usually linguine or fettucine dyed with squid ink." He looked at Lily's ring finger. "You ever been married?"

"No."

"Then let me give you some advice," he said, slipping an arm around her shoulder. "When you get married, have fun with your wedding. Don't let your mother tell you that you can't have pink mashed potatoes because she thinks white would look better. You make a good living as a reporter, don't you?" He did not wait for an answer. "Well, then, if your mother thinks pink mashed potatoes are too expensive, you pay for your own reception, right?"

If only it were that simple, Lily thought. She wished she had parents whose views on wedding financing—if not their tastes—were more like the chef's. That she and Mark had not insisted on paying for their reception was just one of many mistakes it was too late to undo.

Lily tucked one of the chef's brochures into her purse and wandered through the convention hall, stopping at a booth dominated by a poster of a man in a tailcoat partly enlarged by a magnifying glass. It advertised a detective agency called Put a Tail on Your Groom. The owner, a former police officer, told her he worked for brides suspicious of their future husbands. Lily asked if it was really necessary for couples to subject each other to such scrutiny.

The detective looked at her with pity. "I can tell you've never been married."

Lily asked what kinds of things brides wanted him to investigate.

"Oh, the usual," he said. "Girlfriends, jail records, shady financial dealings, children the men haven't told them about. But it's generally the things the brides haven't suspected that upset them the most. An amazing number of men turn out to have other wives they haven't mentioned."

Lily's pen stopped moving.

"Other wives?" she said. "I thought that sort of thing only happened on *Jerry Springer*."

The detective did not smile. Instead, he looked at Lily as though she had stepped directly from the Dark Ages into the convention hall, like a character in one of those time-warp romance novels in which the heroine falls into the moat of a medieval castle and wakes up with amnesia in a hot tub in Fresno.

"You would never imagine the half—the *half*—of what goes on in this country from watching *Jerry Springer*," the detective said darkly.

Lily found this idea ominous enough that she hurried away from his booth. She could not imagine growing desperate enough to hire a detective to stalk someone she was planning to wed. What was getting married all about, if not having a partner you trusted enough not to have to spy on?

But some women clearly had other ideas: They were

thinking of marrying men whom they didn't trust farther than the nearest motel room, while she did not want to marry Mark, a man whom she trusted almost more than she trusted herself.

Faced with such contradictions, Lily didn't see how any woman could be sure that she was marrying the right man. If trust lay at the heart of a good marriage, and trust had come to be regarded as something that was up for grabs between a man and a woman, she didn't see why more couples didn't just live together, or at least forgo the sort of financial meltdowns the bridal fair was promoting.

Lily remembered how surprised she had been when Sally had told her that, if she ever married, she would elope. Her best friend insisted that big weddings were a way of taking women's minds off what a terrible mistake they might be making. Sally added, only half-jokingly, that such weddings let women focus on china patterns rather than on the possibility that they someday might be throwing plates at the groom.

At the time, Lily had viewed her friend's comments as a good-natured commentary on the high cost of New York life: If you lived in Manhattan, after you paid your rent, you probably weren't going to have enough money left over for the tissue-stuffed invitations, anyway.

But she was beginning to wonder if Sally was right. Did fancy weddings merely allow brides to displace their anxieties onto chicken liver or mashed potatoes? How much sooner might she have come to her senses had she not faced the distractions of the place cards and bridesmaids' dresses?

Lily tried to stop second-guessing herself and concentrate on her story. She had promised her editors that she would try to track down a travel agency known for its package deals, which let people get a Dominican Republic divorce from one spouse, then go on a cruise with another. The firm had become famous for its slogan, "A free piña colada in every port."

But Lily could not find its display and had to return to the information booth for help. She had just left, with a marked-up map in hand, when she heard her name.

"Lily! I've been looking all over for you!"

She turned and saw Ed Martinez, the photographer whom she had forgotten she was supposed to meet. Mortified, she began to apologize.

"Don't give it a thought," Ed said, with a grin. "Isn't this place great?"

Ed often covered disasters for the paper—drive-by shootings, lightplane crashes, drownings at places with names like Paradise Falls—and consequently loved assignments that did not involve trying to get the body bags in the photo. He told her he had just taken some great shots of the Ferris wheel.

"Glad to see they finally put you on a story where nobody's big toe gets tagged, Ed," she said.

"Did you see those amazing chicken-liver cruise ships they have over in the food section?"

"Yes, and you'll be happy to know they're going to be in my story."

"That's why you're a great reporter, Lily," Ed teased. "You think like a photographer."

Lily knew, as Ed did, that his pictures of the cruise ships would have a better chance of making page one if she mentioned them prominently in her article. "Thanks, Ed."

"De nada," he said. "What else is in your story?"

Lily told him about a few other exhibits, and he went off to photograph them. As mothers and daughters walked by clutching pastel-colored shopping bags filled with free samples of perfume and stationery, she debated what to do next.

Should she look for the travel agency that arranged Caribbean divorce packages? Or should she try to interview some of the models on the Ferris wheel, to give Ed's pictures a better shot at page one? Watching the mock brides and grooms, Lily couldn't imagine how they kept vertigo at bay.

She moved closer to the Ferris wheel but had trouble getting a good look at the models. Some of their faces were too high up to see clearly, while others were obscured by the rose petals that fluttered past them.

Trying to focus made Lily dizzy, and she thought it might help if she picked one bride and groom and followed their path all the way around the circle traced by the wheel. In seconds she realized that she had made a mistake.

She began to feel shaky, as though she were about to have another attack of carsickness, from which she had suffered as a child. In an instant, Lily felt her knees give way. Then, for the first time in her life, she fainted.

6

First Aid

"A young lady who faints, must be recovered; questions must be answered, and surprises explained."

—Emma

L ily was lying on a cot in the First Aid station at the Convention Center when she came to. Next to her stood a woman in a gray dress whose badge identified her as a Dallas bridal consultant. She was holding a wet paper towel to Lily's forehead.

"Poor baby," she said. "You fainted next to my booth. You hit your forehead on a display table on the way down. It's going to give you a lulu of a lump. Does this hurt?"

"Not too much."

"You don't have to talk if you don't want to. As a bridal consultant, believe me, I have a lot of experience with fainters."

The woman wet the paper towel again and put it back on Lily's forehead. "A few years ago, one of my brides fainted on the way to the altar and fell face-down in a font of Holy Water. You can imagine what that did to her makeup. I tried to tell her that, in the Texas heat, she was going to have problems with any dress that weighed more than the altar boy."

Lily liked the bridal consultant, the only person she had met at the Convention Center who had a sense of humor. "It's nice to know I'm in the hands of a veteran."

"Did all the excitement get to you?"

"It must have. I don't think I've ever been in such a noisy convention hall."

"I meant the excitement of your wedding."

The woman glanced at Lily's ring finger. "Sometimes I can even tell the size of the stone from those white marks. Three-and-a-half carats?"

"Five."

"That's big even by Dallas standards. Is he rich or did he just do something to make him feel extra guilty?"

"Rich."

"Lucky you."

"That's what everybody says."

The woman raised an eyebrow. "You don't agree?"

"I thought I did."

"Then what happened?"

"I'm not sure. One night I just woke up at three A.M. and knew I couldn't go through with the wedding. And the worst of it is I can't tell my fiancé, because he's in California for a week, and I can't bear to break the news to him long distance."

"Maybe it's a good thing you haven't told him."

Lily sat up. "Why not?"

"Well, I'm not saying you'll change your mind. But in my line of work I see a lot of women go through something like you're experiencing right now. A month or two before the wedding, they come into my office weeping and saying that it has all been a terrible mistake. You know, 'Thank you, Jesus, for my wonderful fiancé, but I am bailing out of this wedding.' "

"And you talk them out of it?"

"No, they talk themselves out of it. They realize they'd just had too much of their mothers or their in-laws or writing thank-you notes for wastebaskets with ducks on them. One woman came to my office in tears, saying that everywhere she went she heard imaginary quacking. The next week she came back and said she didn't know why she had been so upset: If her friends had given her wastebaskets with hunting dogs on them, there would have been no problem."

Lily smiled despite her aching forehead. "I know what she means. I have a trivet, two lamps, and four place mats with ducks on them. My fiancé says we should pick our whole house up by the foundation and move it south for the winter." Then she grew serious. "The problem is, I don't want to talk myself out of canceling the wedding. I just don't want to go through with it, with or without the duck trivet."

"I know you think that. But may I ask you a personal question?"

"Let me guess. Am I pregnant?"

"No, but you're on the right track. Have you stopped having sex with your fiancé?"

"No."

"Do you throw up before he comes to pick you up?"

"No."

"Have you considered suicide?"

Lily almost laughed. "No, of course not."

The bridal consultant smiled. "Then I'd give all this a little longer, because in my experience a woman isn't ready to call off her wedding unless she can answer yes to at least one of those questions."

"But—" Lily broke off, feeling like a contestant on the game show "What's My Perversion?" in the Woody Allen movie *Everything You Always Wanted to Know About Sex,* which involved a rabbi, bondage fantasies, and pork chops. She imagined herself standing in her wedding gown in front of a host who was saying, "Can you guess whether this bride is (a) repulsed by her fiancé, (b) nauseated by her fiancé, or (c) the Hemlock Society's Bride-of-the-Month?"

Lily tried to think of a reasonable way to explain herself. "It just seems so—extreme—to say that a woman shouldn't call off her wedding unless her fiancé repulses her, nauseates her, or makes her want to drink strychnine." She paused, unsure of how much to reveal about her private life. "It's true that my fiancé and I have always had great sex. But does that mean we should get married? Sex is partly a matter of technique. I might be able to have great sex with the translator of the *Kama Sutra.* He might be able to have great sex with Shere Hite."

The bridal consultant looked at her sympathetically. "Sugar lamb, I'm not saying that you should or shouldn't marry your fiancé. I'm just saying that, in my experience, those are things that happen when a woman is ready to call off her engagement."

Lily was silent. She touched the lump on her forehead, which felt alarmingly large and painful, and wondered if she were playing out an inverse variation on the woman's Repulsion Theory of romantic destiny: Mark did not repel her, but she might repel him now. Inexplicably, she thought of Caroline Van Allen who, the few times they had met, looked cool and unruffled enough to suggest that Elizabeth Arden had risen from the grave to apply her makeup while Giorgio Armani had hand-selected her wardrobe. Perhaps that explained why men perceived

Mark's partner to be so beautiful. Caroline did not appear to be a woman who would ever allow a black-and-blue mark to interfere with her color coordination.

Trying to banish Mark's partner from her mind, she lay back down on the cot.

"Why did I do it?" she asked.

"Do what?"

"Agree to marry to someone I had only known for three months. For most of my life, I never wanted to get married at all, at least not in the same way that other women seemed to want to. I thought I'd see the world first, maybe live abroad the way my brother, Todd, did. But then I met Mark, and I don't know what came over me."

"What about love?"

"Love?"

"Didn't love come over you?"

Lily realized she had said too much. How could she explain how she felt about love to a stranger? She could scarcely explain it to herself. Nearly everyone she knew believed that, when it came to marriage, nothing mattered more than love. But she thought that the subject was more complicated, and not just because she had never read a better definition of love than E. M. Cioran's, "Love is an agreement on the part of two people to overestimate each other."

Couldn't some things make more of a difference in a marriage than love: maturity, for instance, or how well someone treated or understood you? In New York men were always telling Lily that they loved her without appearing to have any idea of whom they were in love with. On their evidence, "I love you" often meant nothing more than, "I want to sleep with you." Yet she did not think the men were being dishonest with her so much as with themselves. They defined love so narrowly that when they wanted to sleep with a woman they really believed they were in love with her.

Mark had been different: He *had* understood her. He wanted to marry her even though, in the five months they had known each other, she had never told him she loved him. In fact, she had accepted him precisely because she believed he knew her well enough to know that she would accept him without having made such a declaration.

But neither she nor Mark had anticipated that she would find herself, despite her best intentions, unable to go through with the wedding. And how could she ever explain that to a bridal consultant she had just met?

Lily decided not to try but to deflect the woman's question with one of her own. "Have you ever seen the pop-art poster of a woman saying, 'I thought I was in love . . . I think it was the flu'?"

"Many times," the bridal consultant said, smiling, but something in her manner changed. She took a long time to rearrange the paper towel, then looked at Lily with regret.

"You're sure you don't want to get married?" she asked kindly.

Lily nodded. "Yes, and every day that I put off telling my fiancé is costing my parents more money. Today I'm supposed to pick up my bridal shoes and later in the week to have my wedding portrait taken—"

"Then at least one good thing has come out of this fainting spell."

"What's that?"

"Nobody gets her wedding picture taken when she has a lump like the one you have on your forehead."

7

Hard Copy

"Composition seems to me Impossible, with a head full of Joints of Mutton & doses of rhubarb."

—Letter to Cassandra Austen

There were a lot of head cases at the bridal fair," Lily wrote. "Chicken liver head—"

No, too cynical, might be taken as a put-down of *Daily* readers who had visited the fair. Lily hit the Delete key on her computer.

"Feeling black about your wedding?" she wrote. "Your reception menu—"

No, too downbeat, not likely to win over the brides who were actually looking forward to their weddings. Lily hit the Delete key again.

"If you're getting married soon, you're probably thinking a lot about dicks," she wrote. "But have you considered hiring one instead of—"

Now she had gone around the bend. The copy desk chief would drink printer's ink before allowing that double entendre into the paper. If, by chance, he missed it, angry readers would swamp the *Daily* switchboard with calls, and Lily would lose her job. Delete, delete, delete.

Lily had no idea why she was writing such lines. She had always regarded puns as the mildewed basement in the house of wit. Now, she was trying them out for the front door of the *Daily*, the first sentence of a page-one story.

How could she write about an event that had made her physically ill, especially if you counted the bruise on her forehead? She had nothing in common with the radiant women at the bridal fair, whose happiness reproached her with every phrase she wrote.

Lily considered filing a satirical report on the bridal fair, then thought better of it. She had never heard the end of it after she wrote an op-ed-page spoof of the decision to name a candy bar after a famous local ballplayer, in which she had said that several other players might be honored by having illegal drugs named after them. For weeks, the paper had received enraged letters from readers, accusing her of promoting drug use among Ohio children. Mark had tried to cheer her up by suggesting that the legislature might adopt a new state song, "I Left My Heart in San Francisco and My Sense of Irony on the Pennsylvania Turnpike."

Maybe her father had been right, Lily thought. She was trying to do too much. Her telephone rang continually, and after a while she stopped answering it and let her voice mail record her messages. She was still trying to decide how to begin her story when Jack walked up and did a doubletake.

"My God, what happened to you?"

With her eyes fixed on her computer screen, Lily only half-heard him. "What happened to me? I got engaged, that's what."

Jack looked at her oddly. "I mean, what happened to your forehead?"

Lily touched her lump, which had swollen rapidly. "This? I guess I sort of fell at the bridal fair I'm writing about for tomorrow's paper."

"You sort of fell? You look as though a Green Beret bashed you with a rifle."

"I almost wish I had been bashed by a Green Beret. Then I could get out of writing this story for page one."

"I thought you liked writing page-one stories."

"Usually I do. But everything about the bridal fair just seemed so—unreal."

"That's the nature of weddings. They are unreal. But the unreality only lasts for a day. Then you get down to the nitty-gritty of marriage, like arguing over who controls the remote for the VCR and whose in-laws you visit on Millard Fillmore's birthday."

"Jack, a few hours ago you were telling me what a wonderful institution marriage was. Now you tell me it's a lifetime of arguments over Millard Fillmore."

Lily hadn't meant to sound irritable. But her good spirits were wearing thin, and Jack picked up on it.

"I don't mean to pry," he said. "But are you sure you're okay? Lately you've been acting as though you've been planning a wake instead of a wedding."

"Really, I'll be fine once I finish this story."

Jack was about to say something when Ed Martinez walked up carrying several photographs, for which Lily needed to write captions.

"Hey, did you have too much of that free pink champagne they were handing out at the fair and take a spill?" Ed asked.

Lily took the pictures from him without comment. She was having so much trouble with her article that she decided she might as well tackle the captions first. Her head began to throb harder as she saw a photo of a Ferris wheel atop the pile Ed left on her desk.

An hour later, Lily noticed a green light flashing in the upper-right corner of her computer screen. She hit the Message key and saw a note from Frank Gallese, the deputy news editor and her immediate supervisor, who wanted an Estimated Time of Arrival for her story.

"Soon, Frank, soon," she wrote, then hit Send.

Lily knew that her message would bring her supervisor scuttling to her desk in minutes. Frank, though one of the saner people in the newsroom, had acquired the unfortunate nickname of Benito, because he made the stories run on time.

But Lily could scarcely admit that she still had not written the first line of her bridal-fair report. Distracted by two reporters who were fighting for a computer terminal, she reminded herself that sportswriters routinely tapped out their stories while listening to thousands of drunken and screaming fans. Perhaps if she tried to imitate them?

Closing her eyes, Lily attempted to think like a sportswriter, an effort that drove her thoughts deeper into a maw of clichés. As she free-associated herself into a press box, every line that came to her had the word "phenom" in it.

When she opened her eyes, Frank was standing over her desk, staring at her forehead. "What on earth did you do to yourself?"

"Just a bruise, Frank."

"You sure? You look like you had a fistfight with one of Mark's old girlfriends."

"Do I look like the fistfighting type?

"No, but there must be a lot of women out there who are pretty jealous of you at this point. They could bring out your unknown macho side."

"Don't worry, I didn't injure my typing fingers. You'll have your story by seven P.M. on the dot."

"That's cutting it close. Any chance we could have it earlier?"

"I'll do my best."

At that moment, a voice came over the office loud-speaker system and announced that the newsroom computer system had crashed.

By the time the system came back up, Lily had twenty minutes in which to complete her story. She could barely type that fast, let alone write, and the approaching deadline made her almost thankful for the lump on her forehead. It might win her a little sympathy if her story was late.

At the *Daily*, Lily had never missed a deadline. But she could not write a bridal story while sitting at a desk topped by a framed copy of her engagement photograph, in which she and Mark held hands under a rose trellis. Her eye kept returning to the picture like a convicted bail jumper's returning to an eight-count grand jury indictment.

Lily impulsively picked up the photo and shoved it into a desk drawer. It was as though she had stepped out of a dress two sizes too small. With the picture gone, she could breathe again and knew instantly what to do.

She began her story from scratch with an anecdote she had heard from the bridal consultant, which involved a father who had taken out a third mortgage to pay for his daughter's wedding. The tension left him such a wreck that he passed out at the reception, and his toupee fell into the punch bowl. He spent the next hour recovering in bed in a hotel room while his guests did the Chicken Dance in a nearby ballroom.

The anecdote struck Lily as just right: bright enough to

hook readers but bleak enough to reflect her mood. From there she went on to describe some of the more colorful bridal-fair exhibits with what she hoped was a lively wit, then ended by quoting Anne Morrow Lindbergh's *Dearly Beloved*: "When the wedding march sounds the resolute approach, the clock no longer ticks, it tolls the hour . . . The figures in the aisle are no longer individuals, they symbolize the human race." She was proofreading her work when her message light flashed again: another plea for her story.

"It's on the way, Frank," she wrote.

"Okay, don't leave the office until I've read it," he replied.

Ten minutes after Lily sent her story electronically to Frank, he strolled over to her desk.

"You're a natural at these wedding stories, Lil," he said. "This one is even better than your article about the couple who exchanged matching nose rings to the music—and I use the term loosely—of Nine Inch Nails. Maybe we should make weddings your permanent beat."

Lily flinched.

"Are you sure you're all right?" Frank asked.

Lily felt her forehead again. "Yes, I just need to put a little ice on this."

"So go home, already. You look like you could use some rest."

Lily was clearing off her desk when Jack returned.

"Hey, Lily, I just called up your story in the page-one desk," he said. "It was great, especially that part about Jerry Garcia. His fans will be sending you tie-dyed T-shirts forever."

"Thanks. I'll pass all the extra larges along to you."

"Glad to have them," Jack said. "But isn't something missing from your desk?"

"Something like what?"

"That picture of you and Mark that's been there for weeks. I saw it just an hour ago. First, your ring disappears, then the picture—"

"What is this, a newsroom or a belated Iran-Contra hearing?"

Lily knew that her reply would only inflame Jack's curiosity. But in her relief at having finished her story, she had forgotten to put the photo back on her desk.

"Testy, testy," Jack said. "I was just asking—"

Lily abruptly opened a drawer, pulled out the photo, and shoved it back into place.

"There's the picture," she said. "Okay?"

Jack looked around the newsroom to see if anybody was nearby. Having determined that no other reporters could hear him, he leaned toward Lily.

"Something is up between you and Mark," he said, in a mock-conspiratorial tone. "I don't know what it is, but I know."

"How can something be up when Mark isn't even here?" Lily asked.

"That's just the point, that he's not here but off in the land of five-alarm sunsets with Caroline Van Allen."

"I thought we agreed—" Lily started to say.

Just then her phone rang. It was Mark's father, calling from a portable telephone at a charity benefit.

"Lily, where are you?" Buck Slayton asked. "I've been leaving you phone messages for an hour. The dinner is about to start."

The dinner? Lily's mind spun. She thought she was supposed to meet Mark's father at a charity benefit tomorrow night, not tonight. Now she not only wouldn't be able to pick up her bridal shoes after work but would have to face hundreds of people looking as though she had been struck by a five-iron. For a moment, she considered trying to beg off, then remembered that the dinner cost $250 a plate.

"I'm on the way, Buck," Lily said. "Sorry we haven't been able to connect, but I've been on deadline all afternoon."

"We'll be waiting for you in the Grand Ballroom of the Majestic. Black tie."

"Black tie?" Lily said. "I thought . . ." She stopped when she realized that Buck had hung up.

Lily turned weakly to Jack.

"Got to run," she said. "I forgot that I was supposed to meet Mark's father at a benefit after work, and it turns out to be black tie, so I have to race home and change."

As Lily hurriedly cleared her tape recorder and notebooks off her desk, Jack looked at her sympathetically.

"Not your day, is it?" he asked. "A few hours after you take a prize-winning fall, you have to spend the evening with a man who never looked at a half-acre of grass without thinking how much better the land would look with a taco parlor on it."

"Jack, he's my future—" Lily began. But she caught herself just in time.

8

Buck

"This is not my idea of a chapel. There is nothing awful here, nothing melancholy, nothing grand. Here are no aisles, no inscriptions, no banners . . . No signs that a 'Scottish monarch sleeps below.'"

—Mansfield Park

Buck Slayton had two points of pride: He had the largest real-estate empire in three counties, and he had never hired a man who wore leather elbow patches. Despite this, he had an ego that was unresponsive to flattery. He was not unimpressed with his own achievements. Rather, he was so assured of his own greatness that he regarded any allusion to it as a statement of the obvious and, therefore, a waste of time.

Born Walter Dean Slayton, Buck had acquired his nickname in high school, where he earned so many varsity letters that he sold his surplus to friends, who dubbed him Make-a-Buck Slayton. After he had begun to build his real-estate empire, he claimed to have adopted the nickname out of loyalty to the team for which he had played college football, the Ohio State Buckeyes.

But the switch had not kept him from deciding, early in his marriage, to name all of his children after currencies: First came Penny, then Frances, and finally Mark. A family joke said that Buck had only three children because, with the Cold War on, he was too patriotic to name his subsequent offspring Zloty and Kopeck.

How such a man had produced a son as well-liked as Mark was, to many of his associates, a riddle that found its only answer in the heroic contributions to the gene pool made by his late wife, Miriam.

Miriam Peabody Slayton had been, it was agreed, a saint: gentle, thoughtful, refined, and devoted to her family and church. She had come to Ohio, after graduating from Wellesley, to study at the Erie Conservatory, which had an excellent piano department. After hearing her perform with a trio that included the wife of one of his clients, Buck had pursued her relentlessly, and they had wed the day after she received her music degree. Improbable as the match was, it was apparently happy.

Mark's mother turned out to have been well-prepared to withstand his father's chronic battles with zoning boards and city councils. A descendant of a sturdy line of New England politicians, Miriam Slayton was a distant kin of the former Massachusetts governor Endicott "Chubb" Peabody, about whom a rival once said that he had three cities named after him: Peabody, Marblehead, and Athol. As such she knew how to confront her husband without losing her dignity—a trait Lily regarded enviously.

It had been Miriam who carried the day when Mark outraged his father by refusing to apply to Ohio State and setting his hopes on Harvard, which Buck regarded as a school for wimps. Knowing her husband too well to invoke the intellectual superiority of the Ivy League over the Big Ten, she built her case on the illness of her father on the

North Shore, who she said would benefit from his grandson's visits.

The argument, for two reasons, proved decisive: first, because Buck had a loyalty to his family that rivaled that of his loyalty to the Big Ten, and second, because his father-in-law's illness gave him a way to save face among his friends. No one could fault him for sending his son to a school where the linebackers wore boxer shorts—this, true or not, was devoutly believed by Buck—if a family crisis required it.

Miriam had prevailed again when, as a college senior, Mark said that he was thinking of entering the ministry. Buck did not object to his son's working briefly for a company besides his real-estate firm, which he believed would convince him of the inferiority of working anywhere but Slayton Enterprises. But if working for a different firm was one thing, working for God was another, and Buck laid down the law. He would not pay for Harvard Divinity School.

As the dispute threatened to estrange father and son, Miriam took matters into her own hands. Without mentioning it to her husband, she urged Mark to attend Harvard Law School, which also had accepted him. If, after a few years as a lawyer, he still wanted to attend the seminary, she would pay for his degree out of the income from her trust funds.

Mark, a born compromiser, agreed to the plan and liked litigation better than he had expected, especially after he began specializing in civil-rights cases, which helped to satisfy the instinct for social justice that had led him to consider entering the ministry. Then his mother died, dividing her trust funds between her three children and removing the question of how her son might pay for divinity school. Not long afterward, his grandfather had a fatal heart attack, leaving him enough money to endow a small seminary in perpetuity.

Lily had learned most of this from her coworkers at the *Daily*, who had spent years chronicling the activities of the Slaytons on the business and society pages and who warned her not to take her future father-in-law's actions personally. Buck Slayton was the sun and moon of his own universe and ill-attuned to the movements of outlying planets. But their advice did not make it easier to live with his decisions.

The biggest of these, insofar as they affected Lily, involved the house he had given the couple as a wedding present. It looked like a Tudor brothel that had mutated under the influence of a lawn sprinkler-system gone haywire.

As such, it resembled nearly every other house built by Mark's father. An ornate mock-Tudor mansion that sat atop a low rise in Colony Heights, it had been painted a sickly orange that Buck called "tangerine" but made Lily think of the toxic sunsets that might occur in a nuclear winter.

Perhaps the kindest thing she could say about the house was that it fit its neighborhood like a Spandex jumpsuit. Colony Heights had once harbored a Shaker Colony. After the sect had died out, the oil and steel barons of the region honored the Shaker ideals of economy, simplicity, and nonviolence by buying up all the colony's land and erecting bombastic mansions with turrets, battlements, and castellated roofs.

This garish display did nothing to diminish property values in the suburb. Lately, the land in Colony Heights had grown so expensive that few developers could afford to build there, and Buck ranked among the few who remained able do so. He had nearly finished his latest house when Mark and Lily had become engaged and had given it to them soon afterward.

Without telling them of his plans, Buck later customized the property by converting a billiard room into a small chapel, which he kept secret until its completion. He had taken the step, they learned, in the hope that it would give Mark enough of an outlet for his religious impulses to banish forever his idea of entering the ministry.

On the day that construction workers finished the chapel, Buck asked them to meet him at the house for a drink and then led them to its newly constructed east wing.

There they saw it: a private chapel that Buck had equipped with a wet bar, which occupied a corner of a small room just off the sanctuary. Underneath a stained glass window stood a wood-grained unit complete with a sink, refrigerator, and several bottles of single-malt Scotch.

As Buck picked up a plastic coaster embossed with the logo of his company, Lily felt Mark slip his arm around her waist. She could not tell whether he was trying to steady her or himself.

"Dad, this is something we—this is so—it's incredible," Mark said. "How many couples get a chapel with a wet bar for a wedding present?"

"That's what I was thinking, too," Buck said with obvious pride. "Sure, it cost me more money. But I kept thinking how much more convenient this would be for you if you were having, say, a nice chardonnay for a communion wine and wanted to serve it chilled."

Lily was about to speak when she felt her fiancé's arm tighten around her waist.

"You know, chilling communion wine is something I never thought of," Mark said, as though marveling at the wondrous possibilities. Lily's waist started to hurt.

Buck beamed as he turned on a faucet, sending a stream of water rushing into the sink. "See, when you have your first child, you won't even need to go into the chapel to baptize it. You can do it right here under the tap."

Lily could not tell whether or not he was serious. Grinning, Buck shut off the water and turned to her.

"So, Lily, what do you think? Did you ever imagine, when you got engaged to my son, that you would be getting a wedding present like this?"

Lily assured him that she had not, and Mark squeezed her hand gratefully.

"Well, why don't we fix ourselves a drink here and take it out on the deck?" Buck asked. "You're both up for one, aren't you?"

Lily looked tentatively at Mark, who did not answer. He was staring at the stained glass window near the wet bar.

"Dad, what is this?"

Then Lily noticed it, too: In the stained glass window, she saw a cross formed on a football field by figures wearing the scarlet-and-gray uniform of the Ohio State Marching Band.

After seeing the chapel, Mark suggested that they drive to his place in the city, and Lily readily agreed. She loved his riverfront loft, which had dazzled her when she had first seen it: a vast sweep of exposed brick with a grand piano, a two-story fireplace, a cluster of ficus trees, and a wall of books across from a row of windows overlooking the water.

The only problem with the loft lay in its location in a bleak warehouse district that made it impossible for them to live there after they married. At night, the area became so dangerous that the police warned women away from the converted bicycle factory in which Mark lived, which was occupied mainly by well-paid single men. And yet the Bike Factory was regarded as the best residential address in a city with only two high-rise apartment buildings, neither in a neighborhood in which people could safely walk after dark.

On returning to the loft after visiting the chapel, Lily was struck by the gap between her fiancé's taste and his father's. She hated to fault so generous a gift as they had just received. But after she and Mark had settled into bed, she was unable to concentrate on her copy of *Persuasion*. She turned to her fiancé, who was poring over Dawn Powell's *The Locusts Have No King*.

"Mark, how are we going to survive in a house that has a stained glass window with marching tuba players on it where Jesus, Mary, and Joseph should be?"

On hearing her question, Mark put aside his novel.

"By having sex on the redwood deck every night?" he asked, kissing her on the cheek.

Lily glanced out the window, toward a field of dormant smokestacks. Mark started to unbutton her nightshirt, and she removed his hand reluctantly.

"Why couldn't he have been like other fathers and just given us a fake Tiffany lamp?"

"Because, for him, that would never be enough. He'd have to buy us a whole fake-lamp distributorship."

"I'm just not sure I will ever be at home in that house. Who ever heard of a Tudor chapel with a built-in wet bar?"

"We never have to use the chapel. We can close it off and pretend that it doesn't exist."

"It's not just the chapel. It's all that red flocked wallpaper in the halls, and the bowling alley with glow-in-the-dark pins in the basement. Not to mention, the doorbell that plays the Ohio State fight song—"

"Actually, it's the Ohio State alma mater, 'Carmen

Ohio.' And it's set to the tune of an old Protestant hymn, 'Come Christians, Join to Sing,' which I've always rather liked." Mark sang the first two lines. "Remember it?"

"Yes, but I still feel like a cross between a Tudor hooker and a Heisman trophy finalist every time I step inside that house."

Mark laughed, reminding Lily of what had attracted her to him. Since she had returned to her hometown, he was the only man she had met who not only got her jokes but raised them to a higher power. A few days after she told him a line she had heard from her best friend—"What's the national flower of Canada? The satellite dish"—he sent her a dozen tiny plastic satellite dishes tied up with a big red bow and a card that read, "A Canadian Valentine." He did not miss the chance to try to add topspin to her comment about the house.

"Why don't you pretend that you're a Tudor queen, and I'm your king?"

Lily tried to think of a Tudor king besides Henry VIII. She had a vision of her lithe, athletic fiancé as an aging and obese monarch contriving to produce an heir, and the image made her feel guilty: She was acting as though an 18-room Tudor mansion were the Tower of London.

"Oh, Mark, this sounds so ungrateful, doesn't it? Your father is giving us a house that would cost a half million dollars—"

"More."

"More than a half million dollars. And I'm complaining about a window."

"It is pretty ghastly," Mark admitted. "But my father's intentions are good. Or, at least, I think they are. He adores you—which is saying a lot, given what he thinks of the press—and the house is his way of showing it. When my sister Penny got married, my father disliked her husband so much he gave them half an acre of land next to a toxic waste dump."

Lily did not respond directly but glanced at the copy of *Persuasion* in her lap.

"Maybe I just read too much Jane Austen," she said doubtfully, fondling the cover of her novel. "Her houses are never just houses. They always reflect the character of their owners. Elizabetth Bennet would never have married Darcy if he hadn't lived on an estate as handsome as Pemberley, because in Austen's novels, taste is never just taste. It's linked to morality. And your father has built the whole house to his taste instead of ours."

"That's because, unlike Jane Austen, my father doesn't understand that there are any tastes besides his own. All his houses look like that, no matter who lives in them."

"But we're the ones who have to live in this one. I'm afraid that, if move in, we'll turn into the sort of people who have that kind of house instead of—us."

Mark looked at her affectionately. "Aren't you giving yourself too little credit? You're too far strong a person to turn into a Stepford wife just because you live in"—he smiled—"a Stepford house."

Lily wondered if Mark was right. Did her reluctance to live in a Tudor atrocity have more to do with her lack of confidence than with his father's taste? When she said nothing, Mark removed her copy of *Persuasion* from her lap and set it on the night table. He wrapped his arms around her.

"Believe me, I would never have chosen that house, either," he said gently. "But we don't have to live there forever. We can sell it in a couple of years and buy something we like more. In the meantime we can replace the wallpaper, turn the bowling alley into an exercise room, and disconnect the doorbell."

Lily nodded, unconvinced. People were always telling her how much her life was going to change after the wedding, and she was beginning to understand what they meant: Marriage turned women into chronic perjurers. To avoid hurting the people who loved them, they had to act in ways that would have been unthinkable when they were single.

As she reconsidered her fiancé's words, Lily told herself that moving into the house made perfect sense. Turning it down might alienate her future father-in-law permanently after it had taken Mark years to repair the relations with Buck that had eroded while he was in college.

But the idea of living in the house troubled Lily, for reasons that she had difficulty expressing. And, just before they fell asleep, she made a final attempt to define the problem.

"Mark, what would your mother have thought of that house?"

"My mother? She would have loathed every inch of it."

"And moved in, anyway?"

Mark looked at her in surprise. "Oh, no. In all the years my parents were married, they never lived in one of the houses my father built. It would have driven my mother crazy."

9

Benefits

"You ought certainly to forgive them as a christian, but never to admit them in your sight, or allow their names to be mentioned in your hearing."

—Pride and Prejudice

Now that Mark was in California, Lily wished she did not have to spend an evening with his father, who tended to show her off like a new tanning salon at one of his shopping malls. She regretted not having time to ice her forehead before meeting him, which might have eased her physical if not mental distress.

Distracted by the soreness of her lump, Lily couldn't remember who was hosting the dinner at the Majestic. In her mind she ran through the candidates—the Chamber of Commerce, the Downtown Athletic Club, the Business Roundtable—among the organizations to which Mark's father belonged.

Buck Slayton liked to support groups that promoted sports or industry, but that scarcely narrowed the field. Sports and industry were the right and left ventricles of the atherosclerotic Tri-County region; culture and education, for all that civic leaders boasted of them, were its appendix and spleen. Every major industry was expected to support the local sports teams by buying skyboxes at the stadium, and every local sports team was an industry unto itself.

Defeated by her effort to recall the sponsor of the benefit, Lily reached into her closet and pulled out her one good evening dress. It was black and slinky—apt to bring her grief if Buck had invited his daughters—but in New York she had dated the son of a Danish baronet whom she met while wearing it at a ball at the Pierre.

Lily stepped into the dress and saw, to her alarm, that she had lost so much weight that it no longer fit. The black straps that crossed her back no longer stayed in place, and the top would not stay up. Lily thought that she looked like a *Mad* magazine parody of Demi Moore in *Indecent Proposal*—Robert Redford would pay a million dollars *not* to sleep with her.

Flipping through her closet, Lily saw nothing else remotely suitable for a charity benefit at the city's fanciest hotel. "Fancy" was a relative term—at one of the city's best French restaurants, the waiters wore white socks—but in the Tri-County region it invariably meant "conservative."

Lily fell back on her silver tube top and black silk trousers, which at least would not expose too much thigh, and set out for the Majestic. Twenty minutes later, she arrived and learned that a benefit for the head-injury wing of Lakeland Hospital was taking place in the Grand Ballroom. *Naturally,* she thought. How could she have forgotten all the money that Mark's family had given to build the unit?

After taking the elevator to the mezzanine, she saw a frieze adorned with images of classically draped women engaged in spinning, weaving, embroidery, and other household arts. The hotel originally had been called the Athena, but with every decline in the local economy, it had been spruced up, given a new name, and proclaimed a symbol of the city's rebirth. With a grandeur inversely proportional to the fortunes of the region, the names had grown steadily more pretentious until, in its present incarnation, the hotel had become known as the Majestic.

At the entrance to the Grand Ballroom Lily found a registration table presided over by a woman who, on seeing the lump on her forehead, looked up brightly.

"You must be one of our spokespeople," she said. Glancing at Lily's bare shoulders, she continued. "I must say, you have made a remarkable recovery from your tragedy. You don't know how lucky you are compared with some of the people our hospital has helped. Are you representing diving, horseback riding, or household accidents?"

Lily said that she had suffered only a superficial wound, which did not require hospitalization, and asked for the number of Buck's table. Disappointed, the woman directed her to the front of the ballroom. Lily found Mark's father at a large table at which the fruit cups had just been served.

Buck was explaining that he realized the importance of head injuries after an Ohio State wide receiver had been knocked out during a play, causing the Buckeyes to lose to Wisconsin.

"It could have been worse," he was saying. "It could have happened during the Penn State game the week before. But I thought, why take a chance on something like that happening again? Would I want a player to get injured when Ohio State was playing in the Rose Bowl?"

There were murmurs to the effect that, certainly, he

would not, when one of Mark's sisters noticed Lily.

"My God, you look ghastly!" Penny cried. "What happened to your face?"

Lily said that she fell at the Convention Center, where she had been working on a story for the *Daily*. Penny's husband, Dick, looked up from a fruit cup in which the sliced bananas were turning brown.

"Boy, I bet Mark could get you a bundle if you sued the *Daily* for that thing," he said. "Six figures at least, and he probably wouldn't even take all of his usual thirty percent because you're his fiancée."

"Thanks for the tip, but I'm not going to sue anybody," Lily replied. "My fault entirely."

Dick said that she should sue even though it was her fault just to get back at the *Daily* for all the other things it had done without having been taken to court.

"Like my subscription," he said. "I should sue about *that*. At least once a week I don't get any paper at all, and on the other days—"

Penny interrupted him. "Dick, you can talk to Lily about her legal rights later. We haven't introduced Lily to the rest of the table yet, and we don't want her to feel left out, do we?"

Buck's older daughter had a habit of using the plural, as though speaking to a dim-witted child or to a semicomatose hospital patient, when she wanted to make a point. In her presence Lily always felt that she had been cloned.

"Everybody, this is the future Mrs. Mark Peabody Slayton," Penny said.

Lily reminded her that she was keeping her name. That she had planned to keep it after the wedding, she thought, did not obviate her doing so now that the wedding was off. On hearing this, Mark's other sister jumped in.

"Well, of course you're keeping your name professionally," Fran said. "Of course you're keeping it *professionally*. Journalists always do that."

Unlike her sister, who favored the imperial "we," Fran tended to repeat what she said, as though speaking to people too slow to grasp what she said the first time around. The result was that, if Penny made people feel that they had body doubles, Fran made them feel that they were in an echo chamber. This fact, paradoxically, had attracted Lily to their brother.

That Mark had survived decades of exposure to his sisters without becoming cynical left her with the same sense of awe that she had for survivors of hit-and-run accidents, or poison-gas attacks. His good humor seemed a spectacular triumph of character over circumstance that, in the face of relentless challenges from her parents, Lily longed to emulate. Mindful of his example, she told Fran calmly that she was keeping her name socially as well as professionally.

"Oh, Lily, you know that's impossible. Impossible. Think of how awful that would be for your poor children. No woman in our family has ever kept her name. After my first date with my darling husband"—she looked across the table indulgently—"I went home and immediately wrote out my future name every way I could think of. *Mrs. George Henry Platt. Mrs. George H. Platt. Mrs. G. H. Platt. Mrs. Frances Slayton Platt. Mrs. Fran—*"

Lily wondered if the psychiatrists who studied multiple personality disorder had a category for people like Fran. Buck broke impatiently into his daughter's list of aliases.

"Fran, I don't care what name Lily uses," Buck said. "Any woman who can get my son to the altar after thirty-two years must know what she's doing, right?" Buck laughed. "Too bad Mark is in California. Just think of all the malpractice cases he could pick up from the doctors in this room." Lily started to remind him that Mark did not do malpractice-defense work, but Buck cut her off. "What's Mark doing in L.A., anyway?"

Lily said that he was trying an age-discrimination case in which a big corporate client was accused of unfairly firing employees over fifty-five. She added that he had been asked to take the case partly because he had once won a similar case that he had handled on a pro bono basis.

Penny, who had been trying to fish a maraschino cherry out of her husband's fruit cup with a fork, perked up.

"Really?" she asked. "I didn't know Mark represented Sonny Bono."

After Lily explained the meaning of pro bono, Penny said that it made no difference because "I Got You, Babe," wasn't a very good song, anyway. Dick said that, in fact, "I Got You, Babe," was one of the greatest songs ever written, in a class with the Beach Boys' "Be True to Your School," which he began to sing. Fran looked disconcerted.

"Lily, after you're married, you have to make Mark stop representing people who don't have two hundred-dollar bills to rub together," she said. "Every time I talk to him, he's taken on a client who could keep his spare cash in a capped tooth. Last week he told me he's agreed to represent a priest—a priest—who got in trouble with the diocese because he let women serve communion at his church when he was in the hospital with pneumonia. Now, would you tell me how a priest is ever going to be able to pay his legal bills?"

Buck spoke up before Lily could answer. "Fran, I don't care if my son wants to represent the Pope. I'd rather have him working for men who wear dresses than trying to wear one himself." Mark's interest in the seminary clearly still upset his father, who changed the subject. "Now, would you let me introduce my future daughter-in-law to the rest of the table?"

Besides Penny and Fran and their husbands, the group included of two chief executive officers and their wives and a British architect whom Buck was trying to induce to design a chain of sports bars for his company. One seat was unoccupied.

Lily found that Buck had placed her between the architect and one of the executive's wives, whose place card identified her as Mrs. Charles Franklin Gardiner III. The woman wore a long-sleeved, high-necked aqua chiffon dress with a spray of pleats fanning out from an empire waist. Next to her, Lily felt like a nudist. She apologized for her lateness and said she had been delayed by a crisis at work.

"Well, that's one problem she won't have after next month," Fran said, smiling at the executives' wives. "Aren't we all thankful that marriage took us all away from our offices and let us play tennis all day long?"

Fran laughed, and patted her husband's arm. "Only kidding, George." Her husband, excavating a basket of rolls, did not reply. "But, Lily, after you quit work, you'll be able to join our tennis league, too. Ten to noon at the Mt. Garfield Tennis Club, Tuesdays and Thursdays. Your mother said you used to be quite good when you practiced more and didn't spend all your time at the office turning into one of those workaholic career women who have their children raised by illegible alien baby-sitters."

Not for the first time, it occurred to Lily that Colony Heights had skipped the early stages of the women's movement and gone directly to the backlash. She was debating which of Fran's misconceptions to correct—she was only a fair tennis player, she did not spend all her time at the office, and she had never met an "illegible" alien—when the British architect spoke.

"I'm sure Lily is quite good at many things right now," he said, smiling ingratiatingly.

Lily turned in surprise to the architect, whose place card gave his name as Nicholas Monford. As she was about to speak, a waiter began clearing the fruit cups. This distraction allowed Buck to bring up the former owner of the local football team, who had pulled his franchise out of the city.

In Lily's youth the team owner had been admired as a bulwark of the community who contributed heavily to charities in the Tri-County region. The moment he had withdrawn his team from the city, however, he was compared with Benedict Arnold, Saddam Hussein, and Jane Fonda. Shunned by friends and vilified on call-in radio shows, the man had become an overnight pariah. Buck said that he almost felt sorry for him when he saw him at an airport earlier in the week and had been tempted to say hello.

This comment drew a sharp look from Mrs. Gardiner. She said that, had she run into the team owner at an airport, she would have changed her flight rather than eat salted peanuts next to him. It was rumored that he might make a contribution to a hunger-relief fund in her suburb, in which his grandchildren still lived, and she was organizing a campaign to reject it.

"Now, let's not talk about silly things like politics anymore," Penny said. "Let's talk about more interesting things, like my brother's wedding. Come on, Lily, show everybody your ring."

Lily slipped her left hand uneasily into a pocket of her silk trousers and made a mental note to stop by her parents' house later in the week and retrieve her ring. She knew the gossip that might arise if she kept it off her finger for long, and she could not bear that Mark might hear it. If she had to break their engagement, she would at least have the decency to make sure that he heard the news directly from her.

"Come on, Lily," Penny said. "Show Dick the ring. I want him to buy me one like it someday, although it would be totally impractical while I have small children who might swallow it."

Lily fought the urge to ask Penny if she stored her jewelry in jars of strained lamb. With Mark's sisters, conversation followed a logic to which she still hoped, after weeks of fruitless effort, to find the key.

"Unfortunately, I left the ring at home tonight," Lily said, feeling her face grow warm. "I was afraid to wear it downtown after dark. I didn't want to tempt the muggers." In her own defense she told herself that her words, though not strictly true, would have been true if she still had her ring. Not long after moving back to town, she was mugged near her office, an experience that left her wary of going out alone at night.

"Oh, Lily, you're always so foolish about these things!" Penny said. "This city is not like New York"—she uttered the words disdainfully—"where they have such terrible crime problems. Two years ago, when Mark's firm offered him a transfer to its New York office, he said he couldn't imagine why anyone would ever live there, and I'm sure that everyone at this table couldn't agree more. Here you can walk anywhere at any hour of the day or night and be perfectly safe."

At that point Lily excused herself from the table, saying that she had to put cold towels on her bruise. Like a Vietnam veteran who did not remember the Tet offensive, she had forgotten the toll that Buck and his friends could take when Mark wasn't around.

Near the ballroom, she found a ladies' room and slipped into one of the stalls, which had a louvered wood floor-to-ceiling door. She wished she had trumped up an excuse not to attend the benefit and was trying to determine how soon she could leave when she heard two women enter the ladies' room. They were talking, improbably, about postage stamps.

"American flags are so tacky."

"Especially on ecru envelopes."

"On white, it might have been different."

Lily listened interestedly. It had not occurred to her that anything so innocuous as postage stamps could be tacky, on ecru envelopes or any other color. This was a new concept.

"She could at least have used those nice peach stamps."

"Or the pears."

"Flowers would have been good, too."

"Though love stamps are always the best for that sort of thing."

Lily suddenly recognized the voices of Tess Mahoney and her daughter, Erin, both of whom she had invited to her wedding. She was about to leave the stall to say hello when, catching another fragment of their conversation, she froze.

". . . why Charlotte let her do it, I'll never know. She usually has such good taste."

"Can you imagine spending all that money on a wedding and not bothering about a detail like postage stamps?"

Lily waited until she was sure the women had left the ladies' room, then returned to the table. She found Buck and his guests working on Chicken Florentine that, inexplicably, did not include spinach. They were talking about a local pitcher who had been suspended for flipping an umpire over his shoulder during a game. The ball player was appealing his suspension—rather inventively, Lily thought—on the grounds that he had not known the man was an umpire.

Buck argued that the disciplinary action constituted further evidence of baseball officials' bias against their city, a view quickly ratified by his daughters and sons-in-law and the executives. Dick, a psychologist, said that the pitcher had merely expressed appropriate anger at how his team had been treated while the umpire showed hostile tendencies that required professional help. George thought that both the pitcher and the umpire should read *Seven Habits of Highly Effective People* so they could learn how to view baseball games as a "win-win" situation. One of the executives seemed to settle the matter by saying that the whole incident had been blown out of proportion by the out-of-town media, which was biased against the city.

Lily knew that, now that the conversational possibilities of baseball and football had been plumbed, the discussion would move swiftly on to basketball if she did not introduce a new topic. After mentally casting about for a subject that might interest everyone, she asked what the others thought of the strike that the city's public school teachers were threatening to stage.

Buck said that it would be too bad if the teachers struck because, the last time they did, the high school football teams had to play a reduced schedule and missed a shot at a state championship. Penny agreed that it would be too bad but, if parents sent their children to public schools, what did they expect?

Lily was relieved when, a few minutes later, the after-dinner speeches began before Fran had commented on the strike. The speakers echoed so many others that she had heard in the city that, by the time the third man had taken his place at the podium, she began to play a mental parlor trick of trying to predict what he would say next.

"This city has the greatest history . . ." he said.

And the greatest traditions, Lily thought.

"And the greatest traditions . . ."

Not to mention, the finest people.

"Not to mention, the finest people . . ."

In America.

"In America."

It also has the best cultural attractions.

"It also has the best cultural attractions."

And world-class athletic teams.

"And world-class athletic teams."

I don't need to tell you that it also *has the most distinguished hospital in America. (Roar of applause.)*

"I don't need to tell you that it *also* has the most distinguished hospital. (Roar of applause.)

There's only one thing wrong with this city.

"There's only one thing wrong with this city."

It has an inferiority complex.

"It has an inferiority complex."

The speaker had just said that the people of the city needed only to see that they lacked nothing that existed in New York or Los Angeles when the architect turned to Lily.

"I'm afraid that his calling this the greatest city in America doesn't sound like an inferiority complex to me," he said, smiling, in a low voice. "That sounds like my definition of a *superiority* complex. Perhaps you would care to go for a walk later and explain your curious American expressions to me?" The architect paused. "Now that we know the downtown streets are completely safe at this hour . . ."

Lily smiled, grateful that one person in the ballroom had a sense of perspective. "Well, they might not be quite as safe as some people think, but—" she said. Much as she longed to leave, she knew that going for a walk with the architect could give rise to gossip. She suggested instead that he walk her to her car in the hotel garage, if Buck would allow her to leave after the speaker had finished.

The architect told her to leave the matter to him, and as soon as the man had sat down, began telling Buck that he was afraid the injury to his beautiful future daughter-in-law was slightly more serious than she had allowed, and that she really must attend to it. If they would be so kind as to excuse him for a few minutes, he would see her to her car.

This caused a flurry of solicitous comments on Lily's well-being. Everyone who had been silent on the topic during the meal now insisted that she must take care of her head at once. Penny, the only guest who had previously mentioned the bruise, declared that she had known from the start that she should leave but had refrained from saying so because Lily never would listen to anyone but herself. Dick again urged her to think "in the strongest possible terms" about suing the *Daily*.

At last Lily and the architect extricated themselves from the group and headed for the hotel garage. When they passed the bar, he asked if she wanted to have a drink. Lily yearned to say yes—she had not had an intelligent conversation since Mark left town—but wanted to leave enough time to retrieve her ring from her parents' house.

With what she hoped was ample graciousness, she declined.

"Perhaps another time, then?" the architect asked. "I must say that, for someone who has just taken the fall of her life, you look ravishing."

10

Ice

"Seven years would be insufficient to make some people acquainted with each other, and seven days are more than enough for others."

—Sense and Sensibility

Back at her apartment, Lily emptied a tray of ice cubes into a white plastic bag imprinted with a black-and-white sketch of Jane Austen, which she had received at a bookstore. She arranged it on her forehead, settled back against the headboard of her brass bed, and hit the Play button on her answering machine:

1. *"Hi, sweetheart. You're probably not back from my father's dinner yet, but I decided to try you, anyway. Could you call me no matter when you get in? Love you."*

2. *"Miss Blair? This is Fairview Photo Studios calling to remind you of your appointment to have your wedding picture taken Saturday at one P.M. Would you call tomorrow to confirm*

it? As you know, we require forty-eight hours'
notice on cancellations."

3. *"Hey, Lily, it's Sally. Just wanted to let you*
   know my maid-of-honor's dress arrived, and
   it's spectacular! It makes me feel like some-
   thing out of a BBC costume drama on the
   court of Elizabeth I. My next-door neighbor
   stopped by to borrow a Roach Motel while I
   was trying it on, and when she saw me, she
   curtsied. It's after nine here—after seven
   your time—but I'll be up until at least mid-
   night."

Lily looked at the clock beside her bed: ten-thirty. Sally,
like a surprising number of the people she knew in New
York, had never quite been able to grasp that Colony
Heights was in the Eastern Time Zone but invariably sit-
uated it in Central or Mountain Time with Calgary and
Winnipeg.

But Lily was overjoyed to hear from her best friend. In
New York, she had found Sally to have that most precious
of traits in a confidante: She was unshockable. As a police
reporter, Sally dealt with burglars, rapists, murderers, ar-
sonists, and teenage vandals who threw their mothers'
pink bubble bath into the fountain of the Seagram Building, all of whom had taught her to listen to confidences
in a way that implied neither blame nor reproof.

Lily knew she had found her future maid of honor when
she confessed guiltily that she had been working so hard
that she had not filed a tax return due three months earlier. Without saying a word, Sally reached across her desk
and picked up a copy of that morning's newspaper. She
pointed to a photograph on page one.

"This man did not pay income taxes for two years," she said, "and he got elected mayor of New York."

Lily admired her friend all the more after Sally quit her steady job as a police reporter to freelance. With that kind of nerve in a high-rent city like New York, Sally would not condemn her for wanting to call off the wedding. And despite her desire to keep her decision under wraps, Lily resolved to try to raise the issue with her. As she dialed her number, she hoped that a good, long talk with her best friend would fortify her for her conversation with her fiancé.

Sally answered on the first ring and began to bemoan the effects of the heat wave on Manhattan.

"God, Lily, you don't know how lucky you are to have moved to Ohio."

Lily was taken aback. "Lucky? Weren't you the one who told me that anybody who lived beyond a fifty-mile radius of Zabar's was gastronomically deprived? That scientists have pointed to a severe Kosher-pastrami deficiency as a leading cause of pellagra?"

"That was before this heat wave struck. This morning the air-conditioning in my building went out for the third time this week. So for the past three hours I've been sitting beside an air shaft trying to cool off while listening to my neighbors, who are all in the same boat, screaming at each other through open windows." Sally stopped, as though distracted by a hornet. "It's like *Lord of the Flies* here. Listen to this."

Sally held the receiver up to the air shaft, and Lily heard what sounded like a beer bottle crashing against a wall, followed by death threats in Spanish or Italian. She thought she could make out the words *"cochinos"* and *"muerte"* but had no chance to comment before her friend went on.

"You don't know how lucky you are to live in a peaceful, bucolic place like the Midwest."

"Bucolic?" Lily repeated. "I live in a grommet on the Rust Belt."

"You might live in a grommet, but you don't live in a high-rise that has turned into a twenty-seven-story sauna."

"Actually, Sally, I didn't call to talk to you about the weather. I wanted to talk about the wedding."

"Oh, don't worry about whether I can still afford my maid-of-honor's dress," Sally replied quickly. "I'm getting paid pretty well for my articles for *Home Invasion Weekly*."

Lily felt a stab of remorse that she had not offered to help Sally pay for her dress. She resolved, once her news of her broken engagement became public, to reimburse all her bridesmaids for their dresses.

"It's good to hear that you've found a steady market," Lily said. "But your dress wasn't what I was thinking about. I'm just wondering if I did the right thing in getting engaged after three months. Maybe Mark and I should have waited longer before booking the Holy Family Cathedral Choir to sing the 'Hallelujah' chorus for three hundred and fifty people."

Sally appeared startled. "Lily, if it's fate, you don't need to wait a long time. How often do you meet a man who's been waiting all his life to play Julius Rosenberg to your Ethel?"

Lily considered the implications of this and decided to leave Julius and Ethel out of any future conversations about her wedding.

"If it was fate, that ought to have given us all the more incentive to wait a year or two before getting the license. Fate doesn't penalize you for being sensible." She thought about her comment, then expanded it slightly. "For being timid, maybe, but not for being sensible. Fate would have held our places."

"But what would have been the point of having fate hold your places? You're always quoting Jane Austen, and doesn't she say something like that in *Sense and Sensibility*? Sort of like, it's not how long you've known each other but how long you've known yourself?"

"Jane Austen said that intimacy has less to do with time than with temperament, which is precisely my point. Three months might have been enough for Mark, but three years might not be enough for me."

Lily looked, a bit wistfully, at the vacant spot on her ring finger, and went on. "Where did people ever get the idea that women are the more romantic sex? Mark is far more romantic than I am. Once I asked him, after he gave me the ring, if he ever thought that we should have lived together before we got engaged, and he looked at me as though he didn't even understand the question. He just said, 'I've known since the first week we met that I love you and want to marry you. What good would have come of our living together?' He doesn't see what we would have gained by living together, and I don't see what we would have lost. It could have been great to have tried playing house together, in a nice little condo somewhere—"

"To tell you the truth, sweetie, living together always sounds better than it is," Sally said. "Yes, as feminists, we have every obligation to try to avoid the bourgeois, capitalistic, patriarchal institution of matrimony, even if it *is* the only dependable source of sex for women over twenty-five. I know Simone de Beauvoir had some sort of arrangement with Jean-Paul Sartre where they lived in separate rooms of the same hotel—"

Sally broke off, as though trying to remember whatever happened to Simone and Jean-Paul, then resumed. "But all the women I know who are living with men would rather be married to them. It drives them nuts that the guys won't commit to anything more than two names on the buzzer for the intercom. If Mark had asked you to live with him, you might wish he had asked you to marry him instead."

Lily could not imagine that she would have wished this and tried to sidestep the question. "Right up until the day Mark asked me to marry him, I was planning to look for a job in New York as soon as I had been at the paper for a year. The idea that I will never live there again is like—I don't know, having had the world's greatest lover for three years and then suddenly realizing you'll never sleep with him again."

"Haven't you forgotten what New York is like?" Sally asked. "Let me remind you." She held the phone up to the window again, and Lily heard the sound of another beer bottle crashing, followed by the wail of a police siren.

"See?" Sally said. "At least the cops have finally arrived to do something about those hoodlums."

"I sort of liked the street noises when I lived in New York," Lily said, fighting off a wave of nostalgia for the staccato blasts of pile-drivers and jackhammers under her window at 6 A.M. "It made me feel connected to the universe. By the time I left New York, I could tell the difference between a gunshot, a backfiring car, and a small bomb from a distance of ten blocks away. Now, when I go downtown after work, it's like walking through a mausoleum."

"Well, if you miss all the noise so much, why can't the two of you move here? You could freelance—you and I could be a sort of roving investigative team—and Mark could get a job with a New York law firm. You could listen to all the backfiring cars you want on Wall Street or Park Avenue."

"Mark doesn't want to live in New York. He had the chance when he got out of Harvard, and another one two years ago when his law firm offered him a transfer to its Manhattan office." Lily sighed. "It's not even that he loves Ohio. He just thinks that the right person can make the wrong place right, whereas I think that the wrong place can make the right person wrong."

Lily glanced at a photograph on her night table, in which she and Mark were holding hands in a grove of white birches, which had been his idea to have taken. "That's what I mean when I say Mark is so much more romantic than I am. He thinks that, no matter where you live, when you meet the right person, you turn Dante and Beatrice. Whereas I think that, if you live on a heath inhabited by Weird Sisters, you turn into Mr. and Mrs. Macbeth."

"Mark has so much money, you wouldn't be stuck with anything," Sally said. "You can go someplace different every weekend. New York, Chicago, Toronto—"

Sally interrupted herself. "What's that thing that you told me people always used to say about Ohio when you were growing up?"

" 'The great thing about Ohio is that it's so close to everyplace else?' "

"That's it. So you see? You just have keep telling yourself: Ohio, it's not nowhere, it's everywhere."

"But why be nowhere—or everywhere—when you could be somewhere? Like, for instance, New York."

"I wonder if you aren't romanticizing New York now that you don't have to deal with it every day."

"I probably am romanticizing it. But at least in New York you have something to romanticize. Out here I'm still looking for a worthy object of my delusions."

"What about Mark?"

"Mark?"

"Yes, your fiancé. M-A-R-K. What about romanticizing him?"

Glancing again at the spot where her engagement ring used to be, Lily said nothing. Finally, Sally grew restless.

"Lily?" she asked. "I was just wondering, did you and Mark have a fight or something? You sound so different from when you first got engaged."

"No, not at all. Mark and I never fight." Lily realized how improbable her words sounded and sought to clarify them. "I mean, we've only known each other for five months and been engaged for two, and during a lot of that time Mark has been away. So we haven't really had a chance to have any major battles."

"Are you kidding? I've known plenty of people who have major battles after five hours together." Sally seemed to be trying to digest Lily's words. "You haven't had any fights at all?"

"Well, you couldn't really call it a fight. But we do disagree, sort of, over the house his father gave us for a wedding present. It's so wrong for us that I'm afraid to move in. But Mark thinks we should try to live in it, even though it has all sorts of crazy things in it, like a doorbell that plays the Ohio State song."

Sally laughed. "That's pretty funny, a doorbell that plays the Ohio State song. At least it isn't something really bad, like Barry Manilow." As if sensing Lily's chagrin, Sally grew serious. "So disconnect the doorbell."

Lily suddenly realized how much Sally sounded like Mark. "It's not just the doorbell. The house also has a private chapel with a stained glass window that has marching tuba players where Jesus, Mary, and Joseph should be."

Sally began to laugh again, then stopped herself. "I'm sorry, Lily, honestly. I know the house must be much worse than it sounds from here. But how often do you go to church? Twice a year, at Christmas and Easter?"

"That doesn't matter," Lily said, more heatedly than she had intended. "The whole house is just—I don't know—a parody of my dream house, all eighteen rooms of it. It looks like something the Addams Family might have lived in if they'd had more money. I look at the house and imagine my children pouring boiling oil on Christmas carolers from an upstairs window, or taking a pair of scissors to cobwebs growing between the pews in the chapel."

"Lily, I'm Jewish, so there may be some nuances to this that are lost on me. But it seems to me that just because you have a chapel doesn't mean you have to use it all the time. Wasn't Mark going to go to the seminary at one point? And if it doesn't bother him—" Sally hesitated, then went on more sympathetically. "The trouble with turning down the house is that it's like turning down any other sort of wedding present. You hurt people too much by doing it. My Aunt Florence didn't speak to me for five years after I tried to return the leaky fountain pen she gave me for my bat mitzvah. Imagine how your father-in-law would feel if you rejected a house. Couldn't you just think of the house as a big, expensive, eighteen-room variation on a set of salt-and-pepper shakers shaped like outhouses?"

Lily had never had so much trouble getting through to her friend. Lamenting that she had brought up her wedding, she tried to think of a way to make her understand the situation.

"Suppose you were getting married, and your future father-in-law gave you a house with a synagogue attached."

"That's crazy. It would never happen, because Jews don't have synagogues in their houses."

"That's exactly my point. Episcopalians don't have

stained glass windows with marching tuba players in their houses either."

Sally seemed to think about this. At last, tentatively, she began to speak.

"Okay, so let's say my future father-in-law did give us a house with a synagogue," she said, slowly. "And let's say that in this synagogue there was a stained glass window with a picture of Brandeis University cheerleaders on it."

Lily felt relieved. "Right."

"The question is, what would I do about the Brandeis cheerleaders?"

"Precisely."

Uncharacteristically, Sally said nothing for a long time. Lily noticed that the police had not quieted the residents of her building, who were still shouting at each other. A car backfired as Sally began to speak.

"To tell you the truth, I would ask myself: What am I really upset about here? Is it the window that's bothering me, or is the window a symbol of something else? If it were the first, I would replace the window. But if it were the second, I would try to figure out what the window represented. Then I would, absolutely, do something about that."

After hanging up, Lily debated whether she had enough energy left to call Mark. She was afraid that, if she spoke to him, she might say something that would betray her decision about the wedding. Mark had a veteran litigator's radar for anything less than full disclosure.

But she was afraid that if she didn't call she would arouse even more suspicion. Since the first days of their acquaintance Mark had called her daily, and she had always returned his calls. After vacillating for a while, she waited until she thought he would be out to dinner, then dialed the number of his hotel and asked to be put through to his suite.

To her dismay, Mark answered promptly. "Hi, sweetheart," he said. "How are things in the city that has made the greatest comeback in history, with the possible exception of Grover Cleveland's election to a second term?"

Lily could not help smiling. "Not bad, if you don't count the food, the schools, the weather, the crime rate, the poverty rate, the unemployment rate, or my parents. Or the fact that a local theater company is rumored to be doing a stage adaptation of *An American Tragedy* called *An American Comedy . . .*"

Mark laughed. "Well, I see things haven't changed much since I left. I hope—" He broke off as Lily heard a voice in the background. Mark asked if she would wait until he switched to another phone.

When he came back on the line, he explained that Caroline Van Allen and Dave Lynch, a partner in his firm's Los Angeles office, were going over depositions in the next room, and he had not wanted to disturb them. The trial was not going as well as he had hoped.

"Winks Ferguson doesn't just have trouble staying awake on the bench," he said. "He doesn't seem to want to stay awake. He closes his eyes whenever a lawyer is making a point that he disagrees with—which sends a subtle signal to the jury members that he isn't paying attention to the argument, and they don't have to, either. And on this case, he's always wide awake when the plaintiffs' counsel are making their case and half-asleep when we are."

"Can't you protest somehow, or call his behavior somehow to the attention of the jury?"

"It's incredibly difficult, because it's never clear that he's closing his eyes intentionally. If we tried to protest, he might just argue that he was deep in thought. But he leaves such a strong impression of being asleep that it has the opposite effect."

Mark, who had never lost a case and tended to remain upbeat against the most unpromising of odds, quickly amended his comment. "But it was a stroke of luck that our L.A. office put Dave Lynch on this case. If anybody can wake up Ferguson, he can." Mark lowered his voice. "Caroline is—" He broke off again.

"Caroline is?" Lily prompted.

"Well, Caroline has her strengths. For one thing, she's excellent with the male witnesses."

As Lily was wondering what that meant, Mark asked about the head-injury dinner. She gave him a synopsis that left out the discussion of her ring.

"By the way, did you know your father wants to build a group of sports bars?" she asked. "At the dinner I met a British architect he's trying to interest in designing them."

Mark said he heard about the project from his father, who hoped that an imported architect might lend his latest project an air of refinement. "I admit I'm a bit doubtful about whether anything could lend refinement to bars filled with the sort of sports fans I grew up with. My father tends to forget that he's dealing with people who like to show their support for their team by meowing drunkenly and throwing Kitty Litter at the players."

The most ardent fans of the departed local football team, officially known as the Bobcats but invariably called the 'Cats, called themselves the Kennel. At half-time, they got down on all fours and lapped beer out of saucers. Going to 'Cats games was like attending a Mensa Convention in reverse: Everywhere you looked you saw people trying to prove how low their IQs were.

"But who knows?" Mark went on. "Maybe this will—"

Mark stopped. "What?" Lily heard him say, and then, "Later, Caroline." He apologized when he returned to the line.

"Caroline walked into the room, but she's gone now. We haven't had dinner yet, and she says she and Dave are starving, so I'll have to go soon. But the reason I called was—" Mark paused. "I was wondering if you could fly out here this weekend."

The request threw Lily off guard. Mark had tried three out-of-town cases since they had met, and he had never asked her to accompany him on any of them.

"But won't you have to work this weekend?"

"I have to work during the day, but we could see each other at night."

With mild alarm, Lily asked if anything was wrong.

"No, no," Mark said. "It's just that it seems so long since we've seen each other. I know it hasn't even been a week but . . ." He seemed to be groping for words. "But this trial is so grueling that Dave keeps popping Maaloxes, and Caroline keeps—" Mark did not finish.

"Mark, I'm so sorry, but I'm supposed to have my portrait taken on Saturday."

Lily did not regard this statement as a lie given that she had not yet canceled the appointment and, in fact, still was supposed to have the picture taken.

"What about flying out after you have your picture taken, and going back Sunday night?" Mark asked. "I could get you a first-class plane—"

Mark stopped again. "What's that, Caroline?" He listened to what appeared to be a plea. "Oh, all right, just a little longer." Lily had never heard him sound so distracted.

"Sweetheart, I'm so sorry, Caroline and Dave want to eat, so I'm afraid I'll have to go. But would you at least think about flying out here after your photo appointment?"

"I'll think about it, but it's hopeless. My mother has a whole list of things she wants me to do besides getting my picture taken."

"Please try." Mark sounded so unexpectedly dejected that Lily almost relented. "I really need—"

Before he could finish, Caroline entered the room again.

After talking to Mark, Lily could not sleep. From the earliest days of their acquaintance he had asked so little of her—almost nothing beyond that she try to live with his father's house—that declining the trip to California left her uneasy. She could not bear to fly to Los Angeles and deceive him for a weekend, but neither could she bear that he would think less of her refusing so mild a request.

Lily kept thinking about her conversation with her father. What if he had been right about Caroline? Mark had told her repeatedly that he never became involved with women from his firm. That he might deviate from his rule, two months after becoming engaged, made no sense. It didn't matter if it did make sense, now that the wedding was off.

But Lily could not resolve the conflicting emotions that her conversation with Mark had aroused. The ease with which Caroline laid claim to his attention had surprised her; she could not imagine herself interrupting his conversations so easily. Still, Lily told herself, Mark had never complained when she went on out-of-town assignments with male photographers. So how could she object to his spending time with a partner in California?

11

White Lilacs

"I consider everybody as having a right to marry once in their Lives for Love, if they can."

—Letter to Cassandra Austen

The next morning Lily found members of a gay-rights group demonstrating in front of her office building. They were carrying signs that read, "Boycott the *Daily*," "Don't Subscribe to Homophobia," and "Shakespeare Was Gay." Several of the protesters wore T-shirts that bore a photograph of the Republican presidential candidate, Bob Dole, overlaid with a red circle with a slash through it.

Lily hurried past them and into the building, where the elevators were out of order for the third time that week. She climbed the stairs to the fourth-floor newsroom and, on reaching her desk, saw a huge bouquet of white lilacs.

Without reading the card, Lily knew that the lilacs had come from Mark. After learning that she loved white flowers, he had devoted himself to finding different varieties to send her: white tulips from Holland one week, paperwhite narcissus from a Florida greenhouse the next.

But the sweet and hardy lilac was her favorite. On the

card Mark had included a handwritten quotation from
Thoreau: "Still grows the vivacious lilac, a generation after
the door and the lintel and the sill are gone, unfolding its
sweet-scented flowers each spring." Had he dropped it off
at the florist's before he left town? Lily wondered how,
working twelve- and fourteen-hour days, he found the time
for it.

After clearing a space on her desk for the bouquet, she
called Fairview Photo Studios to cancel her appointment
to have her wedding picture taken. Jack stopped by before
she could listen to her first phone messages of the day.

"Out-of-season lilacs," he said, grinning. "That ought to
take the sting out of knowing that every gay-rights group
in Ohio wants to hang you in effigy."

"Me?"

"Sure. Didn't you see those pickets on the way in?"

"How could I miss them? But I didn't pay any attention
to them. People demonstrate here every week."

"Right, and this week it's your turn to be pilloried."

"Jack, that's crazy," she said. "I've never written a word
about gay rights."

"That's just the problem," Jack replied. "Have you
looked at your messages yet?"

Atop the stack of pink slips on her desk Lily saw a note
from the news editor, asking to see her. Bill Schroeder
liked to be known as "Big Bill," a nickname he had earned
as a guard for the only undefeated St. Benedict's High
School basketball team.

Lily was sure the summons meant trouble. Bill usually
left the care of his subordinates to his overworked deputy,
Frank Gallese, while he practiced three-point shots with
crumpled-up press releases aimed at his wastebasket.

"Good luck," Jack said sympathetically.

Lily noticed that a group had gathered near her desk,

led by Art Felden of the grievance committee of the Reporters' Guild. The reporters who surrounded him looked
like rubberneckers at the scene of a two-car collision.

"Don't forget that, if the paper tries to suspend you, the
Guild is here to protect you," Art said enthusiastically.
"First, we'll file a grievance, and then if that doesn't work,
we can take your case to arbitration. If all else fails, we'll
take up a collection and send you a fruit—"

"Art, please," Lily said. "I haven't done anything I could
remotely be suspended for."

"Makes no difference, Lil," Art replied. "It's happened
before. That's why your union is always ready to fight for
the rights of its downtrodden brothers and sisters, any
time, any place, day or night—"

"Honestly, I appreciate your support," Lily said, glancing at the reporters who surrounded Art. "But I think this
is a little premature."

Still, Lily went quickly to the office of the news editor,
which stood half-exposed behind a wall of glass along a
long corridor, like the shark tank at Sea World. Bill was
at his desk, preparing to attempt a foul shot with a portion
of her bridal fair story. He released the paper ball, which
missed.

"Don't stop on my account," Lily said lightly. "The rule
book says you get another shot."

Bill ignored her and began paging through the sports
section of the day's paper. He stopped when he came to
side-by-side headlines that said, PARMA COACH DIES/SOX
DROP TWO.

After making a withering comment about the Red Sox,
he glanced up briefly.

"Lily, you've probably figured out that the demonstrators out front are a little upset that gay marriages aren't
mentioned in your story in today's paper."

Lily had not figured it out. "How could I mention gay marriages when they weren't part of the bridal fair? The fair was filled with mothers and daughters wallowing in the heartbreak of heterosexuality."

Bill turned another page of the sports section. "The protesters say they staged a demonstration—some sort of mock gay wedding—that you ignored. It lasted only about fifteen minutes before security guards escorted them out of the convention hall, but the people out front think it should have been in your story."

Lily wondered how she could have missed the scene, then remembered the half hour she spent at the first-aid station. She gestured toward her forehead and said the gay wedding must have taken place while she was nursing her bruise.

"That's a fairly pathetic excuse, Lily," Bill said. "Plenty of pro basketball players have played in championship games with worse injuries than that scratch. Kareem, Hakeem, Shaq, Michael, Larry—" He stopped, as though he were a coach who had finished calling out his starting lineup. "My point is, I want you to go outside right now and interview the gay-rights people for a story for tomorrow's paper. About seventeen or eighteen inches, and try to keep a lid on the wit, will you?"

Bill looked at Lily sternly. "I've already had one call from some guy who thinks you were making fun of people who like to do the Chicken Dance." He made clucking noises and flapped his elbows like wings.

Lily told him she would talk to the protesters, at which point Bill realized that people had been watching his chicken routine through his plate-glass window. He quickly assumed the limited dignity that remained to a man whose idols consisted exclusively of people whose names appeared on the heels of sneakers.

"No problem. I know we can't expect you to meet the performance standards of greats like Kareem, Hakeem, Shaq, Michael, Larry—" Bill wadded up the page that held the story about the Red Sox and took another unsuccessful shot at his wastebasket.

"By the way, don't be surprised if the protesters are upset about more than your story. They've been threatening to demonstrate here ever since Howard Jones wrote a column calling the Defense of Marriage Act the greatest piece of legislation since the repeal of Prohibition."

Lily winced. Howard represented a new kind of columnist at newspapers, the token redneck, hired during the Reagan administration to counter a wave of accusations that most reporters had a liberal bias. But his columns often backfired, turning into a public relations nightmare for the *Daily*.

At least once a week Howard wrote a column so outrageous that readers besieged the editors' fax machines with angry letters. His column on the Defense of Marriage Act, entitled "Heather Has Two Morons," had managed simultaneously to offend women, gays, children's-rights advocates, support groups for the mentally ill, and people named Heather.

"Was that the column that talked about 'not wanting his son to marry one'?"

"Right, and one other thing. I may hit you up for some tickets to the Garden at some point." Bill paused after mentioning the city's inaptly named basketball arena. "I'm having a little trouble getting the seats I want, and I understand that you have an inside track on these things."

Without answering, Lily hurried to her desk and grabbed her notebook. On the way out of the building she passed the desk of Art Felden, who looked at her eagerly.

"Sorry to disappoint you," she said. "But I'm not suspended. The Guild will have to come to my rescue another time."

Art's face fell. "Oh, well, we tried," he said. "Let us know if the *Daily* tries to retaliate by taking away your vacation time, forcing you to work overtime, or banishing you to the night obit desk."

"Art, I have no seniority or vacation time," Lily said. "I've been working overtime since the day I got here, and at this point the night obit desk might be a relief."

As Lily left the main entrance to the *Daily* building, she saw that the number of protesters had grown. They now included a man who carried an enlargement of a *New Yorker* cartoon that showed one man saying to another: "I wouldn't marry you if you were the last gay person on earth!" Several of the protesters were chanting the words on a picket sign.

"GAY RITES ARE RIGHT. GAY RITES ARE RIGHT."

Television camera crews had just begun to film the protesters when Lily introduced herself to their leader.

"Hey, everybody!" he shouted. "The perpetrator of the article on the bridal fair is here."

The protesters glared at Lily. A small net bag of sugared almonds, like those she had seen at the bridal fair, hit her on the head.

"Ow!" Lily said. "Look, I'm here to get your side of the story." She held up her notebook.

"All right, let's cool it," the leader said. "We don't want to face assault charges. The rest of you go back to chanting, and I'll talk to the reporter."

Lily learned from the man, Mel Goldstein, that the protesters belonged to the Ohio chapter of the Gay and Lesbian Organization for Weddings (GLOW), founded after the Defense of Marriage Act had begun to wend its way through Congress. He launched into an attack on Howard Jones's column on the bill intended to outlaw gay marriages.

With her conversation with Sally still fresh in her mind, Lily asked why gays wanted the right to take part in a patriarchal institution based on outdated ideas of money and property.

"I mean," she added, "isn't it enough that generations of women have been 'given away' like the titles to so many suburban split-levels? Doesn't the issue of gay marriages have any relation to larger issues of class or—"

Goldstein ignored her and turned to a television reporter filing a report that ended with the words "heterosexist media hegemony." Lily tried to regain his attention but, after another bag of sugared almonds hit her, returned to the newsroom. Jack was waiting at her desk.

"Looks like you could have used a SWAT team to defend you, Lil," he said. "Was it that bad?"

"It could have been worse. The demonstrators could have thrown a wedding cake at me instead of almonds."

"Well, at least you have your lilacs to console you," Jack said. "But isn't it unusual for Mark to send flowers to the office?"

This observation gave Lily pause. Mark generally did avoid sending flowers to the newsroom, where she wanted to play down her connection to his father, and had them delivered to her apartment. But his break with habit might reflect nothing more than his desire to persuade her to fly out to California. The enclosed card added that more lilacs would await her if she flew to Los Angeles.

"I don't know, Lily," Jack went on. "That bouquet must have cost a fortune. In my experience, there's only one reason a man sends a woman a bouquet like that."

"Which is?" Too late, Lily realized that she did not want to know the answer.

"He's as guilty as a war criminal of *something*. Might that 'something' have to do with the fact that you're still not wearing his ring?"

For most of the day, Lily ignored her ringing phone and worked on her story, which she wrote easily. To her relief the gay-rights protesters did not affect her nearly as emotionally as the women at the bridal fair. Late in the afternoon, she took a break to listen to her new messages:

1. *"Hi, sweetheart. Winks Ferguson called a fifteen-minute recess—rumor is that he wanted to take a catnap between witnesses—so I'm calling you from a pay phone at the courthouse to see if you've thought any more about flying out here this weekend. You won't be able to reach me this afternoon, so I'll try you again tonight. Hope the flowers arrived safely. Love you and hope to see you Saturday."*

2. *"Hello, Lily, this is Nick Monford, the architect you met last night at the dinner. It was delightful talking with you, and I wondered if you would like to join me for lunch today at the Ritz. Would you call my room at the hotel if you get this message before noon? Hope your forehead is on the mend."*

Lily left messages for Nick Monford, apologizing for not getting back to him, and for Mark thanking him for the lilacs and insisting that she could not fly to California. As she left the office for the day, she glanced at the digital clock suspended above the newsroom and saw that she had just enough time to pick up her shoes at Heart and Sole before heading to her parents' house to retrieve her five-carat diamond. She hardly knew which she dreaded more—another day of demonstrations or another of Jack's innuendoes about her ring.

12

Headaches

"Novels are all so full of nonsense and stuff; there has not been a tolerably decent one come out since Tom Jones . . . "

—Northanger Abbey

On seeing a lump the size of a duck egg on her daughter's forehead, Charlotte Blair's first words were, "You did this on purpose." After a pause, she added, "You did it just to torment me. You know that with that lump you can't very well have your wedding portrait taken."

All her life, Lily had avoided sarcasm, which she regarded as the lowest form of wit after puns. She had shunned it all the more diligently after joining the *Daily*, where it so thoroughly pervaded the newsroom that she feared she might catch it, like pink eye, from the telephones.

But her resistance to sarcasm, as to other things, had worn down after she had become engaged. So when her mother suggested that she had wounded and possibly scarred herself for life, for the sole purpose of defaulting on her appointment with the photographer, Lily was unable to take the high road that had risen up to meet her in the past.

"You're right, Mother," she said. "I snuck into the Commodore's Club in the middle of the night, took a polo mallet out of the equipment room, and smacked myself with it on the forehead, just so I wouldn't have to go the photographer's on Saturday."

"Very funny, darling," her mother said, lending credence to the contagion theory of sarcasm that Lily had developed at the *Daily*. "But you're the one who is going to pay for this, because your appointment will have to be rescheduled for a date closer to your wedding, when you will have more things on your calendar, and it will be less convenient."

"It doesn't have to be rescheduled. I don't need a wedding portrait for a nonexistent wedding."

"You and your father agreed that you weren't going to make a decision about the wedding until after you had seen a psychiatrist."

"Wrong. We agreed that I am going to talk to a psychiatrist because it might change your and Daddy's mind about what's right for me, not because it might change my mind."

"Are you so closed-minded that you can't accept that somebody else might know what's best for you?"

"Are you so—" Lily fought the urge to return her mother's blows in kind. "Can't you accept that I might know what's best for me?"

"Psychiatrists have medical degrees. They have studied these things. You have a degree in English literature. You studied novels about wives who kill themselves on the way to the cleaners."

"Mother, we've been through this before. *Anna Karenina* and *Madame Bovary* are not novels about 'wives who kill themselves on the way to the cleaners.' "

"Just because that wasn't the name of the course—"

"The course was called 'By Her Own Hand: Suicide as an Alternative to Patriarchy in—' "

"In four years at Yale, you never read one book about a happy wife. This is why I wanted you to go to Smith."

"Mother, they teach *Anna Karenina* and *Madame Bovary* at Smith. Besides, I didn't take that course at Yale. I took it at summer school here at—"

"Lily, I don't care if you took the course at dancing school. The point is, in your whole life, you've never read one book about a happy wife. You refuse to read anything but novels about women that are completely morbid, and now they've twisted your mind to a point at which you don't want to get married."

"Books are supposed to twist your mind. And, anyway, I did, too, read books about happy wives."

"Like what?"

"Like—" Lily stopped, brought up short. She couldn't very well count the novels of Jane Austen, which ended, figuratively speaking, at the altar. But in her other favorite books—*Middlemarch, The Portrait of a Lady, Mrs. Bridge*— the views of marriage ranged from mixed to savage. As a her mother's face was arranging itself into an expression of conquest, Lily remembered Natasha Rostov. "Like— *War and Peace*."

This comment briefly silenced her mother, who had not read Tolstoy since Smith. Lily took the opening to say that she had come to retrieve her engagement ring.

Her mother looked at her with satisfaction. "So you admit you are going through with the wedding after all."

"No, I don't admit it. I just want the ring."

"Well, I'm not giving it back just so you can return it to Mark. That man deserves better treatment than this."

"Mother, it's *my* ring." Lily looked around the breakfast nook, where she had again found her mother at her computer, trying to parse place cards. "Where is it?"

Charlotte Blair turned her attention back to her computer screen. "You can't have it, because I put it in my safe-deposit box. I was afraid you hadn't had it insured, and with all the break-ins we've had around here, I didn't want to keep it in the house."

Lily sank onto the banquette in the breakfast nook. She was not sure she believed the ring was in the safe-deposit box. But, if it was not, it was probably in a locked jewelry chest in the master bedroom, and she did not see how she could retrieve it easily.

As Lily was weighing her options, her grandmother walked into the breakfast nook.

"Gran! You're back!" Lily said. She embraced her grandmother joyfully. "How was Maine?"

"Wonderful, although our cottage was so small, the bedroom unfortunately didn't have room for the king-size bed Mr. Brooks prefers. We had to make do with a queen."

Lily thought she saw her mother wince as her grandmother admitted that she and her companion had shared a bed.

"But, Lily, you look so tired," her grandmother said. "You look as though you haven't slept in days."

"To tell you the truth, Gran, I haven't, or least not very well. You might have suspected that I've been a little busier than usual."

"I'm not surprised, although your mother seems determined to take as much of the wedding as she can out of your hands," her grandmother said dryly.

"That's because she has shown very little interest in doing anything herself," her mother said. "Right from the beginning, I've had to do practically everything on this wedding. I never saw a girl take so little interest in her big day in my life."

"Charlotte, perhaps that's because she doesn't see it as quite as big a day as you do."

"Nonsense. She wants to have a big wedding but just doesn't want to do any of the work for it, the same way Isabelle wanted a big wedding but didn't want to pay for it."

Lily, sensing that she had just heard the opening volleys in another of the rare but blistering arguments between her mother and the mother-in-law who shared her home, said that she had to leave for her health club. Her grandmother hugged her and urged her to come back soon to see the pictures from her trip.

"Darling, I only hope that you're having as much fun this summer as Mr. Brooks and I had at the cottage," she said. She looked somberly at Lily's mother. "I'm afraid that fun doesn't rank very high on the list of priorities in this house right now."

13

Toxic Men

"Stupid men are the only ones worth knowing, after all."

—Pride and Prejudice

At her health club Lily found that Edie Vogel had switched from reading *Men and Other Reptiles* to *Toxic Men*. The book had a deep hold on her attention that did not keep her from looking up regularly from her exercise bicycle to consider the new arrivals. Edie waved when she saw Lily.

"Hey, did you fall off your bike when I wasn't here?" she said. "You look like a minor-league hockey goalie."

Edie would not be put off by Lily's assurances that she had taken only a mild spill.

"Honey, you've got to learn to pay more attention to your appearance," she said. "Men don't like women who look tough. Men like women who look delicate and feminine, like little parakeets."

Edie looked impressively birdlike in a yellow leotard with ruffles at the shoulder, yellow head-and wrist-bands, and orange leggings. She went on to give Lily intricate directions for masking her bruise with makeup by applying a blend of lighter and darker shades of foundation.

"Sort of like the way Princess Di straightened out her crooked nose by drawing a white stripe down the center and dark lines on either side, then covering the whole thing with her regular shade, you know?" she said.

Lily wondered why Edie, an apparent font of knowledge about the other sex, never seemed to have dates but spent all her time at the health club advising other women on their social lives. Without having resolved the issue, she went off to the locker room to change into her Yale Athletic Department sweatpants.

On her return Lily found that the only vacant exercise bike stood next to that of Brad Newburger, whom she had dated briefly before meeting Mark. The sight of him was painful.

Lily judged herself severely for having become engaged too quickly, knowing how much grief her decision to cancel her wedding would bring to everyone close to her. She was neither young nor flighty enough to imagine that she would not have to account emotionally for every dish of Grand Marnier sorbet that would not be served at her reception.

But whenever she asked herself whether God would forgive her for the wounds that her misjudgments would inflict on others, she had to answer yes. God was merciful: God would remember her dates with Brad Newburger. Brad would have driven any woman into the arms of the next mature, responsible, adult male who came along. Especially when the man was as attractive as Mark, with whom Lily could never appear in public without fearing that she might at any moment yield to impulses that would lead to her immediate arraignment on sexual molestation charges.

Throughout the city, Brad was regarded as a catch, which meant that he was attractive and well educated enough to have convinced many women to overlook that he was insufferable. Brad spotted Lily before she made it to the locker room.

"Lily! Swell to see you again! Come sit by me."

Brad patted the seat of the bike next to his. He was vice-president of a well-known public relations firm founded by his father, Bradford Newburger & Son, and liked to say that he regarded all women as potential new romantic accounts. This led him to treat them all—even those who had dropped him, as Lily had—with a friendliness that bordered on the pathological.

Lily slid onto the vacant bike and propped up her copy of *Northanger Abbey* on the Lucite stand. She had taken to bringing Jane Austen's novels to the club in the hope that they would discourage men who would have driven across the state to avoid reading anything but *The Baseball Encyclopedia*.

But this effort, she was beginning to conclude, had failed dismally. As soon as she opened *Northanger Abbey*, Brad said that he had read in the gossip column of the weekly *City Lights* that she had become engaged to Buck Slayton's son. "Guess you have a thing for guys who wear bow ties, huh?"

Lily winced. That Mark wore bow ties was widely seen as a peculiarity associated with his having gone to Harvard, which attracted the sons of the region's new money, instead of Yale, to which the city's old guard had been sending its children since the days when a large portion of Ohio was part of the Western Reserve of Connecticut.

But Lily liked his bow ties. She had never understood how men could tie on a yard-long phallic symbol each day without blushing deeply or apologizing to anyone within

earshot. Bow ties neutralized some of the Freudian connotations of the act. Not, of course, that she could ever
say this to Brad, who had a rack full of club ties bearing
the logos of companies he represented.

Lily ignored the remark about bow ties and asked about
his work, dangerous as she knew this to be. Brad was
proud of the range of his clients: a firm that made bowling
trophies, a lingerie store famous for its buy-five-get-one-
free Girdle Club, a condom boutique called Condom and
Gomorrah, and a Lawn-Mower Museum in a distant suburb that he liked to promote as a great day trip for the
entire family.

But he specialized in food accounts, and none was too
unpromising to arouse his enthusiasm. The few times he
and Lily had gone out, he had taken her to places he represented, including a French café that gave the phonetic
spelling of each dish on the menu and a Libyan restaurant
with a picture of Moammar Gadafy taped to the cash register.

Lily had listened in awe as he celebrated each of them
with the easy confidence that came from knowing that he
was not prostituting his ideals, because he had no ideals
to prostitute. His moral vacuity allowed him to excel at his
job. Brad might be promoting the world's most depressing
city, but he was better at it than anybody else.

So Lily was not surprised when Brad said his business
was booming. He had picked up the account for a company that processed flash-frozen catfish for local restaurants and hoped soon to represent a major corn-dog
supplier.

Lily imagined Brad standing in front of a group of executives explaining why he was the man for corn dogs, a
regional specialty that consisted of batter-fried hot dogs
on a stick. She had to admit that he was ideally suited to

selling the food most likely to result in an arrest on public-indecency charges if eaten in public.

After congratulating him on landing the flash-frozen catfish account, Lily could think of no hopeful direction in which to pursue the topic of corn dogs. She left for the locker room and, by the time she came out, Brad had struck up a conversation with Edie, whose threshold for male toxicity appeared to have increased remarkably.

Lily had not eaten dinner before working out, and on returning to her apartment switched on the news and began fixing herself a tuna-and-white-bean salad. She was slicing a red onion when she heard a familiar sound on the television set on her kitchen countertop.

"GAY RITES ARE RIGHT. GAY RITES ARE RIGHT."

Lily put down her knife and stared in dismay at the image of her own face. A camera zoomed in as a bag of almonds hit her in the head and she said something about marriage as a "bourgeois, capitalistic" institution based on money and property. She was startled by how tired and angry she sounded, not to mention how unattractive she looked with a lump on her forehead.

Unable to watch, she flipped off her set. For the first time, she was glad Mark was out of town. No doubt she would face taunts from her coworkers the next day. But Mark, at least, would be spared the humiliation of seeing her being pelted with nuts in front of hundreds of thousands of viewers. Lily remembered that she had an appointment the next day with a psychiatrist she had chosen from her father's list, and she could only hope that the woman had such a full practice that she had no time to watch television.

14

Lightbulb

"We all love to instruct, though we can teach only what is not worth knowing."

—Pride and Prejudice

"How many psychiatrists does it take to change a lightbulb?"

"Only one. But the lightbulb has to *want* to change."

Lily had heard the joke from a medical writer at the *Daily* and, as she sat in the office of Dr. Eloise Lefland, she could not stop thinking about it. What benefit could she derive from counseling that she did not want?

The list of psychiatrists she received from her father had offered her little hope. She rejected one therapist because he was a client of her father's law firm and, if she was going to be told that she had unresolved oedipal impulses, she did not want to hear it from someone who helped pay Oedipus's polo club dues. She rejected another because he treated Tess Mahoney, the one person she knew who grew certifiably loonier every year.

That left Eloise Lefland—a psychiatrist who, besides lacking the disadvantages of the other two candidates, had the advantage of being a woman. Lily could not deny that fifty minutes with a discreet female listener would be worth it if it won over her parents on the issue of her wedding.

The trouble was: Lily had always believed that if you read widely and deeply enough and had the right friends, you had all the therapy you needed. What psychiatrist understood the human heart better than La Rochefoucauld, who wrote, "In love there is always the kisser and the one who gets kissed"? What therapist could sum up marriage more pithily than Jane Austen, who called it "of all transactions, the one in which people expect most from others, and are least honest themselves"?

Lily had banished her doubts long enough to make an appointment to see Dr. Lefland, only to find that her pessimism returned the moment she entered the psychiatrist's office. She arrived fifteen minutes late after getting stuck in a traffic jam caused by the annual Mid-America Polka Challenge, which brought thousands of visitors to the city. But she did not get far when she tried to explain to Dr. Lefland that she had been delayed by a caravan of kielbasa- and accordion-wielding dancers who leaned out of their car windows singing the "She's Too Fat for Me" polka.

"Lily, psychotherapy only works if the therapist and the client have an equal commitment to the process, and that commitment includes being on time," Dr. Lefland said, with what sounded like a distinct undertone of condescension.

Given that she had no commitment to the process and had only shown up to please her father, Lily did not know how to respond to this. Without waiting for an answer, Dr. Lefland gave her the choice of a chair or couch.

Lily took the chair, which faced a cluster of photographs of the psychiatrist and her children, surrounding a bronze plaque that said, "Tri-County Mother of the Year." Below it stood a teak credenza with more pictures, apparently of her grandchildren, and a pink ceramic foot that said "Ashley, Age 3."

This display unnerved Lily. As far as marriage was concerned, she hoped to find another conscientious objector; she appeared instead to have stumbled on the sergeant who followed Teddy Roosevelt up San Juan Hill. Glancing at a group portrait of six grandchildren wearing devil suits and clutching jack-o-lanterns, Lily tried to break the ice.

"Are all these children and grandchildren yours, or did you rent them for special occasions?"

Dr. Lefland ignored the question. "We're not here to talk about me," she said briskly. "We're here to talk about you. So why don't you tell me what brings you here?"

Earlier in the day, Lily had thought about how to respond to such a question. She wanted to tell the truth: that she had come because her courage had failed her. After hearing for weeks that her newspaper in New York might fold, she had taken the first job offered to her, even though her savings would have allowed her to stay in the city much longer.

She had known almost from the start that she had made a mistake, and yet within a year she had agreed to marry a man who would bind her forever to a city in which she would never feel at home. Mark loved her for her energy and optimism, and the city was sapping her of more of her energy and optimism every day. In twenty or thirty years, it would have extinguished them, just as it had extinguished the youthful vitality that had drawn her father to her mother.

But Lily found that she could say none of this to Dr. Lefland, whose frostiness had banished any inclination toward candor that the mother-of-the-year plaque left intact. She groped for a way to answer her with a measure of truth.

"Why did I come here?" she asked, stalling. "In a way, I came because of veal medallions."

"Excuse me?"

"Veal medallions. You know, those little beige—"

"Lily, I am aware of what veal medallions are. I was just wondering how they relate to your being here."

"They relate because I'm supposed to be getting married in a few weeks, but I don't want to go through with the wedding. And when I told my mother I wanted to call it off, she said I can't because of the veal medallions."

"I'm afraid I still don't see how that brought you to this office."

"The caterer's deposit. It's nonrefundable. So my mother thinks I can't call off the wedding. And, if I don't get out of it soon, my parents will go bankrupt."

"I hardly think it likely that your parents will go bankrupt any time soon."

Lily, wondering how she knew this, said nothing. She heard the scratch of Dr. Lefland's pen against her legal pad.

"How has your fiancé reacted to all of this?"

"He hasn't reacted, because he doesn't know yet. He's in California for a week, so I haven't told him that I want to pull the plug on the wedding."

Dr. Lefland went on red alert. "That's an interesting choice of words, pull the plug," she said quickly. "It sounds as though you equate marriage with death and self-annihilation."

Lily looked at her in surprise. "I don't associate *pull the plug* with death and self-annihilation, I associate it with water running out of the bathtub."

"Umm-hmm."

Lily could hear the psychiatrist's pen scratching again and, unsettled by this, tried to explain herself.

"Dr. Lefland, *pull the plug* is just an expression—a cliché, actually. It doesn't mean I equate marriage with gladiola wreaths, a mahogany casket, and 'Abide with Me.' "

"Perhaps your words have a meaning you haven't considered."

"Forgive me, Dr. Lefland, but I'm a reporter. Considering the meaning of words is what I do for a living. *Pull the plug* is a phrase like *bite the dust* or *killing time*. If President Clinton says that a bill bit the dust because of Republican opposition, does that mean he's thinking of sneaking into Newt Gingrich's office and slipping arsenic into his electric coffee-maker?"

"Who knows?"

"You don't know whether President Clinton would put arsenic in a coffee machine in the office of the Speaker of the House of Representatives?"

"We're not here to talk about politics. We're here to talk about why you're afraid of marriage."

"I'm *not* afraid of marriage," Lily said. "I'm afraid of marriage to someone I agreed to marry after three months, as any sensible person would be."

Dr. Lefland ignored this answer and asked a number of other questions that included the words "fear" and "intimacy" or "marriage," as though Lily had misunderstood her the first time. At last, she put down her pen.

"It must be scary," she said unctuously, "to think of standing up there in church and saying 'I do' in front of all those people."

At this Lily began to twitch mentally. Of all the things that made her wary of the psychotherapists she had interviewed as a reporter—their fees, their pretense of omniscience, their willful anti-intellectualism—nothing bothered her so much as their tendency to speak in a sort of glorified baby-talk.

Why did so many of them seem to assume that even the most minor crisis deprived adults of the ability to understand words of more than two syllables? Lily was tempted to ask but realized that she had no more heart for argument, and instead submitted to a battery of questions that she had long since asked herself and answered definitively. At last Dr. Lefland looked at her watch.

"Lily, our time is up," she said, "and I urge you to return next week. In the meantime, I must warn you against canceling your wedding prematurely."

"Prematurely? It's in three weeks."

"There was obviously a reason why you agreed to marry your fiancé, and if you call off the wedding, you may hurt him so badly that you will never get him back again."

"Should I hurt myself instead?"

"This is something I would like to discuss with you in the future, and until then you must be extremely careful about what you say to your fiancé. It's a very tough world out there for single women. Every day I see clients who would love to trade places with you, and I probably don't need to remind you that if you break your engagement, there is a good chance you will spend the rest of your life alone."

"I'm not alone *now*. I have my family, my friends, and my work. If I want more company I could get a cat." She paused. "Or some ficus trees."

"I'm sorry, our hour is up. If you arrive punctually next time, we will have more time to discuss these things. Please make another appointment with my receptionist on the way out."

Lily kept herself from replying, "Over my dead body," sure that she knew what Dr. Lefland would think of that.

Back at her apartment, Lily found a message from Mark, saying that he loved her article on the bridal fair, which his secretary had faxed him. When she returned the call, Caroline Van Allen answered the phone in his suite.

"Oh, hi Lily," she said cheerily. "Dave and Mark and I are going out to meet with one of tomorrow's witnesses in a few minutes, and Mark is taking a shower. Want me to ask him to call you after we get back?"

Lily was so surprised to hear Caroline's voice that she could not at first respond. After she had collected herself, she said that Mark could call whenever it was convenient. Caroline promised to give him the message, and Lily found herself straining to hear whether she could make out Dave's voice in the background.

Before she hung up, Lily asked how the trial was going, and Caroline said, cryptically, that Winks Ferguson was not going to make the cover of *Modern Maturity* anytime soon.

"By the way, Lily," she added, "it's such a shame that you couldn't make it out to California this weekend. One of the partners in the L.A. office is taking all of us on a sunset cruise to Santa Catalina on Saturday night, and we were so hoping you could join us."

Lily could not be certain, but she thought she could detect a note of victory just behind those words.

15

The Morgue

". . . they were never insulted by her real favour and preference."

—Sense and Sensibility

The first call Lily got the next morning came from a reader who said that he used to think she was a great writer but, now that she had done a story on gay rights, he realized that castration would be too good a fate for her. On talking with the man, she learned that he had not read her article but had seen the report about it on television.

Lily tried to explain that she was biologically ill-equipped for castration. But the caller would not be placated and went on to accuse her of making fun, in an earlier story, of people who liked to do the Chicken Dance at weddings. He said that he was not the only one who was upset—two of his neighbors in Elyria had thrown away her story before their children could read it. For no reason, Lily thought of the headline an Elyria newspaper ran with the obituary of Sherwood Anderson: "Former Elyria Paint Manufacturer Dies."

After the caller hung up, Lily tried to work on the next installment in her bridal series. She was studying men's and women's personals ads to see what differences between the sexes emerged from them.

But the story was going poorly. After sifting through hundreds of men's ads Lily had gotten no further than dividing male advertisers into several categories: Figaro ("women tell me I'm handsome and charming"), Hitler ("no smokers or meat eaters/photo a must"), Napoleon ("ambitious, well-traveled executive, can-do type, likes French and Italian food"), and Methuselah ("young-at-heart retiree seeks female companion, under thirty, who believes that today is the first day of the rest of your life"). She spent an hour or two trying to figure out how to give this grim fraternity the upbeat spin her editors wanted, then listened to a phone message that had come in just after the call from the man from Elyria.

To her surprise it was from Mark, full of enthusiasm for her gay-rights story, which his secretary had faxed him. He added that he and Dave and Caroline would be in court all day but that he would try to reach her later.

Hearing Mark mention Caroline's name unsettled Lily, and before resuming work on her personals-ad story she decided to visit the paper's morgue, where clippings of old newspaper articles came to rest in alphabetically arranged envelopes in long file drawers similar to card catalogs. She signed out an envelope labeled "Vallejo–Van Nuys" and took it to her desk.

After emptying out the contents, she began sorting through clippings about people whose last names started with *V*. She realized, after she had been going through them for a few minutes, that Jack was reading over her shoulder. He picked up an article about the columnist Abigail Van Buren.

"Writing about Dear Abby's advice to brides in the next installment in your series?" he asked.

Lily, wishing she had not brought the clippings to her desk, tried to think of a reply that would not betray her interest in the file. "Who knows? If she turns up in front of this office with a picket sign, I might."

"You're certainly taking precautions well in advance. Good old Abby doesn't exactly strike me as the type who would parade up and down in front of the *Daily* just because we use a picture of her taken on a bad hair day."

Jack began trolling through the other articles from the "Vallejo–Van Nuys" clip file.

"Jack, please—" Lily began.

He ignored her and read aloud from a clipping he had picked off her desk. "Magnificent in a beaded gown of Alençon lace . . . Reception for two-hundred-fifty people at the Union Club . . . Met the groom while taking one of his classes in law school." He tossed the clipping back on Lily's desk. "That sounds like Caroline Van Allen, all right."

Lily berated herself for not having taken the clip file to a more private spot. Then she realized that the office had no more private spot: Working in a newsroom meant living in the pocket of hundreds of other reporters.

Jack glanced again at Caroline's wedding announcement.

"You don't need to go through all this if you want to find out about Caroline Van Allen," he said with exaggerated solicitude. "All you need to do is ask me." He paused. "Believe me, I could tell you more about her than this file."

Lily was exasperated. "Jack, you don't know what I was looking for in this file."

"Aha. The old 'refuse to confirm or deny' ploy. You'll

have to come up with something better than that shop-worn trick in a roomful of reporters."

Without speaking, Lily gathered up the clippings on her desk and stuffed them back into the envelope. She excused herself, a bit curtly, saying that she had work to do, and headed for a women's lounge used mainly by the secretaries in the Classified Department.

There she settled onto a couch and emptied the clippings onto her lap. She looked at the longer articles first and was relieved to find nothing on Caroline except for her wedding announcement and the article on Mark's age-discrimination case that had appeared in the paper a week earlier.

Then she spotted a yellowing item from the society pages of the *Daily*, which consisted of a photograph and a few lines of text. The picture showed a radiant Caroline, breathlessly identified as "the beauteous and brilliant student at Ohio's finest law school," at a summer-evening fund-raiser for the Harvard Club on a riverboat. Next to her stood her date, who was partially cropped out of the photo and unidentified in its caption.

Lily looked at the picture for only a few seconds before her stomach seemed to evaporate. The unidentified man in the photo, who looked so happy standing next to Caroline, was unmistakably Mark.

Back at her desk, Lily tried to brush aside thoughts of the picture and work on her story on the personals ads. Although Mark had never told her he had gone out with Caroline, the picture was years old. What obligation did Mark have to tell her about women he had dated long before he met her? Didn't good manners dictate the opposite? Even if not, why should she care whom Mark had gone out with? Had *he* ever grilled *her* about her former dates?

No, he was far too diplomatic for that. But he said he never went out with women from his firm. Had he, the most truthful man she had ever known, been lying to her?

True, Caroline had been a law student in the photo. There was no reason to assume she had been working with Mark back then. But most law students got their jobs at his firm by working there first as summer associates. Wasn't it likely that Caroline had been employed when the photo was taken?

Lily had not resolved the question when she received an unexpected call from Nick Monford. They spoke briefly about the head-injury dinner before he came to his point.

"Since we missed each other for lunch, what about dinner tonight at the Ritz?"

Lily knew she would enjoy nothing more than dinner at the one restaurant in town that was sure not to have corn dogs on the menu. But she also knew that, in a city that amounted to a big small town, the most innocent encounter could be misread. If any of Mark's friends or family saw her with the architect, they would be likely to speculate feverishly about it.

Then Lily remembered her conversation with her father about Caroline. If he had been right, people already were gossiping—if not about her and Nick Monford, about Mark and Caroline. On realizing this, Lily felt the powerful surge of freedom that comes from knowing that it doesn't matter what answers you give on a rigged test, and she agreed to meet the architect a few hours later at the Ritz.

16

Mirrors

*". . . such a number of looking-glasses! oh, Lord!
there was no getting away from oneself."*

—Persuasion

Lily stood in front of her bathroom mirror in the navy
silk bathrobe that Mark kept at her apartment, trying
to remember the directions Edie Vogel had given her for
minimizing the lump on her forehead. Did the lighter
foundation go at the center and the darker at the edges,
or vice versa?

With a sponge in one hand and a tube of makeup in
the other, she dabbed at her forehead until she thought
she had achieved the right balance. By the time she finished, she had to admit that she looked better than she
had in days, even without the sparkle of a five-carat diamond.

That still left open the question of what to wear to dinner at the Ritz now that most of her clothes were too big.
Lily tried on several near-misses before she remembered
the black silk sheath that she used to wear to hear Bobby
Short at the Carlyle—a dress so tight she could have ex-

truded it. She had packed it in mothballs after Mark's sisters said that they did not want their children getting a sex-education course from their future aunt's wardrobe. At least by the standards of Penny and Fran, it would fit perfectly now.

Lily climbed onto a stepladder and found the dress in a box on the top shelf of a storage closet, next to a carton labeled "Colony Heights C.D.S." On an impulse she removed a white-and-gold yearbook from the carton and brought it down, too. She turned on her shower full blast and hung her black sheath on a towel rack, then went into the living room and slipped a Mozart divertimento into her compact disk player.

As she waited for the wrinkles to steam out of her dress, Lily sat down on the sofa and began leafing through the yearbook. She had been one of sixty-two girls in her class, and as she studied their pictures she realized that she had run into at least two-thirds of them since she had returned to town. They were all still living in Colony Heights or the horsier suburbs to the east, married to men who had attended local private schools or who had gone away to Choate, Exeter, or Andover. Mark had attended Lawrenceville before he spent a summer working on a Cumbrian sheep farm, fell in love with England and transferred to a boys' school near London.

Lily was particularly struck by the yearbook picture of a woman named Pansy Hallowell, to whom she had once been linked by dint of the awkward distinction of their being the only girls in their class with flower names. She had reintroduced herself after hearing her former friend explain at a bookstore why she was buying her son *Quasimodo's Busy Day*, based on the Disney movie of *The Hunchback of Notre-Dame*: "It's so important for children to have culture in their lives."

Pansy clearly had not recognized her and, after studying her for a while had said, with the first note of irony Lily had heard since returning home, "My, haven't you turned out to be the glamorous one." Lily had not known what to make of this—she certainly was not glamorous by the standards of anyone she knew in New York—and expressed surprise at seeing her classmate, who after a junior year abroad had professed a loathing for the self-satisfied conformity of Colony Heights and an intention to spend her adult life on the Left Bank. She asked Pansy why she had returned to her hometown, and her classmate appeared taken aback by the question.

"Why would we want to live anywhere else?" she said. "This is the best place in America to raise a family. It has the best private schools and the best art museum, and you won't find harder-working people anywhere in the country. Every woman on my street does volunteer work for the ballet or the Cancer Society at least two afternoons a week while her children are in school."

Pansy asked what charitable organizations she worked for, and Lily replied with some embarrassment that she was still trying to adjust to the demands of a job that often required her to work eleven- or twelve-hour days. Her former classmate did not bother to hide her disapproval.

"You'd better do something about that," Pansy said, shaking her head. Then she added, pointedly, "You can have all the money in the world in this city, but if you don't pitch in and do your share for the Garden Society or the Boosters' Club, nobody will speak to you. If you're going to live here, people expect you to have good values."

Lily did not see the good values reflected in the social ostracism of anyone who declined to work for the Garden Club and had not renewed the friendship. Now, looking at Pansy's yearbook picture, she was struck by how little her classmate had changed. At the bookstore she wore the same hairstyle and the same sort of round-necked dress with pearls—probably more expensive now—that she had favored a decade earlier.

But Lily hardly recognized herself when she came to her own picture. She looked so lost and wistful that she wanted to wrap her former self in a blanket and tuck her into bed. What fear lay behind her tentative half-smile, auditioning for the approval of the camera? And yet, incredibly, her classmates had voted her "Most Beautiful" and "Most Liberated." The caption for her photo read: "Destination: New Haven. Ambition: Not to get married. Motto: *'It is better to do the right thing badly than a bad thing well.'—Louis Kahn.*"

Lily closed the book hurriedly. A bit ruefully, she thought that if her looks had changed and her ambition had been severely compromised, her motto had undergone no such transformation. As far as her wedding was concerned, she was still trying to do the right thing, but she could never have imagined that she would do it so badly.

17

Intersection

"One has not great hopes from Birmingham. I always say there is something direful in the sound . . ."

—Emma

Getting to the Ritz required Lily to drive through one of the city's worst neighborhoods, a place so crime-infested that the *Daily* once refused to send female reporters there alone. Before leaving home, she locked her car doors and windows.

One winter night when her car had failed to start, Lily had taken a taxi home, and the driver urged her not to keep her purse beside her on the seat of the cab. Thugs had been preying on women seated in cars stopped for traffic lights, in what had become known as smash-and-grab attacks, by smashing the passenger's-side window and grabbing a woman's purse off the seat before fleeing.

Lily knew that she had been lucky: She had been mugged only once since returning to town. It happened on a warm summer evening, before the sky darkened, when she defied the warnings of coworkers and decided to walk the five blocks to an enclosed downtown mall known as Renaissance Station.

When she stopped to cross a street in front of the city's largest cathedral, a thief had snatched her purse and given her a shove that left her with a cut lip and scraped knees. No one answered her cries for help—visitors to the mall parked in an underground garage that kept them off the streets—and she limped back to the *Daily* unaided. Even so, she had fared better than coworkers who had been held up at knifepoint near the office, which shared a decaying block with a pawn shop and three bars.

As she drove warily toward the Ritz, Lily realized how much safer she had felt at night on the streets of Manhattan. Of course, she had friends who had been mugged in midtown. But their calls for help had not gone unanswered, because the streets were never empty. That was the great thing about New York: No sooner had your purse vanished than you were consoled by someone who, having just emerged from a Korean market, dashed to your aid carrying a bag of cold sesame noodles. Getting mugged in New York resembled a rough-and-tumble fraternity-initiation ritual after which you went out for drinks with friends and congratulated yourself that it had not been worse.

A few blocks from the Ritz, which occupied a portion of Renaissance Station, Lily stopped at a light, relieved that she had almost completed the trip. At that instant a man who had been slouching in a doorway rushed up to her driver's side window and pounded on it.

"No! No!" Lily shouted.

The man kept beating on her window as Lily calculated whether she could safely run the red light. She could not: No break appeared in the line of cars that, with the green light, whizzed toward the garage at Renaissance Station.

As she prayed for the traffic signal to change, Lily tried not to look at the man pounding on her window. He began yelling something to which she paid no attention. Instead, she made a silent vow: If she made it through the inter-section unscathed, she would begin looking for a job in New York the next day. No more delays, no more excuses, no more telling herself that she could not send out résu-més until Mark had returned and she had extracted herself from the high-stepping MGM production number that her wedding had become.

When the light changed, Lily lurched into the intersec-tion. Just before she made the left turn toward the parking lot for the Ritz, she glanced at her rearview mirror and saw that the man who had been pounding on her window was holding up a copy of the newspaper that the homeless sold to raise money to get themselves off the streets. He walked over to a man and woman with cameras around their necks, who were photographing Renaissance Station, and showed them the paper.

The woman stopped taking pictures long enough to hand him a dollar. The homeless man kissed her hand graciously, then walked off in the direction of a Salvation Army soup truck that served dinner each night in the city's main square.

In her shame at having given so little credit to someone who clearly had meant her no harm, Lily almost lost her heart for dinner with Nicholas Monford. She could no longer deny that the paranoia that she had never known in New York had come to her with a vengeance in the Midwest.

But this thought faded as she stepped into the deeply burnished mahogany elevator at the Ritz. In an aggres-sively and almost defiantly provincial city, the hotel was an anomaly—an island of discreet cosmopolitanism. At the Ritz staff members never boasted that their hotel was better than the Ritz in New York but allowed it to speak for itself, a rare break with the traditions of a city in which any self-respecting institution blew its own horn until it gasped for breath.

Lily sometimes wondered whether she might not have fled town long before her engagement had the city not attracted an American cousin of the Paris landmark in which Ernest Hemingway spent the first days after the Liberation and Marcel Proust ate chilled melon at midnight with Léon-Paul Fargue. On bad days at the office she would sometimes slip away for a lunch at the Ritz and return an hour later, restored by its calming presence.

At the sixth floor Lily left the elevator and made her way to the restaurant, which had a panoramic wall of windows overlooking the river. Nicholas Monford was waiting for her at a table next to one of them.

On seeing her, he rose and kissed her. "How can anyone so lovely exist in such a city?"

Lily smiled. "People here insist that the gloomy weather is good for the complexion—that the perennial cloud cover wards off wrinkles caused by too much sun."

"If that's true, I'm afraid that the gray skies haven't done nearly as much for most other people as they have for you. Buck's daughters appear frightfully jealous of you, and with good reason."

"It must be a bit hard on them to have to share their brother with someone after having had him to themselves for thirty-two years," Lily said, not wanting to appear too eager to agree with a view that echoed her own suspicions.

The waiter took their orders for drinks, and they talked about their impressions of the city. Nicholas Monford said he had concluded that he could not design the sports bars for Buck, whose ideas for the project differed too greatly from his own.

"I can't quite adjust to the idea of a pub—a bar—in which people will eat popcorn out of football helmets."

"You may have saved yourself a lot of trouble by not doing them. Buck can be a bit—" Lily paused. "Buck has very strong opinions, and he might imagine himself to know more about how to design a bar than any architect he hired."

"So I gather. But I must say, he seems to adore you. You had no sooner left the dinner than he began to praise you to everyone at the table as the best writer on the *Daily*."

"Buck may not be the most absolutely reliable source on that topic. He always says he never reads anything in the paper except what I write, so his frame of reference is a bit limited, and unfortunately he is not entirely atypical of his circle. If his friends don't perceive you as one of them, they ignore or vilify you. If they do perceive you as one of them, they overpraise you shamelessly and lose no opportunity to let others know of their link to you."

"Rather like Gopher Prairie on a much larger scale?"

Lily felt a slight chill of truth. In high school, when she had first read *Main Street*, she had identified so deeply with Carol Kennicott that she had cried over the toll taken on her spirit by the willful narrowness of Gopher Prairie. But she ascribed her turmoil to the power of literature— not to any connection between the novel and her life.

"You might compare the city to Gopher Prairie in some ways," she said reluctantly, unwilling to delve too deeply into the idea. Then she smiled. "But, no doubt, people here would deny that to the death. The city's slogan is 'The best location in the nation.'"

Nicholas Monford laughed. "And I'm sure that, in England, people in Manchester and Birmingham say precisely the same thing as they look with pity on the poor souls unlucky enough to live in Mayfair or the Lake District."

The waiter took their orders, and their discussion moved on to Tony Blair and Bill Clinton, Richard Rogers and Michael Graves, Le Gavroche and Lutèce, their favorite Jane Austen novels, and a Magritte show at the Hayward Gallery that they both had seen. They disagreed spiritedly on several points, and Lily found herself wishing that she could discuss their conversation with Mark, with his gift for reconciling diverging views. That she could not did not keep her from enjoying so civilized a discussion immensely.

At the end of the meal, Nicholas Monford invited her up to his room for a drink, an offer that Lily did not regret less because she had been prepared for it. On many trips to London, she had found that English men viewed "American" as a synonym for "available."

But she had to admit that they took romantic defeat more graciously than French or Italian men. If English men took rejection as a signal to withdraw temporarily and reconsider their angle of attack, the French and Italians took it as a sign to that they had attacked with insufficiently heavy artillery. Lily had no doubt that—if a French architect had asked her up to his room—she would have had to remain at the table a half hour longer trying to persuade him that he could not achieve with a howitzer what he had failed to achieve with a slingshot.

As it was, Nicholas Monford accepted his loss with the perfect equanimity of a tennis player who had been allowed to play several highly enjoyable games in someone else's court. He gave her his card, invited her to visit him in Fulham, and walked her to her car, where he looked at her with what appeared to be sadness and disbelief.

"From all that I have heard, you have an entirely admirable fiancé," he said. "But a man who loved you would not make you stay in this rather distressing city. You have nothing in common with anyone I have met here, least of all with your future father-in-law and his daughters. You belong in New York—" He paused, smiling. "Or London. A man who understood you would have no doubt of it."

"And you understand me perfectly?" Lily asked.

"Not perfectly. But well enough not to want to see you give up Pemberley for Main Street."

18

Tornado Watch

"As far as I can understand what nervous complaints are, I have a great idea of the efficacy of air and exercise for them;—daily, regular Exercise . . ."
> —Sandition

Lily studied the clippings on her desk like Ishmael surveying the floating oars of the Pequod. She had nearly finished writing her story on the personals ads and had come up with none of the witty and trenchant observations about the sexes that she hoped it would include.

After days of research, she had drawn no conclusion except that the men who advertised invariably wanted a woman who had "a good sense of humor." But when she searched their ads for traces of a sly wit—or for any other sign that they might be prepared to return in kind what they demanded of women—she came up empty-handed.

Nor did she find comfort in her interviews with men who had met their wives through the personals. Apparently, when they had said that they wanted a woman with "a good sense of humor," they meant that they wanted somebody who would laugh at their jokes. Or, at least, somebody who would not cringe when they showed up in a T-shirt that said, "Beer: The Breakfast of Champions."

Lily finished writing her story in time to see Jack walking through the newsroom listening to a Walkman radio. He approached her desk without talking off his earphones.

"Bad news, Lily," he said, frowning. "Tornado watch in effect for most of the Tri-County region. I just hope you don't have to call off your wedding because of one of these storms."

Lily brightened at the thought that a tornado could achieve what she could not. She and Mark had been so eager to have their wedding before the annual September snow flurries descended that they had failed to consider one thing: Whenever the city had no chance of being hit by a blizzard, it was in danger of getting blown away by a tornado. Each year the region had approximately three days of good weather between the snow and the twisters.

Jack said he was leaving the office early, and Lily decided to do the same. But when she left work, the sky looked only mildly ominous, so she stopped at her health club on her way home. She found Edie Vogel reading a book called *Maybe He's Just a Jerk* as Brad Newburger rode an exercise bicycle beside her.

"Hey, I see you've started using my makeup tips," Edie said. "You wouldn't believe how much better your face looks. It's lost that washed-out, pasty look it usually has. Now all you need is a little teal eye shadow and you won't have to come to places like this to find a man."

"Lily already has a man," Brad said matter-of-factly. "She's engaged."

"You're *engaged?*" Edie said. "Some people have all the luck. I came here for years without meeting anyone, but you've been a member for less than a year, and you've bagged a guy already."

Brad said that Lily had not met her fiancé at the club but through the Young Friends of the Arts, which he knew from the gossip column of *City Lights*.

Edie did not appear to hear him. "C'mon, how'd you do it? How'd you get engaged?"

Glancing at Edie's copy of *Maybe He's Just a Jerk*, Lily tried to think of a diplomatic way to answer her.

"Edie, did you ever think that you might—that men might hesitate to approach you when you're reading a book with a title like *Maybe He's Just a Jerk*? That, maybe, it would put them off?"

"Oh, no," Edie said. "Men never notice things like that."

"How could they not notice that you're reading a book with a title like *Maybe He's Just a Jerk*?"

"Trust me, men don't care what women read," she said. "All they care about is whether women give great————." Edie mentioned a sex act that brought to mind a vision of Brad's bid for the corn-dog account.

Lily started to protest this vicious slander against the worthies of the other sex but stopped when she calculated the number of men fond of the act named by Edie versus the number of men who enjoyed Jane Austen. After trying to reconcile this conflict between theory and practice, she asked Edie if she wasn't oversimplifying men's natures.

"Ask Brad, he'll tell you." Edie turned to Brad. "Do men want anything besides————?" Lily wished Edie had not repeated the name of the act so loudly, which caused several men to look up from nearby exercise bicycles.

On hearing the question, one of the men smirked and shook his head no, but Brad was indignant. "Of course, they want other things." He paused. "Like a good sense of humor."

Lily did not want to hear about humor from a man who had taken her with a straight face to a Libyan restaurant that displayed Moammar Gadafy's picture, and she asked about his new flash-frozen catfish account. Brad spent fifteen minutes describing the exciting new deboning procedures that were revolutionizing the lake-fish processing industry.

When he moved on to a forthcoming blade exhibit at the Lawn-Mower Museum, Lily cast about urgently for a new topic. She noticed that he was reading John Grisham's *The Chamber* and asked about it. Brad said that it was not as good as *The Firm*. Lily thought of Dorothy Parker's remark on hearing of the death of Calvin Coolidge and asked how he could tell.

Brad went on to list the many ways in which he could tell *The Firm* was better than *The Chamber*. These had mainly to do with the number and quality of their BMWs, on which he considered himself an expert, since he owned one.

At that point Edie perked up. She had been listening to Brad with what appeared to be adoration, and Lily suddenly noticed that the two of them were pedaling their bicycles in sync.

"Oh, yes," Edie said. "Brad is definitely right about *The Firm*. He gave me a copy on our first date, and I told him that he was so brilliant, I was sure that someday *he* would represent a law firm where the lawyers all got free BMWs."

Lily could not tell whether she was serious. "Your first *date?*" she asked incredulously. She stared at Brad, who blushed.

"That's right, Lily," he said. "Edie has all kinds of great ideas about the PR business. She's already helped me land a new client, the therapist who wrote *Why Sleep with a Man When You Can Sleep with Your Cat?* Trust me, if you haven't heard of it yet, you will. This book is going to change the whole way women look at men." He patted

Edie on the ruffled shoulder of her leotard. "And Edie has changed the whole way I look at women. Who knows? Someday soon I might be asking her to marry me over a candlelit dinner for two at the Flower of Libya."

Edie beamed. "And you know what the best thing is? If we get married, we won't even have to pay for the reception, because we've been promised all the flash-frozen catfish our guests can eat as a wedding present."

Lily drove home through a dark and lashing rain, along a route that took her past the house she and Mark had received from his father as a wedding gift. The sight made her queasy. In the storm, the house resembled an upscale suburban-Gothic third cousin of the Bates Motel, and she sped past it toward the center of Colony Heights. There she saw a mock-Tudor aromatherapy salon with a pseudo–Middle English sign that had been blown off its hinges.

Twenty minutes after leaving her health club, she arrived home and found that the red light on her answering machine, miraculously, was not blinking. Then she realized the storm had knocked out her telephone.

Despite this, Lily spent an hour revising her résumé. Then she pulled out *Northanger Abbey*, the Jane Austen novel that seemed best suited to the weather. With lighting still flashing, she reread the book until she began to worry that, that if she continued, she would lose the courage to put "writer" on her résumé.

As she prepared for bed, the electricity in her apartment went out. Lily saw, when she opened a window, that the power also had gone out in the other houses on her block. The street was unnervingly quiet, and she thought fondly of Sally's neighbors in New York, screaming at each other through their open windows after losing their air-conditioning. She had no idea whether her neighbors were at home or had decamped en masse for the summer.

She considered driving to her parents'—she was not sure it was safe to stay in her apartment with no phone or lights—but decided against it. If she went to bed, the electricity might have come back by the time she awoke. And given the choice between facing an intruder or her mother, Lily cast her lot with the intruder.

By the next morning, the electricity was working but the phone was not. Lily had not been able to make or receive a call in twelve hours and, as she left for work, she realized that for the first time since her engagement, she had gone for more than a day without speaking to Mark.

19

City Lights

"We have had a dreadful storm of wind in the fore-part of this day, which has done a great deal of mischief among our trees."

—Letter to Cassandra Austen

The morning after the storm, Colony Heights looked as though God had thrown a New Year's Eve party and forgotten to clean up. Lily no sooner left her apartment than she heard two neighbors fighting acidly over whose insurance company should pay to remove a fallen tree—that of the woman on whose lawn the tree had stood or that of the man on whose property it had fallen—and backed her car out of her driveway without speaking to either.

At her office, she found that another sort of storm had erupted after her story on personals ads turned up on newsstands. Never had she seen her desk littered with so many faxes, which a mail clerk had arranged so that she would see the most hostile first.

Lily picked up the fax on the top of the pile and read:

Dear Ms. Blair,

    We the undersigned members of the Ohio chapter of the Men's Rights League are outraged by your portrayal of men as a sex-obsessed beer-drinking gender with no sense of humor. For your information, discrimination against the male gender is a *very serious problem* in this state, and articles such as yours only contribute to the oppression of a group that—

Lily moved on to the next fax, which arrived on the letterhead of a law firm that had once offered Mark a job, which he rejected:

Dear Ms. Blair:

    As a lawyer who recently moved to Ohio from Louisiana, I was dismayed by your article in today's paper, which perpetuates stereotypes of Napoleon as a congenital megalomaniac imperialist. You may be unaware the Napoleonic Code is a fine and subtle legal instrument that—

Good going, Mark, Lily thought. *Glad you rejected that that one.* She reached for the third fax:

Dear Miss Blair,

    If I may read between the lines of your story on the personals ads, I believe you are suggesting that retirees have less interest in sex than men in their twenties. I am in my mid-eighties and must inform you that this is not the case. Two years ago I met a lovely forty-three-year-old woman and want to assure you that we have sex at least—

Lily was losing the heart and stomach to go on but tried to stay open-minded:

> Miss Blair,
>   "Dear" is too good a word for you. Every time I pick up the *Daily*, you are giving this city another sick example of how the young of America have gone to the dogs. In my day men and women did not have to advertise themselves like chewing tobacco just to get married! More than fifty years ago I met my dear wife at the Odd Fellows Hall, and ever since then I have been as proud as any man in this country to call her "my ball and chain."

Okay, Lily thought. *One more fax, and* that's *it*:

> Dear Susanna—

Susanna? Lily stopped reading. The mail clerk must have misdirected the fax. She checked the *Daily* telephone directory to see if the paper employed any Susannas and, on finding that it did not, began reading the letter for clues to the identity of its intended recipient:

> Dear Susanna,
>   You have always been the loveliest reporter at the *Daily*, and the now the city will know that you are also the wittiest and most intelligent. Your story on the personals ads was the latest installment in a delightful series.
>   Perhaps you will allow me to take you to dinner after I return so that I may further express my admiration for your work? Or perhaps you will permit me to show my appreciation for your

exquisite gifts by means unfit to mention on the pages of a family newspaper?

The Count beckons, so I will talk to you later. In the meantime, I love you.

Your adoring,
Figaro

P.S. You were completely right about men's obsession with sex. I *am* obsessed with you.

Lily looked at the letterhead and saw that it was that of Mark's hotel. Carol, his secretary, apparently faxed him the story.

This unsolicited show of affection, to Lily's surprise, brought tears to her eyes, and she fought them back by trying to recall all the Italian words to an aria from *The Marriage of Figaro* that she liked to play on the piano. She had gotten as far as *Non sò più cosa son, cosa faccio* when Frank Gallese called her over to his desk.

He reminded her that he was leaving on vacation at the end of the day and that the last installment in her bridal series was due the following week. She was supposed to try to interview famous wedding experts, such as Martha Stewart, and he wanted her to send her story directly to the copy desk after she had written it.

This instruction heartened Lily. She had been afraid that, while Frank was fishing in Minnesota, her story would be edited by Bill Schroeder, who would make her fill it with anecdotes about the weddings of famous basketball players.

"Thanks, Frank," she said gratefully. "Hope you don't hit too much Friday-night traffic on your way to the cabin."

Frank asked what she was doing for the weekend, and Lily realized that she didn't know. She had been so absorbed in Mark and in her wedding that she could not remember the last time she had two free days in a row. Having canceled her photo appointment, she planned only to work on her résumé, which she could hardly admit to her boss.

In New York she might have spent a low-key Sunday afternoon reading the paper in Central Park or taking a walking tour of O. Henry's Murray Hill. But in a city conspicuously lacking in parks and noteworthy architecture, she would be thrown back on herself.

Realizing this, Lily walked over to Jack O'Reilly's desk after her boss had left. "Jack, have you noticed how there's nothing to do in this city on weekends?"

Jack looked at her in mock astonishment. "How can you say there's nothing to do in this city on weekends? The Laundromats are open."

"Actually, in Colony Heights, they aren't."

Lily explained that the Colony Heights zoning board had banned Laundromats as a way of keeping out undesirables, which presumably meant people who wore clean clothes. This was only one reason single people shunned the suburb: They had no place to pick up dates during the rinse cycle. Lily did her laundry at her parents' house.

Jack protested that the lack of Laundromats in one suburb did not mean that there was nothing to do in the city. He rooted around in the compost heap of papers on his desk and pulled out a copy of *City Lights*, which he opened to a calendar of events entitled "Ohio Living."

Jeff Carter, a reporter who had grown up in the South, looked up from his computer. "Don't believe him, Lily. 'Ohio Living' is an oxymoron."

"Ignore the man, Lily," Jack said. "Jeff has flown back to Virginia almost every weekend since he got here. He has no idea of the great things you can do in this city."

"I've stayed in town enough weekends to know what it's like to be single here," Jeff replied. "This city is to single people what the Sierra Nevadas were to the Donner Party. Anybody who doesn't die of exposure or bad food will die of boredom."

Lily was relieved that she had set aside part of her weekend to plan her escape from the Sierras. She found that Jeff, as a transplant, usually took the pulse of the city more accurately than Jack, who had grown up in a working-class steel-mill town on the West Side.

"All right, I'll prove to you that there's a lot to do here," Jack said, feigning indignation. He held up the "Ohio Living" section of *City Lights* and flipped through it. "See? There are hundreds of possibilities. For instance, the Catholic Slavic Mothers' Association is having a communion breakfast."

"Jack, I'm not Catholic, I'm not Slavic, and I'm not a mother," Lily said.

"Okay, then here's another one. Saturday night is Ladies' Oil Wrestling Night on the West Side."

"What's ladies' oil wrestling?" Lily asked, suspecting that she did not want to know the answer.

Jeff guffawed, and Jack explained that ladies' oil wrestling was a popular local sport in which women in bathing suits covered themselves with Mazola and groped each other in bars.

Lily asked if the city had men's oil wrestling.

"Men's oil wrestling?" Jack asked. "Gee, I don't think so. Why would anybody want to watch a couple of guys rolling around in Mazola?"

"That's exactly my point," Lily said. "Try again."

"All right, here's something I'm positive you'll like: Bauxite Night at the Rock Hall of Fame."

The Rock Hall of Fame was the nickname of the North

Coast Geology Museum, the most visible symbol of what was being hailed as the city's magnificent turnaround. The museum was supposed to attract geologists from all over the world with its unique collection of pebbles and boulders, and to give residents of the city something to do on Saturday nights besides watch ladies' oil wresting. It had become famous for its "Celebrity Rock" exhibits, such as a piece of granite that Bob Dylan stepped on at a Farm Aid concert and a chip from Jim Morrison's tombstone at Père La Chaise Cemetery in Paris. But the number of visitors to the museum was falling short of projections, and officials were trying to make up for it through special events like Bauxite Night.

"Thanks for the suggestion, Jack," Lily said. "But I saw Jim Morrison's whole grave the last time I visited my brother in Paris, so I can't get excited about a chip."

At this, Jack closed his copy of *City Lights*. "Some people sure are hard to please."

"I'm not hard to please," Lily said. "Just holding out for something a little more exciting than Bauxite Night."

"Well, if you want to do something really exciting, you could go out with me."

Lily looked at Jack with mild irritation. "Aren't you forgetting that I'm an engaged woman?"

"I'm not forgetting it at all. But I'm also not forgetting who your fiancé is spending the weekend with."

"Jack, Mark is spending the weekend working on a case," Lily said, with more conviction than she felt. "End of story."

20

Betrayal

"My courage always rises with every attempt to intimidate me."

—Pride and Prejudice

T alking to Jack left Lily all the more determined to retrieve her engagement ring from her parents' house. Her mother's refusal to return it stung her keenly. If she had learned to live with bribery and emotional blackmail, she drew the line at outright thievery. But how could she get the ring back when she had no idea where her mother had put it?

Lily could not think of what to do until she remembered that her parents usually went to the Commodore's Club for dinner on Friday nights while her grandmother went to the Symphony with Mr. Brooks.

What if—? she thought, then stopped herself. The idea of letting herself into her parents' house and searching their bedroom was too unsettling. She had never done anything like it, not even when her friends were raiding their parents' wallets for cash for Red Hots or comic books.

But Lily was emboldened by injustice. Until she returned it to Mark, the ring was *hers*. And she had a key to her parents' house that she used when she did her laundry, so she would not be breaking-and-entering so much as exercising a territorial privilege.

Lily called her parents' house and, getting no answer, drove over. Seeing no sign of activity, she made her way up the expensively carpeted stairs to the master bedroom. Like the rest of the house, her parents' room was aggressively color-coordinated and hermetically neat, a place where a visitor would never find an open copy of *Time* tossed casually onto the bed by someone who had rushed out a party.

It was also, Lily realized, a room that put the maximum distance between its occupants. At one end stood her mother's dresser, with its perfume bottles arrayed as formally as pawns on a chess board. At the other, a curved writing desk fit snugly into a large bay window, allowing her father to pay bills without facing his wife. When both parents used the room at the same time—her mother at the dresser, her father at the desk—they could remain back-to-back.

Atop the dresser sat a lacquered Oriental chest in which Charlotte Blair kept the jewelry, the most likely spot for the ring, if it had not gone into the safe-deposit box. Lily found the chest locked and tried to think of where her mother might keep the key. She opened a few dresser drawers without luck.

Then she remembered that under a green desk blotter her father kept the bills with which he tipped the people who delivered for the florist and liquor store. As she was about to lift the blotter, she saw a familiar return address on an opened envelope in a brass letter holder. Driven by an uneasiness that overrode her guilt, she removed the letter from its envelope.

As she began to read, Lily felt ill. Addressed to her parents, the letter was from Dr. Lefland. Lily scanned it hastily enough to catch only a half-dozen phrases: "Client arrived late . . . gave ludicrous excuse of having been delayed by 'kielbasa-wielding polka dancers' . . . behaved in a hostile manner and expressed anger inappropriately in perceived 'jokes' . . . displayed immature refusal to accept adult responsibilities of marriage . . . may be obsessed with death and self-annihilation."

Lily needed no more than a minute or two to realize that that she had been betrayed, not just by her parents but by her therapist. Hadn't her father assured her that she could speak confidentially to Dr. Lefland? Even if he had not done so, didn't a therapist have an obligation not to repeat what a client said in her office?

As angry as she was by the breach of trust, Lily was all the more outraged by the characterization of their meeting. The therapist stopped just short of calling her a liar, implying that she had made up the polka festival. Didn't the woman read the paper, which had run a long story on the event the day after they met? Did Dr. Lefland wear earplugs when she drove through the city?

But nothing rankled as much as the therapist's cool assumption that her reluctance to wed was a sign of immaturity. Didn't maturity—or the lack of it—have more to do with your character than with whether you had a spouse?

Lily could hardly steady her hand as it held the letter. Never had she felt a firmer resolve not to go through with her wedding. She had to find her ring and return it before she became entangled in another charade played out by people who knew as little of her as they did of the ancient Lydians.

After tucking the letter back in the envelope, she lifted

the blotter on her father's desk and found the key to her mother's jewelry chest. She opened the chest and found her diamond under a garnet necklace that her father gave her mother after Todd's birth. The perfection of the ring moved her deeply. She had almost forgotten how beautiful it was and could not keep from holding it up to the light, a bit wistfully, to admire its brilliance.

Lily had little doubt that her mother would be furious with her for removing the diamond. But by the time she slipped the ring on her finger, she had lost the fear of hurting her parents that preyed on her ever since she had decided to cancel her wedding. Her parents, it seemed, were more than able to hold their own when it came to inflicting injury.

Too unsettled to face Brad and Edie at the health club, Lily went back to her apartment. She had a message from Mark, who said that he thought his trial would end on Monday. If the jury appeared likely to return its verdict in a day or two, he would remain in Los Angeles until it did.

Lily realized that she had not yet thanked him for the fax in which he had cast himself as a lovestruck Figaro, and she decided to acknowledge it by playing a portion of *"Non sò più"* for him on the piano. After unearthing the score for *The Marriage of Figaro*, she ran through the aria and saw that her musical technique had deteriorated badly since she had returned to Colony Heights. She could not manage the faster notes.

Unwilling to give up on the opera, she tried *"Voi che sapete"* and found a section that she could play. She called Mark's hotel and, on reaching his room, left a portion of it on his voice mail.

The poignancy of Mozart's music, and the irony of its theme, made Lily melancholy. Without the distractions of her health club, her emotions gnawed at her, and she longed to talk to a friend.

As she had done so often, she wished that the *Daily* had more single women on staff. Almost all of her female co-workers went home to their children directly after work, which had made it nearly impossible to cultivate the sort of after-hours friendships that had sustained her during her romantic crises in New York.

That was one of the things she had loved about the city: Manhattan was an eight-mile-long Women's Center or, more accurately, a Single Women's Center. From Battery Park to the Cloisters, it was filled with unmarried women who had the gift and the time to become the Picassos of the art of friendship. Lily had made more female friends in five years in New York than she had in all her time in Colony Heights, as a child or as an adult.

Impulsively, she called Sally, who took longer than usual to answer the phone. Sally said that she had been brushing her teeth with Perrier for the third time that week, because the water in her apartment building was out.

"God, Lily, you have no idea how great Ohio looks from here right now," she added. "They should call it, Ohio: The Land of Running Water."

Lily, not wanting to have a replay of their earlier conversation, tried to hurry to her point. "Sally, I'm not calling about plumbing. Remember how I told you in our last conversation that I've been having a few, sort of, reservations about my wedding?"

There was a silence at the other end of the line.

"Sally? Remember how I said I wasn't absolutely, completely sure I'd made the right decision in getting engaged so soon?"

There was another silence.

"Sally?"

"Sure, I remember," Sally said, at last. "But I thought you were having a bad day, like the time that Danish baronet's son told you that, even though he really loved you, he couldn't go out with American women any more because his parents were pressuring him to find some sort of deposed princess of Yugoslavia. You were never really crazy about that guy, anyway."

"It's worse than that." Lily steeled herself against her best friend's disappointment. "First, I'm moving back to New York—"

"That's great! You and I can be a freelance investigative team, after all. Did Mark get a job on Wall Street or Park Avenue?"

"Mark doesn't have a job in New York. I'm not moving back with him." Lily was not sure her friend heard her. "I'm not moving back with Mark, because I'm not getting married at all. I'm not going through with the wedding."

Sally said nothing for a moment, then spoke in a voice filled with disbelief.

"Oh, God," Sally said. "Please don't tell me Mark is having an affair."

"No, no, that's not it at all," Lily replied with consternation. Perhaps, Sally's encounters with ax murderers had left her with a more cynical view of human nature than she had remembered. "Mark's not involved with anybody else." She modified her comment slightly. "At least, I don't think he is."

"What do you mean, you don't *think?*"

"Well, he's been in Los Angeles for the past week, trying a case with a female partner who the men here think is really beautiful. And I guess some people might suspect him of cheating, but I don't. I mean, maybe my id does"— Lily broke off, reflecting guiltily on her trip to the *Daily* morgue—"but my superego doesn't. Mark is just too honest to cheat. He wouldn't do it because, if he did, he would have to lie about it. Some people are pathological liars. Mark is an almost pathological nonliar. He says he's seen too many clients tell their lawyers one thing, then say another thing on the witness stand and get killed for it in court. Once I asked Mark why he had never lost a case, and he said there were two reasons. First, when he takes a case, he makes clear to his clients that they can't lie to him, ever, even if they think they're only telling a white lie. He says that whenever clients tell what they call 'a little white lie,' it turns out to be the size of Antarctica. Second, if a case goes bad—say, if he finds out that a client *has* been lying to him despite the warning—he settles the case out of court."

Lily glanced at her music for *The Marriage of Figaro*. She remembered all the dissembling that went on among the men and women in Mozart's comic operas: The characters in those operas were bigger liars than any client F. Lee Bailey ever defended. Wondering if Mark would have represented da Ponte, she approached Sally's question from a different angle.

"Anyway, we're talking about a man who wanted to go to seminary. Mark's partners rib him about it all the time. They say if you dropped him into a harem via a parachute, he would sit there reading the Book of Revelation."

"My rabbi had an affair with a woman at our temple," Sally said. "One Saturday he got up in front of the congregation and said he was leaving the temple because he had a moral flaw. Then, in the next breath, he said, 'I had a moral flaw with a member of the congregation.' "

"Let's assume Mark is not having a moral flaw with his partner in Los Angeles."

"Okay, let's assume it. But, if we do, why don't you want to get married?"

"In the first place, I never wanted to get married, except for about fifteen minutes when I was seven and a flower girl in my Aunt Grace's wedding. I always thought that, if you got married, you should have a good, solid reason—such as that you were ready to have children—and that until then you should just live together. And I'm not ready to have children. I can barely take care of my scheffleras."

Lily picked a yellow leaf off a tree next to her telephone. "You know, in France, where my brother lives, everybody lives together. One third of the children in France are born out of wedlock—a lot of them to couples who just don't see the need for a marriage license—and, if those children are worse off for it, I haven't noticed it. Every time I visit my brother, I see how much better-behaved French children are than American children. My five-year-old niece was born seven months after Todd and Isabelle got married, and she's a Little Miss Manners compared with Mark's nieces and nephews from Purgatory, who grew up in a city that everybody thinks is such a wonderful place to raise a family."

Lily glanced affectionately at a photograph of Sylvie, who was demonstrating how to eat escargots. "The trouble is that when I moved back to Colony Heights, I lost myself. It was so clear that you can't be a player here unless you're married. It's as though the women's movement flew over the city in a 747 but never stopped to refuel. Or maybe it stopped to refuel before I got here, and now it's in a holding pattern over Boise. And the problem goes beyond women. Gay men are penalized for being single just as much as straight women. There was a big demonstration in front of my office the other day—you know that case out in Hawaii involving gay couples who want to get married?"

"The case that led to the act that sets up some sort of

Star Wars system to defend the universe against gay marriages?"

"Right. The Defense of Marriage Act. At first, I couldn't understand why that case came up in Hawaii, instead of New York or San Francisco, where there are so many more gay people. But now I have a theory. It's because there *are* so many gay people there that it didn't. Gay or straight, in places like New York or San Francisco, you can be single and be accepted for your talent or your money or your great personality. Sort of, strength in numbers. Out in places like Hawaii, or Ohio, it's much harder to be seen for who you are than for whom you're married to. Most people will be perfectly friendly to you"—Lily was suddenly afraid this might leave the wrong impression—"according to their definition of friendliness. But they won't invite you into their homes or want you on their committees. Getting married under these conditions—getting married because you won't be socially accepted until you do—would be buying into a flawed system instead of trying to change the system, or moving someplace where they have a better system."

"Lily, I grew up in Brooklyn and have never lived more than an hour away from Samuel J. Tilden High School," Sally said. "So I don't really know what it's like to live in a place where they don't have all those things that are essential to the mental health of single people, like New School catalogs. But you're talking about your wedding as though it were a political statement. The fact is, you *did* meet a wonderful man, who sounds perfect for you except that he has this tragic flaw: He wants to marry you."

Lily was beginning to realize that New York women, whom she regarded as the highest female life form, did have a tiny defect: If they lived in New York long enough, they found it inconceivable that you could meet a wonderful man without immediately wanting to monogram your towels with his initial.

"Sally, I met a wonderful man who, figuratively speaking, came to pick me up for a date while I was still in my bathrobe. My mother has a saying about marriage: A man finds the woman when the time is right, and a woman finds the time when the man is right. But I keep thinking: Why don't women have the same right that men do? Why can't we say, 'The time isn't right,' the way they can?"

"You mean, other than because we outnumber them the way the Sioux outnumbered the Seventh Cavalry at Little Big Horn?" Sally laughed. "Not a bad analogy. When you think of men, do you identify more with Custer or Sitting Bull?"

Lily said nothing, not knowing how to make her friend see her point. Her silence, paradoxically, seemed to make her see it.

"Lily, I'm so sorry," Sally said, full of contrition. "You must be going through an awful time, and I'm not helping by cracking jokes about Sitting Bull. I'm afraid that freelancing has made me overestimate the charms of the two-income household. I haven't even asked you how Mark is taking the news."

"That's one of my problems. He doesn't know yet, because he's trying a case in Los Angeles and won't be back until next week, and I can't tell him until he returns. That's why I called. I was hoping that you could help me think of how to break the news to him, or at least get through the next few days without losing my sanity."

Sally said nothing for a moment. "You've just been telling me that, if you're single, you can't retain your sanity in Colony Heights. So why don't you come to New York for the weekend? We'll talk about everything here, during a nice walk in Central Park. It sounds like we need more than an hour on the phone for this one."

Lily suddenly could not imagine anything she would like more than a weekend in New York: two days away from her mother, her answering machine and her parody-of-a-dream-house. She could not deny that Colony Heights was taking its toll. Every time she walked by a mock-Tudor pizza parlor, she wondered whether Anne Boleyn's last meal was deep-dish or double-crust. And she longed to see the members of the writers' group that she and Sally had formed in New York.

But she was not sure she should take so expensive a trip. A last-minute plane ticket would cost a fortune in a month in which she would have to reimburse all her bridesmaids for their dresses.

"Suppose you stayed in Colony Heights for the weekend," Sally prodded. "What would you be doing without Mark?"

Lily thought about ladies' oil wrestling and Bauxite Night at the Rock Hall of Fame and her mother's reaction to her retrieval of her ring. Then, instead of answering her best friend's question directly, she told Sally that she would call a few airlines and see if she could get a flight that would get her into New York by noon the next day.

21

"Regulated Hatred"

". . . this exquisite weather . . . I enjoy it all over me, from top to toe, from right to left, Longitudinally, Perpendicularly, Diagonally . . ."
—Letter to Cassandra Austen

Lily booked herself into the Plaza with that false sense of economy that results from the idea that—once you have wildly overspent on airfare—it doesn't matter how much you pay for a hotel room because your budget already has collapsed. She had not achieved her goal of arriving before lunch but checked into the hotel in the early afternoon, which left her with several hours to herself before meeting Sally and several other friends for dinner.

Although Sally had wanted her to stay with her, Lily had declined the offer. Her best friend's studio apartment was so small that, if two people inhaled at the same time, they bumped into each other. So she had pointed out that a hotel room might be a better choice. That way, if the water went out in Sally's building over the weekend, Sally could shower and brush her teeth at the Plaza.

Lily arrived in the city just after the heat wave had broken. As she stepped out of her cab in front of the hotel, the sky was as fresh and blue as all the morning glories in Colony Heights, and throngs of apartment dwellers had taken exuberantly to the streets, sprung from the captivity of their erratically air-conditioned apartments. The sun glinted off the blue necks of the pigeons in front of the hotel fountain and burnished the coats of the flower-bedecked horses waiting to take visitors for rides around Central Park. It was a miraculous day: The whole city looked like an Ode to Serotonin.

As Lily unpacked her suitcase, she could see a kite festival getting underway through a window overlooking the park. Children were streaming toward it, some of them in prams pushed by uniformed nannies. For a while she watched their kites being hoisted aloft: boxy red kites with Chinese characters on them, shiny blue and green polyethylene kites that looked like tropical birds, kites handmade from brown paper bags. Then she decided to walk up Fifth Avenue on the park side of the street, which would give her a good view of the festival.

Lily had gotten as far as Sixty-third Street when man in a ragged shirt and several-days-old beard walked up, smiled shyly, and handed her a long-stemmed red rose, an improbable Lancelot of the streets. When she tried to pay him for it, he gallantly refused to take the money.

A few blocks later, she passed a man swinging a huge boom box, who stared at her. For a moment, she was sure he intended to mug her. Instead, he grinned.

"Hey, blue eyes, you are lookin' fine today," he said, before he went on his way with a jaunty swagger. "You sure do know how to wear a pair of black jeans."

Lily turned around reluctantly at the Frick Collection, wishing she had time to revisit its glass-roofed courtyard, and headed back to the Plaza. She had nearly reached the hotel when she came to a mobile book stall at the corner of Fifth Avenue and Sixtieth Street, run by the Strand Bookstore.

To her joy, she found among its shelves a battered copy of a study that she had been trying to find for months, in which a critic had described Jane Austen's view of her society as "regulated hatred." She quickly found a park bench and began to read it, exhilarated by D. W. Harding's analysis. Why, she wondered, was it so perversely uplifting to know that hatred seethed within the heart of a novelist who appeared to be the very model of female civility and decorum?

By the time she returned to the Plaza, Lily knew that— if she were counting the weekend's blessings—she could stop there with a profit. But the scene was so seductive that she decided to walk for a few more blocks, along Central Park South, where she found herself thinking of Mark.

Why couldn't she have met him in New York, where they would have had a chance? Free of the expectations of their parents and community, they might have dated for a while, lived together for a year or two and finally— maybe—run downtown to City Hall someday and wed when they were ready to push their own pram to a kite festival. In New York, she and Mark could have breathed. They would not have suffocated under the dead weight of a city that kept itself alive by pretending to be more than it was and turning marriage into its badge of certified adulthood.

Looking up at the brick-and-glass co-ops on Central Park South, which had a glorious view of the Kite Festival, Lily could almost envision the two of them living there. Then she remembered, with a jolt, that Mark wasn't the one who was suffocating under the expectations of their city: she was.

22

Home

"With due exceptions—Woman feels for Woman very promptly and compassionately."

—Sandition

At tea time, Lily listened to a string quartet playing Viennese waltzes at the Palm Court of the Plaza before she headed uptown to meet Sally and several other members of their old writers' group. She decided to walk along Fifth Avenue—the weather was still perfect—and turned right at Sixty-seventh Street in order to go by the Regency Whist Club.

The club had always been Lily's second-favorite New York anachronism, after a row house on West Eleventh Street that had a brass door plaque that said THE GRETA GARBO HOME FOR WAYWARD BOYS AND GIRLS. Nobody knew whether the plaque was a hoax or a whimsical exercise in Garbo-esque philanthropy.

No such air of mystery clung to the Regency Whist Club, where members gathered to play whist as men and women had done in Jane Austen's day. Lily had time to make only a brief stop in front of its handsome limestone building, not far from some of the city's best-known sky-scrapers.

Even so, she loved being afoot again in a city hospitable enough to welcome both the Regency Whist Club and World Trade Center, the realm of nineteenth-century English leisure and that of twentieth-century American commerce. So what if its landlords at times treated working plumbing as a luxury? New York was still the country's most accommodating social, cultural, and intellectual carryall.

The walk gave Lily something she never encountered at home: a glimpse of a city willing to seduce her into a heightened sense of life's bright possibilities and to achieve through subtle persuasion what it could not bring about through brute self-promotion. From behind the elegant Italian mannerist and Beaux Arts facades there leaked out a droll wit, as though the city belonged to people who took periodic whiffs of laughing gas.

Lily made a half-dozen detours before, on East Eighty-fifth Street, she entered a graceful weathered-brick apartment building. She was greeted warmly by Patrick, the doorman.

"Good evening, Miss Blair. It's a pleasure to see you again. Didn't you have a fine weekend for your trip?"

Lily was startled to find that the doorman's memory of her nearly brought tears to her eyes. That she might still be recognized by a man in whose building she had never lived moved her far out of proportion to its intended efforts.

After thanking Patrick, Lily took the elevator to the seventh floor. She and Sally had agreed to meet the other members of their writers' group at the apartment of Ruth Bryant, an editor at a publishing house, because it had large rooms and dependable air-conditioning.

As she stepped off the elevator, Lily could hear laughter and the clatter of dinner plates. She saw, when Ruth opened the door, not just the members of their writers' group but several other of her closest female friends. They shouted when she stepped inside.

"Surprise!"

Sally explained that she had made a few calls to let people know that Lily was coming to town and—would you believe the luck?—nearly everybody was free for dinner. *That was another great thing about New York,* Lily thought as she hugged her friends: *On any given Saturday night, you could spontaneously call up six or seven of the most terrific women you knew, and none of them would have dates.* She was amazed that Sally had corralled not just Ruth but a group that included her friend Jane, who wrote children's books, and Ellen, an arts critic for their old paper.

"Lily, you look fabulous!" Ruth said. "You could model for Bendel's. How do you stay so slim?"

Lily smiled and said that, luckily, she did not find it difficult to resist corn dogs. Then, realizing that none of her friends might know what corn dogs were, she tried to describe them objectively.

"Oh, gross," Ellen said. "Do people really eat those things in public?"

Lily assured her that they did, often with Midwestern specialties such as fried catfish on a bun, and Ellen made a face. "Please. Don't they have focaccia bread out there?"

At that moment, Jane began to praise the black leather miniskirt that Lily was wearing with a white shirt. "Where on earth did you find something so stylish?" she asked. "You can't possibly have gotten it at one of those leather shops run by aging hippies on Eighth Street, where all the hookers buy their thigh-high boots."

Lily said that she had found it on her last trip to Paris to visit her brother. She had never owned anything so short, but her sister-in-law refused to allow her to try on skirts longer than five inches above the knee.

"What a great sister-in-law," Jane said enviously. "She definitely knows what looks good on you. But how did you get that lump on your forehead?"

Lily said she had fainted while covering a trade show in an overheated conventional hall, then asked her friends about their latest projects. To her delight, nearly all of them had good news. Jane had sold a picture book on Harriet Tubman. Ellen had received a great rejection letter from the Feminist Press. Sally was working on a groundbreaking report on women's prisons for *Home Invasion Weekly*. Ruth had wrung a promise from her bosses that she didn't have to edit books with Stealth bombers on the cover any more.

By the time the *pastitsio* and the Greek salad had been consumed and most of the guests were working on their second or third glasses of wine, Lily had worked out a new definition of "home": Home is where, when you go there, you don't feel crazy any more. In the presence of these women she could say anything without fear of losing their affection—a realization that eventually allowed her to bring up the reason for her visit.

The bad news, Lily said, was that her wedding was off. The good news was: She would never have to look at another corn dog. She was coming back to New York.

Her friends' joy on hearing of her return quickly gave way to concern about the second and about her job prospects in the city. Was she sure she wanted to break her engagement? (Yes.) Did she plan to give back her ring? (Of course.) Did she have any job leads yet? (No, but maybe with all of their help . . .)

To her relief, nobody suggested that if she called off her wedding she would betray her parents, humiliate her fiancé, hasten her grandmother's death, or otherwise bring dishonor to the human race. Her friends gave her credit for knowing what she was doing and, before long, began to offer the names of New York editors who might want to hire her.

The lone dissenting voice came from her friend Ruth, who had met Mark when she flew out to Colony Heights for a fitting for her bridesmaid's dress and who appeared unsettled by the discussion. Naturally, she said, she would love to have Lily back in New York, and naturally, she would instantly pass along any job leads that she heard about. But the whole thing was so—unexpected.

"I have to admit, the moment I saw you and Mark together, I thought you and he were perfect for each other," she said. "The men you went out with in New York were all amazingly interesting—the son of the baronet, that performance artist who took apart Hondas onstage, the poet who wrote you sestinas on the napkins from coffee shops, because he couldn't afford paper . . ."

"And how often did we all get free passes to watch somebody disassemble fan belts at an off-off-Broadway theater with black walls?" Sally broke in, drawing laughs from the women who had attended the show. "To this day, I can smell the oil fumes."

"But none of them was the sort of man I could ever envision you married to," Ruth persisted. "They were fun, but they were men you'd want to spend a few Saturday nights with, maybe more than a few, but not the rest of your life. I can see you and Mark in your old age, walking arm in arm past the Greta Garbo Home for Wayward Boys and Girls and talking about the grandchildren who have been bestowed on you by your own wayward boys and girls."

Lily adored Ruth but, at that moment, realized why Sally was her best friend. Sally might argue with her but, in the end, would let her make her own decisions. Ruth would never stop trying to shape the plot.

"You might see us that way, and I might see us that way, Ruth. But *Mark* doesn't. He sees us growing old in a city that has pet karaoke nights."

"What's pet karaoke?" Ellen asked.

Lily explained that in karaoke clubs people sang off-key to taped music, sometimes accompanied by their cats or dogs.

"That's *awful*," Ellen said. "Good thing you're planning to ditch that guy while you still have a chance."

"In New York we have play groups for pets," Ruth said evenly. "Are pet karaoke nights so much worse than that?"

"Of course they are," Ellen said. "Pet play groups provide vital interspecies interaction for animals that stay cooped up in apartments all day long. They fill an important social need here in the city."

"Ellen, for some people they do, and for some people they don't," Ruth said. "That isn't the point. The point is, Mark and Lily don't have to go to pet karaoke nights." She turned to Lily. "Do you?"

"The problem isn't just the pet karaoke nights. They're sort of a symbol of everything else that's wrong with our living there, like the ladies' oil wrestling—"

"What's ladies' oil wrestling?" Ellen asked.

Lily explained that on ladies' oil wrestling nights women rolled around on mats, after dousing themselves with Mazola oil, while men hooted.

"That is *totally* sexist," Ellen said. "Get rid of that guy, I tell you. Any man who has grown up in that sort of city is probably completely warped, anyway."

"Lily, I admit that I wouldn't be too happy in a place that had ladies' oil wrestling as the unofficial sport," Ruth said. "But even if the city has all those things, couldn't you and Mark just ignore them all?"

Lily described the weather, the decaying neighborhoods, the 'Cats fans who lapped beer out of saucers, and the house with the doorbell that played the Ohio State song, adding that these were just the beginning of the other things they would also have to ignore.

"They're all part the same problem," she said. "In a sense, the house is just an eighteen-room version of pet karaoke nights. I just didn't think any of these things through carefully enough before I agreed to get married. If Mark and I had known each other longer, if we had met in New York, if we had lived together—" Lily stopped. "You know, we sort of skipped the stage of fighting over how many shelves you get in his medicine chest and went straight to disagreeing over an eighteen-room house."

"Why can't you fight over the medicine chest now?" Ruth asked. "Why can't you live together instead of getting married?"

"Because Mark doesn't see the point of living together. He thinks that, if you love each other, you get married; and that's it."

"Why can't you make him see the point?"

"Because he doesn't want to see it, and, even if he did, he doesn't want to live in New York."

"Lily, this doesn't make any sense," Ruth said. "You could persuade Mark that he does want to live in New York. It's obvious to anybody who has seen you two together that he loves you, and you love him." Ruth turned to her. "Don't you?"

"I never said that."

Ruth, who had been passing a plate of baklava, set it down. "You never said it to us, or to him?"

Lily tried to think of a way to duck the question. She wished Ruth had asked her about sex instead of love: Sex was much easier to talk about, because people were more realistic about it. But it occurred to her that if she could not talk about love with these women, she would never be able to talk about it with anyone.

"I never said it to us or to him."

Ellen looked shocked. "You never told your fiancé that you loved him? Why not?"

"I don't know. It just always seemed to me that when it came to getting married, some things might be more important than love, such as how you treat each other . . . It doesn't necessarily follow that because two people say they love each other, they have the wisdom to act as though they do. Nor does it follow that, if they don't say they love each other, they don't have the wisdom to act as though they do. My French sister-in-law says that in France, there's a saying: There's no such thing as love, there are only proofs of love. Sort of a Gallic version of actions speaking louder than words."

Ellen still did not appear to believe what she had heard. "So you were going to go through your whole married life without ever telling your husband you loved him?"

"I didn't know what I was going to do. I just thought that if it seemed right to say it at any point, I would say it. I wasn't intentionally holding it back, I just never had a compelling reason to say it." Lily could see that most of her friends were baffled. "Why say everything before you marry? Why not retain a little mystery or surprise?"

"Oh, I get it," Ellen said, brightening. "Sort of like the way our mothers used to save their virginity for their husbands, but since we don't have that to save, we have to save something else?"

"Or like when Anne Marie Ramsay got engaged and didn't tell her husband about her trust funds until after the wedding, because she didn't want him to marry her for her money?" Sally asked.

Lily pondered their words, never having thought in such terms. "Well, maybe a bit more like Anne Marie than like our mothers." She paused. "Where is Anne Marie tonight, anyway?"

"In the Hamptons," Ellen said.

"Probably meeting with her lawyer out there," Sally said. "She and Ted are in the middle of an incredibly bitter separation."

"Let's not get into that," Ruth said hastily. "It was obvious from the beginning that Anne Marie and Ted were wrong for each other, just as it's obvious that Lily and Mark are right for each other."

"Ruth, it's not as simple as Mark and I being right for each other or not right for each other. People who are right for each other can become wrong if the deck is so stacked against them that every day they have to—" Lily could think of nothing but the sort of military analogies invoked by Jack. "That every day they feel like Henry V at Agincourt."

"Henry V won at Agincourt," Ruth said.

"He won once. He didn't have to keep refighting the battle over and over. Anyway, I've met somebody else, a British architect, and he's really interesting."

"That's what you said about the son of the Danish baronet when you met *him*. And he lived five thousand miles away, too. The Danish baronet, the guy with the Hondas, the poet in the coffee shops—they were all fantasies. Mark is real. If you love him, you shouldn't let him go just so you can chase another fantasy."

"I told you, I never said I loved Mark."

Ruth, appearing worn down by the debate, began to serve the ouzo-spiked ice cream.

"Lily, you don't *have* to."

23

The Book of Revelation

"Why should you be living in dread of his marrying somebody else?—(Yet how natural!)"

—Letter to Fanny Knight

On her desk on Monday morning Lily found an item from the gossip column in the latest issue of *City Lights*, which had come out over the weekend. An attached note said, "Lil, Did you see this? Jack." The afterglow of her New York trip faded as she read the item:

An in-house joke at the city's largest law firm says that, if attorney Mark Slayton parachuted into a harem, he'd sit there reading the New Testament—a reference to the star litigator's flirtation with the ministry before he repented and became a lawyer for celebrities such as Sonny Bono. But his interest in the Book of Revelation is likely to face its greatest challenge this week as he goes to court to defend TechnoCorp against a multimillion-dollar age-discrimination suit filed by a dozen employees over fifty-five, whose charges include that their bosses routinely referred to them as the "Gee-zers" and the "Geezerettes." The handsome at-torney is trying the case in Federal District Court in Los Angeles with his law partner Car-oline Van Allen, the stunning socialite-turned-lawyer whose previous conquests include a professor at Ohio's finest law school. A *City Lights* correspondent, visiting California last week, spotted Slayton and Allen emerging from a hotel room just as the sun was beginning to rise. (Could the sun also be rising on a new ro-mance?) Meanwhile, Slayton's attractive fiancée apparently does not lack for potential diversions of her own. She was observed the other night at the Ritz with . . .

Lily could read no more. "Previous conquests"? That made it sound as though Caroline had conquered Mark. And wasn't it bad enough that one of his sisters didn't know the difference between pro bono and Sonny Bono? That a writer for *City Lights* made the same mistake left her embarrassed to be a reporter. Unless—the thought made her almost ill—the error had occurred not because the writer didn't know the difference but because he or she had received the misinformation from Penny or Fran.

But nothing in the item bothered Lily more than the mention of her dinner with Nick Monford. She couldn't bear that Mark might think she had been unfaithful to him and was calling off their wedding because of another man. Yet how could she prove she hadn't been unfaith-ful?

As she tossed the paper aside, Lily saw that Jack was watching her.

"Well?" he asked. "What did I tell you?"

Lily felt her anger rising. Jack's satisfied expression added to the insult of the gossip.

"Jack, you know that if they gave negative Pulitzers to the papers that published the most errors in a year, *City Lights* would win the reverse public-service award," she said coolly. "I can't believe that you would take an item like that seriously. It isn't even timely. The item makes it sound as though Mark's case is going to trial this week when the trial is almost over."

"Don't blame me for what appears in that throwback to the days of yellow journalism," Jack said in a mock-aggrieved tone. "Everybody knows that they hand out *City Lights* for free because nobody would pay money for it. I just thought you wouldn't want to miss the article. The paper only printed what I've been trying to tell you all along. Watch out for Caroline."

"That's unfair to Caroline," Lily said. "Not to mention to Mark and me. The trouble with this city is that too many people have never moved beyond the days when it was assumed that any unattached woman was so desperate to get married that she regarded any attractive man who crossed her path as fair game."

"Maybe the gossip columnist for *City Lights* has a source inside Mark's firm that you don't have."

"If so, it's an incorrect source. I don't intend to give two seconds' worth of thought to that item," Lily said. To her chagrin, she realized that she had already given it substantially more than two seconds' worth. "Mark is not having an affair with Caroline."

"How can you be sure?"

"Because Mark has always been totally faithful to me. Ever since he left for Los Angeles, he's been calling me, sending me flowers, writing me notes—" Lily checked herself, realizing that none of this was Jack's business.

"Any man can be totally faithful for a few months. But men are like video-cassette recorders. After a while, their warranty expires, and you can't tune into the X-rated movies anymore."

"You're talking about men as though they were nothing more than household appliances with out-of-control hormones," Lily said. She thought about her household appliances, then went on. "Anyway, my VCR is incredibly complicated. I've never figured out how to program that thing."

"All the more reason not to dismiss the *City Lights* article. Maybe Mark is more complicated than you think. Maybe he was faithful to you here in Ohio but fell in love with Caroline once he found himself alone with her in L.A."

"Jack, Mark is not in love with Caroline," Lily said. "Mark loves me." Lily said this with slightly more certainty than she retained after reading the *City Lights* item. "Given that fact, if you know something about Caroline that I should know, I'd appreciate it if you would come right out and say it instead of continually resorting to innuendoes that do a disservice to Mark, Caroline, and me."

"All right, I will come right out and say it," Jack said. "*I* had an affair with Caroline. It happened a few years ago, when I was covering a big out-of-town bankruptcy case. Caroline and I were staying in a hotel downstate, and one night she knocked on the door of my room and—"

Lily abruptly pushed back her chair and stood up. "I don't want to hear this," she said. "If Caroline knocked on your door one night, you had as much to do with what happened next as she did, and what happened between the two of you has no bearing on what might have happened between Mark and Caroline. It's irrelevant."

"So you admit that something 'might' have happened."

Jack had scarcely uttered the words when he seemed to notice, for the first time, that Lily was wearing her engagement ring again.

"I see that you've regained the ability to type and wear the Rock at the same time," he added cheerfully. "I must say, the jeweler did a fine job with it. That diamond could be an exhibit in the Rock Hall of Fame."

As Lily turned her back to him, Jack spoke again.

"By the way, who's Nick Monford?" he said. "Sounds like a lucky guy."

For the rest of the day, Lily had trouble working on her interviews with wedding-etiquette authorities. That she had not heard from her mother since retrieving her ring made her uneasy. She knew that she would have to pay for her stealth and that the *City Lights* article would raise the fee. The distinction between a scandal and the appearance of a scandal carried little weight among her mother's friends, for whom appearances mattered as much as, or more than, the morality that lay behind them.

Worse, after reading the article, Lily found it harder to dismiss the possibility that a romance had sprung up between Mark and Caroline. If *City Lights* was right, it would mean that she had been wrong. It would mean that she had misjudged the man with whom she had agreed to spend her life, a thought that unnerved her enough to resolve to tell Mark of her decision as soon as her conscience allowed after he returned from Los Angeles. She would give him a day or two to recover from his jet lag but no more. No matter how much pain it might cause him, Mark had to know the truth.

That afternoon Mark called to say that both sides in his case had finished their closing arguments, and he thought the jury might return its verdict the next day. If it did, he would take the next flight back and hoped to arrive in town by early evening. He wondered if they could go out to dinner afterward.

This request unsettled Lily. Mark was usually tired of hotel food by the end of an out-of-town trial. He liked to wind down from the tension of the courtroom by making dinner for her at his condominium, and the TechnoCorp case had been more harrowing than most. Lily asked if anything was wrong.

"No, there's nothing wrong," he said, sounding more tired that he had in days. "It's just that—"

"Just that what?"

"Lily, we need to talk."

Mark's call left Lily in torment. More than a decade of dating had convinced her that no woman ever wanted to hear what came after, "We have to talk." The words were the nonmedical equivalent of, "Your biopsy is positive."

Lily was sure that Mark wanted to talk about Caroline, but what would he say? She tried to convince herself that, if he said he had fallen in love with his law partner, she ought to rejoice that he had found someone who could make him happier than she could.

But Lily could not make peace with the idea that Mark would marry Caroline. For, although she did not want to marry him in three weeks, what if Ruth was right? What if she wanted to marry Mark *someday*?

Lily tried to deflect the question and focus on other possibilities. What if Mark was not going to tell her that he had fallen in love? What if he was only going to say that he'd had an affair with Caroline and wanted to clear his conscience before they married? Mark was so truthful that it was impossible to imagine his going into the wedding with such a secret. Perhaps he had seen the article in *City Lights* and was hoping to make a preemptive strike, to tell her about the affair before she heard of it from another source.

This thought gave Lily hope. If Mark was having an affair with Caroline, that fact might give her an opening to bring up options that would have remained closed had he been faithful. She could say that she and Mark could not continue to see each other as long as he worked in the same office with Caroline—he would have to accept a transfer to his New York office—and that she could not marry him until they had lived together for at least a year and she was sure he no longer cared about his partner. The plan was perfect.

Lily had almost talked herself into believing she wanted Mark to have had an affair—what luck! to have your fiancé take up with someone else on the eve of your wedding!—when reason took command of her once again. She would not want to force Mark to move to New York any more than she would want him to force her to stay in Colony Heights.

More than that: She had been attracted to Mark for his kindness and loyalty and integrity. She had been sure that he understood how devastating an affair would be to her and, for that reason if not for lack of temptation, would be faithful. If Mark had been having an affair, that reshaped their universe.

As she considered these things, Lily found her perfect plan disintegrating. It did not matter whether, when she and Mark next saw each other, they went out to dinner or he cooked for her. She could think of no outcome for their reunion that, wherever it took place, would make her anything but miserable.

24

LOSS

"I do not know what is the matter with me to day, but I cannot write quietly; I am always wandering away into some exclamation or other.—Fortunately I have nothing very particular to say."

—Letter to Cassandra Austen

Late Tuesday afternoon, Lily got a call from Mark's secretary. Carol was near tears. Mark had lost the TechnoCorp case and, after years of working with him on it, she had nearly as much of a stake in the outcome as he did.

Lily was numb. Despite her realization that all was not going well with Winks Ferguson, she had expected Mark to win, if only because he always won.

"How could Mark lose?" Lily asked. "He always says that if he gets a case he thinks he can't win, he settles it before it gets to court."

"He tried to get TechnoCorp to settle for years, but the company refused," Carol said, sniffling. "He told people at the company that they would be in trouble if those Geezer and Geezerette memos were introduced in court. They just kept telling him and Dave that it was their job to make sure the memos weren't introduced, as if lawyers could rewrite the rules of evidence. Mark said that the discrimination was so overwhelming that, in the end, even having a judge as bad as Ferguson didn't make much difference. The memos spoke for themselves."

"Mark never told me he tried to settle," Lily said, surprised.

"That was long before he met you. Mark knew what he was up against as soon as he saw those memos, which was at least two years ago, and he started trying to get the company to settle then. But the president wouldn't hear of it. He just kept telling Mark that settling discrimination cases was like negotiating with terrorists."

Carol sniffled again. "The president, by the way, is a thirty-three-year-old who wears red suspenders with Mickey Mouse ears on them, and refers to his girlfriend as his 'arm candy.' I think Mark sympathized with the plaintiffs much more than with his client but could never show it. Some of those older people lost their houses because the company gave their jobs to younger ones. They would give depositions, and the stenographers had to fight back the tears while they were taking them down. So you can imagine how Mark felt." She paused. "You know, I don't know whether I'm more upset because Mark lost this case or because the firm made him take it in the first place. It really bothered him to have to go against those older people. It was so obvious that they had a strong case, and that they deserved something for what they had suffered. But a lot of the partners didn't want to pass up the chance for a huge fee from TechnoCorp. And once they took the case, there was no way Mark could come out of it ahead. If he won, he would take money out of the hands of people who had been treated unfairly. If he lost, he would upset the partners and take money out of their pockets, if the firm lost TechnoCorp as a client because of it."

Lily tried to make sense of what she had just heard. "It's still hard to believe that given all the evidence against it, a sensible company wouldn't have settled."

"We're talking about a company based in Los Angeles, where they have support groups for people who were abducted by UFOs. Sensible may have been too much to hope for. Dave told me once that he turned down a client who said that she had been impregnated by aliens and wanted him to get custody of the child for her. I think he told her they don't have domestic-relations courts on Venus."

At the mention of UFOs, Carol came back to earth and resumed her usual brisk efficiency. "But I didn't call to talk about the love children of extraterrestrials. Mark had to rush out to LAX to get a plane, so he asked me to call to let you know he'll be back in a few hours."

Lily asked if Mark wanted her to pick him up, as usual, at the airport.

"Gee, I don't know," Carol said. "He didn't say so, and I'm not sure you could, anyway, because he doesn't know what flight he'll be on. All the planes were booked, so he has to fly standby. If only this town had a decent airport, he might have been in the air by now."

Hodgkins Airport was notorious for its too-short runways, which kept the largest jets from landing there and often required travelers to change planes in a city even more blighted than their ultimate destination. Civic officials had all but ignored this fact while pinning their hopes for the city's revival on its new tourist attractions, such as the Rock Hall of Fame. The result was a comeback city that only the most masochistic air travelers would come back to.

Lily regretted that, after losing a big case, her fiancé would have to fly into such an airport and wished she could pick him up. It seemed the least she could do, given that she had not flown to California.

But Carol insisted that if everybody around Mark was falling apart, she was sure he would rebound quickly and call Lily as soon as he got back.

"You know Mark, he's so good-natured, even if he's upset, he won't show it," she said. "He'll spend all his time trying to make everybody else feel better instead of asking sympathy for himself."

Carol ended by saying that she had seen Lily on the news and, hoping to lift Mark's spirits, had sent him a videotape of the broadcast by Federal Express.

"Funny that he never mentioned how he liked it," she said. "He always tells me how much he loves your stories in the *Daily* when I fax them to him. I guess that, by the time he got the tape, the trial was going so badly for his client that he couldn't think about much else."

Lily cringed at thought that Mark had seen her on television but tried not to think about why he had not mentioned it. She had to turn in her story on the wedding-etiquette experts by the end of the day and could not afford a moment of self-recriminatory introspection.

When she could not reach Martha Stewart or other national celebrities, she had fallen back on interviewing a group of local experts on weddings: a bandleader, a videographer, a clerk at the marriage license bureau at City Hall. But with the exception of the man at City Hall—who complained about the low salary imposed on him by ungenerous taxpayers—all of them had largely ignored her questions and spent most of their time sniping at their competitors.

After she got off the phone with Carol, Lily tried out

several openings for her story, each of which could have been written by a GS-4 in the General Accounting Office. Then she remembered a high school journalism teacher who said that, when stuck on a story, students should try to loosen up by writing something else: a letter, a diary entry, a page or two of a novel.

Lily decided to write a spoof of *Martha Stewart Living* based on the premise that the magazine had inspired a new publication about death. After clearing her old story off her computer screen, she began:

"Martha Stewart announced today that her trail-blazing *Martha Stewart Living* had become so successful that she would launch a new publication called *Martha Stewart's Death*.

"Stewart said that her new publication would tell how to have chic backyard funerals by offering tips on cooking, decorating, and gardening to the newly bereaved. The regular features will include a column on fast funeral-planning called 'Martha Stewart's Quick and Dead,' which will address itself to the special needs of the families of victims of heart attacks, car accidents, and international terrorism.

"Faithful to the formula that has made her famous, Stewart added that she would appear on the cover of the first issue in a casket . . ."

Lily had just ended her spoof by describing the food that Martha might suggest for a designer funeral, including black mashed potatoes, when she got a call from Mark's father. He had just heard the news from Carol.

Buck said that there were two seats available in his sky-box for that night's baseball game and that it might cheer Mark up if they attended. Lily was sure that it *would* cheer him up: Mark loved baseball, which he said relieved his tension after a day in court. So she told his father that although they had planned to go out to dinner, she knew he would prefer to use the seats. She would tell Mark of the change in plans when he called, and they would join the party at the skybox shortly before the game.

Just before hanging up, Buck told Lily that he was glad she had made it to the head-injury dinner.

"Nick Monford said he enjoyed meeting you," he said nonchalantly. "Too bad his wife couldn't come. I'm sure she would have enjoyed meeting you, too."

His wife? Nick never mentioned a wife and did not wear a wedding ring. But, then, Englishmen didn't wear wedding rings, at least not the way American men did.

Lily wondered how she could have been so naive. Now Mark would suspect her not just of having been unfaithful but of having betrayed him for a man with a wife back in Fulham. That he might think such a thing was intolerable: If he was having an affair with Caroline, he was at least having an affair with a woman who had no husband.

All of this caused Lily such distress that she abandoned her plan to give Mark a day or two to recover from his jet lag before telling him that the wedding was off. She would deliver the bad news after the ball game. At that point she would explain that—whatever her reasons for not wanting to go through with it—they had nothing to do with Nick. Whether or not Mark believed her, she would never be able to live with herself until she had returned her ring and at least tried to tell him the truth.

25

Detour

". . . it was but a mixture of those who had never met before, and those who had met too often . . ."

—Persuasion

Lily was still working on her advice-guru story when, an hour before the ball game was to start, she heard from Mark. He was calling from the airport in Newark, New Jersey.

"You're flying to Ohio—from Los Angeles—via Newark?" Lily asked.

"Unfortunately, yes. None of the planes leaving LAX this afternoon flew directly to Hodgkins—apparently they were all too big to land there—so the best I could get was one to Newark. My connecting flight is about to leave, and if there are no delays, I should be home within an hour and a half."

Lily was amazed by how upbeat Mark sounded despite a flight schedule that had taken him five hundred miles out of his way. Carol had been right—Mark was amazingly good-natured—and she told him so.

"You might be forgetting how often I've been in this

situation before. Almost every time I've gone to the West Coast, I've had to come back via Houston, or Denver, or Chicago—" Mark broke off. "—or Atlanta."

"Via Atlanta?"

Mark laughed, as though nothing could delight a $250-an-hour lawyer more than spending three hours watching a parade of Bubba Lives T-shirts at Hartsfield Airport.

"Yes. At least twice. And my father can never understand why more businesses don't relocate to the city. He thinks it's all the fault of comedians who make fun of the place on talk shows. I keep trying to explain to him that— if the comedians ever actually visited the city and realized that they had to fly in from Hollywood via Newark—the jokes would be worse." Mark paused. "But the delays almost don't bother me any more. After spending your whole life in the city you get used to living with things that people in other places would consider . . ." Mark laughed again ". . . utterly intolerable."

You get used to things that are utterly intolerable, Lily thought. *I never will.*

Before Lily could respond, Mark said that he had spoken to his father about the ball game and wondered if she wanted to see it as much as he had been led to believe. He knew she liked baseball much less than he did and would be glad to pass up the skybox seats and have a quiet dinner out.

Lily remembered Carol's remark that her fiancé would think of everybody but himself and insisted that she would love to see the game. Mark said that the baseball season lasted until October, but she would not let him go on. She was convinced that he deserved the consolation of the game and persevered until Mark agreed to attend but told her to go ahead to the stadium without him. He might not arrive until the first or second inning and would meet her at the skybox.

Lily wrapped up her advice-guru story and, fifteen minutes later, sent it hurriedly to the copy desk. It was far from her best work—everyone she quoted needed a week in a Cliché Detox Unit—but she rejoiced in having completed it. She had finished her bridal series and, in a few hours, she would have broken her engagement.

If only Mark had won his case, she thought. She hated to give him a piece of bad news so soon after another. But she found comfort in the knowledge that the team was playing the Red Sox, who had added many of their own refinements to the art of snatching defeat from the jaws of victory. With Boston in town, she did not have to fear that an early blowout would cast a pall over the game. For the Red Sox, it was never too late to choke. If she was lucky, Mark would have at least one thing to cheer about by the end of the evening.

On arriving at the skybox, Lily saw Mark's sisters talking to two women whom she did not recognize. Fran was saying something about "the decimated-hitter rule."

Lily avoided Mark's sisters and moved toward several men who were discussing Jean Yawkey, the majority owner of the Red Sox. Too late, she realized that the theme of their conversation was Why Women Are Ruining Baseball.

How can women be ruining baseball? Lily thought. *There* are *no women in baseball.* Lily listened to the men and gathered that their main points were that (1) men who owned baseball teams should not die, and (2) if they had to die, they should leave their teams to experts. Apparently, "the experts" meant "the fans."

Faced with the choice between talking with Mark's sisters or with the men, Lily reluctantly asked the men if she might join them. Of course, one of them replied instantly: They were not talking about anything important, from which she concluded that they meant women and not baseball.

The men introduced themselves as Ray Walters, Max Fried, and Stan Harmon, all of whom were corporate presidents or chief executive officers in the Tri-County region. They were drinking Crooked River Ale, which they had fished from a nearby cooler, out of plastic cups.

Lily did not know how to introduce herself in relation to their host's son—"soon-to-be ex-fiancée" obviously wouldn't do—and said only that she wrote for the *Daily*. This fact provoked much comment.

Ray Walters, who owned several Polynesian restaurants, said that he would read her articles "with more interest" now that he had met her. Lily did not know whether she was supposed to say "thank you" to this and tried to think of a suitable reply: Perhaps that she would eat his pu-pu platters with more interest now that she had met him? This struck her as slightly obscene, not to mention untrue, given that she had never eaten a pu-pu platter.

She had not resolved the issue when Max Fried, a furniture manufacturer, said that he had never read her articles but would start reading them now that he knew that they had such a pretty author. Lily again did not know how to respond. Would it be appropriate to say that she had never bought his furniture but would try out an Early American waterbed the next time she visited one of his factory outlets?

This did not appear to strike quite the right note, and she was almost grateful when Stan Harmon, a bank president, said that he read nothing in the *Daily* except the columns of his great friend, Howard Jones, and did she know him? Lily allowed that she did, slightly, and Stan urged her to study his columns, because this was the way a young person could learn how to write. In his view, Howard should win a Pulitzer for "Heather Has Two Morons," which was the best thing the paper had published since Howard's "America, Sí, Spongers, No" column on how to resolve the country's immigration problems.

Lily remembered the "America, Sí" debacle, in which Howard had urged readers to pool their Frequent Flyer miles to send Puerto Ricans back to Puerto Rico. The diatribe had caused a stir at the paper because a copyeditor, thinking it all a witty joke, had allowed it to stand as written. After the column appeared in the paper and everyone realized that Howard was serious, Howard and the copyeditor had both received one-week suspensions with pay, which Art Felden and the Guild had protested in vain.

When Max and Ray jumped in to offer additional praise for Howard, Mark's sister Penny came up and accused the men of monopolizing her future sister-in-law. She was trailed by Fran, who said that she was glad Lily had not worn black for once because a baseball game wasn't a Sicilian funeral, was it? Lily was slightly hurt by this, having hoped that her black outfits were a bit more chic than a funeral in Palermo, and did not respond directly but asked where Buck was.

Penny said that her father had business to take care of with the front office—he had some sort of limited partnership in the stadium—and would arrive soon. Fran added that they were all upset that Mark had lost his case and that she was sure that either the judge was crazy or the jury was rigged. She then began describing a movie she had seen involving New York gangsters who had broken the fingers of a hostile jury member, and said that perhaps that would be a good idea in this case?

Lily had started to say that, in fact, it would not be a good idea when Buck strode buoyantly into the box. He reintroduced her to the group as his son's "future better half" and mentioned the house he had given them as a wedding present. His friends agreed that he was the most generous father in America, though Penny and Fran remained silent.

Buck was describing the Tudor doghouse when the door to the skybox opened, and Lily's heart rose at the thought that the new arrival might be Mark, who always dealt so artfully with his sisters on topics such as the merits of breaking or not breaking the fingers of jury members. But the latest guest turned out to be a real-estate developer friend of Buck's from Boston, who had flown in for the Red Sox game. He was carrying a Styrofoam box containing a live lobster that he had bought at Logan Airport as a gift for his host.

The real-estate developer looked so harried that Lily asked if his flight had been difficult. He said that it had not but that, on arriving at Hodgkins Airport, he had taken a taxi driven by a man who did not know his way into the city. With the exception of Lily, the group assured the developer that this was an aberration, because the city's taxi drivers were the best in country, and he relaxed a bit.

Buck opened a bottle of Crooked River Ale for the man and suggested that his guests sit down, because the game was about to start. Lily tried to protest when he directed her to one of two empty seats in the front row of the skybox, with the other reserved for Mark. She said that his friends might appreciate the view more and offered to give up her place to the Boston real-estate developer, whose lobster was clawing frantically at its box.

But Buck insisted that Lily sit in the front row, and she yielded after realizing that this position had the advantage of requiring her to make conversation only with the people in back of her and not also with those in front. She took her seat and saw a stadium that, with the team leading its league, did not appear to have an empty seat.

The first inning went scoreless, and Lily used the time to rehearse the speech she would make to Mark after the game, when she returned his ring. Wishing again that he had not lost his case, she found herself distracted by the wound-up crowd and by the lobster flailing away in its box behind her.

Mark arrived in the middle of the second inning and, after kissing Lily, settled into his seat. This upset Fran and Penny, who insisted that he get up and kiss them, too, even though his movements blocked the others' view. Mark took his seat again, and he, too, seemed distracted by the noise, or by the brightness of the banks of white toothbrush-shaped lights that surrounded the stadium.

Although baseball usually held his attention, Mark kept looking at Lily, as though he wanted to make sure she had not dematerialized between pitches. He eventually took her hand, which seemed to make him feel better, though it irritated his sisters.

The Red Sox scored not long after he arrived and, by the end of the fourth inning, had a three-to-nothing lead. Lily's spirits began to fray. Possibly the game had not been such a good idea, after all.

Lily became gloomier when, with the bases loaded, Corky Klingel left the dugout to bat for the home team. She regarded Klingel living proof of Frank Gifford's comment that "There's no place in sports for intelligence"— an egotistical misogynist who stood in chronic need of a long visit to the baseball equivalent of reform school.

As Klingel swaggered cockily toward the plate, Penny became more animated. She said that her husband had told her that the reason Klingel so often got into trouble with baseball officials was that he had low self-esteem. Lily wondered if Klingel's esteem for himself could be lower than her esteem for him and, as she was pondering this conundrum, the pitcher released two balls that appeared to have been aimed at a batter in another state. The three chief executives began to scream.

"Hey, Cork, sock it to the Sox!"

"Yeah, Cork, scalp 'em!"

"C'mon, Cork, show 'em who's got—"

Lily saw Mark wince at the third comment, which would have been unprintable in the *Daily*. The count rose to 3–0, and it appeared that the Red Sox might be about to walk Klingel, one of the team's best hitters. Everybody in the box screamed except for Mark and Lily and the Boston real-estate developer.

"Hey, Cork!" Max Fried shouted. "The cowards are afraid to pitch you anything that's not in the dirt!"

Ray Walters made a comment about the Red Sox manager that impugned the masculinity of the Irish. Stan Harmon followed up with a remark about the mothers of the Irish. Fran began smiling and singing, bizarrely, a verse from "Who Put the Overalls in Mrs. Murphy's Chowder?"

On hearing all this, Mark looked at Lily nervously. He bent toward her and said in a low voice, "We don't have to stay for the whole game."

As Lily was about to answer, the pitcher threw a ball over the plate, and Klingel hit it out of the ballpark.

Once the team had taken the lead from the Red Sox, the comments in the skybox grew steadily less rational and, therefore, easier to ignore. By the last pitch of the sixth inning, Lily had worked out what she was going to say to her fiancé on returning his ring, and she was beginning to relax.

But Mark became visibly tenser with every slur that his father's friends made against their opponents, and he clung to her hand as though trying to keep not just her but himself from bolting out the door of the skybox. At the start of the seventh-inning stretch, he asked if she wanted to take a walk, and she immediately agreed. As they started to leave, Buck jumped up from his seat and demanded that they stay.

Mark told his father that he had been sitting in court all week and needed to stretch his legs. Lily added gently that she also could use a walk.

But Buck was adamant, and the three executives took positions at the door of the skybox, blocking their exit. Lily could see her usually unflappable fiancé starting to become angry.

"Dad, we only want to leave for a few minutes," Mark said edgily. His father again overruled him.

Lily and Mark were facing the skybox door, which the three corporate executives were still blocking, and in the middle of the argument Buck motioned for them to turn around. As they did, a spotlight hit the box, forcing them to shield their eyes.

The light was so bright that Lily at first could not see well, though she could hear fans screaming and the stadium organist playing "The Wedding March." Buck pointed to something in the distance. Lily could not see what it was but could tell, from the alarm on her fiancé's face, that he had recognized it.

Buck was gesturing enthusiastically toward the scoreboard, and at last her eyes adjusted to the light well enough for her focus on it. On a video monitor that usually displayed the names and pictures of the players, she saw a huge enlargement of her engagement photo. Below it, in front of thirty-eight thousand screaming fans, flashing yellow lights spelled out, CONGRATULATIONS, MARK AND LILY!

25

Postgame Show

"Elinor agreed to it all, for she did not think he deserved the compliment of rational opposition."

—Sense and Sensibility

In her twenty-seven years Lily had never known a moment of such perfect clarity of vision as that which descended on her after she saw the congratulations sign on a video monitor applauded by thirty-eight thousand cheering baseball fans. If she wanted a sign from God about her engagement, she had received it.

There was no question of returning her ring now. She would have to go through with the wedding, wait a tasteful length of time and then get a quiet divorce. If Mark told her after the game that he had fallen in love with Caroline, if he admitted to the tawdriest affair of his life, it did not matter. She would still go through with the wedding.

To break her engagement would mean that she and Mark would never escape from the consequences of her actions. Her decision would shadow them for the rest of their lives: She and Mark would be forever known as the couple who didn't get married after their engagement was announced at a sold-out baseball stadium.

The city was simply too narrow to accommodate any other result. Sherwood Anderson had suffered the humiliation of a headline on his obituary that identified him as a former Elyria paint manufacturer. She and Mark would face a similar ignominy—not as obvious, perhaps, and not as insulting, but no less real. At charity benefits and cocktail parties, they would be spoken of as the couple who never made it to the altar. And if she could inflict this pain on herself, she could not inflict it on her fiancé.

Lily knew she could insulate herself from the notoriety by moving to New York. But Mark, who expected to spend his life in Ohio, could not, and she could not ask him to pay that emotional price. It would be far kinder to him to go through with the wedding and, after a suitable interval, fly to the Dominican Republic for one of those sunny-side-up divorces that a travel agency had been promoting at the bridal fair. These days, people got divorced all the time, and nobody spent a lifetime having to account for a brief early marriage that failed. Mark would be hurt by a divorce, but he would recover. As for herself, Lily thought, *If I divorce Mark I may never marry again. But I know one thing: If I do marry again, my next wedding will be different.*

So sure was Lily of all this that, long before the baseball game ended in a 4–3 win for the home team, she had shed all the anxiety of the past week. She was calmer than she had been in months. Like a Death Row prisoner whose appeal for clemency had just been turned down by the Supreme Court, she knew what lay ahead.

Instead of viewing her approaching wedding with dread, she saw it as unavoidable and therefore something she could bear as easily as she had borne finals week at Yale or her appendectomy in the eighth grade. To her amazement, she even found herself accepting a beer, which she never drank, when Buck pressed a bottle of Crooked River Ale on her at the top of the ninth inning.

This new spirit of tranquility enabled Lily to resist the bait when, soon afterward, Stan Harmon began explaining to her that Corky Klingel was a great American but was misunderstood by women, the media, and baseball officials. She did not say—as she had done on such occasions in the past—that she was a woman, that she understood Corky Klingel perfectly, and that what she understood him to be was an embarrassment to the team, the city, and the game of baseball.

Instead, when Buck's friends praised Klingel, she merely turned to her fiancé and smiled. "Hasn't this been a great game?" she asked.

On hearing this, Mark looked at Lily in alarm and asked if she was feeling well. He appeared scarcely reassured when she said that she was fine or when she listed the many virtues of Corky Klingel that were continually overlooked by the editors of *Sports Illustrated*.

After the game, Mark refused to go to a victory party that his father was hosting at the Stadium Club, saying that he was tired after his flight, and steered Lily quickly out of the skybox. He took her hand and, on the way to his car, kept asking if anything was wrong.

Lily, able to respond with perfect equanimity, said that nothing was wrong. What did she have to worry about now?

For the next two and a half weeks, she could put herself on automatic pilot and let her mother direct the emotional roller derby that her wedding had become. She had to do nothing but show up and make all the socially appropriate responses that she had been force-fed since infancy. If she felt herself losing control, she would need only to draw on the lessons of her high school and college drama classes.

She could act her way through her wedding. If her mother was right that she had a theatrical streak, the world would see it now. She might even get lucky and find herself in a screwball comedy, which would provide a few laughs, instead of in *Othello Goes to the Rust Belt*.

Fortified by this realization, Lily remained unperturbed when, on the way to the car, she and Mark passed a group of drunken men wearing T-shirts emblazoned with the name of the softball team for Stan Harmon's bank. Mark flinched as one of the men staggered toward them and called, "Hey, wasn't the Cork great?"

But Lily remained serene. "Yes," she said unhesitatingly. "Too bad he is misunderstood by women, the media, and baseball officials."

This appeared to surprise the drunken man, who looked enviously at Mark.

"Man, you've got a great date," he said. "I've never heard a woman say that before."

Mark shook his head and said somberly, "Neither have I." Then he unlocked his car and helped Lily in as though he were a medic assisting a wounded member of the First Infantry Division onto a stretcher at Omaha Beach.

Back at her fiancé's loft, as Mark unpacked his suitcase, Lily was surprised to see a paperback edition of *Persuasion* in a bag from the gift shop at Newark Airport. On noticing that he had marked his place with a cash-register receipt, she turned to him in surprise.

"Mark, you've already read *Persuasion*, and you have a great edition of it here." Lily removed *Persuasion* from his six-volume *Oxford Illustrated Jane Austen*, which lay within easy reach on the wall-to-wall bookshelves facing the river. "What made you buy another?"

Mark looked mildly embarrassed, as though Lily had

caught him buying a pornographic video entitled *The Devil in Miss Austen*, but soon recovered.

"I just had an urge to reread Jane Austen," he said lightly. "And the only thing you can buy at airports are paperback editions."

"But you were going to be home in an hour and a half."

Mark put his arms around her. "You know, some women would be happy that their fiancés were reading Jane Austen instead of one of those novels with Stealth bombers on the cover. Maybe you'd rather I'd bought one of them out of loyalty to your friend Ruth?"

"No, no," Lily said hastily. "Ruth hates editing those Stealth-bomber books. She says it makes her feel paranoid enough to consider voting for Republicans." Lily scanned the bookshelves for a moment, then turned to Mark in relief. "Mark, I'm so glad you don't own any of those horror novels with red-and-black covers. Ruth hates editing those, too. The first time I saw one of those red-and-black books, I thought it was a new edition of Stendahl. Then I started reading it and found out that it was about a man who cut up the body of his girlfriend, fed it into a wood-chipper, and stored it in his frost-free freezer."

Mark laughed. "You can be sure I don't need to buy any books about cases like that. I hear enough about them from my partners. Of course, all of them are thinking of writing books about their cases—" he smiled "—so that they can see their own names on books with red-and-black covers."

Lily, turning over the paperback edition of *Persuasion* in her hand, remained uneasy. "But there must have been a reason why you had an urge to reread Jane Austen."

Mark put his arms around her again. "Let's just say I had an urge to understand my beautiful fiancée better."

His explanation did not reassure Lily. It reminded her,

though she could scarcely have forgotten, about Mark's comment that they needed to talk. He had not mentioned it since he had returned, and his silence made her apprehensive. She reminded him of his remark, and he suggested that they might leave the matter until the next day. Perhaps she was tired after the baseball game?

This suggestion made Lily even more nervous. Afraid that the news was so bad that Mark believed her unable to handle it without adequate sleep, she pleaded with him to tell her what he had to say. He had to be as tired as she was, and if he didn't mind—

After more prodding, Mark took her by the hand and led her to a window overlooking the river. She could see the white lights of bridges and buildings that by day resembled a decomposing forty-year-old set for *On the Waterfront* but that by night were almost romantic.

"Now, don't be angry with me—" he began gently.

"How could I ever be angry with you? After all you've done for me—" Lily said.

Mark said nothing and studied her face as though he were a doctor trying to decide whether his patient could be moved out of the intensive-care unit.

Lily, sensing his fear of hurting her, went on. "Honestly, if you fell in love with Caroline when you were in Los Angeles, it's all right. I'm not angry."

"Fell in love with *Caroline?*" Mark asked. "I've worked with her for years, and I've never even been attracted to her. Caroline is so emotionally demanding that no man who lived with her would have a moment's peace. No one could sit and read Jane Austen in her presence because she would always want to go out to dinner or dancing instead. Why would you think that, after all this time, I suddenly fell in love with her?"

"For one thing, whenever I called, she was in your suite,

and when I spoke to her she sounded so, somehow, pro-prietary about you. I just want you to know that if you did fall in love with her, it's okay."

Mark looked wounded. "You think I fell in love with Caroline, and you're not upset? It's *okay* with you?" He glanced out the window at a tugboat, as though unable to face anyone who would suggest such a thing. "If you went away on a trip with another reporter and fell in love, I wouldn't be 'okay.' I'd be devastated."

Lily, realizing that she had said the wrong thing, tried to think of a way to undo her mistake. From the pained expression on Mark's face, it was obvious that he not only had not fallen in love with Caroline but was injured by the implication that he had.

"All I meant was, everybody makes mistakes. If you had a fling"—Lily hoped that "had a fling" would sound less accusatory than "fell in love"—"if you had a fling with Caroline, yes, I'd be upset. But I'd understand that you were under a lot of pressure and try to be a mature, ra-tional adult about it."

"If you 'had a fling' with someone, I couldn't be 'mature' and 'rational' about it. I'd be completely bereft. I'd think that, somehow, I'd failed you."

As he said the words "failed you," Mark reacted as though the track lighting in his loft had just come back on after a power failure. "Oh, no. Now I understand what happened. You spent the weekend with Nick Monford be-cause you thought I was having an affair with Caroline."

"Spent the weekend with Nick Monford?"

"Yes. That's what I wanted to talk to you about. You said you couldn't come to Los Angeles because you had to have your wedding portrait taken. But whenever I called you over the weekend, I got no answer. I was so worried that I called your parents' house, and your mother told me you had canceled your appointment and she had no idea where you were."

Lily fantasized about matricide, and Mark went on. "At first, I thought you might be home and taking a break from returning your phone messages. Then, on Monday morning, Carol faxed me the article from *City Lights*, and I realized that my sisters might be right."

"Right about what?"

"That you were interested in Nick. After the head-injury dinner, I spoke to Penny, and she said that my father had invited a British architect and that you seemed interested in him. I didn't give it a thought—everybody in my family can see that Penny is almost crazy with jealousy of you— but Fran said the same thing. Then when Carol faxed me the *City Lights* article, everything sort of fit together. Penny's husband has a theory that all women secretly want to have an eleventh-hour romance just before their weddings."

"Dick also has a theory that Corky Klingel suffers from low self-esteem when, in fact, Corky Klingel has enough self-esteem for the entire Central Division." Lily realized that she was getting sidetracked and tried to rein herself in. "But that's not the point. The point is, I didn't go away with Nick Monford for the weekend. I didn't see him again after we had dinner because it was clear that, well, he would want me to go away for the weekend with him. Instead of going away with him, I went to New York to see Sally."

"You went to New York?"

"Oh, Mark, I know it was wrong of me after saying I couldn't fly out to Los Angeles, and I apologize. If I was going to go to New York, I should at least have let you know, so that you wouldn't worry. But the truth is, women can't live by men alone. They need other women, too, and after a steady diet of my mother and your sisters—forgive me, but I was famished. I was starved for the companionship of spirited and intelligent women."

Mark smiled for the first time since the names of Caroline and Nick had come up. "If you had no more to sustain you than your mother and my sisters, I'm not surprised that you were starved. I wonder that you didn't have indigestion, too."

Lily, starting to relax but unsure that she had convinced him, went on. "I know it sounds implausible that in the whole city I couldn't find one woman I could talk to with any hope of being understood—"

Mark smiled again. "It doesn't sound implausible at all. I couldn't find a woman I could talk to with any hope of being understood until I met you."

"But I can prove to you that what I say is true. If you don't believe me, you can have me investigated by Put a Tail on Your Groom."

Mark looked baffled, as though she had just begun to speak Urdu. "That detective agency you wrote about in your bridal-fair story?"

"Right. Women hire its detectives to investigate the men they are about to marry. But I'm sure they would work for men, too. You could hire them to investigate me: you know, go through my dumpster and root around for credit card receipts that would prove I was in New York."

Mark put his hand on her forehead and pretended to take her temperature. "Sweetheart, in the first place, I'm a lawyer. You don't need to tell me how to find private investigators. My firm has a list of agencies, although they don't have nutty names like Put a Tail on Your Groom. But in the second place, I love you. If you say you went to New York, that's enough for me. I trust you to tell me the truth. Some people say that love means never having to say you're sorry. I'd say love means never having to say, 'I'm sorry I hired some guy in sunglasses to root around in your dumpster.' " He took Lily's hand. "I guess the only thing I'm curious about is why you went out to dinner with Nick in the first place. You know how glad I am that you have male friends. It reassures me that I can keep all my female friends. But from what I hear from my father, Nick is the sort of man who always expects something more than friendship from women."

Lily was so relieved that Mark believed her that she decided she could risk the truth. "This is going to sound crazy—"

Mark smiled again. "Not any crazier than the idea that I might want to have you investigated by a company called Put a Tail on Your Groom."

"—but I had dinner with Nick because of corn dogs."

"You hate corn dogs."

"That's my point. After you left for Los Angeles, the week went so badly that I thought, somehow, it would cheer me up to go to the only restaurant in the city where you know you'll never see corn dogs on the menu."

Mark began to laugh, and Lily was afraid that she had lost the credibility she thought she had won back.

"Please believe me—" she said.

Mark put his arms around her again. "Sweetheart, I do believe you. I'm only laughing because the comment about the corn dogs is so—you. Nobody who knows you would doubt that you would go out for a two-hundred-dollar dinner just to avoid two-dollar corn dogs. That's why I knew from our first date that I wanted to marry you. You always surprise me." He paused. "I just didn't expect you to bring up corn dogs now. I thought you were going to tell me that, say, you were momentarily swept away by Nick's British charm and lost control of yourself. You know, when I was at school in England, I spent two years among boys who, when they wanted to, could have charmed the ermine off the Queen. Unfortunately, in my case, they were usually more interested in putting bugs in my bed—"

"Bugs? That's awful. At Girl Scout camp, we only short-sheeted the beds."

"Well, fortunately, there are no bugs in the bed in this loft." Mark glanced at the bookshelves across the room. "Now, let's do something we can't read about in Jane Austen."

27

Martha Stewart's Death

". . . we met a gentleman . . . in such very deep
mourning that either his mother, his wife, or him-
self must be dead."

— Letter to Cassandra Austen

ow, now, don't cry. I know you'll find a copy of *Martha Stewart's Death* in plenty of time to arrange a
wonderful funeral for your Uncle Arnold."

Lily had no sooner walked into the office the next morning than she heard Deandra Foy, the receptionist, trying
to console a distraught reader. *Truth is stranger,* she
thought. When she had fantasized about a magazine called
Martha Stewart's Death, she had no idea that such a publication actually existed. She was chastising herself for her
lack of originality when the receptionist saw her.

"Lily, thank heaven you're here," Deandra said. "The
phone has been ringing off the hook with readers who
want to know where to buy that new magazine you wrote
about in today's paper. They keep saying they've gone to
newsstands all over the city but can't find *Martha Stewart's
Death.*"

"What!"

Lily ran to a stack of the day's papers near the reception desk and scanned the front page. Near the bottom she saw her parody of *Martha Stewart Living* instead of her collection of interviews with local wedding experts.

Lily closed her eyes. "Oh, no."

"Are you okay?" Deandra asked.

Lily nodded. "But, Deandra, do me a favor, please, and don't tell any more readers you're sure they can buy *Martha Stewart's Death* here, okay? I'll explain later."

"Sure thing. But are you positive you're all right? You look a little weak-kneed."

"Yes, I'll be fine as soon as I talk to the news editor."

Lily hurried to her desk and found it littered with pink slips from Bill Schroeder. She glanced at Jack, who feigned deep interest in the day's comic strips, then at Jeff Carter, who looked at her gravely.

"Think of it as a blessing, Lily," he said. "You'll be able to collect unemployment while you look for a new job in a tornado-free city."

Lily hurried to the office of the news editor and found him hanging his old basketball jersey, framed and matted, on the wall of his office. It had deodorant stains under the armpits. Bill asked what she thought of hanging the shirt at various heights, then put it down.

"Well, Lily," he said, after he had explored all the aesthetic possibilities inherent in a deodorant-stained jersey, "I guess you've figured out that you're benched for two weeks."

"Would you translate that into something besides sports jargon?"

"Watch it, or I'll add another two weeks for insubordination. You're suspended for two weeks without pay, starting immediately."

"For what?" Lily knew her suspension had something to do with her parody of *Martha Stewart Living*, but she had no idea how the spoof had gotten in the paper. She wished she had done a little checking before she rushed into Bill's office.

"Come on, don't give me that innocent look. You think you can just make up all that stuff about Martha Stewart being dead and get away with it?"

"First of all, I did not say Martha Stewart was dead. Yesterday I was having a little trouble trying to write the last installment of my bridal series, so I decided to limber up with a warm-up exercise. You know how Kareem and Hakeem and Shaq run out on the court and sort of bounce the ball around before a game starts?" Lily, who had hoped that a sports analogy would help her boss see her point, could tell by his annoyed look that her effort had utterly failed.

"It's called dribbling, Lily, *dribbling*," he said sarcastically. "Okay? Greats like Kareem and Hakeem and Shaq do not 'run out on the court and sort of bounce the ball around.' They *dribble*."

"All right. They dribble, and I was dribbling with my mind. I couldn't get going on the last installment in my series, so I tried to loosen up by writing a parody of *Martha Stewart Living*. I imagined that Martha Stewart was launching an upbeat magazine about funerals and made up some things that it might include—you know, Ten Tips for Backyard Embalming, How to Make Your Own Shroud from All-Natural Fibers, that kind of thing." Lily searched Bill's face for signs of a smile but saw none.

"But I never intended that parody to go in the paper," she added. "Before I left for the day yesterday, I sent something completely different to the copy desk—a bunch of interviews with local wedding experts."

"Not according to the copy desk. The people on the desk say they edited what you sent, and you sent that 'parody,' as you call it."

Bill pulled out a printout of the previous afternoon's computer transmissions, and Lily saw her initials in a column that showed that she had sent the story to the copy desk.

"Oh, no." Lily realized that amid the calls from Mark and his father, she could have hit the wrong computer key and sent the spoof instead of the article that she had intended to transmit. "Bill, I must have accidentally shipped the Martha Stewart parody to the desk, and I'm incredibly sorry. It was an unforgivable lapse of concentration."

"At least you admit it."

"But why is this all my fault? You just said that somebody on the copy desk edited the story. Don't you think that whoever it was should have realized that it was a joke?" Against all the evidence of her experience at the *Daily*, Lily continued. "Somebody on the desk must have a sense of humor."

"Copyeditors aren't paid to have a sense of humor. They're paid to—well, don't ask me what they're paid to do. I don't have a clue. Can you believe that some of them don't even know that you spell Shaq with a *q* instead of a *k*?"

Lily reached deep into her high school acting experience and said that she could not imagine that anyone might think of spelling Shaq with a *k*, and that the Janet Cooke affair was but a trifle compared with it.

"But that's not the point," Bill said. "The point is, I see you as the Janet Cooke of this paper." He grinned. "You could say your goose is Cooke-d, ha-ha."

"That's totally unfair," Lily protested. "Janet Cooke made up a story about a heroin addict for the *Washington*

Post, and the paper submitted it for a Pulitzer Prize."

"Right, and you made up a story about Martha Stewart being dead—"

"I told you, I didn't say Martha Stewart was dead. And I didn't *make up the story*. It was a parody. You know, *humor*. I made it up the way Russell Baker makes things up for *The New York Times*."

Bill went off on a tangent about how he had met Baker once, and Baker was tall enough so that he probably would be a good basketball player if the *Daily* ever played against the *Times*. Lily, who had no idea what this had to do with her suspension, said nothing until he ended by saying her paychecks would cease immediately and resume in two weeks.

By then she could see she had no chance of getting through to her boss, whose mind seemed to dwell permanently on a foul line in the never-never land, and she started to leave his office. At the door, she turned around and said she might take up her suspension with the Guild.

"Don't bother," he said. "Art Felden is on vacation for two weeks." He wadded up a portion of her parody and tossed it into his wastebasket. "But if you're that upset about this, I still haven't gotten those seats I need at the Garden, and if you have any pull in that area—" he winked "—we might be able to make a deal. For example, your suspension might be reduced to one week."

Infuriated, Lily said nothing. Her boss was not, as some people on staff suggested, a "basketball fanatic." He was a basketball lunatic. She would not have put it past him to have trumped up her suspension to cut a deal on his seats.

But she had to admit that she was almost relieved to be facing two weeks out of the office, which would give her more time to write overdue thank-you notes for her wedding gifts and to look for a job in New York. She even felt thankful that Art Felden couldn't oversee the full-dress battle against her suspension that, had he been around, she would have been inclined to wage.

Back at her desk, Lily swept all of Bill's pink slips into the wastebasket and prepared to go home. As she did, Jack continued to feign interest in the comic strips, and Jeff Carter slipped her a list of names of Virginia editors who might want to hire her.

But Lily ignored them, no longer caring what they thought. She had made her decision about her wedding, and a decision had been made for her about her job. For the next two weeks, she had nothing to worry about but putting herself through the paces of getting married. As she walked out of the newsroom, Lily thought that for the first time she understood what Al Capone had meant when he said there was no peace on earth like a bank vault at midnight.

28

Thorns

"I must keep to my own style & go on in my own Way; And though I may never succeed again in that, I am convinced that I should totally fail in any other."

—Letter to James Stanier Clarke

Lily thought she would spend the rest of the day pulling together copies of her best stories to send to New York editors. But before she had begun, Mark called. He had telephoned her office to say how much he loved her Martha Stewart parody and, on hearing that she had left the newsroom suddenly, was afraid that she was sick. Lily said that, in a sense, she *was* sick, and described her meeting with her boss.

Mark was outraged and said he couldn't believe she was suspended. "Doesn't Schroeder know a parody when he sees it?"

Lily faced the delicate task of trying not to impugn the intelligence of a boss who acted as though Western Literature had peaked with National Basketball Association scouting reports.

"The issue doesn't seem to be what Bill thinks so much as what readers think. They swamped the switchboard with calls asking where to buy *Martha Stewart's Death*, and he had to appease them."

"But Schroeder is punishing you for something that, if the copy desk had been alert, would never have happened."

Lily was taken aback by the intensity of emotion shown by her even-tempered fiancé. Mark agreed when she suggested that he was more upset by her suspension than by losing his case.

"I am more upset, because I knew from the start that we might lose. And if the people at TechnoCorp don't like the verdict, they can appeal. You can't. In most offices, people have less protection against dictatorial whims than they do in court."

"I could appeal my suspension by letting the Guild file a grievance about it. But at this point, I think it would be easier just to go without the two weeks' pay."

"Schroeder suspended you *without* pay? Didn't even Howard Jones get paid when he was suspended for writing that column that maligned every Puerto Rican in America?"

"Yes, but I'm not the only reporter who has been treated this way, so I can't really complain about having been singled out. Bill is so capricious, the treatment you get from him tends to depend on whether or not his team won the night before. Before I started at the *Daily*, he suspended one of the paper's best reporters for rolling her eyes when he asked her to do a story on whether athletes' wives were having trouble sitting through games after the miniskirt made a comeback. He said the eye-rolling amounted to 'insubordination.' A few months later, she got a job at a much bigger paper in the East and, supposedly, still refuses to set foot in the newsroom when she comes back to the city."

For a moment, Lily thought that the Fates had robbed Mark of the power of speech.

"Sweetheart, I wonder if you've ever thought of looking for a new job, or at least freelancing. It's painful to see you working for a boss who treats people so irrationally."

Lily, feeling herself to be on dangerous ground, said only that every reporter who worked for Bill thought about leaving, and tried to change the subject. She asked how his law partners were reacting to his loss in California.

Mark said that he was taking a lot of grief from Kayo Smith, the most flamboyant litigator at the firm, who was said to be in line for managing partner. A specialist in malpractice-defense cases, Kayo had grown rich by representing doctors who amputated the wrong feet or killed babies by prescribing adult doses of medicine for them. But that did not keep him from boasting that he practiced one of the most socially useful forms of law, because it kept medical-insurance rates down.

The differences between the men worried Lily, who was afraid that her fiancé would have to compromise his ideals further if Kayo became managing partner. Mark liked to say that practicing law was like emergency room medicine: "If the Constitution is bleeding, you don't turn people away if they can't pay." Kayo was fond of quoting a Chicago lawyer who said, "The law is like prostitution. If the price is right, you warm up to the client."

Mark did not ease her fears when he went on. "Kayo started up again about all the pro bono cases I've been doing. He said I owed it to the firm to do more corporate work."

"Meaning take on more cases that would make the partners richer at the end of each year."

"Right. But honestly, I'm not worried about Kayo. Almost every lawyer faces pressure to bring in more money, even if it's only self-imposed. I'm more much concerned about you. You've seemed so subdued ever since the base-ball game, and now to have this happen—" Mark stopped. "Why don't I come over and take you out to lunch today?"

Lily would not hear of it—he had told her the night before that he had to see a client at noon. Mark argued that she mattered more than his client and that he could cancel his meeting. But she wanted to begin sending out job applications that afternoon and held him off, though not completely. Two hours later, a dozen white roses ar-rived at her door with a note that said, "Someday you *will* have job with fewer thorns."

29

Compromises

"She was very far from wishing to dwell on her feelings . . ."

—Sense and Sensibility

Free of her usual deadlines, Lily had time to ponder the three pieces of difficult news that she had to break to her parents. She had taken her ring from their bedroom, she had been suspended from her job, and she was going to go through with the wedding after all. The last of these caused her by far the most distress.

Lily had no doubt that her parents would take her about-face on the wedding as proof that they had been right all along. They would treat her as another overeager bride who had suffered a temporary failure of nerve—a silly young woman who needed only a talk with her father, a visit to a psychiatrist, and a bribe no larger than a pair of earrings to set her straight. Then they would never mention the matter again, burying it as they had interred the memory of the time that Todd was picked up by police for joyriding with his teenage friends after one too many beers.

Toward the end of the day, Lily could put off facing her parents no longer and decided to call her father at his office. Geraldine Brooks, his secretary, answered and told her how excited she was to have seen her picture on television while watching a baseball game.

"Lily, you're famous," Geraldine said happily. "All my neighbors have been talking about seeing you on TV. You're almost a movie star."

Only I'll get divorced sooner than a movie star, Lily thought.

Geraldine said that her father had left for the day, so Lily drove to her parents' house, hoping to catch him alone there. Instead, she was greeted by her grandmother, who instantly noticed her ring.

"Thank heavens you have it back!" she said. "Your mother has been frantic about it. A burglar broke into the house while Mr. Brooks and I were at the symphony on Friday night and took the ring before she could have it insured. Your mother didn't tell you about it because she didn't want to worry you. But she's been talking about nothing else for days." Lily's grandmother motioned for her to sit down beside her on a foyer bench upholstered in needlepoint calla lilies. "Your mother seems to see it as a personal insult that the police haven't been able to return your ring to her. Listen."

Charlotte Blair was talking loudly enough on the breakfast-nook phone for her voice to carry into the foyer. She berated a police officer for several minutes before hanging up the phone.

"Wade, is that you?" she called.

Lily apologized to her grandmother for needing to talk privately to her mother.

"No need to apologize, dear. The way your mother has been acting this week, I'm happy to give her a wide berth."

Lily removed her ring and slipped it into her pocket before entering the breakfast nook. Her mother was sitting at the jonquil-sprigged banquette studying the listings for private investigators in the Yellow Pages.

"Why, Lily, this is a surprise," she said, hastily closing the telephone book. "Almost as much of a surprise as seeing your picture up on that big screen at the stadium last night."

Charlotte Blair looked out the window, then turned coolly toward her daughter. "You might at least have warned us about it. Have you thought about the humiliation your father and I are going to face when you bail out of your wedding after Buck has announced your engagement to every sports fan in three counties?"

"That congratulations sign was as much of a surprise to Mark and me as it was to anyone else."

"You might have called us after the game to let us know what we're supposed to tell our friends when you walk away from your wedding after a public exhibition like that."

Lily had not had time to think of a reply when her mother abruptly stood up from the banquette.

"All right," her mother went on calmly. "I admit that when you first told me you were canceling the wedding, I didn't know the full story. I didn't know that Mark had taken up with someone else."

"Mark has not taken up with someone else."

"Lily, I know what's going on. I read that *City Lights* article—not that you told me about it."

"Mother, the editors of City Lights couldn't get their facts straight if they printed them on a ruler."

"Please, Lily, I have something to say to you." Her mother poured herself a glass of sherry. "I know—I realize that it must have been extremely painful for you to find out on the eve of your wedding that your fiancé has been having an affair with his law partner."

"I told you, Mark is not having an affair."

"Well, if not, he's the only one in that crowd who isn't."

"What crowd? Mark's partners don't strike me as more or less faithful than anybody else."

"Not Mark's friends, his father's. Max Fried. Ray Walters. Stan Harmon. All of them. Do you think those men I saw on TV with you are faithful to their wives? I can't tell you how many stories I've heard about Ray Walters chasing his waitresses around those Easter Island statues they have at his restaurants—"

"Mother, Mark has better taste than a man who's made his fortune on pu-pu platters. And even if Buck's friends chase waitresses, Buck doesn't. He was devoted to Mark's mother. If he had an eye for women, he's had plenty of opportunity to show it since she died, and he hasn't. The reporters at the *Daily* have accused him of a lot of things, but never that."

"I'm not talking about Buck, I'm talking about your future, and what I'm trying to say is, yes, it's hard to discover that your fiancé is involved with someone else. But these things have happened to other women, and there are ways of dealing with them."

Lily sat down on the banquette and rubbed her eyes. She was afraid of what she might hear next.

"Your father and I have been discussing this, and he knows a partner in the domestic-relations department of his firm who is very good at drawing up prenuptial agreements covering—this sort of thing."

Lily said nothing, which her mother took as encouragement to go on. "You have never understood that marriage is about compromise. You've always said that you don't want to give up your independence, as though men don't have to give up their independence, too. But marriage is not about freedom, it's about tradeoffs. If Mark has been unfaithful to you, you have every right to expect him to make it up to you. You can have somebody at your father's firm draw up an airtight prenuptial agreement making it clear that if he steps out on you once you are married—"

Her mother stopped, noticing that Lily was looking at the window. "Lily, did you hear me?"

Lily turned to face her mother. "I heard you. You said marriage is about compromise."

"That's right. Just as weddings are about compromise. The only reason you and I have had so much trouble on this wedding is that I'm willing to compromise and you aren't. I told you I was willing to let you have the buffalo chicken wings instead of the veal medallions, and if there's anything else you don't like, such as the flowers or the music, all you have to do is say so. If you don't want your prenuptial agreement drawn up by your father's firm, your father and I would be perfectly willing to pay to have it drawn up somewhere else—not by Mark's firm, of course."

Charlotte Blair drank some of her sherry while waiting for Lily to answer. Lily waved away a glass that her mother had poured for her, then stood up.

"Mother, I have a few things to tell you, and now that I've listened to you, I hope you'll listen to me. First, I've decided for my own reasons to go through with the wedding, and I would prefer not to talk about those reasons."

"You don't have to talk about your reasons for getting married. You're getting married because you love Mark."

Lily let the remark pass. "Second, although I'm getting married, I'm not having a prenuptial agreement. If anybody has the right to demand a marriage contract, it's not me but Mark—and if he hasn't asked for one with all that he stands to lose if we divorced, I'm not going to ask for one, either."

Lily saw her mother's temper begin to flare again and rushed to her next point. "Third, I'm sorry to disappoint you and Daddy this way, but I've been suspended from my job for two weeks. I've been involved in a—a mix-up—and my boss thinks I should stay home for a while."

Her mother looked at her suspiciously. "This wouldn't have anything to do with that story on men who want to marry each other, would it? It was perfectly obvious from that article that you think any homosexual who can afford the caterer's deposit has just as much right as you do to walk down the aisle of Holy Family Cathedral."

"Mother, the courts say—in Hawaii, anyway—that they do have the right. But I didn't get suspended for writing about that. I got suspended because I wrote something that wasn't supposed to get in today's paper but got in by mistake. It was a joke, but the copyeditors didn't understand it, so they approved it for publication."

"Well, I must have missed it. All I saw was your article about that new magazine on death being started by Martha Stewart." She tapped her empty sherry glass against the table. "Why couldn't the paper have suspended you a month ago? Then you could have gone to California with Mark."

"I don't want to talk about Mark's trip to L.A."

"Fine, we don't talk about it. But something happened while Mark was away that I have to tell you about."

Lily remembered her ring, which was still in her pocket, and could not suppress a smile.

Her mother tensed visibly. "Why are you grinning like that?"

"I'm not grinning."

"Oh, yes, you are. But you won't grin when you hear

about the incompetence of the police in this town despite our high taxes. I told you I was planning to take your ring to our safe-deposit box."

"You told me you *had* taken it to the safe-deposit box."

Lily's mother ignored the comment and began to play with the diamond-and-sapphire ring on her left hand. "Well, before I could get to the bank, somebody broke into our house and stole your ring, and of course the police have been so busy ticketing cars illegally parked at the aromatherapy salon that they claim they haven't had one minute to find the thief. Obviously the ring will turn up sooner or later, so you don't have to worry about that. But if it doesn't, I'm sure Mark would be glad to buy you another, especially after what happened in—"

Lily abruptly pulled her ring out of her pocket. "You have no right to slander Mark this way." She shoved the diamond back on her finger. "Now, if you don't mind, I'll say goodnight to Gran and leave."

Charlotte Blair flushed and then turned her attention to the pink geraniums in the backyard, which had regained some of their color. Lily started to leave, but had a thought and pulled her key chain out of her purse. She removed the key to her parents' house and dropped it on the table. "From now on, I'm going to do my laundry at Mark's and my house. Mark's father is putting in a washer and dryer."

Lily's mother did not touch the key. "Really? I wonder if the dryer plays 'Carmen Ohio.'"

30

Presents

"Expect a most agreeable Letter; for not being over-burdened with subject—(having nothing at all to say)—I shall have to check my Genius from beginning to end."

—Letter to Cassandra Austen

With her days empty, Lily vowed to write the overdue thank-you notes that jabbed painfully at her conscience. After deciding to call off her wedding, she had ignored the gifts piling up in her spare bedroom, intending to return them after talking to Mark. Now that she was going through with the ceremony, she began listing her wedding presents and their givers in a white-leather album:

- *Jack O'Reilly*—First edition of *The Longest Day*, inscribed, "Remember, the good guys won on D-Day. Love, Jack."
- *Jeff Carter*—Airline gift certificate with a hand-drawn card reading: "Recipe for a Happy

Marriage in the Rust Belt: First, buy a one-way airline ticket—"

- *Bill and Pam Schroeder*—Matched set of official National Basketball Association coasters with a note from B. S.: "Lily, Hope there are no bad feelings about your suspension. Frankly, I wouldn't mind two weeks away from this nuthouse myself. Thought you might like the enclosed better than a Martha Stewart cookbook, ha-ha, although Pam disagrees with me—as usual!"
- *Sally Levin*—Framed photograph (beautiful!) of Central Park from series by Ruth Orkin.
- *Ruth Bryant*—Needlepoint pillow embroidered with a line from *Emma*, "If I loved you less, I might be able to talk about it more."
- *Todd and Isabelle*—One case Château Margaux 1986.
- *Aunt Grace*—Toaster with ducks on it.
- *Art Felden and "Your Brothers and Sisters in the Guild"*—Fruit basket.
- *Tess Mahoney*—Engraved sterling-silver pill-box.
- *Gwen and Ed Jensen*—An orange gourd shaped like . . .

Lily stopped when she came to the Jensens' gourd. What was it shaped like? Turning it over, she could see no resemblance to anything but an enormous tumescent penis. A Slayton family rumor was apparently true. Gwen Jensen, a passionate gardener, had a collection of X-rated gourds.

But how, Lily wondered, was she supposed to write a thank-you note for such a gift? In her head, she began composing an imaginary letter:

Dear Gwen and Ed,
  *Thank you so much for the gourd shaped like
an enormous penis. I know it will come in extremely handy whenever Mark goes out of
town . . .*

No, no, far too explicit. Wedding thank-yous weren't
supposed to be X-rated even when gifts were. Lily tried for
more subtlety:

Dear Gwen and Ed,
  *Fortunately, Mark and I have always had a
great sex life, but who knows? Ours may yet de-
teriorate, in which case I am sure . . .*

That was hardly an improvement. Why could she think
of nothing but sexual connotations for the gourd? Perhaps
some couples used such things as centerpieces for their
dining room tables?

Dear Gwen and Ed,
  *This fall, when Mark and I give our first dinner
party, our guests are sure to marvel—*

A bit closer to the mark, but still doubtful. Would she,
in fact, have the nerve to display the gourd at a party?
  Lily thought of falling back on a canned, all-purpose
thank-you she had seen in an etiquette book:

Dear Gwen and Ed,
  *What a creative and original wedding gift!
Only you could have come up with something
that was practical yet decorative and goes so well
with the color scheme in our new home. I know*

that, when we are celebrating our silver wedding anniversary, we will still be using the gift and thinking fondly of you—

This note was unlikely to offend the Jensens but its impersonality made Lily reject it out of hand. Perhaps she had made a mistake in trying to compose a note about the gourd first?

Lily wished that Jane Austen's novels had reached the point at which their heroines began writing thank-yous for gourds shaped like penises. Writing letters had always come easily to her, but she did not see how she could come up with hundreds of the sort of notes she wanted to write: heartfelt but clear-headed, honest but tactful, worthy of the occasion but free of the clichés that it so often inspired. She had not been defeated by the gourd but by her wedding itself—an event that drove her deeper into hypocrisy with every gift that arrived.

But if she did not write her thank-you notes soon, she would face the added problem of the hurt feelings of people whose gifts deserved a prompt acknowledgment. With a twinge of guilt, Lily realized that only one solution existed to the matter of how to respond to the gourd: She would ask Mark if he would write the Jensens' note in addition to the thank-yous that he already was writing for his law partners' gifts.

31

Jobs

"A woman especially, if she have the misfortune of knowing anything, should conceal it as well as she can."

—Northanger Abbey

Mark agreed quickly to write to the Jensens about their penis-shaped gourd—too quickly, Lily thought, given how much else he had to do—and she drifted through the days leading to her wedding as though she were already walking down the aisle in a white-tulle wake. She let her mother argue with the church and the florist and her fiancé take on other jobs that needed to be done.

This arrangement left her with her days free to write letters to New York editors and to read Jane Austen, which suited her perfectly. Each morning she would send out résumés, and each afternoon she would sit under an apple tree and read novels—a routine that was just relaxing enough to allow her to keep her uneasy peace with her wedding.

How could she work herself into a panic about an event that required nothing of her and over which she had no control? She felt as though she were waiting for someone else's wedding except during the rare moments when a task arose that she could not delegate to her mother or to Mark.

One of those occasions arose a week or so after she was suspended from the *Daily*. She kept an appointment for a dry run of her hairstyle for her wedding, and her mother went with her to the salon. Lily had planned to wear her hair down, which she and Mark preferred.

At the salon, her mother declared that the possibility of another heat wave required her to wear it up and pulled out a photograph of a bride that she had torn from a magazine. The model looked as though the Trevi Fountain were spouting from her head.

The hairdresser demurred, and Lily protested that she wanted the wedding guests to throw rice at her and not coins, but her mother argued so insistently that customers began to look up from their manicures. At last, Lily gave in. As she walked away from the salon, she half-expected sparrows to deposit twigs on the nest atop her head.

But even her discomfort with her hair did not last. She had decided to take the path of least resistance to her wedding, which was the path of no resistance. On the issue of marriage; she had fought the world and lost; now all she wanted to do was to limp away from her wedding with a minimum of bloodshed. If her mother wanted her to wear her hair up, so be it.

The only thing that worried her, as her wedding approached, was Mark. Since returning from California, he had treated her as delicately as a crystal bell that might shatter if rung too forcefully. He never suggested visiting the house his father had given them and made it clear to his family that he would leave any social event immediately if Penny and Fran criticized her in his presence.

Nor did he tease her as playfully as he had early in their engagement. After his trip, he did not mention the Rosenbergs, *The Marriage of Figaro*, or the almost comically inept *Hamlet* that had helped to bring them together.

None of this struck Lily so acutely as that he lapsed more often into habits that he had picked up in England, asking her for a torch instead of a flashlight and pronouncing *Rousseau* with the accent on the first syllable instead of the second. Mark had once told her that when he first went away to his British boys' school his classmates had teased him so brutally about being American that he had absorbed as much of their speech as rapidly as he could. He had shed that protective cloak on his return, but Lily noticed that he fell back on it under stress. She had never heard him make so many slips as in the week before their wedding.

One day, Mark showed up unannounced in the middle of the afternoon, as she was sitting under a backyard apple tree rereading *Persuasion*. He had such deep circles under his eyes that, had Lily not spent two of the past four nights at his loft, she would have thought he had not slept in days. Mark perched on the edge of her chaise longue and gently took the novel out of her hands.

"Lily, this novel is a fantasy, and life is real."

"What do you mean?"

"There's a reason why, ever since I've been back from California, you've spent almost all your free time escaping into Jane Austen. Please tell me what it is."

Lily tried to think of a convincing answer but could not. "I can't explain it. It's just that I think that, somehow, Jane Austen would have understood."

"Understood what?"

"Everything."

Mark took both of Lily's hands in his. "Sweetheart,

nothing happened between Caroline and me in California. *Nothing.* Do you believe me?"

Lily looked at him and knew once again that—whatever fears she might have had while he was away—he had long since banished. "Yes, I do."

"Then why are you acting this way?

"Acting what way?"

"As though you're facing your funeral instead of your wedding."

Lily said nothing, and Mark spoke again, more softly. "Is it Nick? Have you been having second thoughts and wondering if you brushed him off too quickly?" He paused. "I'm afraid that I might have frightened you away from telling me everything when I said I wouldn't be able to be mature and rational if you found another man. I admit that it would be devastating if you did. But I'd rather hear that truth than see you so distant and withdrawn. You're miles away from yourself."

At the mention of Nick, Lily became alarmed and rushed to reassure Mark that the architect had nothing to do with any changes that he perceived in her. In fact, she had not thought about him in days and, when she did, it was only to compare him unfavorably with her fiancé.

"Then what is it?" Mark asked. "There's a reason why you're acting the way you are. But if it's not Caroline or Nick, I'm lost. Please help me find my way back to you. Please tell me what I can do to make you feel better."

"You've done everything to make me feel better."

"I must have done something to upset you."

"That's just it. You've never done anything to upset me. Since the day we met, you've been nothing but the most loving man I've ever known. This has nothing to do with you, and everything to do with me."

Mark looked puzzled. "How does it have to do with you and not with me? I'm getting married, too."

Lily picked up a small branch that had fallen from an apple tree during a storm and began twisting it. She thought she would never be able to speak, so much heartache did his remark cause her. At last, she tried to explain herself.

"Mark, when you were growing up, did you always assume you would get married someday?"

"Of course."

"The difference between us is that I didn't. Living with my parents' marriage . . . who would have wanted that? For as long as I can remember, I wanted to move to New York, see the world, launch my career, and do anything but spend the rest of my life in Colony Heights, Ohio. The woman I admired most wasn't my mother, who married two weeks after her graduation from Smith, but my grandmother. She didn't get married until she was thirty-two, which she says was almost scandalous in her day, and then she traveled to four continents with my grandfather. She didn't move back to Colony Heights until she was a sixty-year-old widow, and by then she had the strength to—not exactly turn her back on it, but not drown in it, either."

Mark took the apple tree branch from her hands. "And you think you're going to drown here?"

"All I know is that when I got to New York, I saw that when I lived in Colony Heights, I had been swimming underwater. Suddenly, I had air. And I thought that if I came back—with what I had learned there—I could stay afloat here. But when I moved back I saw right away that I changed but nothing else had. I knew I had to get out. Then I met you, and—and everything happened at warp speed. Meeting you was like—oh, Mark, please don't misunderstand this—but like being in a catastrophic car accident in reverse. I was in a great accident, one that changed my life in a good way instead of bad, but still an accident."

"And you think you'll never recover if we get married?"

Lily said nothing, trying to hold back tears. She tried to think of an honest answer. "I just don't know, Mark. Who can say? Doctors are always telling people who have been in terrible accidents that they will never walk again—" she thought she saw Mark flinch—"and somehow they do walk. All we can do is get married and see what happens."

Neither of them spoke as her words hung in the air like an apple tree branch that had been struck by lightning but had not yet fallen to the ground. After a while, Mark left to keep an appointment with a client. Lily remained under the apple tree, reading *Persuasion* and reminding herself that her wedding was only a few days away. She needed to hold on only a little while longer.

3 2

Red Ink

*"My mother means well, but she does not know—
no one can know—how much I suffer from what
she says."*

—Pride and Prejudice

C harlotte Blair was arguing on the telephone, insisting that the bridal limousine was supposed to include a nine-inch color television set.

"Mother, I'm getting married on a Saturday afternoon," Lily said. *"Tomorrow* afternoon. I don't need to watch *Bowling for Dollars* on the way to the church."

Her mother covered the mouthpiece with her hand.

"Hush, Lily, it's the principle of the thing," she said. "The bridal limousine was supposed to include a telephone, television, and minibar. Now they say they can only give us the telephone and minibar."

Lily moved to take the receiver out of her mother's hand. "Let me talk to the limo service. We don't need any of those things. The drive to the church takes twenty minutes. For twenty minutes, I can live without taking a call from the copy desk or drinking one of those little cans of Bloody Mary mix."

Her mother grasped the receiver with both hands. "Don't you dare."

Lily walked to a bookshelf in the breakfast nook and noticed that it contained a copy of *Martha Stewart's Weddings*. She was suddenly curious about whether Martha Stewart had anything to say about the elegant way to get divorced within a year of your wedding. As she began flipping through the book, she could hear her mother resume her argument.

"Well, would you please try harder? It isn't my problem that six high school students want to watch MTV on their way to the senior prom."

Hanging up the phone, her mother looked at the clock in alarm. "What on earth are you doing here, Lily? You're supposed to be at the rehearsal dinner in an hour."

"I called Mark and told him I was running late. He hadn't even left the office yet, so he said that was fine." Glancing up from the book, she went on. "Sometimes I think Mark likes it when I'm late. He told me I'm the only woman he's ever met who doesn't make him feel guilty about how hard he works. He said that if I'm late occasionally, he feels better about the times when he gets tied up with a client and can't meet me on time."

"How many times have I told you that you can't take men at their word on things like that?" her mother asked. "Men always say they don't mind things like lateness when they are courting you. Then, twenty years later, those are the things that drive them straight to the divorce courts. If you don't treat Mark better, your marriage will be over before it's begun. You have to make more of an effort to please him."

Charlotte Blair stuck her head into the dining room that adjoined the breakfast nook. "Isn't that right, dear?"

Lily saw her father sitting at the dining room table with a newspaper folded open to the business section. He was performing his nightly ritual of circling the closing prices of his stocks with a red felt-tip pen.

Taking her book with her, Lily went over and kissed him.

"Hi, darling," her father said, then looked up at his wife, who was still standing in the doorway between the breakfast nook and the dining room. "Excuse me, Charlotte? I'm afraid I didn't hear you. WesTech is down again."

"I said, if Lily doesn't treat Mark better, her marriage will be over before it's begun."

"My dear, it seems to me that a man who proposes to a woman after three months must like something about the way he is being treated," her father replied, looking up from his newspaper. "It took me three years to propose to you."

"That was only because you wanted to finish law school," Charlotte Blair snapped. "Mark finished law school years ago." As her husband resumed reading the stock tables, she turned to her daughter. "Lily, you should not be here," she said, her voice rising. "You should be home getting ready for the dinner. Shouldn't she, Wade?"

Without replying, Lily's father kept circling stock prices in red ink, and her mother approached the dining room table. "Wade, I wish you would take a little more interest in the wedding of your only daughter."

"I take a very great interest in the wedding of my only daughter. I am going over the stock reports, at this moment, to see if we can afford to pay for it."

"At this moment, she should be getting dressed for the rehearsal dinner that her future father-in-law is paying for.

I wish you'd tell her to have a little respect for his money even if she has none for ours." Charlotte Blair turned again to her daughter. "Once and for all, would you please tell me what you are doing here?"

"Gran told me I could borrow her sapphire bracelet for the dinner," Lily said. "I came to get it."

"You can't wear that bracelet to the rehearsal dinner. Those sapphires are much too heavy for a yellow voile dress."

"I'm not wearing my yellow voile dress," Lily said, surprised at how calm she was. "The sleeves are too puffy. It makes me look like a Spanish infanta—an infanta with jaundice. You might as well take it back to Saks while you can still get a credit. If you had asked me, I would never have let you buy it. I'm wearing my navy silk dress, which Mark loves, and Gran's sapphires are just right for it."

"That dress is backless," her mother said. "You can't wear a backless dress to your rehearsal dinner."

"I have to wear it. The yellow voile is out of the question, and all my other cocktail dresses are black, which Mark's sisters said I can't wear. They said it would be morbid."

"Just because those two girls have shown a grain of sense for once doesn't mean they want you to show up half-naked. I won't hear of your wearing a backless dress to your own rehearsal dinner."

"Okay, the next time I get married, I'll wear a frontless one."

"Lily, you are being disrespectful. That dress is completely inappropriate. Isn't it, Wade?"

"Charlotte, a few minutes ago you were telling Lily that she doesn't know how to please Mark. Now you are telling her that you don't want her to wear the one dress that she knows for certain will please him. You'd better make up your mind before she becomes thoroughly confused."

At that moment, Helen Blair walked into the breakfast nook, carrying a narrow velvet box.

"Hi, darling," she said. "I thought I heard your car pull into the driveway."

Lily embraced her, and her grandmother gave her the box.

"Oh, Gran, I love it," Lily said, as she removed the bracelet. "It's perfect."

Lily tried on the bracelet and kissed her grandmother, who looked at her fondly.

"Your grandfather gave it to me for our silver wedding anniversary, and I know you and Mark are going to be just as happy as we were," she said. Then she added, looking at her daughter-in-law, "Although sometimes I wonder how the two of you ever made it to the wedding at all."

"Now, everybody, no arguments tonight," Lily said, just before she left her parents' house. "Tomorrow is my wedding, remember? See you all at the dinner."

33

Luck

*"With such a reward for her tears, the child was too
wise to cease crying."*

—Sense and Sensibility

As luck would have it, Lily and Mark arrived at their
rehearsal dinner at the perfect moment. A crisis had
just erupted involving several of the guests' children,
which drew attention away from their lateness.

Lily and Mark overheard the details as they made their
way toward the bar beside the Suburban Athletic Club
pool, the scene of the predinner cocktail hour. The evening was cool despite the fetid air that clung to the city
during the day, and some of the boys objected to not being
allowed to swim. Their parents tried unsuccessfully to pac-
ify them with peanuts, croquet, Frisbees, soft drinks, and
popcorn served out of Ohio State football helmets.

At first, the boys cried and dropped ice cubes down the
backs of the dresses of female guests. Then, led by Mark's
nephew Zack, they found a box of barbecue matches near
the grill and set fire to the red-and-white Japanese paper
lanterns arrayed around the pool.

When Mark and Lily arrived, firefighters had just put out the blaze, and the guests were still too busy absolving their own children and blaming others' to heed the arrival of the guests of honor. The two of them took their drinks to a white wrought-iron bench under a buckeye tree to wait for the accusations and counteraccusations to clear.

They had just sat down when they heard a shriek and saw Mark's seven-year-old niece, Zoe, the daughter of Penny and Dick, standing on the end of the high diving board in a party dress.

For the sake of family unity, Lily had agreed to have Zoe as a flower girl, although the idea made her nervous. Now Mark's niece was refusing to budge from a spot near the end of the high diving board. As her mother pleaded with her from the edge of the pool, she was screaming and threatening to jump.

"I want my own invitation!"

"Zoe, darling, please come down."

"I want my *own* invitation!"

"Angel, Mommy and Daddy will get you your own invitation to the wedding. Now, please—"

"I WANT MY OWN INVITATION!"

"Sweetie, I said Mommy and Daddy will—"

"I WANT MY OWN INVITATION RIGHT NOW!"

"Angel, sweetie, it was very mean of Aunt Lily and Uncle Mark to put your name on Mommy and Daddy's invitation instead of sending you your own. But I promise—"

Lily turned in alarm to Mark, who understood what was happening an instant before she did.

Zoe screamed again. "MEAN, MEAN, MEAN!"

The other children took up the chorus. "MEAN, MEAN, MEAN!"

Zoe bounced up and down in time to their chant.

"Zoe, darling, you know you don't swim," Penny

pleaded. "You know you insisted on taking karate instead of—"

In despair Penny looked at the adults clustered around the pool, who had fallen silent.

"Does anybody have a spare wedding invitation?"

"I don't want somebody else's invitation! I want my OWN—"

Lily opened her purse to show Mark she had nothing but a comb, lipstick, and a ten-dollar bill. He leaned toward her and apologized for the behavior of his niece.

"Zoe is having a few adjustment problems," he said in a whisper. "Penny says she's jealous of all the attention her brother Zack gets when he starts fires."

Lily tried ease Mark's embarrassment by saying that having a few adjustment problems was probably natural when your brother was an incipient arsonist. Then she heard the familiar drill-sergeant voice of Penny's psychologist husband, Dick.

"All right, everybody, don't panic," he said, in a tone that she could imagine officials at the Centers for Disease Control using if the Ebola virus hit downtown Toledo. "We'll just have to call Lily and Mark and ask them to bring another invitation with Zoe's name on it when they come."

Most of the guests agreed that this was the only thing to do, although one woman turned somberly to Mark and said that she knew someone who had lost a child to death by drowning and that, you'd be surprised, sometimes these things could be a blessing. Lily recognized the voice of Tess Mahoney, whose invitation to the dinner she had protested.

At that instant, somebody saw the couple and began to shout. "Wait a second, they're here! Mark and Lily are under the buckeye tree."

Guests began to murmur and point toward them, ignoring Zoe, who was inching closer to the end of the diving board. Mark waved to the crowd with one hand and,
with the other, refused to let go of Lily's.

"We just arrived and didn't want to disrupt your party,"
he said. "But if you want us to run over to Lily's parents'
we'd be glad—"

There were protests all around from guests who, a few
moments earlier, could think of no solution but for the
couple to bring an invitation for Zoe. Mark and Lily could
not leave their own rehearsal dinner; they were one of the
most important parts of it; the fun had just begun. As the
guests said this, Zoe began to bounce higher.

Penny shouted at her daughter not to jump, and Dick
shouted at his wife not to shout at his daughter, which he
said would traumatize her. Wild-eyed, Zoe jerked her head
in a way that made her resemble Linda Blair in *The Ex-
orcist*.

"Mark, can't we do something?" Lily asked. "She'll kill
herself."

Tess Mahoney started gravely to describe the forms of
death that could be worse than drowning. She had gotten
as far as torture and dismemberment when Mark grimly
handed his suit jacket and watch to Lily.

"Wait here," he said, "and don't worry."

Mark began climbing up the steps to the diving board,
and Dick screamed at him to come down. Dick insisted
that Mark was not a trained mental-health professional
and did not understand the subconscious motivations of
young children.

"I understand the subconscious motivations of young
children in *this* family," Mark said coolly, and kept climbing. At the top of the steps he began to speak soothingly
to his niece about a doll she had asked him for, which was

inspired by a television show and called Beach Blanket Brittany.

"Zoe," he said, "you know that doll you wanted for Christmas? The one that was sold out in all the stores in December?"

Zoe eyed Mark suspiciously.

"Well, Zoe," he said casually, "it's summer now. I bet that doll is back in stores now."

Zoe stared at him but said nothing.

"And Zoe, I was just wondering how much that doll would cost if somebody wanted to buy it."

"Thirty-nine ninety-five!" she blurted out.

"It just so happens, Zoe, that I have forty dollars in my wallet, which I am going to place here on my end of the diving board." He pulled out two twenties and set them in front of him at his end of the board. "And if you want that doll, all you have to do is walk back here and take this."

"I want the surfboard, too!" Zoe screamed. "That's nineteen ninety-five more. And the jet skis and—"

"No, Zoe," Mark said. "I'm putting forty dollars on the board, and that's my final offer."

Dick began to scream at Mark that his daughter would not compromise her integrity by accepting a bribe. Mark replied calmly that his daughter already had compromised her integrity by accepting a bribe and went on bargaining. "You heard me, Zoe," he said. "It's forty dollars or nothing."

"The surfboard!" she shrieked. "And the jet skis—"

"Sorry, Zoe," he said. "No surfboard, no jet skis. Forty dollars, and if you don't make up your mind fairly quickly, it might go down to thirty-five."

"Zoe, if it goes down to thirty-five, your father and I will make—" Penny shouted, and began climbing up the steps to the board in her high heels. Mark said something to his sister, at which she scowled and climbed back down.

Tess Mahoney said that she could not see any lifeguards or life preservers near the pool and that perhaps this was a Sign from God. Fearful of what it might be a sign of, Lily moved away from her slightly. Mark kept his eyes on his niece.

"Well, Zoe, I can see you're having trouble making up your mind. So I'm going to make this easier for you. I'm going to count to ten, and if you don't come get the money by then, these twenties are going to walk off the diving board." He paused. "Oh, and another thing, Zoe, if you take the money, you don't get your own invitation. That's right: *No invitation.*" Mark looked down at Lily and smiled. "Because, Zoe, some things are worth more than money."

Lily smiled at her fiancé as Zoe, perched on the edge of the board, swayed and shook her head violently. Holding hands tightly, Penny and Dick glared at Mark.

Like a leashed dog, Zoe began jerking back and forth in the direction of the money.

"All right, Zoe, I'm going to start to count to ten now." Mark let the words sink in. "One. Two—"

Zoe began to twitch.

"I never wanted any invitation to your wedding, anyway!" she screamed.

With those words, she lunged toward the money, and as she grabbed it, Mark swept her off the diving board by the waist. As Zoe wailed and pummeled him, he climbed down the steps and deposited her in the arms of her father. Dick glowered at his brother-in-law and tried to quiet his unruly daughter.

"Don't cry, Angel," he said. "Uncle Mark doesn't understand little girls like Zoe."

Lily started to protest that, on the contrary, Uncle Mark seemed to be the only person at the dinner who did understand little girls like Zoe. But Mark slipped an arm around her and suggested they refill their drinks.

They had almost made it to the bar when they saw Sally, who had just flown in from New York.

"Sally!" Lily exclaimed. "You look wonderful. Did you get out to the Hamptons for a few days of sun?"

"No such luck. But, miraculously, for the past week all the major plumbing and electrical systems in my apartment building have been working. I've discovered that it's amazing what you can do with tap water—still a little brown, I admit—and a working blow-dryer." She paused to look around the party. "By the way, Ruth and the other members of our group are here, too. But there were a couple of good-looking ushers over by the tennis courts, and I think your bridesmaids realized that they might not meet that many attractive single men in New York in a year. So I'm not sure how much you'll see of them tonight."

Lily smiled and introduced Sally to Mark, who apologized again for the behavior of his niece and said that he hoped she did not think all Colony Heights children were like that.

"Not at all," Sally replied. "Over by the children's pool I saw an adorable little blonde-haired girl with a ribbon in her hair, who sat quietly reading a Babar book to herself the whole time all the other children were screaming along with your niece. Must be an example of those wholesome Midwestern values I'm always told exist out here."

"Blonde?" Lily asked. "That's funny, all the children in Mark's family have dark hair." It took her a minute to realize the implications of what Sally said.

"Oh, my God, Todd and Isabelle are here!"

*   *   *

After a warm reunion with Lily's brother and sister-in-law, Mark and Lily went inside to try to find Ruth and the other bridesmaids. They got as far as the club kitchen, where they encountered a harried chef, who said that Buck had been barging into the kitchen every few minutes to order that more canapés be brought outside.

Mark assured him that the guests were in no danger of running out of food, and led Lily to an alcove overlooking the pool, where they could watch the party unobserved in the few minutes that remained before the dinner began. He commented on a brawl between several of the children on the croquet lawn, and she was pained to hear him pronounce *croquet* with the accent on the first syllable.

Lily asked Mark if he was feeling well, and he did not respond immediately. Instead, he waited until he saw Zoe bring a croquet mallet down on another child's foot.

"You know, everybody says this city is such a great place to raise a family," he said. "But I have to admit, so many of the children I know here are, let's just say, over-indulged. They don't know what to do with themselves if they don't have a half-acre lawn and a pool." He glanced toward Zoe, who was having an angry tug-of-war with her father for a croquet mallet, which she was winning. "Sometimes, they don't know what to do with themselves even if they do have a half-acre lawn and a pool."

Mark had made a trip to his firm's New York office the day before and said that, while he was in town, the daughter of his partner had been visiting the office. "The whole time I was talking to her mother, she sat quietly drawing on a legal pad without once interrupting us. Can you imagine what would happen if I took Zoe—or any of the other children at this party—to my office? They would be standing on the desks threatening to jump and pouring coffee down the backs of the paralegals."

Lily had time only to say that she knew exactly what he meant before they saw that Buck was speaking into a scarlet-and-gray megaphone with the initials OSU on it, announcing that dinner was served.

34

Children

". . . a fond mother, though, in pursuit of praise for her children, the most rapacious of human beings, is likewise the most credulous; her demands are exorbitant; but she will swallow any thing . . ."

—Sense and Sensibility

B y the time the after-dinner toasts had ended, Lily had a headache of symphonic proportions and mild indigestion from the red tide of Madeira sauce on the filet mignon. She was fighting a wave of nausea when Fran came up to the head table with her six-year-old son, Zeke.

Lily remembered that although Mark's sisters professed to loathe being named after currency, they had fetishistically given all their children names beginning with Z. Fran made a show of kissing Lily for the videographer hired by her father.

"We are *so* glad to have you in the family," she said. "So glad. I hope you weren't alarmed by Zoe. She does tend to be a bit high-spirited, but some children are more mature than others. Say hello to your Aunt Lily, Zeke."

Fran's son, who was sucking defiantly on a cranapple-juice box, said nothing.

"Zeke, honey, you're going to be the ring bearer in your Aunt Lily's wedding," Fran coaxed. "Don't you want to tell her how happy you are?"

Zeke, slurping his cranapple juice loudly, remained silent.

"Zeke, Aunt Lily and Uncle Mark will think you don't like them if you don't say hello," Fran said. "Do you want to hurt their feelings?"

Zeke yanked his juice box out of his mouth and stared at Lily. His baby face darkened, and he dropped his drink angrily on her foot. Lily could feel the cranapple juice seeping between her toes.

Mark bent down to pick up the box and started to say something to Lily about the behavior of his nephew. Fran cut him off.

"Mark, for heaven's sake, don't apologize," she said. "Never *apologize*. You'll make Zeke feel bad, and he will think he's done something wrong. Won't he, darling?"

Zeke still said nothing, and Fran looked dismayed. She said that her son had the vocabulary of a college physics major but, because he never spoke, people sometimes found this difficult to believe. Zeke, she added, was obviously going to be a late bloomer like his father.

Lily noticed that Fran's husband, George, was standing glumly a few feet away, trying to get a waiter to refill his wineglass. She wondered if some people were such late bloomers that, well into middle age, the signs of their bloom remained imperceptible.

Ignoring her husband, Fran went on to say that she was not worried about Zeke, because she had read that Albert Einstein did not speak until he was three. Given that Zeke was six and thus three years past the threshold of Einsteinian genius, Lily did not know what to say this.

Her silence did not deter Fran, who went on to list enough other similarities between her son and Einstein to suggest that recruiters from the Institute for Advanced Study would descend at any moment on his play group. Lily wondered if physicists had ever studied such mothers' gravity-defying faith in their children's genius, which remained attached to the branch no matter how hard reality shook it.

Listening to Fran, she thought enviously of Garrison Keillor's Lake Woebegon, where the children were merely "above average." In Colony Heights she was always hearing of second-graders who had IQs of 142, or kindergartners who "tested gifted" at relating squares and circles despite a demonstrable inability to insert sandwiches into their mouths with anything close to scientific predictability.

Lily could feel the cranapple juice congealing between her toes when Mark's sister told her that, although she had her doubts about Zoe's selection as a flower girl, Zeke would be a model ring bearer.

"Trust me, you'll never regret having him in your wedding," Fran said. "Never. A year ago he was the ring bearer for one of my cousins, and he was so darling, he completely stole the show."

Lily tried not to think about the implications of this, which intensified her headache, and excused herself to try to find an aspirin. Mark got up to go with her but, as he did, Fran's husband came over and said he needed some legal advice. George insisted that his question would only take a minute, and Lily slipped away as he began describing an intricate problem involving a faulty sewer line adjacent to his property in Colony Heights.

"By the way, Lily, I wanted to talk to your father about

my problem, too," George said, just before she made her escape. "But your grandmother said he and your mother left a few minutes ago. Funny, your father had a headache, too."

On the way to the clubhouse, Lily saw a deeply tanned guest who appeared to be lost. He introduced himself as Dave Lynch in the Los Angeles office of Mark's firm and said he had just flown in for the wedding.

Lily said she was delighted meet him and hoped that the TechnoCorp case had not been too difficult. Dave replied that it had not been as hard for him as it had been for Mark.

"Caroline never let up," he said, as though her behavior had taken a toll on him, too. "She was after Mark night and day, even though it was obvious to everybody in the L.A. office that he didn't have the least interest in her. The poor guy never had a moment's peace. Caroline kept trying to get him to go dancing, and I don't know what else, when all he wanted to do was to concentrate on the trial." Dave glanced at a senior partner of Mark's firm, who was flirting with Tess Mahoney. "I gather from the people in our Ohio office that Caroline has been after Mark for years and saw the trip as some sort of last-gasp effort to nab him."

"Dave, you don't think that had anything to do with losing the case—"

"Not in the least," Dave said quickly. "Mark has an incredible ability to stayed focused. When he sets his sights on something, he refuses to get sidetracked by nonissues. So he just kept giving Caroline a polite brush-off, which is more than some guys I know would have done. We didn't lose because of him, or because of Caroline, but because the other side had a much better case." Dave watched as two children dueled with croquet mallets. "Even so, you must be relieved that Mark put in for a transfer to the New York office."

"The New York office—" Lily began, trying not to show her astonishment. Dave nodded.

"After about three days of Caroline, I think Mark just decided that he'd had enough. He didn't want to spend the rest of his career working on the same floor with someone so persistent. And he knew that if he wanted to leave the Ohio office, he had to do it before Kayo Smith became managing partner and had a chance to block the move. Mark and I talked about his requesting a transfer while he was in L.A., but I hear from the people here that he didn't formally put in for it until about a week ago." Dave stopped. "Say, didn't Mark tell me that you used to work in New York?"

The news that Mark had applied for a transfer threw her into an emotional tailspin. If Dave Lynch was right, why had Mark not told her of his plans?

After taking two aspirin, Lily lay down on a sofa in the lounge and tried to make sense of what she had heard. Perhaps Mark feared the transfer would not come through and did not want to raise her hopes in vain? This was certainly possible. But it was uncharacteristic of Mark, whose boyish enthusiasm often led him to give her gifts weeks before he had intended to, just for the pleasure of seeing her reaction.

Perhaps he thought she was overtaxed by the strain of the wedding and did not want to raise the idea of a transfer until her life had become calmer? This made even less sense. Mark knew—or she thought he did—that the joy of returning to New York would make up for any hardships that came with the move.

The shrieks of the youngest guests kept impinging on her thoughts. Every time she tried pursue an idea to a plausible conclusion, Zoe found a peanut shell on the lawn and led the others in a piercing rendition of many verses of "Found a Peanut," which Lily had not heard since elementary school.

The children had just moved on from "It was rotten" to "Ate it anyway" when Mark walked into the lounge and sat down beside her on her sofa.

"Feeling better?" he said, smiling, as he bent over to kiss her. "I was worried that you had been tackled by one of my father's friends who had taken the athletic theme of this club a little too seriously."

Lily said that her digestive tract finally had made peace with the Madeira sauce and asked how the dinner was going. Mark replied that it was winding down the way his family's parties usually wound down: A guest had fallen into the pool, Fran's husband had exhausted the conversational possibilities of raw sewage, and the masculinity of the New York Yankees was being called into question by several of his father's friends.

"Oh, and my father's secretary made the mistake of seating the head of the Igneous wing of the Rock Hall of Fame next to a man who proudly calls himself 'Mr. Sedimentary,' so they both stormed out a few minutes ago," Mark added. "It seems that they had an argument over who deserved the credit for the success of Bauxite Night."

Lily, realizing that she had met neither of the feuding men, sat up.

"Mark, how many people at this party would you say that the two of us even know, let alone like?"

"Not enough to keep us here," he said. "Let's say good night to the crowd and go back to your place. I want to give you your wedding present."

3 5

Surprises

*"But people alter themselves so much, that there is
something new to be observed in them for ever."*

—Pride and Prejudice

At her apartment, Lily found messages on her machine from Jack, Ruth, and her mother. Jack teased
her about the "violins of autumn," the code phrase that
the Allies used to let the French Resistance know that the
invasion of Normandy had begun. Ruth apologized for not
having spent more time with her at the dinner but said
that she had so much fun with an usher that—well, perhaps she should not explain on tape. Her mother reminded
her that tomorrow was her wedding day and that "eighty
percent of life is showing up."

The last message struck Lily as bizarre, if not proof that
her mother had at last gone around the bend that she had
been approaching at high speed ever since the engagement
had been announced. Wasn't your wedding the one day in
your life when *one hundred percent* of life was showing
up?

Lily listened to her machine while Mark opened a bottle

of wine in her kitchen. They had agreed to exchange wedding gifts at her apartment after the dinner, and she was so worried about her present to him that she played her messages twice, stalling for time.

Weeks earlier, through an autograph dealer, she tracked down a letter in which Ethel Rosenberg had professed her love for Julius, and she had it framed along with a photo of the couple. At the time, it seemed perfect.

But Mark's avoidance of the Rosenbergs since he had returned from California gave her second thoughts, and she longed for reassurance that he would not think her gift frivolous. At last, she returned to the living room and sat down beside him on the sofa.

"Lots of messages?" Mark asked, smiling. "You were in there a rather long time."

"Not a lot. But I had a strange message from my mother saying that, on your wedding day, eighty percent of life is showing up."

Mark laughed. "I'd say that, on your wedding day, one hundred percent of life is showing up, wouldn't you? But let's not do the math tonight. I want to give you a wedding present that I think will make you very happy."

"Oh, Mark, let me give you yours first," Lily said, fearful that she might lose her nerve if she waited. "After sitting so cheerfully through all of George's tales from the sewer, you deserve it."

Lily went to a closet for his package, which she had wrapped in silver paper and a huge white bow. Mark made several playful guesses about the contents, suggesting that she had given him an Ohio State football team playbook or an affidavit on which Corky Klingel vowed to donate a portion of his salary to the National Organization for Women. He stopped joking when he saw Ethel Rosenberg's signature at the bottom of the letter.

"This is amazing," he said, as he began to read the letter. When he came to the line in which Ethel professed her undying love for Julius, he looked at his fiancée in wonder.

By the end of the letter, Mark had tears in his eyes. He said that, since his mother had died, he had never met anyone who knew him well enough to give a gift that went directly to his heart—but he could go no further. Taking out his handkerchief, he insisted that it was now his turn to surprise her, and he reached into his suit pocket and pulled out a small, flat box.

Lily suspected that it held a bracelet. But on opening the box, found that it contained Polaroid photographs of a half-dozen sunny rooms and terraces. Not recognizing any of them, she looked curiously at Mark, who urged her to read a note that he had tucked into the box.

As she did so, she could not at first believe its words. But Mark was smiling so happily that she at last accepted their truth: The Polaroids were photographs of a co-op on Central Park West on which he had put in a bid on his trip to New York.

36

Talk

"What strange creatures brothers are! You would not write to each other but upon the most urgent necessity in the world; and when obliged to take up a pen to say such a horse is ill, or such a relation dead, it is done in the fewest possible words."

—Mansfield Park

O n the morning of her wedding day, Lily went to her parents' house and found her father fixing himself a cup of coffee in the kitchen while watching a talk show on the topic of homicidal honeymooners. The host was interviewing a somber psychotherapist who was saying, ". . . and so, unfortunately, my advice to newlyweds is to avoid cities with tall buildings."

"Hi, darling," Lily's father said, kissing her on the cheek. "Ready for your big day?"

"I guess that's something you never know for sure until you try to push your spouse out of a tenth-story window in your honeymoon hotel."

Lily's father shut off the white countertop television set. "Now, you know can't take those talk-show therapists seriously. You and Mark will have a great time in Paris."

"At least both of us have been to the top of the Eiffel Tower. That removes one big obstacle to our survival." Lily took a seat across from her father at the banquette in the breakfast nook. "Did you and Mother have a good time on your honeymoon?"

"It's funny, I can't remember much about it now. By the time we got to Venice we were so exhausted we fell asleep in the water taxi taking us to our hotel, and the driver stole our luggage." He took a sip of coffee. "You'll have to get your mother to tell you about it. About all I can remember is that she seemed to take it as a personal insult that I had brought along *Death in Venice* to read. She said the least I could have done was to bring a book about a man who fell in love with a *woman* in Venice."

Lily marveled at the wondrous selectivity of the male memory. How could a man like her father remember the earned-run average of every pitcher in the Central Division but forget the details of his own honeymoon? If women took everything about their weddings personally, men had a genius for taking almost nothing about them personally.

"Where is Mother, anyway?" she asked.

"She's at the church, inspecting the flowers." Wade Blair smiled. "I suspect that she is also giving God his marching orders for the day."

Lily heard a small voice singing, *"Sur le pont d'Avignon,/ On y danse . . ."* She jumped up from her seat as Todd and Isabelle, tired but smiling, walked into the kitchen with their daughter.

"Sylvie!" she cried. All three members of the family, including her five-year-old niece, kissed her on both cheeks and then repeated the ritual with her father. The new arrivals began to talk animatedly about the rehearsal dinner: Todd in English, Sylvie in French, and Isabelle in a mix

of both. Lily was entranced by her niece, who was perfectly behaved and charmingly dressed in a pink skirt and
blouse with a matching hair ribbon tied into a bow on the
side of her head. It occurred to her that, in a similar situation, Zack would be trying to set fire to the ribbon, Zoe
would be trying to strangle herself with it, and Zeke would
say nothing until one of them had succeeded.

After a few minutes, Isabelle explained that Sylvie was
very excited about being "a little girl of the flowers" in the
wedding but that, when she had tried on her dress that
morning, they found that it was too long. They went upstairs to hem it, and Todd suggested that he and Lily take
a walk. Her father reminded them not to take too long,
because the photographer was due at the house soon.

As soon as they left, Lily saw that she had won the Ohio
Weather Lottery. Jeff Carter was always reminding her
that, according to the *World Almanac*, the city had only
seventy-one sunny days the previous year and often had
fewer than sixty.

But somehow, she had landed one of the statistical rarities for her wedding, a fact that cheered her perversely.
If you have to do something you don't want to do, she
thought, *you might as well do it on a beautiful day.* Sunshine was the great natural tranquilizer, the absence of
which no doubt helped to drive her mother's friends toward the artificial kind.

A few blocks from the house they came to a leafy square
known, in one of many such affectations in Colony
Heights, as Lee Oval. After they sat down on one of its
benches, Lily asked Todd about his advertising agency.

"I'll tell you all about the agency later," he said. "Right
now, I want you to tell me what's wrong."

Lily denied that anything was amiss. In fact, it had been
so long since she had given up the struggle against getting

married that she almost believed nothing was wrong. She had met the best man she had ever known at the wrong time, a time when he was ready to wed and she was not, and she had realized it too late to admit the truth: that even if she was prepared to live with him, she was not prepared to marry him. Through a failure of character and self-awareness she had no choice but to commit the biggest mistake of her life.

But Todd would not accept her blithe denials. He said that for weeks he had been getting calls from their mother, saying one day that the wedding was off, the next day that it was on. Then he heard from their father, saying he had tried to send her to a psychiatrist—their *father*, who always said that psychotherapy was the opiate of the masses . . .

"Mother even started calling Isabelle when I was at work, begging her to tell you about how lucky you were to be having a big wedding she never had." He looked at Lily as though she had turned inside out since he last saw her. "What is going on?"

She said again that nothing, really, was going on, except that planning a wedding had been much more complicated than she expected. Todd objected again.

"Lily, even if Mother hadn't called, I would have known that something was wrong just by looking at you. It's your wedding day, and you have circles under both eyes and, as the French say, *tu es maigre comme un clou,* you're as thin as a nail."

Lily was silent. She had not anticipated how much harder it would be to keep the truth from her brother—who had absorbed his portion of their mother's wrath after he eloped—than from others.

Todd did not wait for her to reply. "Lily, I know what our parents are like. And I can only imagine how awful the past few weeks must have been for you if what I suspect is true. But I'm not going to hold it against you if you think you've made a mistake. I won't try to persuade you to go through with a wedding that isn't right—"

"Todd, I admit that I'm a little on edge. But it's just nerves."

"You have never been a 'nervous' person."

"That's because I never got married before."

"Then maybe you shouldn't get married right now."

"It's too late to consider that."

"No, it isn't."

"Yes, it is. If I didn't want to get married, I should have said so months ago."

"Why are you being so hard on yourself? Don't you have the right to make a mistake?"

"Not this kind of mistake."

"So what are you to do—go through with the wedding and spend the rest of your life regretting it?" He took her hand. "Lily, I love you. You can tell me."

Could she do it? Could she tell her brother of the plan that had taken shape in her mind the moment the Congratulations sign flashed on the video monitor at the baseball game? Lily was afraid that her brother would not approve but, given how angry her mother had been after he eloped, she believed that he would understand why she had been drawn to it even if he did not.

At last, Lily took a deep breath and began, "Todd, Mark and I are getting divorced . . ." Then she poured out the whole story of their hasty engagement, her second thoughts, Mark's trial, the baseball game, and her trip to New York, ending with her plan of getting a quiet divorce. Now that they were moving to New York, as apparently they were, it would be almost easy.

When she had finished, Todd was disbelieving. "Lily,

you can't marry Mark only to divorce him."

"It would be better than humiliating him now."

"No, it wouldn't. If you divorce Mark soon after the wedding, everybody will think you married him for his money. Mark will think you married him for his money."

This idea, obvious as it was, had not occurred to Lily. Their families' money had caused so much of her recent pain that she had never considered that others might view things differently. Hadn't her parents' money driven her wedding from the start? Hadn't her father-in-law's fortune enabled him to commandeer a video monitor at the stadium, which kept her from bailing out when she had the strength to do it?

For a moment, Lily thought Todd was right. She could never let Mark think such a terrible untruth as that she married him for his money. Then she saw the solution: She would simply not take any money from him in the divorce but would give up all claims to the ring, the co-op, and anything else Mark wanted. She had been right, after all.

"Todd, I don't care what anybody but Mark thinks, and I can prove to him that I wasn't interested in his money by refusing any sort of divorce settlement. Going through with the wedding is the lesser of two evils. If I divorce Mark, he will survive it, maybe more easily than you or I imagine. A lot of men get divorced in this town without a ripple. Dad told me this morning that he scarcely remembers his honeymoon. Maybe Mark will be one of those men who scarcely remembers his divorce. But if people here get divorced all the time, nobody walks away from a wedding like this. It would follow us for generations. Getting divorced has always been—and always will be—much less scandalous than stranding your intended at the altar."

Todd was so quiet after hearing all this that Lily began

to dread what he would say. She could not tell whether he was frightened or grief-stricken or mute with incomprehension. In the silence she wished Isabelle had come along to make them smile with her fractured English and rich supply of Gallic sayings on the imponderability of love.

"Lily, this is so—" he started to say.

But before he could finish, they heard a horn. Their mother, on her way back from the church, had spotted them on the green and stopped the car.

"What are you two doing here?" she asked. "Get in the car this instant. The photographer will be at the house in ten minutes, and you're nowhere near ready." She opened the passenger's side doors and let the two of them in. "This is going to be the best day of my life, and I won't have you two getting us behind schedule before it's begun."

7

Lilies

". . . I am pleased that you have learnt to love a hyacinth. The mere habit of learning to love is the thing . . ."

—Northanger Abbey

All her life, Lily had tried to avoid unkind generalizations about other nationalities. But when she came downstairs in her wedding gown and saw her sister-in-law weeping operatically and quoting her favorite romantic poet, she was forced to admit that she wished the French would get a grip on themselves when it came to love.

Isabelle was standing in the hallway in her Tudor lady-in-waiting bridesmaid's dress, tearfully repeating a line in which the most prominent words were *"l'amour"* and *"hélas!"* Sylvie was trying angelically to comfort her by offering to give her mother her flower girl's bouquet, petting the skirt of her gown, and murmuring, *"Ne pleure pas, Maman."*

When Lily asked what was wrong, Isabelle only sobbed once again, *"L'amour (hélas! l'étrange et la fausse nature!)."* Todd explained that his wife was quoting a line by Alfred de Musset, which translated to, "Love (alas! how strange and false is nature!)."

Lily wished Isabelle had chosen another time to provide additional evidence that the French confused love and martyrdom more enthusiastically than any other group, with the possible exception of country music singers. In her effort to take a detached approach to her wedding day, she had not expected to have to contend with a histrionic torrent of misplaced nineteenth-century romanticism.

Though it was not yet noon, Lily suggested that her sister-in-law have a glass of wine. This temporarily eased Sartre's misery but soon brought forth another outburst of maudlin verse by de Musset, which Todd swore could be translated as: "Love is all—love and life in the sun . . . What matters the bottle so long as we get drunk?"

Todd said that de Musset was saying that it doesn't matter whom you love but that you love at all. He added that, depending on your point of view, this viewpoint could be interpreted as either incredibly cynical or incredibly romantic. Isabelle clearly fell into the romantic camp.

Still, Lily had no idea why her sister-in-law was crying so hard. Yes, Isabelle had longed for a big wedding that her parents could not afford. But she and Todd were hardly Lydia Bennet and George Wickham, running away amid shame that would shadow them forever. This was not Regency England but twentieth-century America. After five years of marriage and an adorable daughter, hadn't her sister-in-law made peace with her elopement?

More than ever, Lily wished that she and Mark had done what Todd and Isabelle had done: lived together first and wed when marriage was less a decision than an inevitability. She wanted to put her arms around Isabelle and tell her that she had done the right thing.

But Todd had *his* arms around his wife and was trying

to comfort her. Lily could not make out all that he said but heard him insist, "She'll be all right," and saw her sister-in-law shake her head violently. Then she realized that Isabelle was not crying about her own elopement but was crying about the wedding that was about to take place. Todd had obviously told his wife of their conversation.

"Yes, Isabelle, it will be all right," Lily said. But her sister-in-law only shook her head again and said, *"C'est pas bien, le divorce."*

A few moments later, her grandmother came downstairs, and embraced her with great affection. But she, too, looked so drawn that Lily suspected that Todd also had spoken to her. By the time the wedding party began to prepare to leave for the church, the group was so quiet that the sound of the whirring motor-drive on the photographer's camera filled the house with a noise like an onrushing tornado.

Lily's mother had ordered a bridal limousine large enough for the entire family: Lily, her grandmother, her parents, her brother and sister-in-law, and her niece. The car was grotesquely long, resembling a great white shark, yet in some ways too low for its purposes. Lily bumped her head as she entered the limousine and had to reattach her veil. Why on earth had she agreed to such a humiliating hair style?

The day was not just sunny but balmy, almost a meteorological freak show in a region that more often felt like the inside of a hot water bottle in summer. Charlotte Blair had instructed the driver to take the long route to Holy Family Cathedral, which involved making a broad loop around Colony Heights, past the homes of many of her friends. Her mother, Lily realized, was taking her victory lap.

Well, what did she care? If her mother wanted to wrap herself in the flag of marriage, she could do nothing about it now. It pained her only to see the effect of the ride on Todd, who was shaking his head, and Isabelle, who appeared about to burst into tears.

Unable to meet their eyes, Lily focused on the citadel-like houses along their route. Near their entrances many of the homes had black lantern-bearing jockeys, some of which had been painted white, and most had signs warning of their elaborate alarm systems.

The houses became fewer as the bridal limousine approached a small green about a quarter of a mile from the church. In the middle of it stood a gazebo decorated with red and white balloons. Several dozen onlookers clustered around it, some of whom carried bouquets of wildflowers. With unopened picnic baskets arrayed nearby, the scene was lively and festive.

Lily saw a young couple inside the gazebo—a woman in flowing hair and white sailor dress with red piping, a man in a blue blazer and white trousers with a red flower in his lapel—and realized that they were getting married. She rolled down the window and heard a fiddler playing a Scottish hornpipe.

At the sound of the merry tune, Lily had to blink back her tears. The couple in the gazebo were having her wedding, the one she might have had if she had been truer to her own heart and more honest with her fiancé. On the platform, she saw, not a woman in flowing hair and a man in a blue blazer, but herself and Mark, a year or two older.

Not knowing what else to do, she reached up and unfastened her veil. After she had taken it off, she retrieved a comb from a hidden pocket in her wedding gown and began pulling down her hair.

Her mother, noticing this, broke off in the middle of a story she was telling about a friend whose daughter had defied her family by marrying a dentist and soon afterward underwent a series of tragic misfortunes of the sort that are invariably predicted for people who break chain letters.

"Lily, are you out of her mind?" she asked. "Put that veil back on this instant. Wade, tell her to put it back on."

Her father began to say something, but her grandmother cut him off.

"Hush, Wade, I never heard of such a thing as not allowing a woman to wear her hair the way she wants on her wedding day. This is nonsense. If this child wants to get married with her hair down, she is going to wear her hair down."

Charlotte Blair started to reach for the detached veil, which lay across her daughter's lap, but Todd saw her and got to it first. He gathered it up into a ball and tossed it into the front seat of the limousine, next to the driver.

Lily was so grateful to her brother that she could no longer hold back her emotions. Shedding her veil made feel like Samson in reverse, and strength flowed back into her as the tears ran down her face. Her mother frantically pulled a handkerchief from her purse.

"For heaven's sake, stop crying!" she said, wild with anger. "You'll ruin your makeup."

Lily was still emboldened by her success at removing her veil when, moments later, the limousine came within a block of Holy Family Cathedral, close enough for her to see people filing into the church. She spotted several men dressed, ludicrously, in the uniforms of naval commodores. It was her last chance. She leaned toward the driver.

"Sir, please stop," she said. "Don't go any closer to the church."

Todd looked sharply at Lily and smiled for the first time since entering the car. He flashed her an "OK" sign.

"Driver, ignore my daughter," her mother said. "She's only getting married. She'll get over it."

The driver, looking worried, turned around.

"Driver, I said, proceed."

"No," Lily said. "I'm not going any farther."

Todd smiled at Lily again and nodded vigorously. The driver, appearing uncertain of whom to listen to, slowed down but did not bring the to car to a halt.

"Sir, please listen to me," Lily said.

Her mother was livid. "Driver, do nothing of the sort."

The driver again turned around in confusion.

"Sir, have you ever been married?" Lily asked.

"Twice, miss."

"Then please think of that before you go any farther."

The driver stopped the limousine. Her mother ordered him again to go on. Her father said, "Charlotte, I—"

Her mother would not let him finish. "This is an outrage. All she needs is a Valium." She rummaged through her purse, pulled out a pill and handed it to her daughter.

Lily threw it out the window. Isabelle, who finally appeared to understand what was going on, looked excitedly at her husband. Todd was grinning.

"I don't need a Valium," Lily said. "I'm not getting married."

"You will not make that decision until you've had a drink. You need something to stabilize you." Her mother fumbled with the key to the minibar. "I told you we would need this minibar, but would you listen to me?" She retrieved a can of Bloody Mary mix and popped it open. Just then, the car hit a bump, and vodka and tomato juice spilled onto the white upholstery. Lily poured the rest of the Bloody Mary mix out the window.

"If you're not going to have a drink, we're going to proceed to the church," her mother said. "This delay is point-less."

"No, it isn't."

The driver glanced at his watch. "Ma'am—and miss—I'm afraid you'll have to make up your mind because we were due at the church three minutes ago. And we're still a block from the cathedral."

Lily's grandmother reached into her purse and pulled out a $100 bill, which she passed to the driver.

"We'll need a few more minutes to sort this out," she said amiably. "Please don't worry about the time."

The driver opened the dashboard of the limousine and pulled out a *Racing Form,* which he read with studied nonchalance. Lily's mother berated her for keeping the wedding guests waiting.

"Charlotte, why don't you give your daughter a moment of peace?" Lily's grandmother said. "I doubt she's had one since she became engaged, at least not if the grief you gave me over my dress is any indication." She turned to Lily. "Now, honey, why don't you tell me what's going on."

Looking at her parents, Lily said nothing.

"Nothing is wrong," her mother said. "Except that she's too silly to know what's good for—"

"Quiet, Charlotte, I didn't ask you."

Lily remained silent. Tears returned to her eyes as she watched more late-arriving guests enter the cathedral.

"She thinks she doesn't want to get married—" her mother said.

"Charlotte, if you say one more word, I will ask you to leave this car," her grandmother said.

"You can't evict me from this car—we're paying for it."

Lily's grandmother reached into her purse for several more $100 bills and handed them to the driver, who looked up complacently from his *Racing Form*. "Driver, we've had a slight change in plans. I'm paying for this car instead of my son and daughter-in-law." She turned to her granddaughter.

"Sorry, Lily, that money was going to be part of your wedding present. I thought you and Mark might like to take yourselves out to a three-star restaurant with it. But you might prefer this." Her grandmother paused. "Do you think you can talk about it now that you're not going to be rushed into the church?"

Lily hesitated. "I can't," she said. "Not with my parents in the car. I've been trying to tell them what's wrong for the last month. And every time I have, they've told me I need a drink, a pill, psychotherapy, or just to grow up. It's hopeless."

"That's because you're so—" her mother began.

"Charlotte, leave this car," her grandmother said impatiently. "You, too, Wade. It's obvious Lily is never going to get a fair hearing with you two here. Todd and Isabelle, you may stay, and of course darling Sylvie." On hearing her name, Sylvie looked up sweetly and climbed into her father's lap.

"This is an outrage," Lily's mother said.

"No more of one than this child apparently has been enduring for the past several weeks."

"I won't listen to this."

Wade Blair spoke to his wife with deep resignation. "Charlotte, if you won't listen to it, we need to leave, because you're obviously going to have to listen to it if you stay." He opened the car door. "Let's go. It's a lovely day for a walk, and somebody has to keep things under control at the church."

Just before helping his wife out of the car, he turned to

his daughter. "I'm sorry, darling," he said. "I failed you."

As soon as they had left, Helen Blair took her grand-daughter's hand and sighed.

"I was afraid of something like this," she said. "You see, your Grandmother Mead had very definite ideas about the kind of wedding she wanted her daughter to have. She was from a prominent Philadelphia family that also happened to be staunchly Quaker, and she considered big weddings frivolous. Your mother had wanted the sort of grand affair that all her friends at Smith had. But your Grandmother Mead wouldn't hear of it, and she made your parents get married at a Quaker meetinghouse with a reception on the lawn behind it, although Lord knows the Meads could have afforded to make a splash. Poor Charlotte, I felt so sorry for her. She was clearly miserable at having been upstaged by all her New York friends' receptions at the Plaza or St. Regis, and I'm not sure she ever got over it. She's been planning this day ever since you were born."

Helen Blair looked fondly at her granddaughter, then went on. "That's why she named you Lily—for the calla lilies she couldn't have in her bouquet. Her mother in-sisted that she have wildflowers grown on the farm they went to every summer."

This took Lily by surprise. "I never knew that. She al-ways told me that she named me Lily because lilies were her favorite flower."

"They were her favorite flower, but her mother still wouldn't let her have them in her wedding." Her grand-mother glanced at her diamond watch. "And now, if I un-derstand you correctly, you don't want to walk into the cathedral and have the wedding of her dreams."

"That's right," she said. "I love Mark dearly—" She stopped, unable to believe she had said the words. "—at least as much as I could love any man after so short a time. But we just haven't had enough time together to be able to make this sort of permanent commitment. We shouldn't be getting married today. We should be living together in a co-op that he's trying to buy for us in New York."

"Then why don't you do that? You could start by spending a few days there on your way to or from Paris." Lily's grandmother smiled. "Everybody knows that you can't fly directly to Paris—or practically anywhere else—from this city. You've got to stop over someplace. This might be one of the few times when that could actually be an advantage."

"Mark didn't ask me to live with him. He asked me to marry him."

"Did you ever ask him to live with you?"

"No, because by the time I realized what a mistake I'd made, it was too late. This whole D-Day—this whole wedding had gotten completely out of hand."

"Well, what are you waiting for? Ask him now."

"Now?"

"Why not? Call him at the church." Her grandmother pointed to the telephone in the limousine.

"Mark would never agree after I humiliated him this way."

"You haven't humiliated him, and you don't know how he'll react until you give him a chance. Mark is the kindest and most understanding man I have ever met after your late Grandfather Blair. As far as I can tell, he has no false pride at all. He's seen too much of it in his father."

Lily saw Todd and Isabelle smiling and nodding at her. Sylvie, who could not understand the conversation but was caught up in her parents' enthusiasm, began smiling and nodding, too.

Todd whispered in French to his daughter, apparently

giving her instructions. Upon hearing them, Sylvie jumped off his lap and clapped her hands, delighted at having a part in the drama at last. She began speaking in French with mischievous gravity.

"Aunt Lily, my father says you should call up mon Oncle Marc on the telephone and tell him you love him."

Despite Sylvie's gale-force charm, Lily wavered. The idea that Mark might actually speak to her if she called him—let alone agree to live with her—was unbelievable.

Lily's grandmother smiled and took her hand again. "Don't worry. Lawyers settle cases on courthouse steps all the time. Mark is probably much more used to this sort of thing than you are."

At that moment, Lily saw Bill Schroeder walk toward the church with his wife, Pam. Wearing a pin-striped suit and sneakers, her boss approached the door from the right, then loped to the left, and jumped up to touch the lintel, as though executing a reverse lay-up shot. Lily envisioned him at her reception, trying to wrest better stadium seats from Mark's father or doing the Chicken Dance with full sound effects. The thought of having to repeat her vows in front of her boss was, in itself, almost enough to make her walk away from the wedding.

"But, but—I don't even know the number of the church. That's one of those details that my mother always took care of."

Her grandmother picked up the telephone and dialed 411. "Operator, I'd like the number of Holy Family Cathedral in Colony Heights," she said. She wrote the number on a tiny jeweled pad and handed it to Lily.

Sylvie, sensing what was happening, pointed happily to the telephone and exclaimed, *"Téléphone! Téléphone!"*

All Lily could think of was Jane Austen. Had she learned nothing from years of reading her favorite author?

For her thirteenth birthday she had received a leather-bound set of Austen's novels from her grandmother, and in fourteen years none of their lessons had sunk in. She would never be as resourceful as any of their heroines. Jane Austen had never failed her, but she had failed Jane Austen.

Lily sank back against the silver-gray upholstery.

"Elizabeth Bennet," she said, "would never have gotten herself into a situation like this. Elinor Dashwood would never—"

"Elizabeth Bennet might never have gotten herself into a situation like this, but if she had, she would have gotten herself out of it," her grandmother said briskly.

Helen Blair extended the phone toward her grand-daughter. Lily saw her brother smiling at her the way Darcy might have smiled at his sister, Georgianna. With a shaking hand, she dialed the number written on her grandmother's jeweled pad. Rev. McCardle answered on the first ring.

"Lily, where are you?" he asked. "Everybody is here waiting for you, and I just saw your parents in the narthex. I must say that your mother is showing something less than her usual self-possession."

"She'll be fine," Lily said. "I will be, too, I hope. I just need to talk to Mark. Is he there?"

"Certainly. One moment."

This will never work, Lily told herself as she waited for her fiancé to come on the line. Even if Mark still loved her after what she was about to say, he would not be able to forgive her for what she was about to do to him and to all his family and friends. She imagined his father arranging to project a retraction of his congratulations sign onto a screen at the stadium.

Mark, when he came on the line, sounded as though

he had never been so relieved to hear another voice. He said her mother had told him, a few minutes earlier, that the bridal party would be delayed but had refused to say more. She had spoken so cryptically that he had been afraid something had happened.

Then Lily said that something did happen.

"Mark, I love you . . ." she began.

38

Voluntary

"It was a very proper wedding. The bride was elegantly dressed—the two bridesmaids were duly inferior—"

—Mansfield Park

L ily had just explained to Mark why she did not want to marry him but wanted to live with him in New York when, incredulously, she saw what appeared to be the entire Ohio State marching band in the church parking lot. As they played "Carmen Ohio," the members of the band took up positions that spelled out "Mark + Lily 4 Ever."

Looking more closely at the group, Lily saw that it was not the Ohio State band but the Colony Heights High School band, imitating the famous OSU moving "Script" formation under the direction of Mark's father. But she was still so astonished by the sight that she missed part of what Mark was saying.

When she was again able to focus on it, she heard the organist playing a trumpet voluntary so loudly that it drowned out some of his words, and she caught only his last phrase.

". . . and so this is partly my fault."

Lily said that Mark was hardly at fault for what had happened while he was in California. But he insisted on claiming his share of blame. He said he had learned that she was thinking of calling off the wedding soon after arriving in Los Angeles. On the pretext of needing to discuss his Commodore's Club nomination, her father called him and broke the news but added that he thought his daughter was only working too hard and would change her mind if she had a rest. Perhaps if she flew out to California for a few days . . . ?

Mark said he became convinced that she was overworked when he saw her being pelted with almonds on the video of the gay-rights protest he got from his secretary. He had never seen her sound so frazzled, and that bruise on her forehead! That was why he had begged her to fly to California: He hoped that a few days on the beach, away from her mother, would restore her enthusiasm for the wedding.

Then, when his secretary faxed him the gossip column from *City Lights*, he became frantic with fear that she had fallen in love with someone else. He tried to accept her assurances that Nick Monford meant nothing to her. But ever since he came back from California, she had been acting so oddly that he couldn't shake the idea that she was hiding something. Now that he knew she wanted to live with him in New York, not to move five thousand miles away to marry Nick, he was overjoyed.

"But why didn't you tell me when you were in California that my father had told you I wanted to cancel the wedding?" Lily asked.

"Because he swore me to secrecy," Mark said. "Before

he gave me the news, he said he wanted to tell me something about you but made me promise to treat it as though it were covered by attorney-client privilege."

Mark laughed for the first time in the conversation. "It's your bad luck to have had both a father and a fiancé who are lawyers, two of the few people who might respect that sort of promise." Then he grew more serious. "I'm afraid that, during the trial, I didn't really want to know the truth. The case went so badly from the start that I couldn't bear the thought of losing you, too. Having to deal with Caroline made it that much worse. After a few days in L.A. I began to think that it would be worth moving to New York just so I wouldn't have to spend my life turning down her requests to go dancing on the night before a big trial. That Kayo Smith might become managing partner—and make me work on those malpractice-defense cases that he loves—was only part of my reason for wanting to leave."

As he finished speaking, Lily heard the organist begin the trumpet voluntary for the third or fourth time.

"Oh, Mark, what are we going to do now?"

"Well, we have to change planes in New York on our way to Paris, anyway. So maybe you'd like to stop off to see our new co-op? Or try to find another that's more to your taste?"

Lily said that she knew from the photographs that she would love the co-op on Central Park West. Then Mark asked about her work. Even if she loved the co-op, was she convinced that she wanted to move back to New York without a job?

"Actually, I may have a job soon," she said. "I began sending out job applications to New York editors after Bill Schroeder suspended me. But until I find something, I can freelance. Sally keeps telling me what a great investigative team she and I would make. She's always saying that every time she interviews an ax murderer, she wishes she were working with a partner."

Lily glanced out the window of the limousine and saw Tess Mahoney walking up the church steps on the arm of the lawyer she had been flirting with at the rehearsal dinner. "The big problem now is, what are we going to do about all the people in the church?" She looked sadly at her niece. "Poor Sylvie. She was so looking forward to being a flower girl, and she's been such a dear, she deserves her reward."

Lily saw Todd whisper to Isabelle, then to his daughter, with all of them grinning. When he stopped speaking, Sylvie tugged gently on her wedding gown. "Aunt Lily, my father says he and my mother will get married in the church."

"What?" Lily said. Then she said quickly, "Mark, could you hold on a minute?"

Lily covered the mouthpiece of the phone, and Todd said that because Isabelle had always wanted to have a big wedding, they were willing to take her and Mark's places if the two of them would be maid of honor and best man. She and Isabelle were almost the same size—they could exchange dresses at the cathedral.

"Now that's the best idea I've heard all day," said Lily's grandmother, smiling. "Although, I'm afraid, it's a long way from Jane Austen."

Lily returned to the telephone and told Mark that Todd and Isabelle wanted to take their places in the ceremony.

At first, he did not appear to understand what she had said. "Sweetheart, it won't be legal. No court in the country would recognize that marriage if they don't have a license, and there's no way they could get one now."

"Mark, you're forgetting, they're already legally married.

They had a civil ceremony in France. It's just that Isabelle
always wanted to have the big church wedding that she
missed when they eloped."

Mark took a moment to let this sink in. "Okay, Todd
and Isabelle are getting married instead of us," he said
slowly, as though still not quite grasping what he had
heard.

"Yes, Isabelle and I are going to trade dresses at the
church, and you and I will be best man and maid of
honor." Lily took her niece's hand. "And Sylvie is going to
be a flower girl. Now, all you need to do is explain everything to Rev. McCardle and to our parents."

A few minutes later, the limousine pulled up to the
church, and through the open doors Lily could hear that
the organist had switched from the trumpet voluntary to
"The Marseillaise." Upon hearing the French national an-
them Sylvie beamed. *"Allons, enfants de la patrie . . ."* she
sang. Sylvie stopped and explained that she was an *enfant*.

"Yes, you are an extremely good *enfant*," Helen Blair
said, speaking tenderly to her great-granddaughter in
French.

Isabelle glowed. "Sylvie is a very well-elevated little girl,
non?" She added that Sylvie would be a perfect "girl of
the flowers" in her wedding. "All the time, when we take
her to church, she never derange anybody."

Lily was delighted to see Isabelle so happy about the
wedding because she doubted that her sister-in-law would
understand a fraction of the vows she was about to say.
For a moment, she considered trying to explain to the
bride-to-be the finer points of "troth," "asunder," and
"God's holy ordinance."

Then Mark, who was waiting for her at a side entrance
to the church, ran to her and swept her up in his arms,
and Lily decided that Isabelle could do without the En-

glish lesson. It was true that her sister-in-law might miss the nuances of a few "betwixts" or "hereafters." But Lily decided that if ever there was a time just to allow herself to be swept along on a tide of joy, she had found it. The last thing she heard before she walked down the aisle as Isabelle's maid of honor was a familiar voice giving orders to a bridesmaid, who ignored it with the impeccable politeness that was due to the mother of the groom.

Acknowledgments

Johann Sebastian Bach ended many of his musical scores with SDG, for *Soli Deo Gloria*, To God Alone the Glory. In the same spirit, I would nonetheless like to express my debt to a number of others, particularly Bob Wyatt, Abigail Rose, and Flip Brophy, who brought this novel to life. Words cannot express my gratitude to them.

For other acts of grace and kindness toward this book or work that preceded it, I would like to thank Amy Margaret Greenberg, Marianne Jacobbi and Barry Lydgate, Dr. Henry M. Lerner, Tim Page, Jo Ann Pallant, Susan and Bill Samuelson, and Jim Zafris. If knowing how to support writers is an art, in very different ways these friends have been among the Rembrandts of my life.

I also want to say, once again, how much I owe to two wonderful teachers, Eunice Davidson and Donald M. Murray, whose influence has blessed generations of high school and college students.

And let perpetual light shine upon my parents, grandparents, and godparents: Marel Boyer Harayda, John Harayda Jr., Helen Juhasz Haster Harayda, John Harayda Sr., Elsie Fraser Boyer Birdsall, Karl Boyer, Henrietta Haster Gantner, and Matthew V. Pietrucha.

About the Author

JANICE HARAYDA is an award-winning journalist who spent eleven years as the book editor of a major metropolitan daily newspaper. She has been a staff writer and editor for *Glamour*, editorial director of *Boston* magazine, and a contributor to many national magazines and newspapers. A vice president of the National Book Critics Circle, she lives in Princeton, New Jersey. This is her first novel.

THE ONE-CENT MAGENTA

THE
ONE-CENT
MAGENTA

*Inside the Quest
to Own the Most Valuable Stamp
in the World*

JAMES BARRON

ALGONQUIN BOOKS
OF CHAPEL HILL
2017

Published by
ALGONQUIN BOOKS OF CHAPEL HILL
Post Office Box 2225
Chapel Hill, North Carolina 27515-2225

a division of
WORKMAN PUBLISHING
225 Varick Street
New York, New York 10014

Library of Congress Cataloging-in-Publication Data
Names: Barron, James, [date] author.
Title: The one-cent magenta : inside the quest to own
the most valuable stamp in the world / James Barron.
Description: First edition. | Chapel Hill, North Carolina :
Algonquin Books of Chapel Hill, 2017. | "Published simultaneously
in Canada by Thomas Allen & Son Limited."
Identifiers: LCCN 2016038074 | ISBN 9781616205188
Subjects: LCSH: Rare postage stamps — Guyana — History. |
Stamp collectors — Biography. | Stamp collecting — History.
Classification: LCC HE6184.R3 B37 2017 | DDC 769.569881 — dc23
LC record available at https://lccn.loc.gov/2016038074

10 9 8 7 6 5 4 3 2 1
First Edition

Once again
to
Jane

———•———

CONTENTS

———◆———

THE ONE-CENT MAGENTA

ONE

STAMP WORLD

My improbable descent into Stamp World started at a cocktail party that had nothing to do with stamps.

It was in one of those Stanford White private clubs in New York City that was built at a cost of something like a million-plus in the days when something like a million-plus was real money. This was a party for a first-time author whose murder mystery had just been published. He is the younger brother of someone I went to college with. Their father is an author. Their mother was an author. The guy from college published a book that won an award. The brother, a Wall Street type I'd never met, had finally done what everyone else in the family had been doing for years.

What a place for a book party. The Palladian arch just past the front door that you had to walk under—perfectly proportioned. The black-and-white checkerboard floor in the lobby that you had to walk across—immense. The larger-than-life portrait of none other than J.P. Morgan— did I pass him on the way up the marble staircase, or just imagine it?

The party itself was in a basketball-court-size room on the second floor. The ceiling danced with cherubs or horses or celestial who-knows-what. I was early—my college classmate hadn't arrived yet—so I marched across the antique carpet to the only person I recognized.

"David!" I said. "What are you up to now?"

It no doubt sounded like, "What have you done for me lately," because that was exactly what I meant—and he knew it. David N. Redden always has something in the works with the makings of a feature for a newspaper reporter like me. I had written about him before. Little did I know what another round of journalistic recidivism would lead to.

Redden answered by saying that he was about to sell an old postage stamp, but some stamp collectors in London might want to dip it in benzene, and that would be a problem.

He was not talking about just any old postage stamp. Redden never dealt with just any old thing. He trafficked in superlatives—the rarest this, the most expensive that. He was an auctioneer at Sotheby's. He had sold everything from Jacqueline Kennedy Onassis's belongings to a *Tyrannosaurus rex* fossil. He had sold the Duke and Duchess of Windsor's furniture, and one of the pianos from the movie *Casablanca*. There were two. Of all the pianos from all the gin joints in all the towns in the world, this one went for $602,500.

He also sold the first book printed in North America, for $14 million. Twice he sold the same copy of the Declaration of Independence, one of twenty-five from a batch printed in July 1776. The second time, in 2000, it went for $7.4 million; the first time, in 1991, for $2.2 million. That sounds like an impressive profit until you learn that, before that first auction, it had changed hands for $4 at a flea market. The buyer didn't even know he was getting it. It was hidden behind a second-rate painting in an undistinguished frame.

Redden told me that his latest rarity was the one-cent magenta from British Guiana. He read the blank look on my face and all but rolled his eyes, as if to say, "How could you not know about the one-cent magenta from

British Guiana?" He insisted that every schoolboy knows about the one-cent magenta from British Guiana: "quite simply," he announced, exuberantly, "the rarest stamp in the world." He predicted that it would become the most expensive stamp in the world when he sold it in a couple of months.

I would soon learn that the one-cent magenta was issued in 1856, and that until the mass suicide of Jim Jones and his Peoples Temple followers in 1978, it was what the country now called Guyana was known for. This tiny thing was certainly its most famous single export.

That was my introduction to Stamp World, an arcane parallel universe peopled by collectors who are crazed and crazy, obsessed and obsessive. Stamp World exists for something that's practically obsolete—who sends old-fashioned mail when you can post and share on Facebook, Twitter, and Instagram? In our instant-message, Snapchat age, stamps are untrendy and unchic (and unneeded, thanks to scannable barcodes). Stamps are what they have always been: quiet, orderly, proper. And it's certainly true that some stamp collectors are stuffy, stiff-upper-lip types—a high-energy, high-testosterone bunch they are not. "Get ready to freak out, stamp collectors (or, you know, get as excited as you ever get)," *Time* magazine joked in reporting the sale of the one-cent magenta in 2014, after, as Redden had forecast, it became the most expensive stamp in the world. The *Globe and Mail* of Toronto made stamp collecting sound less like a hobby and more like a hang-up. Stamp collectors, it said, inhabit "a fetishistic underworld with little bits of printed paper [that] people licked."

Yes. Well. Welcome to Stamp World.

Stamp World has its celebrities. John Lennon's boyhood stamp album can be seen at the National Postal Museum in Washington. Freddie Mercury of the British rock band Queen was a stamp collector, as was the violinist Jascha Heifetz. The aviator Amelia Earhart, the novelist James Michener, the undersea explorer Jacques Cousteau, and the actor Bela Lugosi, of Dracula fame—stamp collectors all. The tennis star Maria Sharapova is one, too, but she did not sound happy when it became known. "Everyone's calling me a dork now," she said. "I mean, it's just a hobby."

Stamp World delights in catching mistakes: stamps with three horses but only eleven legs, or three men with only five legs. Or the collector on a commemorative stamp honoring stamp collectors who has six fingers on one hand. Or a stamp with a woman and a bald eagle. It's a patriotic image—Neoclassical, even. She's naked. But what gets their attention in Stamp World is that one of her feet has only four toes.

That stamp collectors are known as philatelists does not help. *Smithsonian* magazine's website peppered an article about the etymology of that word with lines like, "Get your mind out of the gutter." *Fowler's Modern English Usage* kept a straight face but lamented that stamp collecting had been burdened with an esoteric-sounding, difficult-to-pronounce term: "It is a pity that for one of the most popular . . . pursuits, one of the least popularly intelligible names should have been found," adding that the word is "irksome to most of our ears."

A dictionary dive only deepened the frustration. I looked in the *Oxford English Dictionary*, which has a stake in all this because its first editor was a philatelist as well as a philologist. The entry for *philatelist* appears, tellingly, after *philargyry*, a love of money, and before *philautia*, a love of oneself.

Some psychoanalysts might insist that philatelists cannot live without one and are driven by the other. And some philatelists love the Post Office much too much. W. Reginald Bray, a turn-of-the-twentieth-century British eccentric, was gleefully enamored of the Post Office. But, as his biographer John Tingey noted, the people at the Post Office were probably less enamored of him, considering the trouble he put them through. He mailed himself. Not once but twice. The first time, he stuck a stamp on his head. The second time, he splurged and sent himself home by registered mail. Bray's house wasn't far from the local post office—the postage was less than a taxi ride would have cost. A bicycle messenger was assigned to deliver him. The messenger happily exacted some revenge. He walked to Bray's house after putting Bray on the bike and telling him to start pedaling.

In Stamp World, I would learn that the one-cent magenta is an accidental icon. It was not supposed to be so special. It was an improvisation, a quick-and-smudgy solution in a nineteenth-century British colony that dispensed stamps printed in London. But sometimes, your ship doesn't come in. When a shipment of 100,000 stamps did not arrive at the dock as scheduled, the local postmaster in British Guiana commissioned a local newspaper to print "provisional" stamps in two denominations. The four-cent stamps were for letters. The one-cent stamps were for periodicals like the newspaper itself. Nobody knows how many were printed, but they only needed enough stamps to last until the next boat arrived with the real thing.

To some collectors, the one-cent magenta is the *Mona Lisa* of stamps, but its face has no face, just a workmanlike image of a schooner and a Latin motto that is usually translated as, "We give and we take in return." Until Redden sent it on a pre-auction tour of libraries and museums a couple of months before the cocktail party, it had not been seen in public since the mid-1980s. It had not been displayed outside of a stamp show since the New York World's Fair in 1940, when it arrived in an armored car, a clever promotional gimmick that a later owner would copy. Once it disappeared at a collectors' convention. Detectives issued all-points bulletins and wondered which philatelic Houdini had made off with it. But it had not been stolen. It had slipped from its mooring and gone on the shortest of trips, drifting for a moment before putting in at the bottom of its own display case.

For all the fuss, the one-cent magenta is not much to look at. In the 1990s, the editor of *American Philatelist* magazine called it the ugliest stamp he had ever seen. That was fifty years after the writer Alvin F. Harlow described it as "a shoddy-looking thing." Another stamp writer mentioned it, but not in his chapter titled "The Postage Stamp as a Work of Art." In the 1960s, L.N. and Maurice Williams, two brothers from Britain who wrote more than thirty books about stamps and stamp collecting, said it was "unsatisfactory to the aesthete."

It is no more satisfactory now. When the one-cent magenta went on display at the Smithsonian's National Postal Museum in 2015, *Smithsonian* magazine's website, bravely telling it like it is, reported that seeing the one-cent magenta in person was "a bit like looking at a red-wine stain or a receipt that's been through the wash a few times." The corners of the one-cent magenta have been clipped off, and it tricks your eye at first glance: Is it square? No. It's three millimeters wider than it is tall, such a slight difference that you have to squint to be certain (and look up the dimensions, just to be sure).

Would anyone in British Guiana have imagined that anyone would ever sit around trying to figure out how many one-cent magentas it would take to cover the real *Mona Lisa*? I did some math. Depending on whose measurements I used, the answer was between 520 and 600, more one-cent magentas than probably ever existed. Five hundred forty-one little stamps would not add much heft to the *Mona Lisa*'s canvas, and at a championship weigh-in, the single one-cent magenta would barely register on the scale. A breeze would carry it off. A breath the strength of a happy-birthday candle blowout would send it soaring (and its handlers panicking, as they did at that stamp show).

But the one-cent magenta has a complexion problem. It's not really ruby or bordello red. I saw it when it was waiting in the wings before Redden sold it, and it was the dull color of dried blood at a crime scene. And then, when it was carried into the spotlight, its red deepened—it's a chameleon, changing in new surroundings.

So what color is it? I called color experts who can tell what shade of white the White House is. Frank H. Mahnke, the president of the International Association of Color Consultants/Designers' executive committee, told me it was a mixture of red and purple.

That is why he did what he did. He could see something in the one-cent magenta that I did not.

I printed a picture of the one-cent magenta and took it to a paint store down the block from where I live. There I asked a color consultant named Ferne Maibrunn to find the color closest to the one-cent's magenta. From among the thousands of paint strips in little holders on the walls, she picked out a shade called "Chili Pepper" after rejecting "Rosy Blush" as too pink.

She asked how the stamp had been printed. By then, I was deep enough in Stamp World to answer,

"Amateurishly." I told her that the font was ordinary, the ink unevenly applied.

I had learned that, like the *Mona Lisa*, the one-cent magenta has its mysteries. Was it always that color, or was it colorized later in life, like an MGM movie? And the back of the stamp is a mystery all its own. It is reddish pink—not the magenta of the front, but not the usual creamy white you find on the reverse side of a stamp. It carries the markings of past owners, a custom in philately. Some signed their initials. But how did it get the unusual-looking wheel-like star on the back?

And if that's not enough to sustain a whodunit, there is the biggest mystery of all: Several hundred one-cent magentas must have come off the press, probably in sheets with four stamps on each page, so why haven't any others turned up? Where was the one-cent magenta for the first sixteen years after it was issued? David Redden understood the importance of raising questions like these, even if he couldn't answer them before the auction, or ever. But to create interest, he had to play detective as well as salesman.

Unlike the famous Inverted Jenny—the 1918 stamp that was mistakenly printed with a biplane upside down—the one-cent magenta is not just rare, it is unique. There are a hundred Inverted Jennies. There is only one one-cent magenta. Lately it has changed hands only once in a generation, leaving some who had the means to buy it—but whose timing was off—panting at the lack of an opportunity to part with their cash. For most of its life, it remained safely out of sight, locked in bank vaults or on a shelf in the palace that is now the official residence of the prime minister of France. Once it got out of British Guiana, it did not go slumming.

It had a presence, a personality. One owner called it the "big baby." Another referred to it by a more romantic-sounding term, the "magenta lady." Redden, while not an owner, possessed it for a while—on consignment, of course. As its custodian, he thought about how it affected those who did own it, even as he himself became the latest character in the life of this stamp, and there had been some characters. Among them was its last owner, John E. du Pont, who, besides being an heir to the chemical fortune, was a collector's collector. Long before he bought the one-cent magenta, he had amassed sixty million shells, two million birds, and thousands of stamps. He once slept with the one-cent magenta under his pillow in a hotel when the staff could not open the safe for him. He even paid a broker who dealt in such things to put his picture on a stamp from Redonda, a "micro-nation" in the Caribbean, really an uninhabited island that was named by Christopher Columbus in 1493 and later mined for fertilizer.

Intriguing as they were, those details about du Pont were largely forgotten when he died in 2010. Most of the obituaries about him began by saying he had shot a famous wrestler—Dave Schultz, an Olympic gold medalist who had lived and trained on du Pont's Pennsylvania estate—and was serving a thirty-year sentence for third-degree murder. The obituaries did not report that two hours before the shooting, he was in a stamp store, shopping. I talked to the sales clerk who waited on him—who assumed, when he heard there was trouble at du Pont's estate, that du Pont was the victim, not the gunman. Nor did the stories about his death say that he had tried to use the one-cent magenta as his get-out-of-jail card, offering it to the National Postal Museum in return for a pardon. ("I said, 'How can I get him a pardon? He's in jail for life,'" the museum's director, Allen R. Kane, told me.)

Before du Pont, the owner of the one-cent magenta was a man who traveled with the stamp in a briefcase he handcuffed to his wrist.

Before *him* was the upholstery and seat-cover manufacturer with wife trouble. She deprived him of his final wish, which was to deprive *her* of the one-cent magenta. But Arthur Hind left behind the one anecdote about the one-cent magenta that everybody remembers. Later, deep in Stamp World, I would read the original version in the yellowing pages of a long-defunct stamp magazine that published an anonymous letter accusing Hind of buying a second one-cent magenta for one reason—to destroy it, preserving the uniqueness of *his* stamp. But there wasn't much in the letter that Redden left out when he told it at the cocktail party.

"According to the story," Redden said, "he lit a cigar and used the same match to light the stamp and burn it. Part of the delight of the story is the cigar and the plutocrat. The image that creates in one's mind is indelible. Nobody knows if it's true."

Redden also told me at the cocktail party that he wanted to have this one-cent magenta "expertized" in London. Redden is the son of an American diplomat and spent much of his childhood in London, and he pronounced it the British way, or so I assumed—"exper-teased." But there was, um, a negotiation. He said this with an inflection that conveyed the notion of "a problem."

And then he said the negotiation was about the benzene.

I laughed.

Benzene—the word, not the chemical itself—was a madeleine. Almost any mention of benzene that hasn't exploded and hurt or killed somebody brings back a memory of the apartment I lived in when I was a year out of college. It was a find: spacious, distinctive, and almost affordable, and the brownstone next door belonged to a man with a thunderous Orson Welles–like voice. He said that when he was in the OSS in World War II and assigned to drive the magazine publisher Henry Luce around, he had made up the answers to every question Luce asked—and that, in time, every made-up answer appeared in *Time*.

That left me wondering what to believe when he began insisting that my landlord was storing benzene in the basement in a fifty-five gallon drum. Whenever we ran into each other, the neighbor would talk about the benzene in the basement and how it was going to blow us all up. Sometimes, after a particularly dramatic pause, he would whisper, "To smithereens." He had Welles' profundity, Welles's gravitas, and in my mind, "benzene" became the takeaway, the "Rosebud" of West Seventy-fifth Street.

Nobody really keeps benzene in the basement, right? But there are alligators in the sewers, aren't there? Why not benzene in the basement?

Hearing Redden say "benzene" took me back not to childhood, as "Rosebud" did for Charles Foster Kane, but to that moment of absurdity in my early twenties—and, inevitably, to other memories from those days, when, it seemed, you could still keep track of the world in time-honored ways. It was a world with newspapers, though not as many as there once were, and television networks, though not as many as there soon would be. And it was still a world with old-fashioned stamps.

But now "benzene" was carrying me to a new place, Stamp World. Redden's mention of benzene would send me hunting down the story of the one-cent magenta—and the resourcefulness of the local postmaster who commissioned it, the charming boyhood dreams of the men who chased after it, and the fulfillment, as adults, for the few who owned it, including du Pont, who bought it sixteen years before he shot Dave Schultz.

Redden didn't see anything funny about my benzene story. Of course he didn't. He was preoccupied with getting what he wanted, a certificate from the Royal Philatelic Society London attesting to the stamp's authenticity. The Royal, as it is known, is the world's foremost body of stamp collectors. On questions of whether a stamp is what it appears to be, the Royal has had the final say for generations. It was the Royal that had vouched for the one-cent magenta in the 1930s. And, in the 1990s, when another one-cent magenta was discovered in Romania, it was the Royal that declared the second one-cent magenta to be bogus.

For Redden, the issue was whether officials of the Royal would insist on dunking the one-cent magenta in benzene, which, he said, stamp collectors sometimes do when they want to check the paper on which a stamp was printed. A benzene bath, really little more than a dip in a few drops of the stuff, would show more than watermarks on the paper that are hard to see any other way. If a stamp had been tampered with, the ink would run and the fake markings would disappear. The risk of dipping a one-of-a-kind stamp in what is basically lighter fluid is that, authentic or not, it could be destroyed. Dunk. Poof. No more stamp.

It was not a risk Redden could afford. Not if he was to sell the stamp for at least $10 million.

TWO

TRAVELS WITH DAVID

———◆———

David Redden is a master of the aristocratic soft sell, urbane and airily entertaining in his pinstripe suits, shuttling between potential sellers and potential buyers, operating quietly, stoking interest. He arranged the Magna Carta auction so quietly that Sotheby's did not tell its own employees why it was rescheduling other auctions. James Zemaitis, the director of Sotheby's 20th-century design department, was asked to give up a room at Sotheby's headquarters that he had reserved for a pre-auction exhibition of his own. "All they told me was: 'David Redden is selling this really important document, the most important document of all. Can you give up this room for us?'" he recalled. "'And I'm like, 'Sure, but what is he selling, the Magna Carta?'"

Redden was thrilled to be selling the one-cent magenta. "I was born a collector," he said in a voice that masks ambition, determination, and, sometimes, the extreme patience needed to convince the owners of some rare object to part with it. He told me that he spent years courting the elders of the Boston church that owned the Bay Psalm Book, the first bound volume printed in the North American colonies. In 2013 it became the most expensive book ever sold at auction, when he gaveled down a bid of $14.165 million (equivalent to $14.4 million today).

How much effort he had to put into corralling the one-cent magenta is unclear. Redden said he approached Taras M. Wochok, John E. du Pont's lawyer, who was charged with selling du Pont's holdings after he died in prison. Redden told me that he pursued the one-cent magenta because of the emotional pull. He had collected stamps when he was a boy.

When I told Wochok about that, he said flatly, "We called him."

Later I would also learn that no one uses benzene in authenticating stamps anymore. And that every schoolboy does not know about the stamp he was pursuing.

That pursuit took Redden to Pennsylvania to inspect the one-cent magenta in the bank vault where it had lain during du Pont's years in prison—and take it away, on consignment. It was mounted on an album page. Redden realized how unlikely the scene was: five or six people—Redden, Wochok, a couple of bank employees, and a couple of assistants—were hunched over a dot of paper, the rarest stamp in the world. Redden told me later that he had been "terrified of damaging it in some way" as he prepared a condition report, a routine auction-house document describing an item that was anything but routine. "You're looking at a tiny, tiny slip of paper which is worth millions of dollars with the obvious concern that any little scratch or nick is highly consequential," Redden said.

Gently, Redden put the stamp in a box that he had brought along, and put the box in his briefcase. He walked out of the bank and climbed into a car-service car that drove him to the 30th Street Station in Philadelphia, where he boarded a train for New York, accompanied by a security guard.

• • •

Redden went to London a few weeks later for one reason. He wanted a piece of paper about the piece of paper in his briefcase—the one-cent magenta. He got the piece of paper he wanted in an afternoon, far faster than anyone thought he would. What it said, though, was more than he wanted. With its careful language, that piece of paper would put experts on one side of the Atlantic at odds with experts on the other—and cause headaches for Redden later on.

Redden traveled light, as he usually does. He carried nothing more than his briefcase and a small suitcase with a change of clothes. At John F. Kennedy International Airport in New York, he stowed the briefcase above his seat and settled in. A couple of hours later, as the plane bucked against the late-winter wind above the North Atlantic, he realized that the in-flight movie was about an elaborate caper to steal $20 million—Ridley Scott's thriller *The Counselor*, about a corrupt Texas lawyer and a drug cartel. Redden chuckled at the thought that, right there on the plane, he had something in his briefcase that could be worth that much.

Only one other person on the plane knew that: the taciturn guy in the seat across the aisle, the security guard Sotheby's had hired to safeguard the stamp (as well as Redden).

The nine people with the power to issue the piece of paper Redden wanted were eager to see the one-cent magenta, if only to be able to say they had examined something that had been out of view for so long. These nine people were the Expert Committee of the Royal Philatelic Society London, a best-of-the-best group that gathers about nine times a year to pass judgment on stamps. The Royal traces its roots to a stamp group founded in 1869 and is a peculiarly British institution; both eccentricity and good manners are the norm in its corridors. The Royal's library is a haven for active-duty research. Some of the books on its shelves are scarcer than a rare stamp. It has writing tables and dark wood, and as they enter, visitors might suspect that they are crossing the threshold of a private club.

But the Royal's members know that appearances could backfire on them. They know that an outsider could see them as cantankerous, wacky, and quaint types with bad teeth whose lives are invested in obscure books like *Swaziland Philately to 1968* or *Sudan: The Postal Markings, 1867–1970*. They know how lucky they were that *Monty Python's Flying Circus* did not mock the Royal the way it mocked so much else in British life.

Perhaps that is why the Royal had a "mission statement" that read, "We may be venerable . . . but we are not stuffy." Still, the Royal's history is formidable. Its president from 1896 to 1910 was the Duke of York (who was also the

Prince of Wales from 1901 on). The historian David Cannadine writes that the Duke of York had been pointed toward philately when he was in his thirties by his uncle, the Duke of Edinburgh, who sold his own stamp collection to his brother, who was the Prince of Wales at the time and was known in the royal family as "Bertie." And Bertie passed the stamps along to his son, the Duke of York. Another biographer, John Gore, wrote that "it was in this hobby that he found the most effective means" of escape from World War I. He was serious about philately and serious about not being disturbed while he was tending to his stamps. "For some thirty years or more, whenever in London he devoted around three afternoons a week to his collection," according to a monograph from the Royal Philatelic Collection. He "is said to have been interrupted by his page on only two or three occasions."

He was the royal who was a regular at the Royal. He attended the society's meetings and once read a paper on "postal issues of the United Kingdom during the present reign," the reign at that moment being Bertie's, who was King Edward VII. The society reported that he "showed a most interesting and valuable display of essays, proofs and specimens."

He relinquished his position with the Royal to take

on a somewhat larger one, as King George V, but his passion for stamps did not diminish with his ascension to the throne. The biographer Kenneth Rose wrote that "courtiers . . . were pressed into service" to track down stamps and send them back to London. Rose quoted a note from one royal attendant to another: "The King is delighted to hear that you are endeavouring to pinch as many stamps for him as you can during your travels." During World War I, a young diplomat named Harold Nicolson was assigned to obtain a rare batch of stamps on which the word "Levant" had been misprinted. Nicolson—who was elected to the House of Commons after quitting the Foreign Office and who later proved to be a prolific author, turning out everything from political disquisitions to murder mysteries—thought that he (and the king) had more important things to do while the Tommies were in the trenches. Nicolson dismissed stamps as "mere scraps of paper" and complained in his *Diaries and Letters*, published in the mid-1960s, that for years "George V did nothing at all but kill animals and stick in stamps."

One young diplomat even worried that stamps could kill the king. After a case of smallpox was reported in a Mideast printing plant, Rose wrote that the anxious attaché was scared that "the royal tongue might be contaminated," presumably if George V licked the stamps, which he was unlikely to do. Still, the diplomat "assiduously boiled his entire offering of four hundred stamps in a saucepan" before sending them to London. Reading about the episode when I was deep in Stamp World, I imagined the diplomat reciting the witches' chant from *Macbeth*. But he probably landed in hot water himself, if only briefly. Sterilizing stamps in a stove-top cauldron would be as destructive as the benzene dip that would so trouble Redden in 2014.

While still the Duke of York, the would-be king had acquired the penny and two-pence Post Office Mauritius stamps of 1847, the first stamps issued by a colonial post office. That fact is often mentioned in the same breath as a delightful anecdote as dubious as the one about Arthur Hind and the cigar: The Duke was asked if he had heard that "some damned fool" had paid £1,400 for one of those stamps. "Yes," he said. "I was that damned fool."

The Royal celebrated King George's jubilee in 1935 as only it could, with an exhibition of seven hundred pages of rarities assembled by ninety of its members. The Royal still enthusiastically describes it as "the greatest gathering of rare material of the British Empire to be shown together in a single exhibition."

For all the pride the members radiated as they hung their pages on the Royal's display boards and all the pomp and pageantry that went with the king's tour, there was one stamp that he did not see: the one-cent magenta. It would not arrive until several months after his death, and then only for the same kind of validation that Redden would seek nearly eighty years later. Indeed, it was the Expert Committee's verdict in the fall of 1935 that set the stage for the stamp's return, in Redden's briefcase, in the spring of 2014.

One person on the Expert Committee in 1935 had examined the one-cent magenta decades earlier, before the Expert Committee had even been established. The British philatelic pioneer Sir Edward Denny Bacon had confirmed the stamp's one-of-a-kind status in 1891. That would complicate the Expert Committee's work later on, because anyone who questioned the stamp's authenticity would be questioning the authority of one of the Royal's most respected members.

Bacon had a nose for forgeries. He had been so troubled by the proliferation of fake stamps in the 1890s that he had proposed setting up the Expert Committee to decide what was real and what was not. He even made the use of technology, such as it was in the late nineteenth century, a part of the Expert Committee's mandate, directing the committee to photograph each and every specimen it analyzed.

But the one-cent magenta was not photographed in 1891 because it didn't officially go before the committee. Bacon saw it in Paris, where it resided at the time. The question was whether it was genuine. "Doubts have more than once been expressed about the 'face' value of this stamp," Sir Edward wrote, "but after a most careful inspection, I have no hesitation whatever in pronouncing it a thoroughly genuine specimen." But in the next sentence of his account, Sir Edward created a problem for later Expert Committees: he recorded that it was "somewhat rubbed," which left open the possibility that it had been altered. That possibility would plague the stamp for generations. Even after World War II, the collector Maurice Burrus argued that the one-cent magenta had been created from a somewhat less rare four-cent stamp. In other words, someone had "doctored" the stamp."

Sir Edward, though, was adamant: "This was never done," he declared.

There is no way to know what Sir Edward himself believed was the cause of the "rubbing"—he didn't say—but in 1935, Sir John Wilson was well aware of Burrus's claim and "took extreme precautions in vetting the specimen." He had it photographed by Colonel W.R. Mansfield, another stalwart of the Royal. Wilson wrote that he "warned Colonel Mansfield of the suggestion that the 'FOUR CENTS' label could have been altered, and [Mansfield] was very definitely of the opinion that no such thing had been done." Wilson reached the same conclusion after a close look at the little stamp: "[T]he magenta-surface paper of British Guiana is material extremely difficult to handle from the faker's point of view," he wrote, "and it is quite impossible to take out a letter, alter two more, take out another letter and, what Monsieur Burrus seems to have forgotten, the full point after it, without creating tremendous abrasion of the surface which should readily be observed by any trained eye[.]" The stamp had to be the real thing.

Redden was determined to have the Expert Committee repeat that finding.

First, though, he took the stamp to the one place in London that mattered more than the Royal: a room in St. James's Palace, built by Henry VIII as he was breaking with the Roman Catholic Church and establishing a more flexible alternative so he could divorce and remarry as he pleased. Inside St. James's, over two fireplaces, are the initials 'HA,' for Henry VIII and Anne Boleyn. This is where she spent the night of her coronation.

Prince Charles (the Prince of Wales) and the Duchess of Cornwall (the former Camilla Parker Bowles) live within the grounds of St. James's. Its Chapel Royal is where Prince William paid his last respects to his mother, Princess Diana, in 1997, and where William's son, Prince George, was baptized in 2013. And that's only the recent history.

But St. James's is considered a "working palace," with offices for the Royal Household. The Marshal of the Diplomatic Corps works there (and the United States ambassador to the United Kingdom is, officially, the ambassador to the Court of St. James's). The Yeomen of the Guard have their headquarters there. And it is home to the Royal Philatelic Collection, the most complete collection of British postage stamps in the world. The albums contain every stamp ever issued by Great Britain and its colonies except one—the one-cent magenta.

So, for a few hours on a blustery March day, the Queen's collection was complete.

And it *is* the Queen's collection. The crown jewels, the artwork, and furnishings in the royal palaces, from the chandeliers to the china, are all owned by a royal charitable trust. The stamp collection is owned personally by the monarch and has been for generations. Prince Charles might well inherit the stamps on his mother's death, assuming he succeeds her, just as she inherited them from her father, King George VI, who inherited them from his father, King George V. But she could leave the collection to the royal trust or to the British Library.

The writer David McClure, the author of the first full-length book on the royal family's wealth in twenty years, estimated in 2015 that the philatelic holdings were worth £10 million, or about $14.8 million. But he noted that some estimates put their value as high as £100 million, which would amount to more than a third of the royal net-worth statement.

The philatelic assets are impressive, whatever they are worth. George V's stamps are kept in 328 red album, George VI's in more than a hundred blue boxes. The stamps issued since the coronation of Queen Elizabeth II are in green albums and green boxes.

One reason for Redden's visit to the palace was to compare the one-cent magenta with some of the four-cent stamps from British Guiana in the Royal Philatelic Collection. Michael Sefi, the keeper of the Royal Philatelic Collection, told me that he had never seen the actual one-cent until Redden walked in.

Sefi told me he was surprised to learn, from me, that Redden was an American. Redden's plummy voice and pleasantly formal manner seemed so British that they did not talk about American sitcoms—Sefi remains partial to *Friends*, which Redden had never watched—or major league baseball in the United States. Redden is no fan, but Sefi has been devoted to the St. Louis Cardinals since 1987, when the World Series was carried on television in Britain and the Cardinals lost by one game. Sefi told me that clinched "the notorious British affection for the underdog." He is so passionate about the team that he took time off in the spring of 2016 to fly to St. Louis for a seven-game home stand.

Redden told me that they spent a few hours comparing it to other stamps "and, I think, satisfying [Sefi's] own curiosity to look at this stamp." Sefi said he was surprised that another one-cent magenta had never turned up, just as there has never been a single two-cent rose from 1851. Ten copies of that stamp exist, but all are in pairs on cover. (In Stamp World, "on cover" usually means on an envelope.)

But studying stamps was not Redden's only purpose in going to see Sefi. He was making a sales call. Redden is discreet, and Sefi would not discuss their conversation with me either, but Redden did not need to be explicit.

Sefi knew that in ninety days, the one-cent magenta
would be available. Perhaps Sefi would consider bidding?

"There's always something we'd quite like if it would
come on the market," Sefi told me later. "That's the nature of collecting, isn't it?" But he had heard the rumors
that the Royal Philatelic Collection bid for the one-cent
magenta at Redden's auction, and he tamped them down:
"We did not."

• • •

Redden breezed into the Royal a couple of days later and
hit a speed bump.

The Expert Committee's command post is down a narrow corridor with old floorboards that creak beneath blue
carpeting. Behind an unmarked door is a long, L-shaped
room dominated by a conference table that is useful for
spreading out pages from stamp albums. Leather-bound
albums fill the shelves against the walls: albums for actual stamps from the British Empire, albums for mere
photographs of stamps from the British Empire, albums
for stamps from the rest of the world, and albums for
stamps determined to be forgeries. The Royal keeps the
forgeries, just in case a forger is dumb enough to try the
same caper twice.

The Expert Committee is the Supreme Court of

stamps: it handles only the most important cases, about three thousand a year, and like the Supreme Court, it keeps no official notes of its deliberations. There the comparisons to jurists in long black robes end. The members of the Expert Committee are unpaid volunteers, which means that they tend to be retired or semi-retired people. The workload is punishing, requiring detailed research before each of the committee's meetings. Someone with a day job would surely fall behind, and that would be noticed—and whispered about.

No one really questioned the authenticity of the one-cent magenta as Redden opened his briefcase and laid it on the conference table; its years in du Pont's safe-deposit box were well documented. For the Expert Committee, the next few hours were about scholarship, and probably bragging rights—"I held the one-cent magenta. With my tweezers, of course."

For all its old-fashioned scholarship, the Expert Committee does more than look through magnifying glasses and make educated guesses. It does cutting-edge scientific sleuthing with the same kinds of machinery found in crime labs around the world. The Expert Committee uses the same kinds of devices that customs agencies use to spot doctored passports or birth certificates.

The company that makes the centerpiece of the

Expert Committee's arsenal, a machine known as a video spectral comparator, says similar instruments have examined disputed lottery tickets, contested wills, and suspicious stock certificates. The technology was perfected in England in the 1970s, and similar machines have put detectives on the trail of counterfeiters who turned out fake driver's licenses, and medical-malpractice lawyers on the trail of doctors who altered patients' hospital records. The machines have looked at contested maps of the Middle East where billions in oil revenue was at stake. The FBI, the Secret Service and the Department of Homeland Security all have the same equipment; many have the same model. The author Patricia Cornwell rented one for her research on Jack the Ripper. And a stamp figured in that. It had been licked by the person who put it on the envelope. Cornwell had the DNA on the stamp tested and found that it belonged to the British painter Walter Sickert, and Cornwell declared him the Ripper. ("Ripperologists" tore apart her findings; she countered that continuing the mystery served them better than did closing the case.)

This is the height of nondestructive testing: a camera that can zoom in to take images that make the grain of the paper look as jagged as a mountain range, and can be adjusted to examine a stamp with different filters and types of light—everything on the spectrum from ultraviolet to infrared. It can, among other things, expose different inks on a single stamp. It can show when a stamp has been rubbed or scuffed.

• • •

And the certificate that the Expert Committee approved said just that—the stamp suffered from "surface rubbing," wear and tear from being scuffed, pressed against other stamps in albums. This was a particularly British way of saying the face of the stamp was far from pristine. For all anyone knows, it could have been scuffed when it was still on the newspaper wrapper in British Guiana.

The next sentence was the one that would cause problems for Redden, for it raised the question of whether the one-cent magenta had had some cosmetic work done. It said the "surface rubbing" had been "reduced by overpainting at some time in the past," meaning that someone had attempted to cover up the blemishes. In its crudest form, "over-painting" would involve mixing some magenta paint and swabbing it on the stamp. Perhaps one of the greatest collectors of all had ordered it done during the not quite forty years he owned it starting in 1878.

The 2014 committee referred to the problems because it had to reckon with Bacon, who had mentioned a slight disfigurement after seeing the stamp in Paris. "It was described in Bacon as rubbed," Christopher G. Harman, the chairman of the Expert Committee and a past president of the Royal, told me the first time I met him. "It's part of the history of the stamp," and he did not care if spelling out that history complicated things for Redden. "We don't always have one-hundred-percent satisfied customers," he declared when I interviewed him a second time. "We are after the truth. We are trying to give a true evaluation of an item, which will include observations. Something that's one hundred fifty years old is not going to be pristine."

The committee knew it had been rubbed when Bacon inspected it. The committee also knew it did not appear rubbed when Redden brought it in. "It's perfectly logical," Harman explained. "Most of these stamps had the surface rubbed and then touched up. We accept the fact that this was enhanced by painting."

The mention of the rubbing would leave some American collectors scratching their heads and saying that since the committee could not establish who had done it or when or why, the committee need not have mentioned it.

But that bit of cosmetic work, if that is what it was, was not Harman's only concern. "The color in the center is unnatural, and if you look at the front, there is no white showing." This might or might not have been a liability: "Many of these get painted on the front. It was perfectly acceptable in those days. Today, you'd get scolded."

Harman had seen the stamp twice before, in 1965 when it was shown in London and in 1986 when it was shown in Australia—but only the front was shown then. He told me that the real surprise in 2014 was what was on the back—the large wheel-like star symbol on the back of the stamp. "We'd never seen one before," he said.

That was a footnote that did not deter the committee from reaching its verdict. Nor did the committee delay because the documentation was incomplete. Improbable as it sounds, Harman told me that the Royal's copy of the 1935 certificate was nowhere to be found. "I know I've seen it," he told me. "I remember seeing it." But the folder containing it was missing.

No matter. The new certificate was quickly written out by Peter Lister, a retired chemistry teacher. He had filled out dozens of certificates in his years on the Expert Committee, but No. 217,796 was different. He felt a sudden sense of wonderment and pride. It was his signature that the public would see, his signature that would figure in the continuing history of one of the icons of philately. His hand shook from the first letter to the last.

• • •

"Here's our patient, as they called it in London," Redden announced brightly after shaking hands with another world-class expert, this one at the Smithsonian Institution's National Postal Museum, next door to Union Station in Washington. The patient was the one-cent magenta, looking tiny and fragile on a velvet bed. The expert was the museum's research scientist, a philatelist named Thomas M. Lera, who had agreed to put the stamp through its paces so the data about the one-cent magenta would be available to stamp collectors.

Redden and I were taking an early-morning train from New York with a security guard in tow. I met Redden at Pennsylvania Station, and I asked—quietly—where the stamp was. He half-whispered that, as always, it was in his briefcase, which he set in the luggage compartment over his head. Between Philadelphia and Baltimore, I asked him to take it down. I had been flirting with photography— like philately, another addictive hobby—and I had brought along a new camera that I wanted to try out. I watched the guard squirm as Redden moved the briefcase to the seat opposite his. A moment later, Redden lifted it onto his lap and hunched over it as the miles rolled by outside the window.

In New Jersey, someone else with an interest in the one-cent magenta boarded the train: Robert P. Odenweller, a philatelist so highly regarded that he was invited to serve on the Royal's governing body even though he is an American. Odenweller wears many hats in Stamp World. He is also a member of the postal museum's Council of Philatelists, and du Pont's estate had hired him as an adviser—he had been a friend of du Pont's. In his advisory role, he was firm about one point: nothing could undercut the Royal's findings. Minutes after settling in next to Redden, he was telling me that the postal museum can do tests, but unlike the Royal, the postal museum does not render expert opinions. As it happened, that was the first thing Lera said after leading the way to his airy workroom, which had more devices than the Expert Committee's room at the Royal. "More toys," someone joked as Redden opened his briefcase and took out the stamp.

Redden, of course, had more in mind than just

collecting data. He wanted to generate buzz about the auction. He already knew, from conversations with postal museum officials, that they would not bid on the stamp. But they had offered to display the stamp if the buyer would agree to a long-term loan.

First on the agenda was a procedure that would involve sliding the patient into a video spectral comparator like the one at the Royal. Lera also wanted to run some X-ray scans. These are not like hospital X-rays of broken bones; they do not yield images that a layman with a displaced wrist fracture can make sense of. Instead, they provide data points that a computer can assemble in a graph.

But Redden, worried about possible damage to the stamp, was not sure that he would let Lera put all the tools to use. Redden all but body-blocked Lera when Lera showed him a micrometer that could measure the thickness of the stamp. It had a lever and looked as if it would clamp down on the stamp like an embossing device. Redden worried that it would leave an impression, an indentation, on the surface of the stamp. He called the micrometer "the torture instrument."

An infrared spectrometer also gave Redden pause, because it, too, had a lever that snapped down like a clamp. Redden saw the spectrometer as the Stamp World equivalent of a horror-movie hammerhead. It could ruin the stamp in a single chomp. For the rest of the day, the theme from *Jaws* played in my head.

"Doesn't even put a dent in it," Lera said, as he flipped the lever on notebook paper.

"I hope not," Redden said, unconvinced. The *Jaws* music in my head got louder.

What followed was a physics lesson that turned into a rebuttal to the Royal on the abrasion issue—the "rubbing" that Sir Edward had noted and the Expert Committee had mentioned on the certificate—and the coloring problem on the back that had troubled Harman.

Lera, writing in a scientific journal, once described his work as "exciting electrons in the atoms. These atoms then emit photons." The photons can be charted, and from that data, someone like Lera can assemble a biography of a stamp different from the usual description in words.

Lera began by demonstrating what his machines could do. He slid in a pair of one-penny stamps from Mauritius into the spectral comparator. As Redden and I looked over his shoulder, with Odenweller a few feet away, Lera said that the two stamps were about the same age as the one-cent magenta, but far less valuable. And something was wrong with the postmark on one. The machine showed the postmark contained two colors of ink. The line of the circle had been altered. "I'm pretty sure it was done with a Sharpie," he said with a chuckle.

Lera had promised that his examination of the stamp would be noninvasive, and the stamp was all but untouched. Even so, I was still hearing the *Jaws* music as Lera looked at the brightly colored lines in a graph on a computer monitor and announced, "It's the original ink." He changed some settings as he showed us the postmark. Redden declared happily, "That's the first time I've seen the 1856 so clearly delineated."

The readings showed that the pigment that gave the paper its magenta color was identical all the way through. No one could have created an exact match to the pigment later on. It was this finding that put Lera at odds with the Royal and its notion of over-painting. Lera would have detected a color wash, a dye job to bring back the original color and rid the stamp of its tired, rubbed appearance.

Redden understood the implications: the entire sheet must have been painted before it went through the printing press. Whatever scuffing or rubbing that Bacon remembered from his look at the stamp in 1891 was nothing more than normal wear and tear.

So Washington was at odds with London over a small point. But Stamp World lives for small points. What was important, what mattered to the world beyond Stamp World, was that there were no doubts on either side of the Atlantic about the authenticity of the one-cent magenta.

Redden, elated, could go home to New York with only one item left on his to-do list: sell the stamp.

• • •

As an auctioneer, Redden does not babble into the microphone at dizzying speeds. Nor does he induce reluctant bidders to put up their paddles by glaring at them. He is not one for cajoling or browbeating, at least not in public. He is traveling the road paved by Peter Cecil Wilson, who was Sotheby's top executive from 1958 to 1979. "The cunning of Wilson," a colleague once said, "is that there is no cunning."

It was Wilson who introduced the marketing and hype that became everyday tools in Redden's trade but were unknown in the 1950s. Wilson turned a sale of post-Impressionist paintings into a black-tie evening, with A-list celebrity guests like Lady Churchill, Somerset Maugham, Margot Fonteyn, and Kirk Douglas.

But the post-Impressionist auction was more than a party; it was the beginning of a transformation. Auction houses had been, in effect, wholesalers—middlemen—selling to dealers. Under Wilson, Sotheby's became a retailer tantalizing, and selling directly to, collectors. Out went the quiet certainty of the private sale; in came the hubbub of the sales room, and with it a certain theatricality. Some art-world historians even credit Wilson with making auction houses the force that supplanted museum curators and cloistered scholars as arbiters of taste. Wilson—and, eventually, Redden—could not resist the ever-rising spiral of "record price" auctions.

It was the day of the sale, and about two hundred people, by one bartender's estimate, were mingling at a cocktail party in a large, bright space outside the auction room. It was far fewer than at the 1970 sale, when the turnout was about six hundred, or the 1980 sale, when du Pont was one in a thousand.

Finally the doors parted, and the crowd moved into the auction room. Redden was wearing a microphone like a television personality, and the room had the layout and trappings of a television studio—the antiseptic chill of the air, the wide stage area, the shopworn lectern that would look just fine on camera. A giant video screen dominated the high-ceilinged space, and a row of cameras had been set up in the back. They had unobstructed views of the stamp, up front in a clear plastic column. One middle-aged man in the room said the column reminded him of one he had seen at a birthday party for a hip-hop mogul, except that there had been an almost-naked woman dancing inside the column at the party.

• • •

"This is like a horse race—it will be over in four minutes, just like Belmont," Redden had told me earlier. But actually, it was over in two, about as long as the first couple of commercials on *Jeopardy!*, which in New York was being broadcast at about the same time. But sitting in the plush studio-audience seats at *Jeopardy!* would have been more comfortable. The audience at Sotheby's ended up squeezing into chairs with shiny metal frames and hard-plastic seats that had been jammed as close together as possible.

No one said, "All right, Mr. Redden, the stamp is ready for its close-up." No one had to. Its moment had come, and he knew it. He pulled on too-tight cotton gloves— "We wouldn't want to leave any fingerprints, now would we?" he said as he opened the back of the column. The stamp itself was in no danger of being touched. It was lying in its little see-through carrier, face up, the same position as when it had gone on display on its pre-auction tour. Newspaper and wire-service photographers rushed forward. For a moment the buzz of the audience was drowned out by a metallic beating of wings, the sound of all those shutters flapping—the sound some of the same cameras have made when this or that celebrity was on a red carpet or this or that disgraced public official finally resigned. It was a frenzy, and watching it, Frank J. Buono, a stamp dealer from Binghamton, New York, told me, "I don't think they'd get that coverage for a van Gogh."

Just out of camera range is a long desk occupied by young assistants, each with a telephone or a computer. Those with the telephones tell unseen bidders how the auction is going and get Redden's eye when the person on the phone wants to get in on the action. This lets buyers acquire their treasures without having to interrupt their schedules to attend auctions in person. David M. Rubenstein, the hedge-fund manager who bought the Bay Psalm Book, called in from Australia. But bidders can also use telephone bidding to remain anonymous. The assistants who place their bids do not identify them by name, only by the number they were assigned when they registered to bid. Unless hackers strike, their secrets are safe with Sotheby's.

Before he opened the bidding, Redden plodded through

the preliminaries, a kind of throat-clearing that quieted the crowd and satisfied Sotheby's lawyers, who wanted the fine-print dicta in the back of the auction catalogue read aloud, just in case the winning bidder was such a newbie that he was unaware that "on the fall of the auctioneer's hammer, the winning bidder will immediately pay the purchase price or such part as we may require." It's the same kind of uninspiring wording that the *New York Times* art critic Holland Cotter once observed in a different context was "as joyless to read as it must have been to write." Redden also read the Royal's certificate, including the line about over-painting.

Sotheby's had prequalified the bidders, requiring them to hand over certified checks before they got their paddles. So, in the standing-room-only crowd, Redden was really playing to only a few, and he knew exactly who they were.

Not all of them were in the hard chairs facing the lectern. Sotheby's has what Redden called "skyboxes"— suites for preferred customers that ring the room. They are not as lavish as the skyboxes at the Super Bowl, which can go for $400,000 and up. Cream-colored curtains guard the plate-glass windows. Some bidders pull them wide open; some leave them closed. Sometimes faces peek through a

slit, like a nervous performer before a talent show. Once
the bidding begins, they do not hold paddles up to the
glass. They communicate with the young assistants on the
telephones.

Downstairs on the floor, heads turned to see who had
the paddles, and the deep pockets, to buy the one-cent
magenta. Many in the crowd, maybe most, are Stamp
World types who do not plan to bid. For them, the auction *is* like a horse race. They are nothing more than eager
spectators. They want to be able to say they were there
when the one-cent magenta was sold. They just want
bragging rights: I was there. That was what Buono told
me as I took the seat next to him. Buono did not register.
No paddle for him.

Redden, determined to set a record, opened the bidding at $4.5 million.

THREE

ONE CENT

———◆———

1856: Printed, Sold, and Forgotten

Some stamps begin with tantalizing stories. A governor's impatient wife mails the invitations to her fancy-dress ball, and the stamps on the envelopes—the handful that are not thrown away the morning after—become rarities: the Post Office Mauritius stamps. Or a pressman makes a mistake, and the biplanes are printed upside down—one hundred stamps bought at the post office for $24 and soon sold to a collector for fifteen thousand: the Inverted Jenny stamps.

The one-cent magenta's appeal came not from being an error but from being overlooked and forgotten. This was also pretty much the story of the place it came from, a place on the right shoulder of South America. Like China and India, Guiana was one of the places Columbus missed on the way to wherever it was that he actually went. It was a backwater before there were backwaters. Later it was picked off by one European monarch after another.

But first it was El Dorado. Lesser explorers like Amerigo Vespucci in 1499, followed by Vicente Yáñez Pinzón in 1500, sailed away repeating the stories that transformed Guiana into a destination. But since none of them had actually found any treasure, it was nothing more than hearsay, really: an unconquered paradise deep in the jungle, a place with endless gold, silver, and jewels, as well as mermaids and headless men. Spain promptly claimed the wild coast, as did Portugal. Neither sent settlers to hack away at the jungle and establish colonies, though, and in Europe, the monarchs feuded. They didn't take the law into their own hands—they went to an unusually high court, the Vatican. A series of papal bulls fixed a line of demarcation that gave Brazil to Portugal and made Guiana a no-man's-land.

Somewhat later in the parade of frustrated explorers came Sir Walter Raleigh, who wanted the political riches as much as the gold. He wrote a best-selling account with a tell-all title: *The Discoverie of the Large, Rich and Bewtiful Empire of Guiana, with a Relation of the Great and Golden Citie of Manoa (which the Spaniards call El Dorado) and the Provinces of Emeria, Arromaia, Amapaia and other Countries, with their rivers adjoining.* The text—at thirty-four thousand words a fraction of the length of, say, Lewis and Clark's journals—was as exaggerated as a tourist-office brochure. Guiana "hath more quantity of gold, by manifold, than the best parts of the Indies, or Peru," Raleigh postulated, adding that all corners of Guiana "appear marvellous rich." His little rhapsody was so tantalizing that the Pilgrims weighed pointing the *Mayflower* toward Guiana. Apparently they gave more weight to the inconvenient truth that Raleigh had failed to find gold in South America. (Back in London after a huge but fruitless expedition to Guiana, Raleigh was executed because an earlier death sentence had never been lifted.)

Next came the Dutch, who saw the possibilities of a tropical Holland in what they called Novo Zeelandia. They chartered a trading company and established three colonies, but like Raleigh, they overstated things. Pamphlets aimed at would-be settlers described the fortunes to be made in Novo Zeelandia and stated that "there were many advantages in Guiana as compared with the New Netherlands [New York]."

Guiana went through several turnovers—first Britain invaded the three Dutch colonies, then the French ousted the British and returned the colonies to Dutch control.

Finally the British seized them again in the Napoleonic Wars and began making British Guiana distinctly British. But the British never fully rinsed out the tastes of the past. Well into the twentieth century, the central district of the capital was known by the original Dutch name, Stabroek. In contrast to Barbados, which became known as "Little England," British Guiana never really satisfied the British. "The museum is somewhat superior to those in other British colonies in the region, but there is no decent library," sniffed the historian W. Adolphe Roberts, who wrote extensively on the Caribbean colonies.

Far more famous visitors stopped by. Evelyn Waugh was welcomed like a celebrity, although he denied that competing reporters from local newspapers had trailed him because he was well known: "*All* first-class passengers are given column interviews on arrival at Georgetown." But few are grilled the way Waugh was. One of the reporters in the capital city pulled out a clipping of a newspaper article in which Waugh had declared—facetiously, he now insisted—that "the beetles in Guiana were as big as pigeons, and that one killed them with shotguns." The reporters warned that if he had come to take aim at the beetles, he would be disappointed.

They asked what he knew about Guiana's natural resources. "This was their stock, foolproof question," he said, "because most visitors to Georgetown came there with some idea of prospecting for diamonds or gold"—El Dorado, first and always. But Waugh was no prospector. His itinerary called for him to sail into Brazil and find the Amazon. The disappointed reporters put their notebooks in their pockets and went off to write their stories, leaving Waugh "to tackle the old problem of getting through the afternoon, which, next to the problem of getting through the morning, is one of the hardest a lonely man can set himself." He went for a walk. He, too, visited the museum— it "took some finding"—and he, too, complained about it, from its musty smell and faded photographs to its collection of "the worst stuffed animals I have seen anywhere."

Anthony Trollope had gone to Guiana for his day job as a postal inspector, which was separate from his sideline as a writer. He had already "[raced] about England and Ireland doing official (and officious) work for the Post Office . . . extending rural service [and] installing letter boxes (which he invented)." He had walked backward through the General Post Office in London, even on the staircases, as he led a tour for a queen—"I think Saxony," he wrote in his autobiography. The barons with her tipped him half a crown for his effort. "That," he wrote with understandable understatement, "was a bad moment."

If this "incarnate gale of wind" had blustered into British Guiana sooner, we might know more about how the one-cent magenta came into being, for surely he would have written thousands of words about the cooperation between the local post office and the local newspaper. But he did not arrive until 1860, four years after the one-cent magenta had been printed, sold, and forgotten.

Trollope liked British Guiana. "There never was a land so ill spoken of—and never one that deserved it so little," he wrote, calling it "the transatlantic Eden." He pronounced British Guiana well run, with "no noisy sessions of Parliament as in Jamaica [and] no money squabbles as in Barbados." Trollope reported that the government posted a surplus and that trade was thriving. His hotel was the best in town, but he complained about holes in the curtains, "the mosquitoes having driven me to very madness." They were a problem on the road, too. Trollope rode in a horse-drawn mail carriage with five paying passengers. It took the bumps hard. An axle snapped, and they had to wait for a couple of hours "among the mosquitoes! . . . Ugh! Ugh!"

Mail coaches—and mail itself—had helped bind Britain together. But using the mail as a unifying force proved difficult in British Guiana, where roads had yet to reach into the jungle. The real roads were the rivers, and the boats that navigated them were not dependable. Without land routes, few settlements sprang up. And to have a postal system, you need destinations, places where the mail can be delivered.

• • •

Now for the part that's inevitable in a book about a stamp, the part that another book about another stamp described as "philatelic facts, which are usually dry." But nothing like a good martini.

In 1840, there was a notable development for British Guiana: steamships picked up mail for the first time. The little colony was now connected to London by the newest and fastest means.

Of course, nothing was terribly new or British about mail. The Dutch West India Company had set up a mail system in 1796. Smallish sailing vessels made the rounds, using a hub-and-spoke system centered on Barbados. It was the same kind of arrangement that airlines would adopt later: to get to Omaha or Abilene, you have to go through Chicago or Dallas. But the Dutch mail was plagued by dishonest captains, and slow voyages made delivery less than reliable.

The changing casts in government in Guiana—Dutch, British, French, and British again—did not help. The postmasters installed with each takeover came and went with their superiors without improving mail service. In 1820 the postmaster was found to have "let out the Office . . . to different persons" for fourteen of the sixteen years since he was appointed. Even in the early years of British rule, the postal system was a low priority, and corruption sometimes lurked behind the post office counter.

By 1856, when the one-cent magenta was commissioned and printed, there was more for the postmaster in British Guiana to worry about than just running out of stamps from London. Past accounts of the one-cent magenta have overlooked racial tensions that had been simmering for years—tensions that would have raised the anxiety level of anyone who ran a business that dealt with the public, especially one that reached across the different elements of a frazzled colony. A race riot erupted early that year, but there was nothing new about racial unrest in British Guiana. In 1847, a Portuguese man had assaulted and injured a black laborer. Black residents "felt exploited by the Portuguese, who controlled the retail shops," the scholar George K. Danns has written, and when a rumor spread that the black man had died, a mob formed and looted Portuguese-owned shops.

In late 1855, a street-corner preacher returned home to British Guiana after leading anti-Catholic disturbances in England, Scotland, and Ireland. John Sayers Orr brought his trumpet—his nickname was "Angel Gabriel," and as always, he blew on the horn to draw attention as he traipsed through the streets of Georgetown. "Nobody expected any trouble," the historian V.O. Chan wrote in 1970, adding that as far as Orr was concerned, "sensible people probably thought he was an amusing and harmless crackpot."

But he rekindled black anger at the largely Catholic Portuguese, whom the white British ruling class also resented. In fact, the authorities tacitly encouraged black residents to attack Portuguese businesses. The police response was slow, perhaps deliberately so. Eventually, though, Orr was jailed in a government crackdown. That set off what the governor called "open insurrection," and soon the black rioters overpowered the police. Troops from the West Indies had to be called in.

The post office in Georgetown was apparently untouched. But the turmoil must have concerned the postmaster, Edward Thomas Evans Dalton. Short on inventory in early 1856, he might even have worried that shipments of stamps from Britain would not survive the shortest leg of the journey, from the dock in Georgetown to his post office. Whoever was supposed to carry them could be ambushed by an angry crowd. If that happened, the stamps themselves could be burned, or dumped in the Atlantic. So, as he had in past years when he was running low on stamps and shipments from London did not arrive on schedule, Dalton went to the *Royal Gazette* for "provisionals"—stamps printed locally. The little newspaper in Georgetown had a printing press—not as large or as fancy as the ones in London, and not equipped the way presses in Britain were. The machine at the *Royal Gazette* could not handle engravings, but even if it could have, no one in British Guiana could have produced an engraving fast enough.

The *Royal Gazette* prepared the provisionals the only way it could, by hand setting type, letter by letter. A printer reached into a type case, no doubt divided into little sections for each letter and number. At least this time the *Gazette* spelled all the words right. In 1853, when the *Gazette* printed a batch of one- and four-cent provisionals for Dalton, the word "Petimus" ("We give and ask in return") had been misspelled as "Patimus" ("We suffer in return").

"Patimus" probably expressed Dalton's feelings better. Dalton lasted thirty-seven years as postmaster despite tussles with his Colonial Office bosses in London. Time after time they suspended him, only to reinstate him, and for the most part he managed to sidestep inquiries about perpetual deficits and irregularities. The questioning from London must have been humiliating. Dalton came from a well-connected family that established a dynasty in the post office, ending the rapid turnover of the early years under the British. Dalton's father had been the postmaster before him, after giving up on a career as a sugar planter, and Dalton's son took over as the postmaster after him.

The *Gazette*, though privately owned, was as much a part of the official fabric of British Guiana as the post office, and it had learned the hard way to be careful about what it published in its bland-looking pages. Benjamin Penhallow Shillaber, later the editor of the *Boston Post*, had worked as a printer at the *Gazette* in the 1830s. In a memoir, he described a morning when Georgetown was rocked by a salute from an artillery detachment in the harbor, followed by an announcement: "The King is dead." A sailing vessel had arrived with news of the death of King William IV. "The papers brought by the ship gave all the details," Shillaber wrote, but when the *Gazette* published the news that afternoon, the Colonial Secretary stormed into the *Gazette*'s office, demanding to know why the Gazette had not waited for orders. "The King was not yet dead, officially, and such elaborate demonstration of grief, under the circumstances, was not called for." The official announcement arrived a week or so later, and when it did, the *Gazette* treated it as if it were new news.

Shillaber liked one of the *Gazette*'s owners, William Dallas—"a more perfect gentleman and a better printer I had never met with." Shillaber's only mention of the other owner, Joseph Baum, had to do with Baum's wife, a fellow passenger on the ship that had carried Shillaber from New England to British Guiana. She got him talking about print shops he had worked in—and used the information to get her husband some help in the composing room, because skilled labor did not arrive every day.

Baum and Dallas wanted their provisional stamps to look like stamps. They pulled the image of a ship from among the cuts that would have been stowed away in any nineteenth-century print shop. Some postal historians have said that image appeared with the shipping news column in the *Gazette*, but the *Gazette* carried no such column in the 1850s.

They probably ran off sheets of four, a two-by-two grid. That's the best guess. No one knows. Philatelists have long wondered which position the one-cent magenta occupied before the sheet was cut and the stamps initialed by post office workers—in the case of the one-cent magenta, E.D. Wight. The initials were said to guard against fraud, though it is hard to imagine counterfeit stamps in British Guiana.

Wight seemed not to care that a stamp he had handled and marked went on to become famous. When Sir Edward Denny Bacon, the unquestionably authoritative collector and curator, published a paper on the stamps of British Guiana, he said he had been assured that "Mr. Wight is still alive and living in the colony, but he is in his dotage and either cannot or will not remember anything about these old stamps except that he initialed them. He has been so pestered on the subject that the mention of old stamps to him is like a red rag to a bull."

FOUR

SIX SHILLINGS

——◆——

1873: Found by a Twelve-Year-Old

It was found seventeen years after it was issued, perhaps in an attic, perhaps in a closet, perhaps in a forgotten drawer—the details are fuzzy. The finder did not realize, when he grabbed the one-cent magenta and took it home to soak it off whatever it had been stuck to, that he had stumbled across something. And that created the kind of story that fueled long-shot dreams of fledgling stamp collectors who cracked the bindings on their brand-new stamp albums and plunged in, hoping to find that one precious stamp someday. It was like panning for gold, something else people did in British Guiana.

Louis Vernon Vaughan, twelve years old and caught up in the then-new fad of stamp collecting, found that one precious stamp in 1873 but did not know it. He sold it for six shillings, or about $16.83 in today's dollars. "The worst stamp swap in history," the stamp writer Viola Ilma called it.

Vaughan grew up to be a tax collector in British Guiana—he lived there all his life—and as an old man was teased about not striking it rich when he had the chance. The one-cent magenta "was always referred to as the one that got away," one of his descendants told me.

Vaughan found it at the house of an uncle. Andrew Hunter came from a line of resolute Scots who became sugar planters when they immigrated to British Guiana, but he had given up. He had moved to Barbados after forty-some years in British Guiana, and the house he left in British Guiana was a mess. Vaughan, tracked down by reporters long after the one-cent magenta had become famous, did not explain why Hunter had left behind so much junk that had to be cleaned out, only that the mess included "a whole lot of old family letters" with stamps that Vaughan could hardly wait to add to his album.

Among them was the one-cent magenta, tattered-looking even then. Surely little Louis ("Louie" to his descendants) had memorized the stamps that had been issued in British Guiana—the provisionals that Dalton had commissioned over the years, as well as the regular issues that were printed in London. This was not one he recognized, and he was not impressed. The one-cent magenta's "condition . . . would not be tolerated by discriminating collectors in a much commoner stamp," the stamp experts L.N. and Maurice Williams wrote a century later.

But Vaughan did not understand its rarity. From the first, he considered the one-cent magenta "a very ordinary one . . . not a particularly fine specimen," and certainly not unique. "I was quite certain that it could easily be replaced by a better specimen when next I took the trouble to reach through the old family letters," he told the London *Daily Mail* in 1934.

He did not say when it dawned on him that he would never find another one-cent magenta, and there were other mysteries he did not explain. He certainly did not admit whether he had been responsible for the one-cent magenta's strange shape—whether it was he who had snipped off the corners, or whether they were already gone when he found it. Vaughan the adult was as uninformative as Vaughan the boy had been impatient.

The one-cent magenta "was not in my album for long," he recalled. He wanted something—a batch of more attractive stamps that a dealer in England had sent him on approval. The dealer was Alfred Smith and

Company, which had jumped on the stamp-collecting bandwagon in the 1860s, targeting boys like Vaughan with advertisements in magazines that reached throughout the English-speaking world. Smith believed in magazines. From 1863 to the mid-1870s, he and his partner, his brother Henry Stafford Smith, published the *Stamp-Collector's Magazine*. (Another Smith, the early philatelic writer Bertram Tapscott Knight Smith, mentioned the *Stamp-Collector's Magazine* and the *Timbre-Poste* of Brussels as "the foundation of all philatelic knowledge." The *Timbre-Poste* would later provide a forum for charges that the one-cent magenta was a fake.)

Addicts know the desperation of desire. Vaughan felt it as he thumbed through his album, thinking about new stamps he could buy. He probably had not seen the July 1, 1865, issue of Smith's magazine, which carried an article about stamps from British Guiana. The article was written by Frederick Adolphus Philbrick, who used the pseudonym Damus Petimusque Vicissim, a play on the motto on stamps from British Guiana that means "we will now turn."

British Guiana came late to an endeavor whose origins are hazy—whoever picked up, sorted, and delivered the primordial mail is unknown. The Persian emperor

Cyrus established a more or less permanent postal system in the sixth century BC, the first in recorded history. The Roman emperor Augustus developed post roads with relay stations stretching out from Rome and "public couriers," but they were public in name only; they stood ready to carry official messages and nothing else. Centuries later Charlemagne pushed the nascent postal grid into Germany and France. Later still, kings and bishops relied on their own messengers until the mid-fifteenth century, when Franz von Taxis fashioned a monopoly on the mails that reached from Vienna to Brussels, the first lasting postal link between nations.

The word "post" began to appear in English after Edward IV set up relay stations where messengers could change horses in the last years of the fifteenth century. "Post" was derived from a Middle French term for men on horseback responsible for transporting letters along a route and the relief riders who took over along the way.

Britain's General Post Office dates to the mid-seventeenth century, although the crown had conferred titles like "Master of the Posts" or "Chief Post-Master" long before that—and the royal posts served the royal family and their court but were allowed to carry the occasional private letter, so long as the carrier did not have to go out of his way to deliver it. That reflected the British preoccupation with efficiency. A seventeenth-century entrepreneur named William Dockwra recognized the need for speed. He promised delivery of letters that absolutely, positively had to go across London quickly. James E. Casey, who in 1907 founded, with a hundred borrowed dollars, the crosstown messenger operation in Seattle that became United Parcel Service, was just following in the footsteps of Dockwra and his men. Dockwra opened special receiving stations across a seven-mile stretch of London. His carriers collected letters on an hourly schedule, hustled them to sorting centers—one was in Dockwra's own house—and hurried off to deliver them by hand.

Dockwra's biggest innovations involved the charges to customers. "Just a penny per item—regardless of the length of the letter," Duncan Campbell-Smith wrote in his comprehensive account of the British postal system. Even more revolutionary was who paid the penny: the sender, not the recipient.

Dockwra's operation was "known to all as the Penny Post." Dockwra himself called it a "New and Useful Invention," and its success was immediate. So was its nationalization. Dockwra did not profit the way Casey did—in fact, he was hit with "a hefty fine for infringing on the Crown's postal monopoly" before his system was absorbed into the General Post Office (though it remained a separate unit and retained its penny pricing). Dockwra even had to fight for a pension.

Through the eighteenth century, the main postal routes stretched out from London, but cross-country service remained iffy and rates prohibitive. The system was plagued by hard-to-calculate charges for the distance a letter had to be carried. Different clerks could arrive at different fees for letters to the same address. The bewildering rules, the confusing zones, the imponderable add-ons—the clerks had discretion, and they made mistakes. And mail became more expensive. Postal rates increased five times between 1784 and 1812. Sending a one-page letter cost a minimum of four pence (as much as $92.81 in today's dollars), but because postage was calculated by distance, that initial charge took the letter only fifteen miles. It cost as much as fifteen pence, or as much as $347.81 in today's dollars, to go five or six hundred miles.

Postmarks were a much earlier invention. The credit apparently goes to Henry Bishop, Britain's postmaster general in the late seventeenth century. A Bishop postmark was wordy and promotional: "The post for all Kent goes every night from the Round House, Love Lane, and comes every morning." Mail sent through Dockwra's system received two postmarks, but they were concise, for they served a purpose other than marketing. One read, "Penny Post Paid." The other, in a heart shape, listed the time at which the letter was due at its destination. "Mor 11," for example, for eleven o'clock in the morning, or "Af 3" for three o'clock in the afternoon.

With the takeover by the national postal service came spelling errors like "Penny Post Payd" that surely had literate Londoners tut-tutting. Nor could the civil servants of the Post Office show their love. The heart-shaped postmark became circular.

• • •

The list of the world's serendipitous inventions is long. Consider these five: LSD, originally synthesized to boost circulation and respiration; corn flakes, originally made from bread dough left out too long; the microwave oven, reverse engineered because a candy bar melted. (The gooey mess appeared in the pocket of a scientist too close to the radar components he was testing.) And there are the twin *V*'s, Velcro and Viagra, the first developed by an electrical engineer who noticed stuck-together burrs in his pants, the other by researchers who observed a side effect of the heart drug they were working on.

The case can be made that the modern postage stamp belongs on the list.

Rowland Hill, who created it, was an ambitious schoolmaster who followed his father into teaching. He was also an amateur engineer—he had designed his school's innovative central heating system and its observatory—and he was a painter, a sideline that would figure in postal history later on. But above all, he was a systems analyst, although no one used that term in the 1830s when Hill prepared a pamphlet called "Post Office Reform: Its Importance and Practicability."

Perfectionist that he was, Hill assembled figures and facts that were "unpleasant," the postal historian Laurin Zilliacus wrote, "but hardly surprising to the authorities or even the public." He documented the stark reality of continually rising mail charges, declining revenues and substandard service. But improving the Post Office's performance was not all that he had in mind. Hill was first and foremost an educator, and he had an educator's vision of the role that an institution like the Post Office could play in British life. He cared less that the public was not getting its money's worth. His concern was "the obstruction thus raised to the moral and intellectual progress of the people; and that the Post Office, if put on a sound footing, would assume the new and important character of a powerful engine of civilization." The Post Office could function as a classroom beyond the classroom, promoting literacy and sensibility.

But the Post Office did not want him behind the counter, much less making postal policy, just as it had not let him observe its operations from within: "I applied for permission to see the working of the London office, but was met by a polite refusal." *Smithsonian* magazine's website speculated that when they read Hill's pamphlet, narrow-minded postal officials uttered "things like 'crikey!' and 'I say!' and 'what hufflepuffery' and other exclamations popular among the blustery Victorian bureaucrat set."

It was as if he had called for an all-out intervention. Hill became a polarizing figure at the center of a national debate. The philatelist David Beech pointed out to me that others advocated reforms—he mentioned Sir Henry Cole, who invented commercial Christmas cards—but Hill is the one who is remembered. The Post Office's chief secretary bellowed: "Fallacious, preposterous, utterly

unsupported by facts and resting entirely on assumption."
But some influential Londoners were not so sure. "Mr.
Place, a prominent citizen noted for his crusty temper and
far from radical . . . views, took up the pamphlet ready to
enjoy some snorts of indignation over the crackpot author," Zilliacus reported. "His reading was at first inter-
spersed with 'Pish' and 'Pshaw.'" But by the last page,
Hill had won him over, and he "turned his snorts on
opponents."

Hill advocated monumental change: prepayment.
Like Dockwra before him, Hill called for the sender to
pay the postage—but now for all letters, not just those ex-
pedited by messengers. He fretted that the public would
reject his startling departure from the time-honored custom of the recipient's paying; he gambled that making
the rate uniform and slashing it to a penny would "neu-
tralize all pecuniary objection to its being invariably paid
in advance." Collecting postage on delivery was "an important incentive, it was thought, to the post boys" on the
streets, but at best it made for sloppy accounting; at worst,
it opened the door to corruption. The populist in Hill also
wanted to address an unfairness he remembered from a
childhood in a schoolteacher's cash-poor household. "Every day that brought post-letters brought also a demand

for payment, the postman waiting at the door till he had received his money," he wrote. "In the very early period, when we were most straitened in means, his rap was not always welcome." And there was junk mail even then, and he objected to the strain it put on the postal system and the financial pressure it put on addressees. "Tradesmen's circulars, in particular, which sometimes came from a considerable distance, and always unpaid, were great causes of disappointment and irritation," he wrote.

It did not take much to see that people were giving the mailman the slip or that avoiding postage was a preoccupation of the rank and file. Hill quoted the poet Samuel Taylor Coleridge: "One day, when I had not a shilling which I could spare, I was passing by a cottage . . . where a letter-carrier was demanding a shilling for a letter, which the woman of the house appeared unwilling to pay." Coleridge stepped in and paid the money, but as soon as the postman was out of earshot, the woman told Coleridge he'd been had. "The letter was from her son, who took that means of letting her know that he was well"—he sent such letters regularly and never wrote anything inside. Together, Coleridge and the woman opened the letter, and sure enough, it was blank. (Hill eventually became so famous that some accounts mistakenly report it was Hill, not Coleridge, who happened by and paid the tab on the empty letter.)

That was hardly the only dodge. Hill complained that "hundreds, if not thousands, of newspapers were annually posted which no one particularly cared to read." What people read were the wrappers, on which they wrote their private codes. Hill detailed the ciphers that a grocer in Edinburgh had worked out with a friend in London. There were six different ways for the friend to write the grocer's name. Each told something about the price of items that fluctuated. Variations on the address—"Street" or "St."—provided additional information about whether to mark up the prices of merchandise the grocer already had on hand in anticipation of the next, more expensive shipment.

Hill also argued that the postal system catered to the haves over the have-nots. One target was franking, the privilege of sending mail without having to pay postage (the term frank came from the Latin *francus*, for free). Franking was available to many British officials—and through them to people who were not using the mail for government business. Lawmakers in the United States later tried to ward this off with statutes making it a crime to use government mail for anything that is not official.

But in Hill's London, it seemed that anyone with a friend in Parliament could easily get his mail franked; those who needed free postage the least abused the privilege the most. Hill complained that "members of the favoured classes" had sent everything from a piano to actual people—specifically, two "maid servants"—and all kinds of animals: at least one cow, a horse, and hounds.

Even more significant than proposing prepayment and doing away with franking, Hill suggested abolishing the distance-based rates. What he said that Britain needed was a flat nationwide rate of a single penny. Birmingham to Edinburgh? One penny, the same as for London to Oxford.

Barred from looking at the Post Office's ledgers, Hill tallied what losses he could. He figured that mail "refused, mis-sent or redirected" cost the Post Office £122,000 or as much as $629.3 million in today's dollars. Startling as those numbers were, another number that Hill came up with was startling because it was so small: one thirty-sixth of a penny. That, according to Hill's calculations, was the most it cost the Post Office to transport a letter from London to Edinburgh—and it did not cost much more to move one piece of mail from Plymouth to Newcastle upon Tyne. But the postage from London to Edinburgh was one shilling and one penny, and Hill, always focused on efficiency, was unhappy that the Post Office wasted time calculating the mileage for each letter.

Hill had friends in Parliament who pushed for his changes, and the post office was overhauled according to Hill's blueprint, even as postal officials took issue with his notion of supply and demand—that lowering postage rates would drive up volume and revenue, because more people could afford to send more letters. Hill was indeed wrong about that: revenue went into a nosedive and took nearly a decade to crawl to break-even levels. But public attention had shifted to the innovation that Hill had played down, if he even foresaw its potential—the postage stamp.

Most letter-writers had depended on pre-stamped stationery, and Hill did not expect "government sticking plasters" on "little bags called envelopes" to eclipse all-in-one letters. Too inconvenient. Too much of a do-it-yourself project. Too foreign to the habits of Englishmen, as one of Hill's opponents put it. And, for the Post Office, too problematic. Envelopes in all shapes and sizes would make sorting the mail more difficult. Different thicknesses of paper could add weight, burdening anyone and anything carrying mailbags, from long-distance stagecoaches to village postmen.

But stamps caught on because the pre-stamped stationery introduced with Hill's rate change was a fiasco. The Post Office had commissioned the well-known artist William Mulready to design the one-piece cover. As the historian F. George Kay, a fellow of the Royal Society of Arts, later explained it, Mulready's design "was supposed to be 'highly poetic,' but was in fact in execrable taste." It was also laughable, because Mulready's seven winged messengers had a total of only thirteen legs. Britain had a good chuckle, the Post Office discarded and destroyed the unsold Mulready covers, and the public turned to the "sticking plasters." The first was an endearing, enduring hit, the template for British stamps ever since. It was the stylized silhouette of Queen Victoria, the Penny Black.

Hill's fingerprints were all over it, because he roughed out the design himself—he was a painter, after all—based on a medal of Queen Victoria, then only two years into her reign. She loved it, and George Kay, who was so scathing about the Mulready cover, could only rave. "The lovely portrait of the eighteen-year-old queen, the bold lettering, the simple background and the aesthetically satisfying border design have never been improved in all the tens of thousands of British and foreign successors since—the vast majority of which are, of course, imitations of this first stamp."

One of those imitations was the one-cent magenta. It shared the Penny Black's simplicity, even if it showed a sailing vessel, not the queen. When it was printed, Victoria had been on the throne for nineteen years, less than a third of her reign.

• • •

By then, or by the 1870s, when young Louis Vernon Vaughan was building his collection in British Guiana, stamps were novel and cool and—believe it or not—high-tech. Stamps had to be printed and perforated and gummed. It took machinery to do all that when machinery was new and intricate and intriguing, and in a backward crown colony like British Guiana where such machinery was slow to arrive, accounts of the way stamps were made in far-off London must have been almost as fascinating as the stamps themselves. Stamps—real stamps, not improvised substitutes like the one-cent magenta— were mass-produced on the latest steam-powered presses, shiny machines that people way off in British Guiana could only dream about. Boys like Vaughan—as well as plenty of adults—were captivated.

And so philately was born. But it always comes back to that word. There are those who maintain that "philately" is the wrong word for what philatelists do. For that they have one of their own to blame. Celebrated as the world's first stamp collector by some who have followed in his tracks—or perhaps as the founder of the first club for stamp collectors, a group that lasted only a few months—Georges Herpin was one of stamp collecting's early elite, a regular in the Parisian salons where stamps were being talked about and the shops where they were being traded. He complained in the mid-1860s that stamp collecting was becoming known as *timbrologie*, or "timbrology" in English; stamps in French are *timbres*.

He wanted a word that would convey the culture change that had come with the widespread introduction of postage stamps in Europe and the United States in the 1840s and '50s. Herpin sought a word that would denote the monumental shift that stamps had brought on with the idea that once a letter-writer had purchased a stamp and affixed it, the letter would go through, period. No one would demand any more money.

Herpin reached to ancient Greek and concocted the word *philatélie*—in English, "philately," from "philo," denoting "loving" or "affinity for," and "ateleia," meaning, as he put it, "free of all charges of duties [when] affixed" to an envelope or a package.

It would have been Greek to the Greeks. "Unfortunately," as the Scottish philatelist James Alexander Mackay wrote, "his knowledge of Greek was not as faultless as his logic. He wished to convey a love (philos) of things which signified that no tax (telos) had to be paid, e.g., a stamp denoting prepayment. Strictly speaking, therefore, the word should have been atelophily."

Or perhaps "timbrophily," a term mentioned by Stephen Satchell, a longtime collector who is an economist and fellow of Trinity College, Cambridge, and J.F.W. Auld, a stamp auctioneer, after dismissing "philatelist" as describing "a lover of postmarks rather than a lover of stamps."

Philatelists may feel passion for postmarks, but they are even more passionate about stamps. Herpin's term—philately—has set the tone for stamp collecting ever since, at least in the mind of the general public: studious, dry, maybe boring, especially in Second Empire France, with racy Offenbach operettas, the Théâtre du Vaudeville and—four years after Herpin's grumblings—the Folies Bergère. And later, much later, an American philatelic writer declared that a stamp was nothing but a tax receipt. What could be less thrilling than a tax receipt?

And stamps were also time-consuming—who knows how many countless hours Vaughan would have spent poring over albums—but then, they still are. In 2015, Yahoo reported that fantasy players spent an average of five hundred minutes a month creating dream-team rosters in football, baseball, or basketball on its site—only about forty-five minutes a day. To stamp collectors, that is no time at all. Surely teenage boys in the mid-to-late nineteenth century had that much time to spend sifting through canceled letters in the hunt for the one-of-a-kind stamp. They were infected with collection-itis, even if they never stumbled across the one great stamp.

Vaughan was not looking for a megabuck payoff, but still the one-cent magenta proved to be hard to get rid of. He wanted money for more stamps and decided it had to go. He took it to Neil Ross McKinnon, who was well known in British Guiana, not only as the first mayor of New Amsterdam, an outlying town in British Guiana, but as an early philatelist. McKinnon turned him away, at least at first. McKinnon objected to the cut corners and grumbled that the stamp "appeared to be a bad specimen," as the *British Guiana Philatelic Journal* put it.

Vaughan tried persuasion, telling McKinnon he wanted money for nicer stamps, an argument that apparently melted McKinnon's resistance. "After some hesitation," the *Journal* reported, "[McKinnon] said he would risk six shillings on it . . . duly impressing on [Vaughan] the great risk he was running in paying 6s."

Maybe McKinnon really believed that he would be stuck with the homely stamp, that its value would sink to one or two shillings—or, worse, to nothing at all. Maybe he worried that he would feel foolish, that other collectors would make fun of him for buying something so obviously worthless.

Five years later, when McKinnon sold the best of his collection, he posted a profit of 800 percent.

Vaughan would live to nearly ninety and never lose interest in stamps. In the 1970s, W.A. Townsend and F.G. Howe, in their study of stamps of British Guiana, would write that Vaughan "rose to the top of the British Guiana Philatelic Society" and wrote "many accurate notes" for its journal. Coming from two famous British experts who prided themselves on exhaustive research, that was high praise indeed.

Townsend and Howe were exacting. Philately is exacting. It demands an eye and a memory for details, for the intricacies of designs, for tiny differences between one batch of stamps and another. No wonder philatelists prize mistakes—easy-to-spot mistakes like the Inverted Jenny, and subtler ones. In 1967, Guyana, then newly independent, reproduced the one-cent magenta on a five-cent commemorative that carried the words "the worlds rarest stamp." The lack of an apostrophe earned the commemorative a place as a howler on a website called "Postage Stamp Design Errors."

Stamp collectors have been mocked often enough—or belittled or disparaged—to have learned that, yes, it takes one to know one. "Devoted philatelists don't go around announcing their predilection," the British writer Simon Garfield wrote in 2008 in explaining why it was easier to tell his wife about his fling with another woman than to tell her about his thing with stamps. "Only fellow philatelists completely sympathize with the obsession. Socially [stamps] may embarrass me ('You collect stamps? You? Who once followed The Clash on tour?')."

But why? Why do stamp collectors collect? "Do we collect in order to touch the past and thereby escape the present, thus making collecting a form of nostalgia?" John Bryant, an English professor whose academic work centers on Herman Melville and the Transcendentalists, asked in the *Handbook of American Popular Culture* in 1989. "Do we collect because we want to know the world, or because we enjoy pretty things? Do we collect, quite simply, because the things, pretty or not . . . are begging to be collected?" Bryant did not answer those questions directly, but his biographical sketch in the first volume of that multivolume work answered another—what, exactly, do philatelists do? "Of an evening," it said, "he will fiddle with a stamp collection that he has maintained since the age of ten."

Many collectors started earlier than they could have started following punk bands. James Alexander Mackay claimed to be a Mozart of stamps, having discovered philately at age four. They know the euphoric highs. They also know there can be a dangerous progression beyond casual stamp collecting. Maybe they didn't plan to spend the rest of their lives amassing stamps—it just happened. "It's an obsession," the Israeli billionaire Joseph D. Hackmey told me, explaining why he had spent so much time (thirty years) and so much money (tens of millions) gathering stamps from New Zealand—among them the only three-penny lilacs from 1862 known to exist.

New Zealand was not his only specialty. Hackmey also assembled a prize-winning collection of Ceylon stamps, and his collection of Romanian material expanded beyond stamps to include the single most expensive copy of a newspaper. For $1.1 million, he got what the later owners of the one-cent magenta never did: the newspaper that came with the stamp. Or, in the case of the November 11, 1858, issue of *Zimbrul și Vulturul* that Hackmey acquired after outbidding the Romanian Ministry of Culture and National Patrimony, the *stamps*. Eight rare Moldavian "Bull's Head" stamps were pasted across the top of the front page before the newspaper was mailed.

If it's any comfort to philatelists, collection-itis is not confined to people with a passion for stamps. People collect anything and everything: baseball cards, Matchbox cars, Homer Simpson bobble-head figures, vintage lunch boxes. There was the dentist who collected incandescent light bulbs—sixty thousand of them, including the world's biggest, a fifty-thousand-watter. There was the teetotaling nonsmoker who collected miniature liquor bottles and, from cigarette packs, Alberto Vargas pinups. And there was the funeral director whom the *New York Times* described as a "Giotto of Maryland" for carving the masterpieces in a duck-decoy museum. A series of books called "Pleasures and Treasures" in the 1960s covered everything from arms and armor to French porcelain. And stamps.

The definition of collectibles changed as fads and fashions came and went. But the reason people collect has not changed. "Collecting fills a hole in life," Garfield wrote, "and gives it a semblance of meaning. When men get together to talk about their passions, we don't just talk about what we love—our cars, our sports, our romantic yearnings—but also how these desires have cost us, and what we have lost. We try to regain what we cannot. We talk about the one that got away—the prized possessions—as if that would have made everything right."

That's Stamp World for you.

FIVE

£120

———•———

1878: Glasgow and London

Neil Ross McKinnon had snapped up much of his collection when "old" stamps from British Guiana were cheap. He probably figured that prices—which had risen somewhat in a "stamp rush" in the 1870s, as stamp collecting became more and more popular—would climb even faster as the years went by. The money must have seemed alluring, considering how low the prices had been for McKinnon and Vaughan and anyone else who had bought and held British Guiana stamps from the beginning: Vaughan remembered selling British Guianan cottonreels for £1, equivalent to about $5 in today's currency. But those were cottonreels, and everyone knew that there were only so many cottonreels. There were other already-recognized rarities, and the race was on to locate them. Advertisements promising cash for stamps, any stamps, sent would-be philatelists scavenging "among private letters, in banks, merchants' offices, government offices, etc., as opportunity offered, with the result that hundreds of the early issues were found," Arthur D. Ferguson, a founder of the British Guiana Philatelic Society and the longtime editor of the *British Guiana Philatelic Journal*, reported nearly fifty years later. It wasn't always the original owners who profited, and it wasn't always committed collectors who were the treasure hunters. Unlike Vaughan, many had no legal claim to the stamps they snapped up and sold. Ferguson complained that some of the stamp hunting was done "without permission by clerks, office-boys, etc."—who sold the stamps and pocketed the money.

McKinnon assembled what would have been an enviable collection of stamps from British Guiana, except that in the mid-1870s, there was nothing enviable about it: no one cared about a collection of stamps from British Guiana—not yet, anyway. Stamps from British Guiana were still too new, and British Guiana was too far from the mainstream, as it always had been. By 1878, McKinnon owned the five most precious stamps from British Guiana: the four known copies of the 1850 two-cent cottonreel on rose-colored paper, which was also a provisional, a stamp printed locally rather than in London— as well as the one-cent magenta (though, of course, he did not understand that it was unique and would someday be the most valuable stamp in the world).

Collectors who resisted the temptation to sell early certainly did well. A middle-aged London barrister with a preposterous double last name, William Hughes-Hughes, started a stamp collection in 1859 and became so immersed in philately that he joined the high-powered coterie that met on Saturday afternoons at the Rev. Francis John Stainforth's rectory. It was the world's first local stamp club, but when it came to collecting, stamps were not Stainforth's only passion. He was also a conchologist (mollusks and shells) and assembled a large library of plays and poems by women, which is intriguing, because women were not allowed in the philatelic group. His catalogue—of course a consummate collector like Stainforth would catalogue his holdings—contains some six thousand entries, but judging by his "Wants" list," there were nine hundred more items that he never acquired.

Historians of philately recognize Hughes-Hughes and Stainforth's club as the one that eventually formed the Philatelic Society, London, the forerunner of the

Royal Philatelic Society London, which David Redden
visited with the one-cent magenta. Historians of Parliament remember Hughes-Hughes's father as "one of the
most thoroughly unpopular" MPs in the nineteenth century, mocked by Charles Dickens for "barking tremen-
dously," like a firefighter's dog.

The younger Hughes-Hughes's passion for stamps
did not last. He stopped collecting in 1874, calculating
that he had spent £69 on holdings that included one of
the blue four-cent stamps from British Guiana that were
probably printed at the *Gazette* at the same time as the
one-cent magenta. But he was not ready to part with his
collection. Twenty-two years later, when it was finally
liquidated, it went for £3,000, or more than $441,000 in
today's dollars.

Stamps were also appreciating in British Guiana by
then. In 1896, the same year in which Hughes-Hughes's
stamps were sold, a church asked members of the congregation to bring in old stamps. The church was in debt,
and the minister wanted to pay off the mortgage. He
hoped to raise money by selling the stamps to collectors. A
woman rummaged around at home and discovered two
early four-cent stamps, enough, she thought, to knock a
few pounds off the church's debt. The minister went to

thank her, and asked if she had any other treasures. She said she did not, but handed the minister a basket with envelopes containing old bills and receipts. One caught the minister's eye. It was addressed "Miss Rose, Blankenburg" and carried a pair of two-cent cottonreels.

Miss Rose was in the room, and when the minister said the envelope was worth a great deal, she exclaimed, "Thank God! I am at last able to give something worthwhile." The minister sold her envelope for £200, all but putting the church in the black.

McKinnon, though, had decided to cash out long before then, and enlisted help from another Scottish expatriate in British Guiana, one who stood to inherit a considerable fortune back in Glasgow. Just as everyone who was anyone in Paris after World War I seemed to know Gerald and Sara Murphy, everyone who was anyone in British Guiana in the mid-1870s must have known Robert Wylie Hill. (He was apparently not related to Rowland Hill, who invented the postage stamp.)

Unlike expats in British Guiana who set their sights on the nineteenth-century sugar frontier and worked as managers on plantations with distinctly Scottish names like Glasgow or Edinburgh—or who found their way to government jobs, as Vaughan did when he grew up—Wylie Hill seemed to see his mission as only slightly different from Columbus's. He wanted to go where few white men had gone—up the Amazon, into the rain forests, and he wanted to take the evidence back to Scotland and sell it. He was absolutely confident that there was a market back home in Scotland for stuffed birds from South America. Wylie Hill had returned to Glasgow by the late 1870s and had used his inheritance to build a department store, where he sold his birds.

For McKinnon, trying to dispose of the one-cent magenta, the problem was that it had not been discovered yet. It was not listed in any of the stamp catalogues. The philatelic experts in Britain had heard about other provisionals from British Guiana, including the blue four-cent stamps that were printed at the same time in the same place, but they knew nothing about the one-cent magenta. McKinnon had to bring it to their attention in a way that legitimized it. He realized that this was a job for someone else, someone who was as close to being an insider as there was—someone in Britain, of course, and someone who could serve as the one-cent magenta's advocate and publicist. He had someone in mind, a man who was already an established authority in the nascent universe of philately, an expert who could weigh in on the one-cent magenta's authenticity—and who, if he believed in the stamp and gave it his imprimatur, could spread the word. The only problem was that McKinnon did not know him, except by reputation. But McKinnon knew just who could put the one-cent magenta in front of him: Wylie Hill.

And so McKinnon had sent his five most precious stamps across the ocean to Wylie Hill in Glasgow with a request to get them to the renowned stamp expert Edward Loines Pemberton and, if Pemberton wanted them, to sell them to him.

It was a pragmatic choice. Pemberton was the co-author of a groundbreaking work on philatelic forgeries, which were flooding the market and threatening the value of legitimate rarities. If Pemberton vouched for the one-cent magenta, collectors would believe it was neither a forgery nor a fake. Anyone who wanted to make the case that it was, say, a four-cent stamp that had been altered would have a hard time going against Pemberton.

Pemberton was a prodigy. Before stamp collecting was weighed down by "its ponderous monographs and its obese catalogues," as the *Philatelic Journal of Great Britain* put it in 1922, there was Pemberton, an authority who spoke as if he had been present at the creation, and he pretty much was. He had caught the stamp bug when stamps were in their infancy and had "mastered every minute peculiarity," according to *The Philatelic Record*, which was written and read by masters of those peculiarities. By the time he attended the very first stamp auction ever held in London—in 1872, when he was twenty-seven—Pemberton was an old-timer in the stamp business. As a mere teenager, he had been considered as much of an authority as "many others who were his seniors by nearly half a century!"

Forgers hated Pemberton, but collectors respected him as the coauthor of a groundbreaking work on forgeries. He happily did more than just name names. His *Journal* promised the "addresses of all ascertained dealers in forgeries."

Pemberton had heard about the four-cent stamps from 1856 and had dismissed them as "purely provisional." "Ship with motto in plain oblong lettered frame," he wrote in *The Stamp Collector's Handbook*, which he described as "a plain and strictly accurate list of postage stamps."

But it was incomplete.

• • •

It arrived at Pemberton's house in a package, a dowdy twenty-two-year-old stamp. But Pemberton recognized its historic significance, and pushed it into the spotlight with his eyes, his memory, and maybe a magnifying glass.

His tools were rudimentary. If he had a microscope, it was probably little more than a couple of lenses in a tube. If he had other tools that modern stamp collectors take for granted, they, too, were rudimentary—tongs, perhaps, to keep dust and sweat from his fingers from damaging the stamps he examined. He had his pick of what was available, and the *Philatelic Journal of Great Britain* sighed that "it [made] one's mouth water" to think about the stamps that he got to see. "There are collectors who are just better at seeing things than others," Ted Wilson, the registrar of the National Postal Museum in Washington, told me. "I've seen people look at things, and they're able to see something that somebody who's looked at it a hundred times didn't see. You can tell the difference between people who are good and people who are incredible that way. He fell into the latter category. He had the eyes." Somehow, Pemberton saw everything, remembered everything, before everything was in catalogues.

But Pemberton had another advantage in examining

the one-cent magenta when he did. Wilson speculates that the stamp has faded with age and looked "significantly better" when Pemberton saw it than it does now. "He was in a better position to make a judgment than we would be today—if we didn't have the fancy equipment we have," he said.

Pemberton did not travel to the places that stamps came from. The mail brought them to him, directly or through intermediaries. When Wylie Hill sent him McKinnon's stamps, Wylie Hill quoted a price of £110, or just over $26,000 in today's dollars.

Pemberton, then thirty-three and already frail from rheumatic fever in his late twenties, looked over McKinnon's collection and judged the one-cent magenta to be the real thing, an authentic stamp that the philatelic world had never seen. He wrote to Sir Edward Denny Bacon, another pillar of British philately, in November 1878 that "the lot included a 'ONE cent, red, 1856!!!" When E.L. Pemberton talked, philatelists listened, and E.L. Pemberton was practically shouting.

If he had not ratified the one-cent magenta as he did—if Pemberton, the reigning expert on fakes, had ruled that it was bogus—it would have gone back to

Wylie Hill. Perhaps Wylie Hill would have returned it to McKinnon with a note that began, "Sorry, old chum." Or maybe Wylie Hill would not have bothered to send it back: "Sorry, old chum—I took the liberty of destroying the worthless and rather ugly one-cent magenta. I'm sure you will agree that I did what was best under the circumstances."

As it was, Pemberton called the one-cent magenta "queer" and "a dreadfully poor copy." But it was authentic. Pemberton never got around to writing out a detailed explanation of why he was sure it was real, but with his capital letters and exclamation points, he cemented the one-cent magenta's place in history.

He cemented its place in history in another way: by not buying it.

All he had to do was to send Wylie Hill a check, perhaps only a deposit if he did not have the money in the bank. Pemberton was Pemberton, and Wylie Hill would have accommodated him. Instead, according to the Williamses, "for some reason Pemberton dallied." He returned McKinnon's stamps to Wylie Hill without making clear that he wanted them.

If he thought he still had the right of first refusal, he

underestimated the wily Wylie Hill, who, "after waiting for some time in vain," moved on. David Redden maintains that Hill was simply following McKinnon's orders when he sent letters offering the collection to other stamp dealers, among them Thomas Ridpath of Liverpool, who hopped on a train to Glasgow, examined McKinnon's stamps, borrowed the money to buy them, and caught a train home to Liverpool, all in twenty-four hours. Ridpath paid £120. Already the one-cent magenta's price was climbing.

But while Ridpath was rushing off to Scotland, Pemberton changed his tune. Now he wanted the one-cent magenta.

Speedy as the British mail service was, Ridpath was not to be beaten. Pemberton sent along a check, but by the time it landed in Wylie Hill's mailbox, it was too late. McKinnon's stamps now belonged to Ridpath. The transaction could not be undone, not even for Pemberton.

Ever since, philatelists have wondered whether Ridpath understood the coup he had pulled off. Pemberton certainly did. He realized the opportunity he had missed.

Ridpath did not hold on to the one-cent magenta. Within days of his marathon trip to Glasgow, the stamp was off to Paris. Ridpath was confident that he could un-load the strange little stamp for more than he had paid for it.

Like McKinnon, he had someone in mind—someone who, just by buying it, would make the one-cent magenta famous.

SIX

£150

——◦——

1878: The Man in the Yachting Cap

Late one afternoon in May 1886, three thousand members of the moneyed aristocracy in France—a thousand more than could have squeezed into the lavish and still fairly new home of the Opéra de Paris—strolled into a palace that had once belonged to the diplomat Talleyrand, who had made himself indispensable to regime after regime. Princes and princesses, dukes and duchesses, viscounts and barons, the wedding guests passed under a balcony with sculptured lion's heads and sauntered through some of the most opulent rooms in Paris. Wedding gifts poured in, too, for the occasion was a marriage, an arranged marriage that united two of Europe's royal families. But it was "undoubtedly a love match," the *New York Times* wrote, surprised that

that thing called love had quickened the groom's humdrum heart.

One of the presents was a stunning tiara commissioned by the bride's father-in-law, King Luís I of Portugal, who was as popular in Lisbon for translating *Hamlet* and *Othello* as for handling the affairs of state. *The Times* noted that the bride's father—"a tall, robust, powerful looking man" who had spent his thirties in the United States and had served under General George McClellan in the Union Army during the Civil War—was a published author in his own right: "The most important of his literary productions is his *History of the Civil War in America*, a large and exhaustive work."

The bride, who carried a lovely wreath of orange blossoms, was "rather too tall," the *Times* carped, but she had the look of royalty behind her lace veil: "It would not be easy to find more aristocratic looking hands or smaller, more shell-like ears than those of this princess."

The one-cent magenta knew all about the wedding. It was close enough to hear the buzz of the crowd, the swish of the dresses, the airy sound of the orchestra. The one-cent magenta knew who flirted with whom, who got tipsy on the champagne, and who made a toast so inflammatory that Parliament said never again—a law passed the following week banned gatherings of that many nobles, for fear they would decide to overthrow the government.

The one-cent magenta knew all this because the palace, known as the Hôtel Matignon, where the wedding took place, had been the one-cent magenta's home for eight years. Later on, the stamp's neighbors on the Rue de Varenne, down from Les Invalides in the seventh arrondissement, would include Rodin, Rilke, and Edith Wharton.

The stamp's owner was an eccentric aristocrat, though he had long since shed his many titles. He tolerated Paris, though he disliked the French and insisted that his heart was with "my beloved Austria and my dear Germany." Philippe Arnold de la Renotière von Ferrary bought any stamp that came on the market, it seemed. His huge collection even included any number of fakes, and he knew it. He patronized one dealer who not only trafficked in forgeries but printed ersatz stamps in a back room. Ferrary supposedly bought one that was printed while he waited in the front room. The ink was still a little wet when the stamp was brought out and he touched it, but he did not mind.

"I would sooner buy one hundred forgeries than miss

that variety I could not find elsewhere," Ferrary said. Collectors soon dubbed the forgeries he accumulated "Ferrarities."

The one-cent magenta was the real thing. Ferrary was the stamp's first owner who lived in a grand setting, who amassed an astonishing collection, and who kept philatelic experts on his payroll. There are other parallels between Ferrary and another, later owner: brief marriages that didn't last, deep attachments to their mothers, passionately conservative views on politics and patriotism. At their deaths, the one-cent magenta was auctioned off with lawyers and executors looking on. Ferrary, though, did not kill anyone and did not die in prison. But that is getting far ahead of the story.

After Ferrary bought the one-cent magenta, it wasn't seen again in public until 1922. That only added to its allure. Stamp collectors still wonder what the one-cent magenta looked like when Ferrary owned it: how bright was it the first time he saw it, bundled it up, put it on a shelf. Whether he had it recolored after Bacon described its surface as rubbed in 1891. How much it had faded by the time he died nearly forty years later. And how often he took it off the shelf, turned it over, studied the initials, held a magnifying glass over the smudgy type, and defended the cut corners. Surely he loved the cut corners. Ferrary was known to cut stamps off covers long after his advisers pointed out that no one did that anymore, that the fashion in philately was to save the whole envelope containing a rare stamp. Maybe he sliced the corners off the one-cent magenta. There is no way to know.

By all accounts, Ferrary was a reclusive man who let in only a few trusted friends. Charles J. Phillips, the philatelist who had owned the venerable London dealer Stanley Gibbons and Company since 1890, was "one of the few people privileged to have the run of the collection whenever desired." The rest of the world had to imagine what the one-cent magenta looked like. As the stamp writer Alvin F. Harlow observed, "When a good stamp fell into his collection, it was spoken of as having gone to the graveyard"—it was not seen again, or so philatelists believed. Ferrary wrote little except for a couple of articles in philatelic journals when he was young and, when he was older, complaining letters to the editors of stamp magazines that used his royal titles. He or his assistants let Sir Edward Denny Bacon examine the stamp in Paris in 1891, and Bacon pulled out all the stops. If anyone had doubts after seeing Pemberton's exclamation points, Bacon meant to settle the matter.

For his part, Ferrary was all about Ferrary: he knew that the one-cent magenta was spectacular—by most accounts, he had paid £150 for it—and he didn't mind letting his friends know that he knew. He probably knew, too, that they would spread the stories about his collection. That would make it more valuable than if he allowed ordinary people to see it—the mystery would be gone—and he even turned down requests from people who were anything but ordinary. Ferrary supposedly said no to George V, who invited him to bring the best of his collection to London. Surely George V wanted to see the one-cent magenta. But Ferrary would not take his stamps across the Channel. Ferrary's excuse was that he had promised his mother that his stamps would never leave the opulent surroundings of the Hôtel Matignon. And they were opulent. The Hôtel Matignon set the standard on the supremely fashionable Rue de Varenne. In 1905, when Ferrary was in his fifties, the artist Eugène Atget photographed a fireplace there with a riot of candelabras on the mantel. The chandelier, the tall gilded clock, the floral-print slipcovers on the couches, the plasterwork on the walls—it was all so grand, and so big. Those three thousand wedding guests gossiped and dined and danced without angering the neighbors.

On her death two years after the wedding, Ferrary's mother bequeathed the palace to Emperor Franz Joseph for use as the Austrian embassy. But not all of it. One wing was to be Ferrary's, for the rest of his life, and his stamp business occupied three "philatelic rooms." Stamp dealers who showed up with treasures to sell had to run a gauntlet—big watchdogs had the run of the court-yard and had to be tied up before visitors entered. In-side was a retinue, Ferrary's philatelic secretaries and a business manager who put bundles of cash on nails in one room—every denomination up to a thousand francs, fifty thousand francs a week, week after week. Ferrary lived by the honor system. The sellers simply took what they were owed. And when Ferrary went shopping, the stamp-shop clerks knew not to stand too close. They opened their albums and looked the other way. Ferrary turned the pages, removing the stamps he wanted and putting them in his pocket. Then he left, and the clerks would go through the albums, noting what stamps were missing. The boss sent an invoice. Ferrary's people sent a check.

But maybe the one-cent magenta did not spend all its days in the palace. It is possible that Ferrary slipped the stamp out of the palace from time to time for a little show-

and-tell. Ferrary didn't advertise this, of course—why tempt the pickpockets of the world? But pickpockets who read a syndicated newspaper article one Sunday morning in 1906 probably wished they were within easy reach of Ferrary's threadbare coat. Smoothly, invisibly, they could have slid their fingers into his pockets and stolen his treasures, because—without meaning to—the article portrayed him as the easiest of marks.

"Ferrary was inspecting an art collection," the article reported, "when a large and handsome canvas that occupied a great portion of wall space was pointed out to him as the most valuable picture in the salon. 'It is worth all of eighteen hundred pounds,'" he was told.

"'Then it is not the most valuable picture here,' replied Ferrary, and he produced a small card case from the depths of a pocket. Inside was a tiny piece of paper, which he carefully held up. 'This,' he continued, 'is far more costly than your beautiful painting.'"

It was the one-cent magenta, which the article described as "a crude affair whose typographical appearance would not be endorsed by the humblest printer in all Christendom." The reporter asked how much it was worth, for as is so often the case with newspaper articles, big money was the point. This article appeared under a nine-word headline: "Most Valuable Bit of Paper in the Whole World."

"'I prize it so highly,' answered Ferrary, 'that if you were this instant to offer me three thousand pounds for it, I would not take it.'" How much was £3,000 worth in 1906? The headline writer saved pickpockets the trouble of doing the pounds-to-dollars calculation. The secondary headline read, "Owner Would Not Take $15,000 For It." That works out to at least $307,000 in today's dollars.

Ferrary stored his stamps not in albums but in packets in cupboards in alphabetical order. No one knows how often Ferrary went to the section where he kept the one-cent magenta—or had someone reach there for him—and untied the packet from British Guiana. No one knows how often he marveled at the stamp. The implication is not often. There are accounts that some of the bundles in his stamp rooms were dusty, that no one touched them for years. This suggests a household that was not attended to. That cannot have been the case. Ferrary's mother had been the richest woman in Europe. There was no *Downton Abbey* squeeze on the household staff. But perhaps Ferrary allowed no one in his quarters, even to clean.

Ferrary was named after King Louis Philippe of France, the "citizen king" undermined by the emerging industrial class. If Ferrary was born in 1848, as some accounts maintain, his namesake was out of power before he was out of diapers, and the Ferrary family was soon playing up to Napoleon III. And if Ferrary's mother was wealthy, his father was almost as well off from holdings in old-fashioned banks and newfangled railroads in Europe and Latin America. His father also had a hand in financing the Suez Canal. The library in the palace contained shelves filled with leather-bound books. After Ferrary's father died and his mother stepped inside the library for the first time, she discovered that the shelves did not contain the collected works of Montesquieu or Rousseau or Racine or Voltaire; they contained the collected works of her late husband. But his works were not filled with words. Each page of the volumes held a government bond—more than twelve million francs' worth in all.

Ferrary hated his father, who, it turned out, wasn't his father at all. In his twenties, Ferrary—and probably the rest of the household—heard Ferrary's parents quarreling. The duke had apparently just learned that the duchess had had an affair with an Austrian army officer around the time Ferrary was born. Some years later, the officer, by then Count de La Renotière von Kriegsfeld, adopted the middle-aged Ferrary. At the same time, the count adopted a second man, said to have been Ferrary's half-brother.

Most accounts agree that Ferrary never married. But in 1893, the *New-York Tribune* told Ferrary's story with a twist. On the same page as articles headlined "A Bride-Hunting Prince" and "From Mr. Greeley's Pen," it divulged that after renouncing his titles, Ferrary had found work as a tutor in mathematics "and lived modestly but honestly on a small income." He may have moved to a Left Bank apartment for a while when he was in his twenties, but he had the money to be welcomed in the right Right Bank circles. And in one salon, the article revealed, he met a Russian princess who was "rich, beautiful and [possessed] all the attractions of the high-class Tartar." It was love, the *Tribune* wrote, "and to please her, [Ferrary] laid claim to the parental millions." The Russian emperor even awarded him a title: the Duke di Ferrari.

"The marriage took place," the *Tribune* reported, "but it proved to be unhappy," and Ferrary and the princess "decided to live apart." It was the same Ferrary: "He has one hobby—the collection of postage stamps—and his collection is said by many experts to be the finest in Europe."

Not only did Ferrary have some ambivalence about his wealth and titles, he did not look the part of an aristocratic Parisian. The stamp writer Fred J. Melville noted that Ferrary was "anything but spick and span, rather dowdy, in fact, apparently careless of his attire, except for the yachting cap he always affected." The cap was emblazoned with three stars, and in stamp shops across Europe, the clerks snapped to attention when they saw it. One account has a worker whispering to a buddy, "Look sharp, for Gawd's sake! Here comes Martell's Three Star." Apparently Ferrary's cap had stars arranged like those on the label of bottles of Martell's cognac.

Ferrary had taken up stamps as a distraction from the worries that preoccupied his parents. When he was ten years old and traveling in Germany, Ferrary was upset by bad news from the front: French forces under Napoleon III had beaten the Austrian army. This was when he first became intrigued by stamps. Ironically, considering the subject at hand, the Austrians lost the Battle of Magenta. (Ferrary had nothing to do with designating the stamp's color as magenta. That had happened even before it left British Guiana.)

His mother approved of his hobby—she may have been the one to nudge him to start collecting. She paid for whatever caught his eye. By the time he was a teenager, he had encountered the Parisian dealer Pierre Mahé, and after years as a regular customer, Ferrary hired Mahé to oversee his holdings in 1874. Thomas Ridpath, who had bought the one-cent magenta from McKinnon in 1878, must have dealt with Mahé when he offered to sell it.

Ridpath sold him only the one stamp. No doubt Ferrary would have bought more. He bought the Australian collection of Sir Daniel Cooper, the governor of New South Wales, in the same year. A couple of years later, he bought a two-volume Japanese collection from Edward Denny Bacon. A couple of years after that, Ferrary bought much of the renowned Frederick Adolphus Philbrick collection for £8,000, as much as $12.1 million in today's dollars. Mahé maintained that even without Philbrick's British stamps, which were not included, this "made" the Ferrary collection. Later still Ferrary snapped up Baron Arthur de Rothschild's collection. That brought to seven the number of Post Office Mauritius stamps that Ferrary owned. And in 1894, he acquired the Swedish Treskilling Yellow from 1857, another stamp discovered by a teenager hunting for treasure stamps among old family papers. The Stockholm dealer Heinrich Lichtenstein realized the mistake: the teenager's three-skilling stamp was the color of an eight-skilling stamp. Like Louis Vernon Vaughan, the teenager walked away with a lot of money (for a teenager, anyway)—seven kronor, or about $223 in today's currency.

By the early twentieth century, some philatelists tallied and toted and guessed that Ferrary had spent as much as $1.2 million on stamps (equivalent to $34.9 million today). But he did not like to see his name in the papers. "For years," L.N. and Maurice Williams write, "the very name of Ferrary was spoken in philatelic circles, almost in a whisper, and reference in print to him and his stamps was usually in the form of 'a Parisian collection.'" Those who knew, knew; those who did not, wondered.

• • •

Ferrary's pro-German loyalty made his life complicated as World War I spread across Europe. Breaking his rule about not traveling with his stamps, Ferrary played the part of a rich man on the run, fleeing to neutral Switzerland, carrying along only a few stamp albums that held mostly Greek stamps. As the fighting continued, Ferrary managed to crisscross Europe in pursuit of stamps. He died in a taxi in Lausanne, on the way back to his hotel after trying to buy yet another stamp. He had a heart attack in the back seat.

Ferrary had spelled out the details of what was to happen to his stamp collection after he was gone. His will said it was all to go to Austria—specifically, to the Reichspost Museum in Berlin. The French would not hear of that. The French government seized the stamps in the Hôtel Matignon, and after several years of legal wrangling, interrupted by the necessary sorting and cataloguing, announced a sale. This was no one-day affair. There were so many stamps in the Ferrary collection that it took fourteen sales between 1921 and 1925 to auction them all. The one-cent magenta was not even included in the first sale.

When it finally went on the block, the catalogue described it in French: "GUYANE ANGLAISE. 1856. 1 c. noir sur carmin, catalogué chez Yvert et Tellier sous le no. 12 et sous le no. 23 dans le catalogue de Stanley Gibbons. C'est le seul exemplaire connu, obl." The only known example.

But the one-cent magenta's uniqueness was not why it set off a bidding war. Ferrary—secretive and obsessive, and the quintessential Mr. Big Spender—would have

Lot No. 295 opened at 50,000 francs, and the price climbed in 5,000-franc increments to 200,000, with Burrus matching Griebert at every step, even as other bidders dropped out, unwilling or unable to risk so much money. The denouement was exactly what Burrus imagined. At 295,000 francs, Griebert indicated that he would go to 300,000. Burrus decided to end his charade, and dropped out. Griebert's total, once the French sales tax was added, was 352,500 francs, or $32,500 ($459,000 in today's dollars).

Redden's pre-sale catalogue in 2014 dismissed the tale of the overheard conversation because, among other things, Burrus had acquired another important item from the early days in British Guiana at one of the earlier Ferrary sales, an 1851 two-cent cottonreel pair on cover that went for $19,000. But Burrus turned the one-cent magenta into the single most expensive item in any of the Ferrary sales, and he had spent not a penny on it. That distinction went to Griebert's American client, the richest man in Utica, New York—Arthur Hind.

loved the caper that unfolded: the intrigue, the preposterousness and the money. Especially the money. The enormous bids made Ferrary look like the smartest stamp buyer in history, not just the most voracious. Suddenly, his purchase of the one-cent magenta looked like a bargain, for in a matter of minutes, it became all the more unaffordable.

The auction opened after an intriguing twist that John le Carré would have loved, the curious incident of the stamp men in the restaurant—an overheard conversation that tipped off one potential bidder about how much his main rival could spend. The two antagonists were seated within earshot of each other, although if the story is to be believed, Hugo Griebert, a London dealer, did not see Maurice Burrus, who was, like Ferrary, wealthy and willing to spend. Burrus, whose money came from a family tobacco business, had been the biggest individual buyer at the first Ferrary sale. He had bought a two-cent Hawaiian "Missionary" for $14,150, setting the record for a single lot at that initial auction.

Burrus might have wondered why the one-cent magenta was not on the block that first day. The philatelic writer Kent B. Stiles asked the question in a stamp journal, estimating that the one-cent magenta would sell for between $10,000 and $15,000 ($139,000 to $208,000 in today's dollars). But he said that eyebrows had been raised by its absence: "Is that stamp still in the Ferrary collection? If so, have any other rarities been sold privately[?] If they have, who are the purchasers and where are those stamps now?" Stiles suspected the French government of strategizing, of taking a wait-and-see approach, of wanting to gauge the interest in the lesser treasures "before it placed the more desirable items . . . on the market."

If that was the French strategy, it paid off quickly. "Everyone is asking in London when the unique 'Ferrarity' will be offered," the philatelic writer Fred J. Melville observed in *Stamp Collecting* magazine amid suspicion that the one-cent magenta really was *that* kind of a Ferrarity: "The old story that it's a defective four-cent" was making the rounds. Gerard Gilbert, the Parisian expert commissioned to catalogue the Ferrary collection, had examined it, but Melville noted that "until M. Gilbert has decided that it is good, the stamp may not be put to the test" of an auction.

The test came eight months later, shortly after the scene in the restaurant. Griebert was the chatterbox, and Burrus said later that he could hear every word of the story Griebert told at his table. And what a cynical story it was: Griebert blithely said his client was an American

who had given him a nearly unlimited bid—a bid with the then unheard-of maximum of $60,000 (equivalent to just over $850,000 in today's dollars). That was all Burrus needed to know, but Griebert could not stop yammering away. He announced that he himself "did not believe" in the one-cent magenta—he had doubts about its authenticity and suspected it was a four-cent provisional that had been altered and fobbed off on the philatelic world.

By coincidence, that was exactly what Burrus had deduced. He maintained—even as late as 1951—that the one-cent had been created by rubbing out the *F* "FOUR" and the *S* in "CENTS"—and transforming the *UR* after the *O* to *NE*.

Burrus decided to show up Griebert. He thought that the game he had in mind would be amusing. It would also be expensive, but he knew that Griebert's client had money. Never mind that the big names of philately had vouched for the one-cent magenta, starting with Pemberton's simple declaration nearly more than forty years earlier. The eminent British philatelists W.A. Townsend and F.G. Howe noted that the Mahés—"father and son, both of whom worked for Ferrary over the years— "accepted and approved it, as [had] Sir Edward [De] Bacon." Burrus still wanted to make Griebert's client until it hurt.

SEVEN

$32,500

———•———

1922: The Plutocrat with the Cigar

In the story about the plutocrat and the cigar, the plutocrat was Arthur Hind, and the cigar was a Pennsylvania stogie, not a hand-rolled Cuban Cohiba. Hind looked like a down-market Daddy Warbucks—fleshier and not so worldly. Daddy Warbucks, according to no less an authority than Little Orphan Annie, had ten zillion dollars. Hind, according to no less an authority than Hind himself, had at least $7 million, and he bought a lot of stamps—thousands and thousands of stamps, so many he could not keep track of them all—before the Depression knocked his net worth down to only a million or so. A careful inventory of his stamp holdings ran to hundreds of pages, as thick as a telephone book. But the plain little one-cent magenta was his most important purchase, for it was the one that brought him what he cherished the most: fame.

Like Daddy Warbucks, Hind was an industrialist, self-centered and self-important. He was a fussy dresser, as one might expect of a multimillionaire in the fabric business. But he remained puzzlingly rough around the edges. There he stands in a fine-looking suit, a blank expression on his wide face as the camera snaps the photograph, but one trouser leg is noticeably shorter than the other. Surely he could have found a competent tailor.

Hind had been born in England, and like the very real Andrew Carnegie before him, had struggled and sweated in a textile mill when he was barely beyond grade school. And like Carnegie, who was only five feet tall, Hind was unusually short. Anyone who asked about Hind would have been told that when he was not quite sixty, he had taken up with a woman who was less than half his age and that they lived in upstate New York, far from the spotlights and celebrities—so far away that the stamp expert Kent B. Stiles commented that Hind "was never publicly identified with philately" until he bought the one-cent magenta.

Once he had it, though, he lived for the attention it

brought him. Hind capitalized on the one-cent magenta the way a politician would, but for Hind it was an impolitic move. Philatelists do not promote themselves with souvenir cards. His carried a reproduction of the prize and a braggart's caption: "The most valuable postage stamp in the world. The only known copy of the British Guiana one cent." As if that were not enough—as if he had done anything more than spend extravagantly—he put his signature on the card.

The story about the second stamp and the cigar surfaced in a Virginia stamp magazine in 1938, five years after Hind's death. The claim, in a long letter to the editor, was straightforward: "I had one too!"

The letter writer said he had been a cabin boy on a steamship that sailed to British Guiana from time to time. On a trip years before, he had bought "a packet of old local letters, some bills and receipts of a real old man" who was a relative of a drinking buddy. The purchase "cost me a few rums," he wrote. "I mounted the stamps in an album I made myself, and that was that"—until he read about the Ferrary sale. "I said to myself, 'D--- if I don't think I've got its twin!'"

The man described driving to Utica and, after calling Hind on the telephone, finding his way to Hind's house. He took out his stamp album and handed it to Hind, who grabbed his magnifying glass. "He went over to a place like a vault built into the wall of that room and got out his stamp, his one-cent Guiana. They were as alike as peas." There were only two differences: the original postmaster's signature on his stamp had more of a flourish than the signature on Hind's, and his stamp had a slight tear. (He did not say whether his also had clipped corners.)

Hind "looked at me, and you could hear my heart thumping," the man wrote, "and I guess he heard his, he was that still with excitement."

"Well?" Hind asked.

The man replied: "One of us has to own both, that's the way I figured it." The letter writer named a price he was willing to pay Hind—"a big sum," but exactly how much, he did not say.

Hind said, "If it's worth that to you, it's worth twice to me"—but insisted on secrecy: "Not even my secretary must know." Hind promised to pay in cash—"I'd rather not give a check"—and directed the owner to return the following day to complete the deal. Even with a fireproof safe within reach, Hind apparently did not keep that much money around.

The man stuck to the schedule Hind prescribed and showed up the next day, dreaming about life after surrendering the stamp and fretting about the money he would walk away with. He feared he would be robbed on the street as he left.

But first he had to close the deal. Hind took the man's stamp. "He held it in his hand and compared it with his again," the man wrote. "Then he put his away." Hind handed the man the money and offered him a cigar—"I put it in my pocket; I don't smoke, but I wanted to keep it."

Hind lit one for himself. Hind "looked at my stamp again," and then did the one thing the man had not imagined. Hind touched the stamp he had just acquired to the flame of the match he had just struck. The man tried to grab the burning stamp but it was too late, and Hind knew it. He smiled mischievously and said, "There's only one magenta one-cent Guiana."

So what if the story is too good to be true. It presented Hind as the stamp world saw him, with his devil-may-care extravagance, and it bared the resentment that collectors harbored against him. "He had more money than knowledge of stamps," Sir John Wilson, the British expert who was Keeper of the Royal Philatelic Collection from 1938 to 1969, wrote in the 1950s. "Where he was advised that a stamp was sufficiently rare and sensational, he would pay almost any price for it." No doubt some philatelists snickered at the mention of Hind's name. Hind must have known. He himself repeated a story he said had originated with a British clergyman during an "antiphilatelic outburst." The minister imagined the dialogue between Hind and Saint Peter at the gate of heaven.

"I crave admittance," Hind announced.

"Have you fed the poor, visited the sick, relieved distress?" Peter asked.

"No," Hind replied, "I really hadn't time, but I have a one-cent British Guiana stamp in a greaseproof envelope, for which I paid £7,000. Even His Majesty the King of Great Britain personally congratulated me upon [my] acquiring it. Would you like to see it?"

"Such tiny fragments will readily burn in hell," Peter declared, slamming shut the gate.

And there were other stories about Hind. "The difficulty in showing stamps to Hind was that he always thought he had something better," Wilson wrote in a passage about Hind's pride at one-upping King George V. He damned Hind even more by implying Hind did not understand the differences between similar stamps in his own collection—differences that mattered to collectors.

Hind did not care. The author Alvin F. Harlow described him as "headstrong" and a reckless buyer, and the philatelic historian Stanley M. Bierman called him "opinionated, cynical and strong-minded." For his part, Hind could bristle with arrogance, as was apparent in an article he wrote for the catalogue of an international exhibition in Australia: "The unfortunate side of being prominent in stamps is that so many of the correspondents who have no knowledge whatsoever about stamps or their value, must be disappointed when not receiving replies to their simple but ignorant questions."

• • •

Some philatelists disdained Hind for buying, some for buying indiscriminately, like Ferrary. But the Ferrary of America was no Ferrary. Hind was more like William P. Brown, a New York coin dealer who began trading stamps around 1860, when philately was beginning to catch on with the public. "[A]s [Brown] had no knowledge of market values or rarity[,] he was guided by instinct," L.N. and Maurice Williams wrote. The stamps Brown felt were worth featuring in his shop "he fixed onto the boards alongside his coins—with the nail through the middle of each stamp!"

Hind did not nail his stamps in place, and he did not nail cash to the wall for dealers, the way Ferrary did. But neither did he assemble his collections patiently, one important stamp at a time. Like Ferrary, he snapped up whole collections that others had put together. He shelled out $15,000 for a complete collection of Hawaii and $63,000 for a highly regarded collection of France. Shortly before he bought the one-cent magenta, he spent $50,000 to acquire the one- and two-penny Mauritius stamps.

Hind glued many of his stamps in stamp albums, all but ruining them forever. Some stamps he affixed to the pages with adhesive bandages. A deep student of philately would have known better than to risk damage to the stamps, but as the prestigious *London Philatelist* curtly observed, "We do not think Mr. Hind ever claimed to be a deep student of philately." Hind simply plunged in, for he had so much to glue down. By the time Hugo Griebert pocketed the one-cent magenta for him at the Ferrary sale, Hind owned three or four of the world's most valuable stamps, including a second pair of the famed Mauritius— the so-called Bordeaux Cover. It bore the orange one-penny and the blue two-pence Post Office Mauritius stamps and was described by the French dealer Roger Calves as "la pièce de resistance de toute la philatélie."

Even A.J. Sefi, a famous British stamp dealer who was friendly with Hind, seemed to damn Hind with faint praise. Sefi—a distant cousin of Michael Sefi, the keeper of the queen's collection whom Redden visited in 2014—maintained that Hind paid too much for the Mauritius cover. A.J. Sefi said he and Percival Loines Pemberton (the son of Edward Loines Pemberton, who had not been fast enough with his check in 1878) had gone to Paris to buy it months before Hind did. Sefi said they decided not to go through with the deal because the price was too high and one of the stamps showed some slight damage.

Sefi went on to indict Hind's approach to collecting, faulting Hind for remaining an across-the-board generalist rather than limiting himself to stamps from only one or two places. "Collecting, as he did, the whole world," Sefi wrote in *The Philatelic Journal of Great Britain*, "it was impossible for him to devote the hours of study to any one particular country that would have been possible had he been a 'one-country' man, as are so many of our great philatelists." Sefi did defend Hind against criticism that he was "a wealthy man just accumulating vast quantities of the rarest obtainable stamps for the pure joy of possession . . . Hind was a much more knowledgeable buyer than the world gave him credit for," Sefi wrote, and he "took the greatest interest and care in every one of his purchases."

Sefi knew Hind's habits because he had visited Hind in Utica. "Wrapped in a voluminous dressing-gown," Sefi wrote, "he would spend the entire day in his simple study, working upon his collection, the whole of which was immediately available a few steps away, in the strong room built into the wall just before where he sat." Hind put in long hours: "I remember one day that we never left the room from nine thirty in the morning until tea time, lunch, as was his wont, consisting of a few sandwiches as we worked."

The one-cent magenta escaped the glue and the adhesive tape because Hind kept it in a cellophane envelope—and at least once, he forgot where he had stashed the envelope.

• • •

Hind was unusual among philatelists: he came to it late in life. He had not collected stamps as a boy. There wasn't time. A seventh-grade dropout, he had gone to work young. He went on to make a fortune in imitation furs and seat covers for automobiles, but he was a hardly a conventional capitalist. From his late forties on, he spent much of his time traveling the world and living large, "a thrifty, hard-headed, meticulous although sometime vacation-minded businessman," as one New York historian remembered him. Hind was known to send telegrams to his home office outside Utica with disarmingly relaxed-sounding accounts of what he was up to: "Might do some business in Calcutta. Things dull in Johannesburg."

His fortune soared, thanks to a straightforward formula: always be the low-cost producer, even in bad times. But his was not the Horatio Alger story it appeared to be. The mill in Yorkshire in which he started out belonged to his family; he quit school because business had soured and he was needed at the mill. He worked his way up from the factory floor, and by the time he was seventeen, he was the firm's rainmaker, bringing in new business.

Hind moved to the United States in 1890, the year he turned 34, because of protectionist tariffs. Republicans had championed such tariffs since the Civil War. The latest round carried the name of William McKinley, the chairman of the House Ways and Means Committee and a Republican congressman from Ohio, the state where Firestone, Goodrich, and Rockefeller had gotten their starts. In Washington, as one biographer noted, McKinley was more often a mediator than a gladiator, and he assumed that the most punishing tariffs in his bill would be reduced by a House-Senate conference committee. The committee let them stand. Hardline protectionism eventually boomeranged on the Republicans, but if McKinley was oblivious to the connection between tariffs and the accumulation of wealth in the Gilded Age, Hind was not. From across the Atlantic, he had seen possibilities. Congress might make laws abridging the rights of foreign firms to profit from their exports, but Congress would never impose limits on American manufacturers. So Hind set out to become an American manufacturer.

He did it the way he would later make himself a stamp collector. He bought his way in.

He decided to move the family company's "plush" division—the unit that made velvet-like fabric from worsted yarn—to the United States, machinery, workers and all. The only thing he needed was a mill. With his checkbook in his pocket, Hind and H.B. Harrison, who handled the finishing and dyeing of Hind's fabrics in England, went shopping.

Together they placed advertisements in newspapers and scouted failing factories that had "for sale" signs out. He and Harrison went as far as Hudson, New York, once a booming port city that later became infamous as "the

little town with the big red-light district." There they ne-
gotiated for a building they thought would do. But before
the contract had been drawn up, Hind and Harrison decided to go sightseeing—specifically, to Niagara Falls—
and before they departed, the one and only reply to their
"factory wanted" advertisements reached them. It was
from Clark Mills, New York, "a place," in the words of
the stamp dealer Charles J. Phillips, "they would never
have considered if they had not planned this trip" to Niagara Falls. They put Clark Mills on the itinerary as the
first stop. Phillips did not say whether they made it to
Niagara Falls.

Hind liked the empty factory building in Clark Mills,
a "virtual ghost town" where hard times had left "vacant
houses pockmarked with broken windows." He wanted
the deal done fast. He stayed up all night in his hotel
room, poring over documents that had to be signed to
make the mill theirs. Then he sailed back to England to
export the company, returning a few months later on the
SS *Majestic* with five employees, the first of hundreds he
brought over.

Clark Mills immediately became a company town, but
the Boss complained that there was too little to do there
after the closing whistle had sounded in the afternoon.

He heard the call of the city—not the big city but the one nine miles away, Utica, the one that the historian Edmund Morris described as little more than a "shabby canal town." Hind took his money there, eventually purchasing a hotel and a parking garage. He also picked up a stake in a golf course that was soon rechristened "Arhipaca." People wondered if it was an Indian name. It was not. It was the first two letters of his first and last name and the first two letters of the first and last names of Hind's partner in the deal, Patrick Casey.

By Utica's standards, Hind was fabulously rich and, according to the stamp historian Bierman, "never took much advice." But he took Harrison's advice when Harrison urged him to take up the pursuits of the rich. It was Harrison who persuaded him to try philately.

Harrison had heard that a collection was available right there in Utica. Hind snapped it up and thus became the owner of twelve thousand stamps. The collection had belonged to a doctor, presumably a pillar of the community in Utica, something Hind aspired to be. "Despite his great wealth," Bierman wrote, "he seemed basically insecure, and overcompensated for his presumed shortcomings by grandiose acquisitions as if to justify his raison d'être."

Hind's insecurity was on display almost as soon as

he completed his most grandiose acquisition. Less than a year after Hind brought the one-cent magenta to the United States following the Ferrary sale, he carried it back to Europe. The occasion was a stamp exhibition in London in 1923. It was probably the first and only time the stamp was seen by the philatelist-king, George V. Sir Edward Denny Bacon, the king's secretary for stamps, reported that George "didn't want a cripple in his collection," meaning the stamp held no appeal because of its cut corners. Sir John Wilson echoed that idea in his history of the royal stamp collection: "While [George V] acknowledged its interest and rarity, he regarded it as too poor a specimen to be worth anything like the figure which it [had] realized" in the Ferrary sale.

But when Hind and about a hundred other philatelists called at Buckingham Palace, Hind "repeatedly pointed out to his gracious host"—the king—"that his own collection was superior in rarities to the Royal Collection," Bierman wrote. "When shown the king's Post Office Mauritius, Hind was quick to mention that he had a better set." Still, the king accepted one of Hind's cards with the image of the one-cent magenta.

Hind was no more diplomatic on a trip to the Collectors Club in Manhattan in 1923. The club's magazine reported that the scheduled events—a dinner at a fancy hotel and a talk by Hind, who had promised to show part of his collection—broke the club's attendance records and brought together "a veritable Who's Who among the leading United States specialists." The Collectors Club counted among its members most of the boldface names of philately, including the dealer and auctioneer J.C. Morgenthau, who had sold Hind some of his Mauritius holdings, and Theodore E. Steinway, the son of one of the sons in Steinway & Sons, the piano company.

But Hind said not one word at his "talk." The club's magazine played the apologist. "The fact is that it was hardly necessary for Mr. Hind to do any talking," it said. "His stamps were there to speak for themselves."

He pulled three albums from a satchel. One was filled with Confederate stamps.

The collectors took issue, however politely, with Hind's glued-down, adhesive-bound stamp albums. The magazine wrote "the mounting is not terribly attractive." But "this is only a temporary condition, as Mr. Hind is shortly to have the collections remounted in better albums."

• • •

Thanksgiving Day 1926 should have been the happiest of days for Hind, who had turned seventy earlier in the year. It was the day he married Ann Leeta McMahon. She wore a dress made of dark-green velvet—no doubt the finest that Hind's mill could produce—and carried an orchid. The small bungalow in which the ceremony was held was decorated with chrysanthemums and lilacs. The Reverend Philip Smead Bird, a Presbyterian minister, officiated.

The newspapers did not mention some intriguing details. One was that the groom had an affectionate nickname for the bride—Bob, although when I ran across a mention of "Bob" in a surrogate court file, I wondered if the judge or the stenographer had misunderstood something gruffer and more colloquial, like "Bub." Another detail was whether the ceremony was a sham. The couple had been living together for years, sometimes traveling as husband and wife. On a passport application she filled out in 1925, she wrote that she had married Hind two years before.

Ann was the daughter of a harness maker who went to work in a textile mill—not Hind's—as the horse-and-buggy days disappeared in rear-view mirrors. It is not clear how she met Hind. David Redden's first question to me, in a conversation months after the auction of the one-cent magenta and after I had begun reading up on Hind, was unrestrained: was she a showgirl? If she was, that occupation did not appear in census records. One listed her as an attendant in a psychiatric hospital in upstate New York when she was in her early twenties, some years before she took up with Hind.

"She was the girl he escorted around town," Richard L. Williams, the current historian for the Town of Kirkland, New York—which now includes Clark Mills—told me. But for years Hind had escorted her far beyond Utica. She had signed a second passport application in 1925 "Leeta Ann Hind" (and had written that her stops on an upcoming trip would include "Maderia, France," suggesting that spelling and geography were not strengths). It was the same name she had used ten years before, when they boarded the SS *Cartago* for the trip through the Panama Canal and on to New Orleans. She was Mrs. Hind again when they boarded a ship in Yokohama, Japan, in 1917. The passenger manifest listed her as married; her name appeared below Hind's, and he paid for more than her ticket. Along the way, Hind bought her a strand of pearls that year for $15,000 (equivalent to $278,000 in today's dollars). When they were sold at an auction in the

1940s, one bidder said, "He was a better philatelist than he was a jeweler."

She registered as Leeta A. Hind in 1918, when they sailed from New York to San Juan on the SS *Brazos*, promoted by its owners as "specially built for tropical travel." Again, she affirmed that they were married. But in 1919 in Liverpool, in the country whose citizenship Hind had renounced after moving to Clark Mills, she boarded the SS *Carmania* as Leeta A. McMahon, using her first husband's name. She was Passenger No. 25, several lines below Hind in alphabetical order on the manifest, but still listed herself as McMahon's widow on a passport application.

Through all of this, Hind worked on his stamps, but his interest in philately faded after they finally married. He said there was nothing more to collect. In 1928, when the stock market was roaring, he put a part of his collection on the market, but not the one-cent magenta. He wanted half a million dollars for much of the collection ($6.9 million in today's dollars). He turned down an offer for $480,000.

Hind's timing was terrible, but before long, he had things on his mind other than stocks and bonds that were worthless after the crash. By their fourth official anniversary—Thanksgiving in 1930—he apparently had had it with Ann. He more or less disinherited her for what he said were infidelities. He never got around to divorcing her, but he did revise his will. He left her their house, and in nine lines of tiny type, listed the possessions she was to have after he was gone, from jewelry and clothes to furniture, silverware, and "bric-brac." He also spelled out what she was not to have: "My stamp collection." It was "expressly excluded."

Leaving her the "dwelling" was generous of Hind. The little bungalow had been hers to begin with, from her first marriage. But there was one possession that she was determined to have, willed or not.

EIGHT

$40,000

———•———

*1940: The Angry Widow, Macy's,
and the Other Plutocrat*

Arthur Hind died in March 1933 believing the one-cent magenta was in a vault at his bank in Utica. He had moved his stamp collection there several years before—most of it, anyway. But his executors, officials of the very same bank, did not find the one-cent magenta when they conducted an inventory. They searched frantically, checking and rechecking the albums and envelopes in the vault. Finally they turned their attention to the bungalow he and Mrs. Hind had shared. There, in Hind's fireproof safe or in a drawer of his desk, was the stamp. It had been sent back from a stamp exhibition in late 1932, while Hind was still alive, and was still in the registered-mail envelope in which it had been returned. Apparently Hind had forgotten to forward it to the bank.

Of course Mrs. Hind claimed it. It was her lottery ticket, if she could just cash it in.

To do that, Mrs. Hind, the one person Hind did not want to have the one-cent magenta, would have to do the one thing that was not possible in the 1930s: sell it.

Hind had tried and failed to sell some of his stamp holdings. In 1931, a disastrous year that began with the Dow Jones industrial average at 169 and ended with the Dow at 74, Hind showed his contrarian side, or perhaps his delusional side. He raised the price from $500,000 to $600,000. There were no takers.

Mrs. Hind did not have the whole collection to sell. She did not have her husband's Post Office Mauritius stamps, his Inverted Jennies, or his Confederates, and she did not demand them. She could really go after only one stamp, the one found in her home. It just happened to be the most valuable single item her husband had owned, the one-cent magenta.

First, though, she had to establish ownership, which meant tangling with Hind's executors. She staked her claim to the stamp on a tale that seemed improbable, considering the explicitness of Hind's will. There was no question that Hind had lavished gifts on Mrs. Hind over the years. The surrogate's court mentioned a necklace that had cost Hind $25,000, as well as a $6,000 mink coat, a $5,000 platinum watch with diamonds, and the two cars, both Pierce-Arrows. Hind had paid $6,000 for one and $4,800 for the other. But she asserted that the one-cent magenta had also been a gift from Hind.

She also claimed a third of the remainder of Hind's estate under a recently enacted state law that allowed widows to do so. Hind's lawyer had tried to preempt such a challenge with a clause in the will. The new law was intended to empower women whose husbands had blindly left everything to the children. But it applied equally to widows from marriages gone bad.

She did not admit to friction in the marriage. She told a tale of comfortable domesticity, of a couple who were relaxed and easygoing around the house. She said she herself had taken the stamp out of the vault in December 1931 because he needed it. He had to mail it to London for display at a stamp show. Soon after the stamp was sent back in February 1932 and returned to its place in the safe, she made her move.

"Arthur Hind was sitting in his study," a surrogate's judge wrote later in summarizing her account. Hind's safe was in the next room. Mrs. Hind knew the combination and dialed it in. She took out the one-cent magenta, carried it to the table where Hind was working and placed it in front of him. "Hind turned and observed the stamp," the judge wrote. "He said to her in substance, 'Bob'"—the judge duly noted that this was Hind's pet name for his wife—"'do you know the worth of that stamp and would you appreciate it if I gave it to you?'" Yes and yes, Mrs. Hind said. Hind said the four words she wanted to hear: "You may have it." The judge said that Hind "turned to the regular work in which he was engaged at the moment" and that Mrs. Hind put the stamp back in the safe. It was just another day around the house.

Now it was Mrs. Hind who took the stamp out of the safe from time to time and looked at it, the way Hind had done before his interest in philately faded. Or so she said.

By then, Hind was an old man. He was in his late seventies. He had lived nearly twenty years longer than the national average. A lesser man—less wealthy, less determined—would have retired to a rocking chair. Hind apparently still saw himself as a man on the go. In December of that year, Hind signed a six-month lease on a house in Miami Beach. He came down with pneumonia in February 1933 and died on March 1.

The funeral was held at the bungalow in Utica; the honorary pallbearers "were all prominent Utica men and old friends of Arthur's," the stamp dealer Charles J. Phillips wrote. There were eulogies by executives and employees of Hind's company and by his bankers.

Mrs. Hind was not terribly convincing as a grieving widow. Her next husband was the man who sold her the tombstone for Hind's grave. Pascal Costa Scala was thirty. She was forty-five.

Scala was a "well-known young Utican," one of the newspapers wrote, although exactly what was meant by that phrase was not explained. Scala was definitely a local. He had grown up a couple of miles from Mrs. Hind's bungalow. Across the street from his family's tenement, home to Pascal and his brothers and sisters, was a funeral home run by a relative. Another relative ran a meat-packing business (and would tangle with Ann over a $20,000 loan during the Depression). A 1925 state census listed Scala's occupation as "auto salesman," but he had given that up by the time the next census-taker made the rounds. The 1930 federal census had him selling "monuments."

They kept their relationship secret while Mrs. Hind parried with Hind's executors and relatives, but tongues in Utica must have been wagging, especially if whispers had escaped that they had married in Pennsylvania just months after Hind's death. The news did not make the papers until later, after she had settled with Hind's heirs in Britain—and kept the one-cent magenta.

• • •

She sent the stamp to London, where the experts at the Royal Philatelic Society examined it and pronounced it genuine. She consigned it for an auction in London in October 1935, with a reserve—a minimum selling price— of $42,500, or at least $590,000 in 2016 dollars. The bidding opened at £3,500 ($16,000) and topped out at £7,500, $4,500 short of the threshold. The stamp was withdrawn without being sold, disappointing a Pemberton yet again. The final bid came from Percy Loines Pemberton, perhaps to avenge his father, Edward Loines Pemberton, who had declared the stamp genuine but had been late with his check in 1878.

Back in the United States, Colonel Edward Howland Robinson Green was prepared to pay $40,000 for the one-cent magenta. The *New York Times* reported that Green would have, "had he lived a month longer." Green was an eccentric multimillionaire in his late sixties who, like Hind, bought everything in sight. He was the genial counterpoint to his mother, Hetty Green, who was known as the "Witch of Wall Street"—famous for her success, infamous for her stinginess, her pettiness, her nastiness. But his death in 1936 dashed the deal for the one-cent magenta. Later the *Times* said Mrs. Hind turned down another $40,000 offer, this time from a British collector. Like Hind in 1931, she then raised the price. She insisted she would not sell for less than $50,000. In 1938, she turned to another stamp dealer, Ernest G. Jarvis, who set a more realistic price of $37,500. Still it did not sell.

She had steadily increased the insurance coverage of the stamp over the years, eventually valuing the stamp at $48,800. But she had no passion for stamps, and probably no patience for them, either. "She has none of the reverence for the stamp that collectors feel for [the one-cent magenta]," a reporter observed, noting the irony of her claim on it: "A woman who never collected anything in her life owns a stamp that makes stamp collectors shiver in awe." She did not express awe or affection for her most valuable possession. She merely said it was "terribly homely." She tried to rid herself of the stamp, but not at a loss. She turned down offers ranging from $25,000 to $38,000 in 1940 before she entrusted the stamp to a retailer that was bigger and more "Barnumesque" than any that had handled the stamp before—Macy's. Macy's had a stamp department in those days (as did its rival, Gimbel's), and promised exposure.

The promises came from Finbar B. Kenny, the precocious—he was in his twenties at the time—manager of Macy's stamp department. He became the stamp's guardian and promoter. Mrs. Hind became the stamp's escort. He arranged for the one-cent magenta to go to the World's Fair. She dressed the part, in a fur jacket, and was photographed looking at the one-cent magenta. In newspapers that did not print color photographs, caption writers had to explain: "That little black spot on the table [in front of Mrs. Hind] is worth $50,000."

Not quite. When she finally sold it, soon after her appearance at the World's Fair, the check was for less than that. The *New York Times* said she got only $40,000. But the auction catalogue for a later sale said she pocketed $45,000.

• • •

Mrs. Hind's marriage to Scala lasted nine years. This time, apparently, it was Mrs. Scala who was the wronged spouse. The judge who handled the case set two conditions. One was that Mrs. Scala could call herself Ann

Hind again. The other was that she was free to remarry, but her ex-husband was not. The judge said that Scala was to seek the court's permission if he wanted to marry while Mrs. Hind was still alive. Nothing in the record explained what Scala had done to prompt such an unusual requirement.

Mrs. Hind died of heart disease in 1945 at age fifty-seven. Scala returned to court the following year, seeking to have the divorce set aside. His lawyer said Mrs. Scala had "forgiven and condoned the acts of her husband and had done so before the decree had become final." The judge turned him down but said he could file suit against his ex-wife's estate. He did, and settled for $6,500.

• • •

Finbar B. Kenny, the manager of Macy's stamp department, arranged the deal for Mrs. Hind. Her sister said Mrs. Hind never knew who bought it. If Mrs. Hind did not know who the new owner was, neither did the public. The buyer was not identified until shortly after he sold the stamp thirty years later. He kept quiet for a reason, and the reason was a grumpy remark attributed to Hind. Soon after the purchase, the *New York Times* reported that the new owner was "withholding his identity because dealers had deluged Mr. Hind, after he had purchased it, with offers to sell other rarities, often at exorbitant prices." The new owner recalled a comment by Hind that the pressure had interfered with his business operations.

His silence did not stop ever-higher numbers from being bandied about. In 1949 the *New York Times* said that the owner had turned down an offer of $60,000 and would not even part with it for $100,000.

That sounded like the kind of damn-the-torpedoes attitude that Hind had taken in tougher times, and like Hind, the new owner of the one-cent magenta, Frederick Trouton Small, was another immigrant who was in the textile business. Small presided over a huge fiber and weaving plant in Maryland for years. But there was a difference. Hind had owned his mill and his company. Small was an employee, however prized he was and however much stock he held—the plant manager for twenty-five years, later a vice president at corporate headquarters in New York.

The company was the Celanese Corporation, which made synthetic yarn and wove fabric from it. Small, an Australian who had been the company's head of production in Britain when Celanese was turning out a million pounds of acetate yarn a week in the years just after World War I, was instrumental in putting the Maryland plant into operation. The installation of the machinery—indeed, the construction of the factory buildings—ran behind schedule because of a flood. Small arrived with a mandate to get the plant going, apparently even if the rank and file had to work weekends and holidays. The first spool of acetate yarn was finally produced on Christmas Day in 1924. It was marketed as artificial silk.

Small did not take the one-cent magenta home once it was his. He told some reporters that he kept it in his office, first at the plant in Maryland and later in New York. Perhaps when Small's secretary said he was not available, he was not holed up studying sales figures or reading memos, he was working on his stamp collection. Then again, perhaps not. He told other reporters that he saw the one-cent magenta only once in the thirty years he owned it. That was at the beginning, after he bought it and Kenny sent it to him by registered mail. Small looked at it and sent it back to Kenny for safekeeping, again by registered mail. The *New York Times* went so far as to write later on that Small "was not a stamp collector. He was an investor in stamps."

Still, Small had the background of a philatelist. He

had collected stamps as a boy in Australia. "It was a lad's collection," the *Times* reported, and his parents gave it away while he was serving in the Australia and New Zealand Army Corps in World War I, first in the defense of the Suez Canal and later in the failed Gallipoli campaign for control of the routes from Russia. He was a mechanical engineer who directed the placement of underground explosives that were used against the Turks. One device exploded sooner than it was supposed to, and Small suffered a knee injury. Later he was trapped in an underground mine that was gassed before he could get out. Later still he was sent to England, where he worked in the Department of Aircraft Production in the Ministry of Munitions. Through a connection there, he met the Swiss brothers who started Celanese. They hired him and sent him to the United States as the company expanded.

He gravitated back to stamps "after seeing the destruction of many classic things" as a soldier in World War I. "Stamps, like everything else, tend to get destroyed," he said, "and the worth of those that remain go [*sic*] up." He owned a fabulous collection of stamps from British Guiana. He also laid claim to specialized collections of stamps from Bavaria and a number of other German states, as well as four collections of Russian stamps that filled forty-five albums—all bought through Kenny at Macy's.

. . .

Small's identity as the owner of the one-cent magenta may have been the worst-kept secret in philately for thirty years, but his name was not revealed publicly until after he sold the stamp in 1970. The public face of the one-cent magenta for all that time was Kenny. It was Kenny who put his initials on the back of the stamp, a small "FK."

He left Macy's to join the Army in 1942 and joined a smaller, stamps-only firm that established itself as a power-house in philately after the war, and it was Kenny who was quoted when the one-cent magenta went to stamp shows. Presumably, it was Kenny who made the arrange-ments, letting the stamp be seen, but not too often. And it was Kenny who recounted the all's-well-that-ends-well anecdotes that had just enough drama to keep the stamp in the news.

Kenny—and the stamp—traveled only a few blocks to a stamp exhibition at the brand-new New York Coli-seum in 1956. Kenny carried the stamp in a back pocket. He stashed a copy of the stamp in another pocket "to foil thieves." Whether they were real or imagined, it was an irresistible detail in newspaper stories, for there were crowds outside the Coliseum and crowd-pleasers inside. The stamp show, officially the Fifth International Philatelic Exhibition, known as FIPEX, was one of three inaugural events at the Coliseum; the others were the far larger International Automobile Show and the National Photographic Show. The United States Post Office took note of FIPEX by, among other things, issuing a three-cent commemorative stamp showing the chunky, cream-colored Coliseum complex and the statue that stood yards away in Columbus Circle.

For Kenny, there was none of the nail-biting at FIPEX that there had been at CIPEX, the Centenary International Stamp Exhibition, nine years earlier. For that show, also held in New York, the one-cent magenta was, as usual, accompanied by police and plainclothes detectives. The stamp simply vanished, Houdini-like. Its display case had not been broken open. "Despair and suspense mounted as worried officials at CIPEX scurried about, comparing the apparent loss of the British Guiana to the theft of the Mona Lisa," the philatelic historian Stanley N. Bierman wrote. Eventually, someone noticed that the stamp had slipped from its place and drifted to the floor of the display case. The CIPEX officials called off the search and remounted the stamp, this time on a stamp hinge that would not give way.

Kenny sent the stamp to Australia in 1963 and London in 1965 for exhibitions that went well. The 1970s were not kind to Kenny. The decade began with Small selling the one-cent magenta through a firm other than Kenny's. In the mid-1970s, the firm Kenny worked for was sold, and Kenny went out on his own. The decade ended with Kenny becoming an unfortunate footnote to history, the first person to plead guilty under a new federal law that made it a crime for Americans to bribe foreign officials.

Congress had passed the law and President Jimmy Carter had signed it in 1977 after an investigation by a high-level task force had found evidence of bribery and other problems by "a significant number of America's major corporations." The task force described "facilitation or 'grease' payments," apparently in response to extortion demands by foreign officials, as well as off-the-books slush funds and falsified business records. Senator William Proxmire, the maverick Wisconsin Democrat who had long crusaded against waste and corruption in government, and Senator Frank Church, who had moved to curb "criminal activity" by intelligence agencies after the Watergate scandal, pushed the bill through. But the first case brought by the Justice Department did not name a major defense contractor or a multinational retailer, it named a stamp dealer—Finbar B. Kenny.

Kenny's business had come to involve more than brokering deals for rare stamps. He was also designing and printing stamps for emerging nations. In 1965, the year in which the Cook Islands in the South Pacific won independence from New Zealand and became an eight-island nation unto itself, Prime Minister Albert Royle Henry struck an economic development deal with Kenny. It promised a faster, surer payoff than, say, building factories for low-cost manufacturing. Kenny would supply limited-edition stamps for the Cook Islands, and he and Sir Albert's government would divide the profits. The Cook Islands were just following the lead of other tiny countries like Liechtenstein and San Marino, which depended on stamp sales for revenue, mainly from collectors. Kenny was counting on them to buy first-day covers from the Cook Islands.

By 1978, the Cook Islands were posting roughly $1.5 million a year in stamp revenues, about 20 percent of the government's budget. But Sir Albert—"somewhat of a Huey Long of the South Seas," according to one account—

was in political trouble. A representative of Sir Albert asked Kenny for help. The prime minister wanted an advance of $337,000 against the following year's stamp revenues, the amount in the budget for old-age pensions. In return, Sir Albert's government would continue Kenny's worldwide distribution rights for Cook Islands stamps.

Kenny agreed to the plan. Sir Albert transferred the money from a shell company that Kenny set up, and then used the money to charter six airplanes to fly in 450 Cook Islanders who would vote for him in that year's election. Sir Albert saw the free trips as the only way to win. He needed the votes. But the Cook Islands had no provision for absentee ballots, and not even he could push one through in time. Under the law, Cook Islanders who lived elsewhere could not cast ballots unless they were on the Cook Islands on Election Day.

Sir Albert won by the slimmest of margins, but the Justice Department said the money from Kenny had been used to rig the election. Prosecutors said Kenny and Sir Albert had schemed to make the arrangement secret, meeting in Honolulu and agreeing on a code to be used in telex messages. Prosecutors also said Kenny's shell corporations were intended to disguise the payments. Kenny paid a $50,000 fine—and paid the government that toppled Sir Albert's another $337,000 to cover the old-age pensions.

• • •

In 1940, perhaps prompted by the stories about the stamp's trip to the World's Fair and its sale to Small, RKO assigned a script that became *The Saint in Palm Springs*, the sixth in a series of eight "Saint" potboilers. From first pitch to final cut, each probably cost $40,000 to make—by coincidence the amount Mrs. Hind got for the stamp—and could be shot in five days. For a B movie with a crime-solving hero, there had to be a crime. The novelist Leslie Charteris and the screenwriter Jerry Cady concocted one about the theft of the world's rarest stamp at a resort in Palm Springs, California (where, as it happened, Charteris lived). *The Saint in Palm Springs* made a profit of $90,000, not as much as RKO's Tarzan movies or *Bringing Up Baby*. But Bosley Crowther's review in the *New York Times* dripped with sarcasm. Simon Templar, the "Saint" of the title, "is entitled by detective-union rules to a vacation every now and then. And that, from the patron's point of view, is what his scriptwriter has given him in 'The Saint at [*sic*] Palm Springs.'" Crowther wrote that "it isn't in the least entertaining to watch the sluggish plot unfold. If the familiar name of director Jack Hively weren't prominent in the list of credits, we'd suspect he'd taken a vacation, too. Obviously the scriptwriters did."

Precious stamps like the one-cent magenta figured in other movies while Small owned it, notably *Charade* in 1963. The Audrey Hepburn character ran around with an envelope to which several world-class rarities had been affixed. The plot revolved around hiding them in plain sight, right in front of a cast that included Cary Grant and Walter Matthau.

But the largest single audience heard about the one-cent magenta on a quiz show. On January 18, 1951, five days before he collected an Emmy Award, Groucho Marx lit a cigar and settled into his seat on the quiz show *You Bet Your Life*. The program was a vehicle for Marx's zaniness—the audience tuned in for Marx's one-liners, which appeared to be ad-libbed (although the director let slip that Marx depended on writers scribbling on an overhead projector, out of camera range, that only he could see). The show had been running on radio since the 1940s, and in 1951 it was still running on radio. But it had added a television broadcast the year before, with cameras whirring away.

In the episode filmed that January evening, George Fenneman, the announcer-sidekick, introduced two contestants: a letter carrier and a stamp collector. Marx joked with the letter carrier about playing post office. Then he turned to the other contestant, Alice Backes, and said, "You're a stamp collector, is that right, Alice?"

She said she was. "Although I'm more of a philatelist."

"You're more a what?"

"A philatelist."

"Well, I am, too," Marx deadpanned. "What is a philatelist?"

"Well, it's, it stems from a Greek word meaning, um, lover of taxes," she said.

"Lover of taxes?" Marx said. "There isn't a philatelist in the house." The studio audience laughed.

Then Marx asked what was the rarest stamp she knew about, and she started talking, knowledgeably, about the one-cent magenta—that it was issued in 1856 and that it was worth $50,000.

Marx, then approaching sixty, made a joke about himself and his longevity: "If I'd only known. I bought a dollar's worth of those when they first came out, and like a fool, I wasted them all writing mash notes to Dolley Madison."

Alice Backes wasn't just a starlet the producers had brought in to flirt with Groucho, as they often did. "She did collect stamps," recalled her younger sister, Virginia Baxter, who said she had helped with Alice's album when they were girls. "I would get mail and ask if she wanted the stamp," Virginia Baxter told me. "Sometimes she would and sometimes she wouldn't."

Alice Backes went on to a long career as an actress, appearing on programs like *Dragnet*, *Bachelor Father*, *Gunsmoke*, *The Andy Griffith Show*, *Mayberry R.F.D.*, and *Columbo*. She died in 2007 at age eighty-three. Her sister told me Ms. Backes kept her stamp album for years, but it was apparently destroyed in a house fire.

NINE

$286,000

1970: *The Wilkes-Barre Eight*

The distance to Manhattan from Wilkes-Barre, Pennsylvania—a fading little city in coal country—is 134 miles. For the ten years that the stamp was owned by eight people from Wilkes-Barre, it stayed in a safe-deposit box in a Fifth Avenue bank. The one-cent magenta went to Philadelphia for the nation's bicentennial. It went to Canada. It went to India and Australia. But it never went to its owners' hometown.

I did, on a Sunday morning, because I had decided that Wilkes-Barre was another important stop in my journey through Stamp World.

From reading up on Wilkes-Barre, I had a sense that it was a shot-and-a-beer town, and like so many blue-collar strongholds across the nation's industrial crescent, it was in decline almost before people realized it. From 1950 to 1960, the postwar boom decade when white-collar jobs surpassed blue-collar jobs, Wilkes-Barre's population fell 17 percent; by 1970, it was two-thirds its size in 1940. After so many years of industrial losses, Wilkes-Barre was a past-tense kind of place, a place to have left after growing up. The actor Jerry Orbach did. Even Joe Palooka, the naive comic-strip prizefighter, did.

But clearly a few of those who remained in Wilkes-Barre, or who moved back after a year or two in Manhattan during their twenties, did well there—very well. The stamp's new owners were wealthy enough to put up $50,000 apiece (as much as $834,000 apiece in 2016 dollars). Seven of them were not stamp people. The eighth was, and the whole adventure was his idea—the partnership to buy the stamp, the trips to display it at philatelic conventions around the world, the stunts to promote it. His name was Irwin Weinberg. For more than half his life, his business address had been a suite in a bank building: two cluttered rooms and an old-fashioned vault with a military-green door that swung open when he dialed in the combination.

Which is what he did when my wife and I finally got there, and it took him a couple of tries. Inside the vault were stacks and stacks of stamps on shelves that reached to the ceiling. Weinberg said, proudly, that the shelves were rigged with an alarm that would go off if anyone touched anything. The words "booby-trapped" popped into my mind, and I wondered whether "anyone" included Weinberg himself. He showed us any number of stamps in the vault, but he pulled them from boxes on the floor, not the trip-wired shelves. (I'd bet that Ferrary, another shelf-storer, would have rushed back to Paris to install the same kind of security setup if he had tiptoed through Weinberg's vault.)

We had gone to Weinberg's office after a couple of hours at his house, which turned out to be a large, comfortable *Leave It to Beaver* kind of place a mile or so from downtown Wilkes-Barre. The front door had swung open as my wife and I started up the walk, and a tallish blonde woman had stepped out. She was wearing a fur coat over what looked like pajamas.

We were deep in Stamp World now.

She introduced herself as Weinberg's daughter. She managed an expression that I remember combined a smile and a scowl. She said they were dealing with a domestic disaster. The boiler had blown up the day before and could not be repaired until the following day.

Weinberg was wearing a heavy topcoat over layers

of jackets and shirts. They led us into his dark, wood-paneled library, in which someone had set up a couple of space heaters that thrummed and glowed but did not heat the space. He did not care. He wanted to show us a photograph from a White House ceremony in 2002 at which Coretta Scott King had presented President George W. Bush with a portrait of her husband, the Rev. Dr. Martin Luther King Jr. Weinberg still sounded thrilled to have been invited and to have met Mrs. King and the Rev. Al Sharpton, another guest.

Weinberg asked what my wife did for a living, and when she said she is a doctor, he launched into his medical history. I began to worry that we would never get around to stamps, but one of his ailments seemed as unique as the one-cent magenta: a malignant tumor inside his ear. It was treated with radiation that weakened the muscles on one side of his face, as if he had had a stroke. I could see from photographs around the room that he had once been handsome and charismatic, and he was still happy to be alive, even if the treatment that saved his life had left him damaged. He was the opposite of Ferrary and Small, who had owned the one-cent magenta before him, and du Pont, who owned it after him. He was more like Hind, an extrovert. He enjoyed people.

But we were shivering. He showed us souvenirs he had brought home while squiring the one-cent magenta to exhibitions around the world. Then we decamped to his office, trailing him as he drove his yellow BMW convertible to a tall, fortress-like building in downtown Wilkes-Barre that had once been the headquarters of a bank. He explained that the bank was gone and the building was being converted into apartments. He told us he had worked out a deal to stay—the only tenant from the old days, when office space upstairs, on the floors above the bank, was filled with lawyers and doctors.

Weinberg settled in behind his big desk and told us that he had done well in the stamp business when he was young. He had also owned a rug-cleaning operation that he bought in the 1950s with a loan from the same bank. He said that a friend at the bank had heard it was for sale and told him that the bank would finance the deal for him. When Weinberg said he knew nothing about running a professional cleaning business, the friend said, "The man who owns it now comes in every Friday with a big deposit. That's all you need to know."

But by the late 1960s, he was edgy. An ugly war in Southeast Asia was dragging on, and the economy was sluggish. Wall Street sensed it. Weinberg, an assiduous reader of the *New York Times* and the *Wall Street Journal*, sensed it. Weinberg knew from his reading that industrial production was continuing to rise as defense contractors kept pace with the escalation in Vietnam. He was also concerned that unemployment rates were close to historic highs. Weinberg knew that those two elements together would put pressure on the third variable in the economic equation, consumer prices, and that the result would be inflation.

He was right: the cost of the most basic items shot up. The Consumer Price Index climbed more than 4 percent in 1968 and more than 5 percent in 1969, and would jump nearly 6 percent in 1970. Weinberg suspected that the country was sliding into its worst money crisis since the Depression. Conventional economic thinking held that runaway inflation and high unemployment were mutually exclusive—they could not happen at the same time. But the frustrated chairman of the Federal Reserve, Arthur Burns, could say only, "The rules are not working the way they used to."

Weinberg thought he knew how to beat the dismal economic forecasts: buy famous stamps.

And then he heard that the rarest and most expensive stamp of all was going on the block.

• • •

Weinberg got hooked on stamps in the late 1930s, when the policymakers in Washington, concluding that the Great Depression was over, cut spending and raised taxes—and the economy slipped into a recession that came close to destroying the still-new New Deal. Weinberg was nine or ten years old, and a boy in his Wilkes-Barre neighborhood made what sounded like a puzzling offer: he would give Weinberg some stamps—and some hinges. Weinberg said to himself, "Hinges. How am I going to fasten a stamp to the page with a door hinge?"

Weinberg soon learned what stamp collectors' hinges were. And Weinberg saw the potential for making money from stamps. "I thought to myself, you know, there are stamp dealers out there, and I wrote to one of them and he sent me stamps to buy. And I spent a good twenty-five cents or something, and as time went on, I thought to myself, I'd like to be a stamp dealer like that."

Weinberg got a glimpse of the one-cent magenta at the World's Fair in New York in 1940. There was so much to see: the icons of the fair, the Trylon and Perisphere;

Futurama, with its promise of automated highways; the giant cash register atop one building; even little Lorin Maazel, the future music director of orchestras on both sides of the Atlantic, making his New York conducting debut at nine years old.

Weinberg was twelve and staying with cousins who lived in Newark, New Jersey. At the fair, $1 million worth of stamps were on view at the British Pavilion, celebrating Rowland Hill's legacy, the hundredth anniversary of Britain's first postage stamp. Weinberg and his cousins followed the crowd to where the one-cent magenta was on display, courtesy of Mrs. Hind. Weinberg did not see her and was not overwhelmed by the tiny scrap of dark reddish paper. "I never thought about it again"—until, he told me decades later, he owned the stamp.

Weinberg had after-school jobs as a grocery-store stock boy and as a Fuller Brush salesman—"I'd knock on the door, put my head down and say, 'I'm your Fuller Brush man. May I come in?' and then just go right through, dump all the stuff on the floor." He was persuasive, and from his house-to-house rounds, he made money he could spend. For $5.18, he bought himself a bus ticket from Wilkes-Barre to New York.

The bus dropped him off near Times Square, but

he was not interested in the lights of Broadway or the heights of the Empire State Building. The destination he had in mind was Nassau Street downtown, not far from the New York Stock Exchange, where the stamp dealers were. Many were there because they had been stockbrokers before the crash of 1929; a few were refugees who had arrived in the United States with the only thing they could carry, a pocketful of stamps.

Weinberg spent $18 on a box full of stamps, which he then sold, making about $25 by the time the last one was gone. He took the $25 and went back to New York and bought more stamps, again selling them for more money. Eventually, one of the dealers promised him a thirty-five-dollar-a-week job when he graduated from high school. Weinberg accepted the offer, rented a room for $5 a week and, by advertising and selling his own stamps on the side, did better than he had expected. Then, on a trip back to Wilkes-Barre, he toyed with the idea of opening his own stamp business there. The overhead would be lower than if he set up shop in New York. He could work from his bedroom in his parents' house. So that's what he did.

But Weinberg kept in touch with the big-city stamp dealers in New York. One of them asked what Weinberg did with the names of the people who answered the ads Weinberg placed in stamp magazines. "Nothing," Weinberg said. The dealer said that was a mistake. He told Weinberg he should build a mailing list from the ad responses and send out a list of "other merchandise"—meaning other stamps he had in his inventory. "I said, 'Oh. I don't have any other merchandise,'" Weinberg recalled, but the other dealer offered to lend him stamps to sell. He and Weinberg split the profits for a year or two as Weinberg sent out the first of his lists, which he typed up like a newsletter. *Miner's Stamp News,* he called it.

Seventy years later, Weinberg was still typing lists and sending them out every Monday. The only difference was the way he printed them. In the 1940s he had spent $5 on a used mimeograph, a smallish machine that did not take up much space in his bedroom. By 2015 he had a massive copying machine that filled the lower half of a wall in his office. He complained that the array of buttons and touch-screen controls was confusing, and that the mimeograph machine worked better. And, on the Sunday afternoon we visited Weinberg—deadline time for *Miner's Stamp News*—the paper jammed deep inside the new and complicated machine. He looked befuddled, so I started opening the many doors and drawers on the copier. It took a few minutes, but eventually I cleared the jam for him.

• • •

Buying the one-cent magenta was, Weinberg told us, "sort of an afterthought." His plan, in the late 1960s, had been to buy rare stamps as a hedge against the inflation he was certain was coming—stamps that were better looking than the one-cent magenta and that would be appealing when the time came to sell them and cash out. "He [was] bullish on 'conservation of capital,'" the stamp writer Viola Ilma reported after meeting Weinberg. "He says, 'True investment must have withstood the test of time, have protected its capital consistently in terms of purchasing power and . . . be instantly liquid.'" He said that other luxury investments—gold, diamonds, even real estate—were dangerous, but "the great classic stamps are first of all known unchangeable quantities." Nothing else held the promise of stamps.

By 1968, he was mulling over the timing. He was so sure the economy would overheat and inflation would become a bigger headache than it had been in 1966 and 1967 that, chatting with his mother-in-law one day, he said, "It's almost a sure thing unless the war ends." She said, "If that's all that's holding you back, get going with it, because Nixon will never end this war."

Weinberg recruited eight investors and set up a limited partnership. None of them knew much about stamps. One was a lawyer, another owned some hotels, another was a furniture manufacturer—"but," Weinberg said, "they all could see what I thought I saw." Weinberg, as the partner in charge, would make the decisions on what to buy. He was so confident in the investment power of the Inverted Jenny that he bought two in one week in 1969—one for $29,000, the other for $33,000—and in 1970, he bought another, for $34,000. He would go on to spend $10,000 for some extremely rare Alexandria Provisionals from the 1840s. Like the one-cent magenta, these were apparently printed at a local newspaper, the *Alexandria Gazette* in Northern Virginia. They were issued before the United States introduced postage stamps that could be accepted anywhere in the nation. Not many Alexandria Provisionals exist. The one that Weinberg bought took longer to be discovered than the one-cent magenta. It was not found until 1894.

Weinberg proselytized about stamps as an investment. He would tell people that stamps were "the only investment that has not had a major recession." "Inflation and devaluation are twin specters that Weinberg often plays on," Joseph L. Lincoln later wrote in the *Sunday Bulletin* in Philadelphia. "It's not a question of how high stamps will go, but how low your currency will go."

Most financial advisers would caution that stamp collectors should never expect anything other than enjoyment from what is, after all, a hobby. But Weinberg was betting on something more than fun: solid returns from relatively modest investments in stamps. Until the day a reporter from the local newspaper dialed Weinberg's number.

The reporter had seen a wire-service story that said the one-cent magenta was coming up for sale for the first time in thirty years. The reporter wanted to know if Weinberg planned to bid on it.

Weinberg faked his way through the conversation. He did not tell the reporter he had not heard about the sale, saying, "We will probably be interested."

There was no probably about it. Once he hung up the phone, Weinberg went into high gear, even though, as he put it, "This was way out of proportion for us." He had not contemplated spending as much on any one stamp as he would have to bid for the magenta. Nor had his original strategy included bidding against better-known collectors who probably had deeper pockets. Still, he called his investors together. They urged Weinberg on, insisting he almost had to buy the one-cent magenta if they were to reign as leading investors in rare stamps.

Weinberg was surprised. "I really didn't think they'd all react this way," he said, "and of course there was the unknown as to what the price would be." After so many years in the stamp business, he assumed it would be high. "I told them it was going to be a number significantly larger than any we had used to buy anything," he said. Weinberg guessed the bidding could climb toward the half-million-dollar mark. "It's the only one like it," he said. "I knew the world was going to be interested. The queen [of England] was rumored to be interested. And there are other people out there."

Each partner put up an extra $50,000. Not quite $200,000 remained in the partners' account—money Weinberg had not yet spent on less expensive purchases. They agreed that Weinberg could go to $500,000. If the bidding for the one-cent magenta went higher, he would have to drop out.

• • •

Now Weinberg was in the big leagues. The lavishly printed catalogue for the sale confirmed it: seventy-six pages bound inside a blue velvet cover designed for this annual "rarities of the world" sale. The one-cent magenta was shown in color on the title page and in black and white on page seventy-one, where it was listed, a bit breathlessly, as Lot No. 279 in the sale: "Unique, the rarest and most valuable stamp in the world." The other pages of the catalog were packed with lesser treasures. A one-cent Benjamin Franklin from 1861 with a minimum bid of $9,000 was described as "fresh, fine, [a] handsome example of this great rarity." An 1869 block of six ninety-cent stamps with Abraham Lincoln's portrait was "very fine, a fabulous showpiece." The next line said that only one other block of six was known to exist—and that the minimum bid was $13,500.

Some mistakes were expected to bring big money. Four lots featured one-cent stamps known as Pan-American Inverts from 1901. The stamps celebrated "Fast Lake Navigation," according to the legend above the words "Postage One Cent," but the impressive-looking ship in the center, like the Inverted Jennies later on, was upside down. Lot No. 136 was a two-cent Pan-American Invert that saluted "fast express." Its train, with a smoke-belching locomotive trailed by old-fashioned coaches, was also upside down. A few sheets of the inverted stamps had somehow escaped whatever checking was done at the Bureau of Engraving and Printing. Philatelists assume that someone at the Bureau stopped the presses and turned the sheets around before they went through the second time. About two hundred misprints apparently slipped out and were spotted—and quickly sold—in at least four post offices.

The owner of the one-cent magenta, Frederick Trouton Small, had chosen Robert A. Siegel, a leading New York stamp dealer, to handle the sale. At the firm's office in Midtown Manhattan, there was discussion about how to showcase the one-cent magenta as the star of the sale. Siegel's wife, Miriam, hatched the idea of the velvet cover. She had two prototypes made, a green one and a blue one. She decided on the blue velvet cover. The firm also ordered brandy snifters with the firm's logo on one side and a reproduction of the one-cent magenta on the other.

Despite the assurance on page seventy-one that the one-cent magenta was unique, in one respect it was not. It was one of three lots in the sale that were so rare that they did not carry estimated prices. The Apollo 11 first-day cover that comprised Lot No. 203 was practically brand-new. It had been issued six months earlier to celebrate the

Apollo 11 moon landing and had been engraved with a die that had been aboard the lunar landing craft. Nearly nine million first-day covers were processed, more than for any other stamp in United States postal history. But this one was different. The colors were not aligned correctly. The dark blue of the earth was on the surface of the moon, and the red stripes of the American-flag shoulder patch on Neil A. Armstrong's space suit almost at his elbow.

But it went unmentioned in the three-page introduction in the front of the catalogue, which was all about the one-cent magenta. The introduction recounted the "emergency shortage of regular stamps" in British Guiana that prompted the postmaster to order provisional stamps—and the improbable journey of this stamp from Vaughan to the unidentified "present owner." Small's identity was revealed only after the catalogue had gone to the printer.

"The eyes of the philatelic world are focused on the Louis XVI Room of the Waldorf-Astoria," the catalogue announced, hinting at how the Waldorf was synonymous with New York itself. The Waldorf was where presidents and princes and playboys stayed. Herbert Hoover and General Douglas MacArthur had lived there. As stamp collectors knew, James A. Farley, the Postmaster General under Franklin D. Roosevelt, had lived at the Waldorf since the 1940s. What the catalogue did not hint at was how many people would want to be on hand. The auction had to be moved to the far larger Grand Ballroom to accommodate the crowd, which the *New York Times* carefully reported was "likely the largest ever for a stamp auction."

The "rarities of the world" sale was a rite of spring for stamp collectors. Siegel's stepson, Andrew Levitt, then thirty years old, presided, gavel in hand. In the crowd were notables like Robert Price, a former deputy mayor under John V. Lindsay, who repeated the rumor that "a band of Englishmen" had designs on the stamp and would bid for the queen, a prospect that had frightened some collectors into keeping their paddles in their laps when the one-cent magenta finally went on sale.

Another was Martin Apfelbaum, a dealer from Philadelphia who had grown the stamp business he took over from his father into the nation's largest retail stamp operation. Apfelbaum's father had sold his own collection in the Depression to make ends meet, and Apfelbaum, just out of college, would load his car with books of stamps and consign them to hobby shops and drug stores. By the

1960s, he was in the hunt for rarities, and he had money to spend. He bought a tractor-trailer-load of stamps for $150,000 in 1957. It took seven years to sell the twenty-five million stamps inside.

Though Weinberg presented himself as a small-town guy, he was not as unfamiliar with glamor and glitz as he claimed. For years he was a regular in Atlantic City, and with stamps as his calling card, he had connections. He became friendly with Frank Sinatra's business manager, a fellow philatelist, and with a Manhattan hairstylist who introduced him to the salon's A-list clients, among them Patti Page, Greer Garson, and Lena Horne.

Weinberg booked a suite at the Waldorf and holed up in it during the afternoon, away from the crowd that was building in the ballroom. He was jittery. He could not afford to tip his hand. He did not want to risk someone overhearing him make a casual remark and figuring out how much to bid against him. Weinberg feared that even his facial expressions would give him away, that competing bidders would realize he had other people's money—lots of it, by Stamp World standards—and the authority to spend it, up to a point. Weinberg knew the major players, and they knew him. Siegel, the patriarch of the prestigious firm running the sale, was on hand; his stepson was its public face.

Andrew Levitt had started in the Siegel firm's mailroom as a teenager. His stepfather had promoted him to auctioneer and then to vice president, and it was Levitt who would bring down the gavel on Lot No. 279. In his career he would sell scores of rarities, not all of them stamps—checks signed by Charles Dickens and Calvin Coolidge, and land grants signed by James Monroe. But he would brag about selling the one-cent magenta for the rest of his life, during which, by his tally, he sold more than three hundred million dollars' worth of stamps.

Weinberg looked nervous when he walked into the Grand Ballroom. He tried to stay out of sight behind the curtains at the back of the room. Finally, when Levitt announced the one-cent magenta, with a minimum bid of $100,000—the crowd quieted down. Looking out from his lectern, Levitt saw several hands go up. They stayed up as Levitt pushed the bidding along, first in jumps of $20,000, then in spurts of only $10,000. At $200,000, Robson Lowe, perhaps the leading British dealer at the time, lowered his hand. Joseph L. Lincoln, a senior at Princeton who had been the stamp columnist for the *Sunday Bulletin* in Philadelphia since junior high school, recalled a "staring contest" between Weinberg and the Weills—Raymond and Roger, well-established New Orleans dealers with whom Weinberg did not want to duel. *The New Yorker* magazine noted the Weills had looked "calmer and calmer" and Weinberg "more and more nervous."

"We figured this meant that the Weills weren't going to go for it and Weinberg was," *The New Yorker* concluded. The *New York Times* wrote that the Weills dropped out at $250,000. Weinberg kept his hand up. So did a Boston dealer, but not for long. After only one more round back and forth, which drove the price $30,000 higher, all the other hands had come down and Weinberg was the only bidder still standing—literally. He had been on his feet the whole time, pacing in the back of the ballroom. Levitt said what auctioneers always say before they pound the gavel—"fair warning." Following the custom of not identifying buyers by name, he said the one-cent magenta was "going to I.W." He did not have to say who Weinberg was. Well-wishers surrounded him.

It was over in about ninety seconds. Weinberg told me that he felt "euphoric"—and more than 40 years later, he was still so excited that he spelled out the word forward and backward. "A lot of people, including Mr. Weinberg, thought that Mr. Weinberg had acquired a bargain," *The New Yorker* observed tartly. Weinberg was happy that the price was so far below the partners' $500,000 limit. Apfelbaum said the chatter about possible British bidders had shaved at least $100,000 off the price.

There was some grumbling, louder than when Small bought the stamp, that Weinberg and his noncollector partners were transforming what should be a pastime for amateurs into a business. "A lot of people questioned spending that much," Ken Martin, the executive director of the American Philatelic Society, told me. "Some questioned whether he was turning it into a commodity." David Lidman of the *New York Times*, who covered the sale, quoted one of the Weill brothers as saying they preferred a customer "who has a warmth for stamps. It's a waste to sell a rare stamp to someone who sticks it in a safe and forgets it."

• • •

Weinberg stuck it in the safe, all right, but he did not forget it, and he did not let the world forget it. He marketed the stamp more exuberantly than Hind had. "What do I know, huh?" Weinberg told me. "I believe in 'Camelot.' I believe in stuff like that, I really do. I believe in *The Great*

Gatsby." He identified with Nick Carraway—"but I was going to become a Gatsby. That was my thinking."

He was going to do it with hoopla and hype. The stamp was coddled and cooed over, and he was comped. Baby-boomer philatelists who had grown up figuring they would never see it marveled at—well, not its beauty. But taking it to stamp exhibitions was an element of Weinberg's strategy. He wanted to build interest that would pump up the price when he decided it was time to part with it—or, as he put it, "I was trying to introduce it to the world, and maybe find a buyer."

It turned out that Weinberg had a knack for stunts that generated publicity far beyond stamp magazines. In return for press releases and photo ops, airlines offered him free seats. Weinberg stole an idea from Mrs. Hind and once asked an armored car to take the stamp from the bank on Fifth Avenue to the airport—again, in return for the publicity. His plan was to slip the one-cent magenta into his briefcase, climb into the armored car, ride to the airport and fly off with the briefcase clutched in his lap. He even drummed up television coverage simply by telephoning a station in New York. A camera crew met him at the bank.

"It was uneventful," Weinberg told me, "excepting

that the armored car got lost on the way to the airport."
Weinberg rushed onto the plane with the stamp safe in
his briefcase. Everything else he had packed for the trip—
the luggage he checked at the gate—was lost.

The word spread. A Japanese delegation arrived in
Wilkes-Barre to invite Weinberg to Tokyo. He was reluctant or coy—or both. "I said I really didn't think I want
to do it," he remembered in 2015. "They said, 'You don't
realize what this could be.' I said, tell me. They said it
would be shown in Tokyo the same way the *Mona Lisa*
was, plus all expenses, plus ten-thousand dollars for my
partners." Off he went. He rode the bullet train and was
the guest of honor at "parties galore."

"Most of the time, I was in nirvana," Weinberg said—
even when things went wrong.

In 1978, Weinberg booked a trip to Toronto and another stamp show with an acronym—CAPEX, for Canadian Philatelic Exhibition. It celebrated the Universal
Postal Union, the main forum for international cooperation among nations with postal networks, which Canada
had joined one hundred years earlier.

Weinberg needed a new gimmick. The armored-car
ride would no longer generate attention or press coverage, but he hit upon an idea that would: he would chain

himself to his briefcase. He sent his teenage son to an army-navy store for a pair of handcuffs.

Weinberg was not afraid that the briefcase would be snatched and the stamp stolen. He did not even snap the handcuffs onto his wrist until the plane was about to land in Toronto. The handcuffs were a prop that would get the attention of the photographers he knew would surround him as he emerged from the jet bridge. Officials from the stamp show would promptly whisk him off to a news conference.

The reporters asked the usual questions—how much was the stamp worth, where had it been, what were his plans for selling it. As the news conference dragged on, Weinberg figured the photographers had their photographs, and the handcuff felt tight on his wrist. No one noticed as he slipped the key from his pocket and pushed it into the handcuff, and he kept his game face on as he turned the key and felt it break in his hand. "I thought it best not to say anything. I thought, just keep talking and worry about it later," he said. "So, as things went along, one of the reporters said, 'When are you going to take the handcuff off?' I said, 'A little later on, when I get to the room.'"

The reporters left. Weinberg broke the news to one of the organizers: He would remain shackled to his briefcase unless they found someone to free him. "He said, 'Don't worry about it, I'll get somebody in here to help you,'" Weinberg recalled. Security guards borrowed hairpins and paper clips but could not open the handcuffs with them. A firefighter arrived a bit later and announced, "I have just the thing that will do it." He left the room, only to return with a saw.

He was just starting to cut into the handcuffs when the door opened and one of the reporters returned. "He said, 'I saw this guy coming in with a handsaw,'" Weinberg said. "'Would you mind if I did a story about it and took a picture?'" Weinberg told me that he had not thought about mining the mishap for publicity, but he believed that any publicity was good publicity. Weinberg remembered thinking, "This is exactly what I would want if I could dream up a thing like this."

The firefighter, though, would not hear of it. He said the fire department had rules, and one was no publicity. The reporter pleaded: "If you let us do this, I promise you it will be world news by tomorrow."

The fireman relented when the reporter promised to keep him out of the photograph, and went back to sawing off the handcuffs.

The reporter was right, of course. The story was picked up around the world and in *People* magazine (which wrote that the steel was too thick for the firefighter's hacksaw, and that Weinberg was freed with the help of a police officer's key).

Weinberg became a minor celebrity. The one-cent magenta became a part of Weinberg's identity, just as it had once become a part of Hind's identity. He appeared on the game show *To Tell the Truth* and on Mike Douglas's talk show.

By then, he was saying the stamp was worth between $500,000 and $1 million.

TEN

$935,000

———◆———

1980: "The Man Showed Up"

Weinberg cruised through the 1970s—literally. He crossed the Atlantic on the *Queen Elizabeth 2* with his briefcase in tow and the stamp locked inside. But by 1980, he was ready to cash out. It was time. He had watched his predictions come true, one by one. The economy had soured, inflation had surged, and so had interest rates—the prime was heading toward 20 percent. The stock market was languishing, and suddenly the most appealing investments were collectibles like stamps, which seemed immune to the ups and downs that were causing so many headaches.

A stockbroker quoted by the *New York Times* said he was fighting to break even on his stocks and bonds but making money on his collectibles. *New York* magazine echoed that idea with a page of investment advice head-lined "Better Than Blue Chips." It was about the intangible market for tangibles like stamps and more esoteric items, from cigar-box labels to Louis XVI armoires. Salomon Brothers—ruled by one of Wall Street's monarchs, John H. Gutfreund, who had risen to power as the pre-eminent bond trader of his generation—began keeping track of what it diplomatically called "nontraditional investments" that were not traded on the stock exchanges. From 1969 to 1979, Chinese ceramics led the list with compounded annual yields of 18 percent, followed by rare books at 16.5 percent, and stamps at 15.4 percent. The conventional economic indicators in those years measured misery. The Consumer Price Index charged ahead at an annual rate of 6.1 percent.

The returns from collectibles seemed limitless, but some economists wondered about a modern-day tulipomania, one of the celebrated boom-and-bust episodes in economic history. The question was, how long could the bull market for collectibles—and, in particular, stamps—continue? When *Stamps* magazine asked Andrew Levitt, who had brought down the gavel at the auction of the one-cent magenta ten years before, he answered, "Possibly two more years." That was in 1979.

Weinberg's investors were not so sure. A couple of them threatened to force a distress sale and buy the stamp out from under him if Weinberg did not get the kind of price he was talking about, which was anything above $500,000. Weinberg dissuaded them and took the stamp to Robert A. Siegel, whose New York auction house had handled the 1970 sale.

Weinberg seemed to lurch from one nail-biting encounter to another. The night before the sale, Siegel, obviously upset, tracked him down: "What am I going to do? We don't have a bid." Weinberg told Siegel to sell the stamp no matter what. Siegel replied, "My God, it will be a disaster, wreck my reputation." Weinberg shrugged: "Nothing I can do about it."

Weinberg told me that Siegel's mood had turned sunny by the time they saw each other on the morning of the auction. Siegel told him: "Irwin, everything I said to you last night, forget it. He, the man, showed up."

Weinberg did not ask who "the man" was, and Siegel did not tell him. And if Weinberg saw a thin man in his early thirties slip into the second or third row as the bidding began, Weinberg did not notice.

Stamps were one of John E. du Pont's passions. He loved buying them, loved assembling them into first-rate collections: stamps from Canada, stamps from the early days of the American postal system on cover, stamps from obscure places like Samoa, stamps that were the kinds of rarities that unlimited wealth could buy. He had other early stamps from British Guiana: du Pont amassed cottonreels, lots of cottonreels, as if he were assembling the most complete collection of cottonreels in private hands. "The queen had only twenty cottonreels," du Pont's one-time business manager, Victor Krievins, told me when I called him in early 2015. "John had thirty-three."

Du Pont was thrilled to own the one-cent magenta. He beamed when he whispered to insiders that he had bought it even as he used a pseudonym to use at stamp shows—Rae Maeder, an anagram of Demerara, the region in which the one-cent had been printed and issued. But du Pont did not see the stamp or handle it for the last fourteen years of his life, the fourteen years he spent in prison after killing the wrestler Dave Schultz. The one-cent magenta languished in one vault or another, in one bank or another, seen by almost no one—and after du Pont died in a prison hospital, could not be found.

But only for seventy-two hours or so. Someone had put it in the wrong box.

• • •

On the surface, the 2014 film *Foxcatcher* is about one man's obsession with wrestling, but it is also about extreme wealth—and about who can afford expensive possessions like rare stamps. With its purchase by du Pont, the one-cent magenta had passed back into a world of money and privilege, and into the odd life of someone who used the fortune he inherited to purchase what he lacked: friendship, respect, and self-esteem.

The title of the film referred to the estate on the Main Line outside Philadelphia where du Pont lived with his mother. The mansion itself was a work of art, an exact copy of Montpelier, the Virginia plantation that belonged to James and Dolley Madison. Du Pont's grandfather had bought the original Montpelier as the twentieth century was dawning. Montpelier's last private owner was du Pont's aunt Marion duPont Scott [her preferred spelling]; after her death, du Pont joined his brother Henry in a lawsuit that they won. She had stipulated that Montpelier would go to the National Trust for Historic Preservation. They moved to block the transfer unless they received compensation. Under the settlement that was worked out, they sold Montpelier to the National Trust for $2 million each—$4.57 million each in today's dollars. The money to pay them came from a separate multimillion-dollar fund for upkeep of the house that she had also bequeathed to the National Trust.

Du Pont's early life had been a curious blend of overwhelming privilege and emotional isolation. Du Pont himself was born in 1938, the fourth and youngest child of Jean Liseter Austin and William du Pont Jr., the great-grandson of Éleuthère Irénée du Pont, who had built the Delaware gunpowder mill that was the cornerstone of the world's largest chemical company. William left when John was two and had little to do with the family. As du Pont acknowledged to the *Philadelphia Inquirer* in 1986, William's absence left a lasting scar. "I spent a lifetime looking for a father," he declared. He claimed to have found one in Villanova's legendary track-and-field coach, Jumbo Elliott. But that was before Villanova repudiated du Pont, shutting down the wrestling program he had underwritten with donations totaling more than $15 million.

Du Pont also considered himself an athlete despite his lack of special talent. He had one great victory when he was in his late twenties, in the 1965 Australian national pentathlon. It was "a triumph that was essentially bought," the *New York Times* said.

The closest he came to the 1968 Olympics was in the comic pages of newspapers. He was the model for "Jeff

Newtown, Olympic athlete" in the action-adventure comic strip *Steve Canyon* that year. Du Pont finally went to the Olympics in person in 1976, when he was thirty-eight, but not as a competitor on the pentathlon team. He was the team manager.

His mother—an heiress to another old-money fortune, from a company that had built railroad locomotives—was competitive, and she passed that trait along to her son. She won more than three thousand ribbons, cups, trophies, and awards at horse shows, cattle shows, and dog shows. Du Pont said she encouraged his interest in collecting—Victor Krievins told me he saw invoices in Mrs. du Pont's name for stamp purchases made by du Pont—but stamps were not his only fascination.

Du Pont also assembled world-renowned collections of seashells and birds; he is credited with discovering some twenty species, including a Philippine parrot and a Mexican sparrow. He built the Delaware Museum of Natural History outside Wilmington to house his trove. He assembled enormous collections of everything from expensive silverware to tin toys to fine Staffordshire china. He also had an impressive cache of weapons, including a Civil War–era Gatling gun that he kept in the library of the family mansion. And then he focused on stamps and wrestling. Of all the rarities he owned, the centerpiece was the little red stamp he called the "magenta lady."

Some philatelists worried that he would damage it. Warwick Paterson, a New Zealand stamp dealer who knew du Pont, visited him once and "noted with dismay du Pont's tendency to smoke whilst looking at his prize stamp," Paterson's son wrote after his father's death. Warwick Paterson "feared that [the smoke] would further cause deterioration" to the stamp.

He fancied himself a modern renaissance man but lived mostly out of the limelight. The Sunday papers did not show him in the boldface-name crowds at society parties and charity balls. He spent his money in other ways. He provided the local police department with equipment, including bulletproof vests and body armor developed by his family's company. For more than thirty years, he let officers train at his private shooting range. He invited some of them to live on the estate. He gave one a second job raising quail and pheasant. Du Pont allowed the officer to sell the eggs—and a certain number of quail and pheasant—so long as he provided some for the house.

In return, du Pont was permitted to play police officer, driving around with a badge and a siren as an honorary, unpaid officer. He even had a uniform. The organizations he financed mostly dismissed him as harmless. Officers regarded problems like excessive drinking as private matters.

• • •

Du Pont took a seat in the audience at the 1980 auction, but he was so concerned about preserving his anonymity that he did not place his bid himself. The man sitting next to him did that—Krievins, who would later go to work for du Pont but who was on the auction-house staff at the time. One of Krievins's jobs was to represent "secretive people who bought things quietly." And du Pont was secretive. He wanted to grin inscrutably when asked if he was the owner—not saying yes, but not saying no, either—so Krievins acted as a surrogate who was under orders to be equally tight-lipped. "I bid on the stamp, and people said, 'Who bought the stamp?' and I said, 'I don't know,'" Krievins told me. Krievins kept the secret for years. "I never disclosed it, not even to my ex-father-in-law, who was a stamp collector," he told me.

Du Pont hired Krievins away from the Siegel auction house in 1984. Krievins told me he functioned as a business manager, reviewing bills and approving payments, among other things: "It was a curse to be a du

Pont. People saw that name and thought right away it was a license to steal. People were trying to double- and triple-bill him." But most of all, Krievins had a hand in du Pont's stamp purchases, two million dollars' worth in the ten years he worked for him. When the stamps were sold after du Pont's death, they went for a total of $17 million. "I always bought the best of the best," Krievens told me, proudly.

The bidding on the one-cent magenta opened at $325,000. The auctioneer this time was Robert A. Siegel himself. Andrew Levitt, the auctioneer in 1970, had left Siegel's firm several years earlier. Weinberg, fretting that he and his partners would not see a big payday, relaxed as the bidding heated up. He had planned a gathering in his suite no matter what happened. Very soon he knew there would be nothing funereal about it. In less than a minute—fifty seconds—the sale was over. It sold for $935,000, a 337 percent profit for Weinberg and his partners. As the stamp was gaveled down, he sent his son to call the front desk and double the order of champagne.

• • •

With forty-some stiffly formal rooms, du Pont's mansion was, as the Philadelphia reporters Bill Ordine and Ralph

Vigoda wrote in their book about du Pont, "more fief-dom than home." It had its serfs and vassals, its peasants and knights, buzzing around a temperamental master. Of the people who came to surround du Pont as he bought more and more stamps, two—Robert P. Odenweller and Taras M. Wochok—had toyed with philately as boys. They did not grow up with du Pont's unlimited cash. They scrimped and saved nickels and dimes from their allowances. They spent their dollars on a stamp they could mount on a page in an album, and then they would stare at the empty spaces on the rest of the page and long to buy another stamp, and another, and another. But there was something about philately—the near-obsessive joy of inquiring about obscure stamps and acquiring them—that would continue to captivate one of them as an adult: Odenweller, the would-be astronaut.

The son of a West Pointer whose love of the Army ran so deep that he was buried on the grounds of the United States Military Academy, Odenweller graduated from the United States Air Force Academy in 1960. His ambition was to be an astronaut, and he had his sights set on the astronaut-training program. He was too young for the Project Mercury flights—the first seven astro-nauts had been chosen while he was in school, and he was thirteen years younger than the youngest of them, Gordon Cooper. But the wait was long. Years earlier, he had been treated to a flight with the record-setting test pilot Chuck Yeager. That only served to make him more determined. But there was a problem. He was too tall.

The original seven astronauts were only five feet eight inches tall. The second group was two inches taller, and eventually six-footers joined the space program. Odenweller stands six feet two inches tall. A space suit is not a tank top or a hoodie—one size will not fit all, and he could not have squeezed into the first space suits, which were custom-made for the first astronauts (although the astronauts could swap suits if necessary). Odenweller knew all this, and hoped for another two-inch step, but it never happened. Faced with that reality—and a gall-bladder operation—he resigned from the Air Force and became a pilot with Trans World Airlines.

The career choice was deliberate. Flying for TWA would let him visit the far-off places whose stamps had intrigued him since childhood. "When I was seven years old," he recalled when I met him in 2014, when he was in his seventies, "I was told by a guy who was at least triple my age, 'If you ever want to be a success in stamp collecting, you have to pick a country you like, learn everything you can about it, get everything you can from it and, in short, become an expert.'" This was the path not taken by Arthur Hind. But Odenweller decided to specialize. "A year or so before that, I had spent the princely sum of two dollars on one New Zealand stamp. And my allowance was twenty-five cents a week, so I figured, with that much capital invested in New Zealand, I was committed for life."

Not until years later did he realize the difficulty of that commitment. It is considered particularly challenging to collect stamps from New Zealand because of the papers its stamps were printed on, the watermarks that were embedded in the papers, the inks that the printers used and the perforations—minutiae to someone mailing a letter, but matters of paramount importance to someone like Odenweller, who went on to spend his life analyzing and categorizing the differences in extreme detail. And he branched out beyond New Zealand.

Life as an airline captain provided time during layovers for him to explore such things—and to meet and make friends with local experts and top exhibitors. Over the years, he immersed himself in what amounted to a decades-long graduate-level course in stamps from places like British Guiana: British colonies, or former colonies, with philatelic histories that dated to the earliest days of stamps. He edited a three-volume encyclopedia of nineteenth-century mail from Hawaii, whose history has enough of a British flavor that the state flag incorporates the Union Jack. He also assembled a prize-winning collection of stamps from the Australian island-state of Tasmania, which, after a long flight across the Pacific, is little more than a short hop from Sydney.

There were other destinations, with other stamps and other postal histories to explore, and by the time Odenweller encountered du Pont, Odenweller had become a recognized expert. He joined the Royal Philatelic Society London, whose Expert Committee had declared the one-cent magenta to be real when Hind's widow tried to sell it in the 1930s, and eventually was appointed to its governing council. And the Royal published two books that he wrote—in its usual limited editions. Odenweller had suggested that the Royal print six hundred fifty copies of his massively detailed study of nineteenth-century Samoan postal history and stamps. The chairman of the Royal's publications committee was willing to allow only three hundred. But he stepped down before the book went to press, and after working through the manuscript, his replacement told Odenweller that the Royal would raise the print order, to five hundred copies. They sold out within a month.

Each copy was numbered. No. 1 was sent to the queen and deposited in the Royal Philatelic Collection at St. James's Palace. No. 2 went to someone who owned many of the stamps that Odenweller described in the book, a man who was in prison at the time it came out—John E. du Pont.

Odenweller had met du Pont in 1980, not long after du Pont bought the one-cent magenta, when du Pont agreed to be a courier for Odenweller, or, more precisely, to be a courier for Odenweller's insurance agent. Du Pont had taken his proud new purchase to a stamp collectors' exhibition in New Zealand—under a pseudonym, of course. At the show, du Pont stopped at Odenweller's exhibit, which won the top prize, and a dealer who was accompanying du Pont was explaining a page of stamps in Odenweller's display.

"How much is something like that worth?" du Pont asked.

"Oh, about a quarter of a million dollars," the dealer answered.

Odenweller, recalling the conversation for me, added, "That got John's attention."

Odenweller planned to leave his collection in place for the rest of the show. His insurance agent, who had policies on a number of philatelists, said he might or might not be able to take Odenweller's stamps home. But the agent decided to go to Australia instead of the United States, and approached du Pont about returning the collection to its owner.

Du Pont's response was: "Sure, who does it belong to?"

The insurance agent told him, and du Pont said, "Odenweller. Does he have a brother named Charlie?"

He did. Du Pont remembered Charlie Odenweller from pistol shoots they had conducted a few years earlier in eastern Pennsylvania. And so du Pont agreed to carry Robert Odenweller's stamps home.

Du Pont soon invited Odenweller to Pennsylvania, sending a helicopter for him, and showed Odenweller around. It was Odenweller's introduction to the world du Pont inhabited when he was not trying to be an athlete. It was the world of du Pont the collector.

The mansion du Pont and his mother shared may have looked like Madison's Montpelier, but Madison never installed a bank-vault door just off the main floor. Du Pont did, to seal off a large room that held a museum-quality diorama that looked like a slice of unspoiled

Pennsylvania woods, with stuffed deer and other items not sent to the museum that housed his seashells and birds. The room also had a movie screen that dropped from the ceiling when du Pont wanted to watch first-run movies from Hollywood.

The walls were lined with reminders of du Pont's successes in philately. While his mother's horsemanship trophies were downstairs for everyone to see, the ribbons and certificates that du Pont accumulated were relegated to this room. He only had to look up to see how good he was, how well he had done at this stamp show or that exhibition. Over the years, he did very well indeed: he won more grand prix awards than anyone in the United States. The grand prix awards are the best of the best of the best; only collectors who have won multiple gold medals in international exhibitions are eligible for grand prix awards.

But even with the bank-vault door, du Pont did not keep the one-cent magenta in the mansion. It lay in a safe-deposit box in a bank in Bryn Mawr, Pennsylvania, in which du Pont was the largest safe-deposit customer, and he drove Odenweller there to look at the stamp. Just outside the vault, at a narrow counter, du Pont opened his safe-deposit box. There, on a card, sat the rarest, most expensive stamp in the world. Du Pont picked it up, but the one-cent magenta fell to the floor. Du Pont offhandedly reached to retrieve it with his bare fingers. Odenweller blanched, careful collector that he is, and distressing thoughts flashed through his mind: What if dirt or sweat from du Pont's hands damaged it? Worse, what if it tore?

In an instant, Odenweller waved off du Pont and picked up the stamp with a pair of small tongs that he always carried in a pocket. Thus began a relationship that lasted nearly thirty years and included prison visits in which Odenweller delivered news from Stamp World.

Odenweller and du Pont had more in common than stamps. They were close in age, and Odenweller excelled in things that mattered to du Pont: flying, shooting, and wrestling.

Still, du Pont had a way of compartmentalizing the people he brought into his life. Odenweller was a "stamp person," and du Pont did not want a "stamp person" mingling with the others he invited to the estate. Du Pont told Odenweller not to mention his philately to the people he met when he visited. "I was to dissemble to a degree, just to keep them in the dark as to what I was doing, why I was there," Odenweller told me. "I'd just say, 'I'm down here, just a friend of John's,' or something like that." Du Pont also insisted on secrecy in the outside world. Once, when du Pont and Odenweller had lunch before a stamp sale in Manhattan, du Pont worried that they would be seen together when they arrived at the auctioneer's. "You and I shouldn't appear to get off the elevator at the same time," he told Odenweller. And above all, despite his wrestling background, Odenweller was supposed to remain separate from the wrestlers who lived on du Pont's estate—Dave Schultz among them.

Du Pont and Odenweller were close enough, though, that du Pont's mother said du Pont looked on Odenweller as the brother du Pont never had. She told Odenweller, "You're the best thing that's ever happened to John. You've done what he wants to do. You don't need anything from him. Everybody else is trying to get something." At du Pont's wedding in 1983, it was Odenweller who escorted du Pont's mother down the aisle as the ceremony began. (Du Pont filed for divorce after ten months, and his ex-wife sued for $5 million. She alleged that he had not only tried to shove her into a fireplace but had threatened her with a gun.)

Odenweller's flying skills were a particularly appealing calling card—and another part of their lives that showed how different he and du Pont were. After the Air Force, Odenweller had risen through the ranks at TWA, putting in his time, just as he had put in his time with stamps and stamp collecting. Du Pont had bought his way into flying, just as he had bought his way into philately—acquiring whole collections the way Ferrary and Hind had, and then filling in the gaps. Du Pont had purchased a helicopter and, with a pilot on his payroll, had learned to fly it.

One Christmas Eve in the 1980s, TWA assigned Odenweller to fly to Baltimore, about a hundred miles from du Pont's estate. Odenweller, chatting with du Pont a few days before, said that he was facing a two-day lay-over. Du Pont asked what Odenweller planned to do for Christmas. Odenweller, contemplating a holiday in a hotel, told him: "There's not much you can do except stare at the walls and watch TV until you get bored." Du Pont's response was immediate: "I'm going to come get you. I'll bring you up here."

Odenweller landed the Boeing 727 and walked to the office where pilots file their flight plans. There stood du Pont, wearing his "chief of helicopter police" uniform. Together they crossed the tarmac to the place where du Pont had parked his helicopter, and soon they were in the air, on the way to du Pont's estate. Odenweller told me it was an eye-opening visit. He witnessed "the people who worked on the property coming to the landowner—you know, I'm talking medieval times now, coming up with little gifts" for du Pont and his mother. Maybe the rich are different, but not when it comes to gift wrap. Odenweller watched as the du Ponts saved the wrapping paper from each little package, and also the ribbon.

On December 26, du Pont flew the helicopter to Baltimore in time for Odenweller to go back to work.

• • •

The other person who figured in the life of du Pont and his stamps was Taras M. Wochok, a lawyer who eventually became the unlikely guardian of the one-cent magenta. But that came later, much later, long after Wochok had lost track of Mr. Ducylowicz.

Wochok's parents helped Ukrainians who had been held in displaced-person camps in World War II find homes in their North Philadelphia neighborhood—Wochok told me his mother sponsored nearly two hundred Ukrainian immigrants who arrived in the late 1940s. Ukraine had been victimized by the Nazis, who imposed forced labor on Jews and non-Jews alike. After the war, the Soviets sent, involuntarily, hundreds of thousands of Ukrainians in Germany back home, but eighty to eighty-five thousand left for the United States.

Wochok's mother welcomed the new arrivals, offering them a bedroom until they found places of their own. Most stayed only a couple of days. But one remained for several years—Mr. Ducylowicz, a man in his late fifties who worked in the print shop of a Ukrainian-language newspaper for a while. As a teenager, Wochok also worked at the newspaper, translating articles from Ukrainian to English and English to Ukrainian. There was a definite formality in the Wochok household, and Wochok, who was six or seven when the man moved in, was taught to address him as "Mister Ducylowicz." Decades later, Wochok still referred to him that way, not as "George," which was his first name. Sitting in the conference room of his law office, Wochok taught me how to pronounce Ducylowicz—"doots-uh-LOW-vitch"—and talked about how Ducylowicz had introduced him to philately.

Wochok told me he had spent hours watching Ducylowicz sift through his stamps, which were mainly from Germany. Ducylowicz told him that six or seven was a good age to begin collecting and even suggested stamps Wochok could start with. For a while, Wochok haunted stationery stores in the neighborhood, buying packets of canceled stamps from metal racks on the counter. But stamp collecting did not take. Wochok found the process too time-consuming, too isolating. "Baseball cards are one thing," he told me. "Stamps are quite another."

Wochok went on to college at La Salle University in Philadelphia and law school at the University of Notre Dame, and to a career as a prosecutor. By the early 1970s, he was an assistant district attorney in Philadelphia under Arlen Specter, a Democrat-turned-Republican who was serving his second term as the district attorney in Philadelphia. In 1973, Specter put Wochok in charge of his campaign for a third term. Wochok figured that if things went well, he would be tapped to manage Specter's campaign for governor the following year, or at least to play a major role in it. But on Election Day, things did not go well: Specter lost, though he was later elected to the United States Senate. Wochok went job-hunting, signing on with a medium-size suburban law firm.

As a prosecutor, he had become friendly with Dr. Halbert Fillinger, a forensic pathologist who was an assistant medical examiner in Philadelphia and knew John E. du Pont. He told Wochok that du Pont had a lot of legal work.

Fillinger introduced them in the spring of 1973. Wochok said he could not handle outside legal work while he was still on Specter's payroll. But he told du Pont that he could give him second opinions on specific questions—friendly advice, really, at no charge.

Soon du Pont was inviting Wochok to the mansion every few weeks. The schedule never varied: cocktails were served at six o'clock and dinner at seven, and there was conversation after that. Those evenings were Wochok's introduction to the kind of opulence he, like Odenweller, had never been aware of. One night in 1974 or 1975, du Pont said, "After a dinner like that, we ought to have a nice after-dinner drink." Du Pont led the way to the basement and through a bank-vault door.

"My first thought is, this is improbable, to see a safe in a basement," Wochok told me, "but, you know, he's got a lot of money—I guess I can understand it, except that I didn't see anything of any value in there except cases of liquor." Du Pont said some of them had been there for as long as he could remember—some had come from relatives who had died. He pulled out a brandy from 1864. "That's followed up with a visit maybe a month or two later when he hands me a bottle," Wochok recalled. "He says, 'Here, take this,' and it's a bottle of champagne from the maiden voyage of the *Queen Mary*."

Forty years later, Wochok still had that bottle of champagne, and it remained unopened. (Victor Krievins told me that du Pont had also given him a bottle, and that when he finally popped the cork, it was undrinkable.)

Du Pont followed Wochok from one law firm to another, assigning him more and more work. Some years, du Pont accounted for 80 percent of Wochok's billable hours; other years, far less. But du Pont was as secretive with Wochok as he was with Odenweller, and did not tell Wochok everything he was up to. Du Pont did not mention his philately until Wochok had been his lawyer for several years, and not because there was a dispute about stamps but because du Pont wanted a traveling companion. He called Wochok and asked if he were free the following afternoon. Wochok checked his calendar and said he was, and du Pont said, "OK, we're going to Toronto." Wochok asked how long they would stay, and du Pont said, "Oh, we're just going up and back." Wochok figured that with commercial flights, they would have to spend the night in Toronto, and told du Pont he could not go—he had appointments the following morning that he could not reschedule. Du Pont said Wochok could make the trip and still see his clients in the morning. "He said, 'I've got the Lear. We're going to take the Lear.'"

Off they went in du Pont's private jet. They spent an hour looking at stamp exhibits. They put in an appearance at a late-afternoon reception. "He said, 'OK, we're out of here,'" Wochok recalled. "Next thing I know, we're back on the Lear, back home, and I'm in my house by seven o'clock at night."

At some point, du Pont confided to Wochok that he owned the rarest stamp in the world. Wochok told me he was wonder struck: "This was so much more impressive and so much more significant and so much more important that I remember thinking, 'Gee, if I'd have maybe collected some stamps and spent some time meticulously collecting them, maybe I would've found something somewhere along the way." It is the dream boys had even before little Louis Vaughan.

• • •

Du Pont's eccentricities worsened with his descent into mental illness in the 1990s. He fired a gun at the ceiling while changing a light bulb. He believed his estate was filled with mechanical trees that slid across the land on orders from unseen remote controllers. He believed there were tunnels beneath the mansion that people used to come and go without being seen. (In fact, there *was* one tunnel, four hundred feet long, from the main house to the powerhouse, and it was du Pont who would use it during his standoff with the police after he shot Dave Schultz.) He was so suspicious he decided Jean could not have been his mother. His "real" mother had been a maid who he believed had had an affair with his father and had been buried outside the mansion. He ordered a plot dug up. "Of course no bones were found," the reporters Bill Ordine and Ralph Vigoda wrote in their book about the Schultz case.

Inside the mansion, du Pont was so sure that people were walking behind the walls that he paid one of the wrestlers who lived on the estate to do just that, to prove it could be done. Someone who wasn't paranoid—or rich, with a retinue that never said no—would simply have called in an exterminator to set out traps for mice.

Du Pont was turning into "a Howard Hughes–type figure: long, greasy hair, unkempt beard, his teeth literally rotting in his mouth," Ordine and Vigoda wrote.

"Frequently, he did not shower." But he could just as easily appear normal, even charming. There was no telling which he would be, the sane du Pont or the insane du Pont.

The sane du Pont went shopping in a stamp store on the afternoon of January 26, 1996. The man behind the counter who waited on him was Steve Pendergast, a onetime insurance broker who had decided that selling stamps was "a much more interesting way of spending my time." The first time Pendergast handled a du Pont transaction, he dealt with an assistant named Georgia, who picked up an expensive stamp album and some stamps from the store. Before long, she called and told Pendergast the album was unacceptable. Then Pendergast got another call that began, "This is John." Pendergast realized who was on the line, and a philatelist himself, he felt his pulse quicken. Pendergast knew that du Pont owned the unique one-cent magenta along with thousands of other important stamps, "but he never talked about it, so I didn't talk about it."

Pendergast told me that du Pont "couldn't have been more normal" as he left the store that January afternoon. Du Pont told him he would be back on Monday to pick up yet another stamp album.

The insane du Pont shot Dave Schultz less than two hours later. When Pendergast first heard there had been a shooting at du Pont's estate, he figured someone had tried to kill du Pont, not that du Pont himself had been the gunman.

Du Pont never saw the one-cent magenta again, except perhaps on television while he was in prison. A cable program did a segment on du Pont and the stamp, and du Pont's cellblock buzzed about the famous prisoner with the famous stamp. Wochok told me that du Pont enjoyed the attention.

The film *Foxcatcher* was less flattering. It is mostly about du Pont's fascination with athletes and athletics, his wealth and his deranged behavior—and his murder of Dave Schultz. Stamp World had a problem with the one scene that refers to du Pont's stamps.

It is the scene in which du Pont's helicopter takes off from the lawn of his mansion. Du Pont and Dave Schultz's brother Mark are aboard, and du Pont hands him the pages of a speech he has written for Mark Schultz to read at an event at which du Pont is to receive an award.

Du Pont is intent on rehearsing the speech, which calls for Schultz to name du Pont's accomplishments:

"ornithologist, author, world explorer, philatelist." But Schultz cannot say those highfalutin words. He pronounces the first one "orny-thologist." The last one stops him completely. "Fuh-lay" is all he can manage.

"Stamps," du Pont says, by way of explanation.

"Can we say 'stamps'?" Schultz asks.

"No," du Pont says, sounding stern. He has chosen the word he wants Schultz to say, chosen it deliberately, and he is determined to make him say it. "Philatelist."

Schultz is nervous about standing at a lectern and speaking to a crowd, and du Pont compounds Schultz's jitters by saying that the audience at the dinner will number four hundred. Du Pont snorts cocaine and invites Schultz to try some. "Well, I'm not so sure that's such a good idea," Schultz says.

Du Pont looks annoyed. Schultz inhales the cocaine, but du Pont has already gone back to rehearsing the speech. And, as usual, du Pont wants perfection.

"Fuh-LAY-tuh-list," Schultz stammers.

"Smoother," du Pont commands.

Soon Schultz is tackling the string of nouns, but he skips a few. Du Pont wants nothing left out, and launches into a pronunciation drill as if he were an instructor coaching the laggard in the class.

"Or-nuh-THAH-luh-gist, fuh-LAY-tuh-list, fuh-LAN-thruh-pist," du Pont says. "Again."

In Stamp World, the problem was not the cocaine but the long *A*. Steve Carell, the actor who played du Pont, did not pronounce the word as prescribed by every dictionary since the word *philately* took its place in Webster's *Supplement of New Words* in 1880, with an *A* that rhymes with "cat."

ELEVEN

$9.5 MILLION

———◆———

*2014: "I Expected to See Magenta,
and I Saw Magenta"*

I understand you want to have a conversation with the person who bought the stamp. I will leave you my number," the message on my voice mail began. The voice was a man's: deep, powerful, and commanding, one that would have carried to the balcony in a theater or sustained a long career in radio or television.

"Zero one one, as I'm calling you from overseas," he said, but he sounded like a New Yorker on a cell phone. He recited a twelve-digit number that began with the country code for Spain.

When I called back, he answered on the first ring. He said his name was Stuart Weitzman.

Yes, the Stuart Weitzman who has designed strappy

gladiator sandals, sultry thigh-high boots, and dozens of other shoes. The Stuart Weitzman whose creations have been photographed on Kate Moss in ads and Kate Middleton in paparazzi shots—and on Taylor Swift, Lady Gaga, Beyoncé, and Charlize Theron. The Stuart Weitzman who refers to first ladies by their first names: "Michelle has bunches of our shoes," he told me.

He is also the Stuart Weitzman who was once a boy in Queens with a couple of stamp albums—and who stared at the empty space for the one-cent magenta.

Now, for nearly a year, the man behind a best-selling sandal known as the Nudist had owned that stamp, which is barely big enough to cover the birthmark on a supermodel.

After du Pont died in prison in 2010, liquidating du Pont's holdings kept Taras Wochok busy. He arranged the sale of Foxcatcher Farm to a real-estate developer. The house that Dave Schultz and his family had lived in was leveled, as was du Pont's athletic training center, but du Pont's mansion was not. It became a clubhouse and—ironically—the fitness center for a new gated community.

When Wochok turned to selling off du Pont's possessions, the one-cent magenta was a priority item. Wochok consigned the rest of du Pont's collection to a philatelic auction house in Geneva. The one-cent magenta did not go there. Nor did he send it to an American firm that specialized in stamps like Robert A. Siegel Auction Galleries, which had once counted du Pont as its number one customer. He entrusted it to one of the big names in the auction world—and, specifically, to one man at that firm: David Redden of Sotheby's.

I saw Wochok at the auction, but not the buyer. Redden told me that the person who bought the one-cent magenta did not want to be identified. Protecting a buyer's privacy is not unheard of at high-profile auctions, and at first Redden would not even say whether the buyer was a man or a woman. This complicates matters for reporters like me, trying to write a newspaper article about a record-breaking sale without knowing which pronoun to use. Redden slipped up this time and said something about "him," so it was a man. The collectors on the salesroom floor tried to guess who had the best poker face—that is, who was not admitting that he was the new owner. A few had bid in the early stages, but they shook their heads when I asked, jokingly, if they had arranged a private signal with Redden that let them stay in the running after they put down their paddles. They rolled their eyes when I said something about bidding by telepathy.

They did not see Weitzman. Neither did I, and I wouldn't have recognized him—I'm not a regular at fashion shows or Oscar-night after-parties. But he was there, above it all. Weitzman told me on the phone from Spain that he had sat through the auction behind the curtains of a skybox at Sotheby's, which is why no one in the crowd noticed him. And he told me that it was not his first time in a skybox there. He told me about being outbid at another Redden auction, and I wondered if he was the mystery owner of a 1933 "double eagle" gold coin. Like the one-cent magenta, it was one of a kind, the only 1933 double eagle that was not melted down and disposed of when the United States went off the gold standard. Redden sold it for $7.59 million in 2002, at the time the highest price ever paid for a coin.

A unique object, sold by Redden to an anonymous bidder. It sounded like something that would appeal to the buyer of the one-cent magenta. And Weitzman knew too much about the lengths to which the New-York Historical Society had gone to display the precious coin.

• • •

Weitzman told me that he pretty much gave up stamp collecting in his late teens. In college he studied real estate and accounting, and aspired to be what he called "one of these geniuses on Wall Street." But drawing and painting had been a hobby, and he sketched some shoes when he was an undergraduate that got noticed—first by a classmate, who showed the sketches to his father, a shoe manufacturer. The father called Weitzman in and asked where Weitzman had copied them from.

"Nowhere," Weitzman said. "I didn't copy them."

The father ripped up one of the sketches and told Weitzman to draw it. He did. The father bought the rest of Weitzman's sketches at $25 apiece and started making shoes from Weitzman's designs. Weitzman figures that he made $12,000 drawing shoes while he was in college—although, as he told the story nearly fifty years later, he was still annoyed he had never been paid for the sketch he had to redraw.

He forgot about the Wall Street career, but he never forgot about the one-cent magenta. He heard about the coming sale from Redden. They knew each other from past auctions, none involving stamps. Redden said the one-cent magenta was being consigned from, as Weitzman described it later, "the estate of this guy who was in prison"—du Pont—and eventually it would be put up for sale. Was Weitzman interested? "Of course I was,"

Weitzman said. He lined up some partners, but after they dropped out, he decided to go all in and bid on his own.

And then Redden showed him the stamp. "It took me back to my childhood," Weitzman told me. "It was sort of like going back to the house I grew up in"—which he did once, in the 1990s. "I thought I grew up in this giant house—when you're six, you're seven, it's all you know, but of course it wasn't when I was fifty and I took my kids to see it."

The stamp also looked tiny. He took in the color, and dismissed the naysayers who complained that the stamp had faded almost beyond recognition. "I expected to see magenta, and I saw magenta, darkened over time, but it was magenta," he said. "I wouldn't call it bordeaux, burgundy, red, or fuchsia. It was magenta, it is magenta."

From past auctions, he had learned to play down Redden's numbers. "He puts out these estimates. I said to him, 'David, it's not going to get close to ten million.' He said, 'No, it's at least fifteen, it may go to twenty.'" This was Redden's pre-auction salesmanship, trying to get likely bidders so excited that they would send more than they were inclined to spend.

In the end, Weitzman's calculus was better than Redden's—the price was not that far from $10 million, but nowhere near $15 million. "When it hit eight, there were only two people left, and that guy didn't want it as much as I did," Weitzman told me.

"Or he didn't have that childhood album that had stuck with him for sixty years."

• • •

His older brother had tried stamp collecting, and Weitzman picked up where he had left off, using the same albums, "partially filled up with easy-to-find stamps." His hobby took on an urgency when he broke his leg playing baseball in the street. "I made a really fantastic catch on a deep fly ball off the handle of a shovel—that's how you got your best bats, you cut off your father's snow shovel hoping he never found out," he said. "I caught this ball one-handed, and when I landed, my foot landed on the curb but my heel went down to street level. That snapped the bone that connects the ankle to the shin, but I held on to the ball. I was so proud of hanging on to that ball."

It was such a bad break that he finished the school year at home. He was not going to live out the cliché about all work and no play, but he could not play in the street, so he played with stamps, even sending his mother to the post office to buy whole sheets of new issues. "I started filling albums with things I could find—once in a while, things you thought were worth a penny were worth fifty dollars," he said.

He knew what the one-cent magenta looked like from the image in his hand-me-down album. He knew what it was from a comic book.

Donald Duck and the Gilded Man was published in 1952, when Weitzman was ten. It had an operatically complicated plot that sent Donald Duck and his nephews to Guiana in search of the one-cent magenta. There they hired a helicopter to take them into the jungle, where, a reliable source had told them, they would find the man who had the stamp, Mr. El Dorado, the gilded man. Young comic-book readers might or might not have understood the playful twist on the name of the rich and surprisingly forgetful stamp collector Philo T. Ellic, whose name was a clumsy play on *philatelic*. But surely they were rooting against a conniving rival of Donald's who turned out to be the sole heir of Miss Susiebell Gander. And of course the envelope bearing the stamp had been addressed to her.

Every page had some development that could induce a fresh fantasy in a boy's mind, but Weitzman was realistic. He figured the comics were as close as he would

ever come to the one-cent magenta. Years later, an art history professor in college said much the same thing to him
about post-Impressionist paintings: "You will not own
any of these, museums will. You will never get to own
them."

Weitzman was not interested in owning post-
Impressionist paintings. But he took the words "you will
never get to own them" as a challenge. Someday, he had
to own the one-cent magenta.

• • •

Once he did, two things happened: he went looking for
his boyhood stamp albums, and the overtures began—the
overtures from museums that wanted to display the one-
cent magenta.

He could not find the album with the blank space for
that stamp, but he found his other album, which had had
a blank space for the Inverted Jenny. Filling that space
now presented a problem for Weitzman. It could hold
only one Inverted Jenny, and not long after Weitzman
bought the one-cent magenta, he acquired four, not just
any four, but the plate block, a four-stamp square, the
quartet from the original sheet that was next to the serial number of the printing plate—8493. On most plate

blocks, the number is marginalia. Philatelists are passionate about marginalia, which they call selvage, but anyone can see its importance on this plate block. The digits, in blue, like the little airplanes, are upside down.

As for the feelers from museums about the one-cent magenta, Weitzman was secretive, just as he had been at the auction. He told Redden to tell officials at each museum nothing more than, "You'll be getting a call from the owner's representative."

So Allen R. Kane, the director of the National Postal Museum in Washington, scheduled a meeting with a deep-voiced caller who gave his name as "Stuart Alan." Kane told me he believed Stuart Alan was an adviser to the owner—an adviser no one at the museum had heard of. Maybe he was more of a business adviser than a philatelist, maybe a marketing type who could evaluate a plan for displaying the one-cent magenta and generating the publicity to bring in crowds. "I was told a team was going to come down," Kane said. "I didn't put one and one together."

The museum occupies a block-square building built just before World War I as part of a master plan to revive sleepy Washington in ways that suggested Rome and Paris. Those were the days when post offices were temples—grand structures that imparted confidence in government. And the Washington post office was one of the grandest. As a museum, its collection includes six million objects, from tiny stamps to full-size mail trucks to the anthrax-laced letter sent to Senate Majority Leader Tom Daschle in 2001.

Stuart Alan passed through the metal detectors inside the tall brass doors, and Kane led him into the main gallery. It was a fast-food restaurant after the building was decommissioned as a post office—philatelists marvel that Kane managed to reclaim it—and it is named for the hedge-fund billionaire William Gross, a stamp collector who was the major donor to the fund for its remodeling. The first time I visited the museum, in 2014, Kane was ebullient, racing through the gallery, showing me President Franklin D. Roosevelt's sketches for stamps. Those sketches, now brown ink on brownish paper, reminded me that I had read that FDR, a lifelong stamp collector, had "assumed complete control over stamp issues." One year when he was in office, the Post Office even reported a million-dollar profit.

Kane also demonstrated a computer that took my photograph and put it on a replica of a stamp—my face, right-side up, where the Inverted Jenny belonged—and he asked me a question he had asked Weitzman: "What do you think was the biggest-selling American commemorative stamp?" On the wall was a poster of the thirty-two-cent Marilyn Monroe stamp from 1995. The power of suggestion being what it is, I gamely gave the same answer as Weitzman: Marilyn Monroe.

Wrong, Kane told me, probably with the same glee as when Weitzman had stood in the same spot. The record belongs to the twenty-nine-cent Elvis Presleys from 1993. (Two versions were issued. The portrait of Presley holding a microphone was the same on both. One said "Elvis Presley," the other simply "Elvis.")

Kane showed Weitzman an alcove where he wanted to install the one-cent magenta in a case with special lighting and special glass to keep the stamp from fading. Kane's team talked about promoting the exhibition online. They talked about the museum's technical specialists and, as Kane put it, "what we could do to clean it up or whatever." Kane was succinct. "It's kind of dark. We have the best paper conservators in town, and they're ready to go."

Kane's team was puzzled about Stuart Alan and why he seemed preoccupied with shoes. "We have this one interactive display in the museum where you can do a search for any topic," Ted Wilson, the museum's registrar, told me. "He does a search for shoes—stamps with shoes on them. We're looking at each other like, what's with the shoes?" The top officials at the museum, Wilson said, were "a bunch of guys who have a limited knowledge of women's shoes."

Stuart Alan listened to their pitch and said he wanted the other person on his team—his executive vice president, Barbara Kreger—brought in. Someone asked where she was, and Stuart Alan instructed them to go to the street corner in front of the museum. A staffer went outside, and there she was, a stylish-looking woman carrying a small hard-shell case.

Just as they were clueless about Stuart Alan, they did not realize that she was the woman who had launched more than a million shoes, Weitzman's output since he hired her in the late 1970s. "She has a model's foot," Weitzman told me, explaining that his designs don't go into production without her approval. (In 2015 Weitzman's company was owned by Coach, but he retained creative control over the shoes.)

Kane's people found a chair and seated her next to Stuart Alan, who said, "You won." Now Kane's people were even more puzzled, until Ms. Kreger put the case on the table and they saw what was inside. She had had the one-cent magenta the whole time, and Stuart Alan—Stuart Alan Weitzman—finally came clean and identified himself as the owner.

Weitzman told me later that he had considered lending it to the British Museum. He said the curators there had offered to display the one-cent magenta in a gallery with an original copy of Magna Carta that drew 250,000 visitors a year, but London was too far away. Patriotism also tugged at him. "I'm American," he said.

Besides, with 400,000 visitors a year, the postal museum packs in more people.

• • •

These days, stamps are museum exhibits, relics of a world that knew the world from stamps. Once, stamps were tantalizing because they had gone places. And they depicted places most people would never see: exotic destinations. "We can capture a giraffe stamp from Tanganyika, even if we cannot go there and shoot one, and we can trap a kookaburra bird for our stamp album even if we never see Australia," Ellis Parker Butler observed in 1933. The writer William Styron recalled that "[d]uring the philatelic period of my late childhood," he thrilled to the stamps from Greece and Guatemala in his album, but "none so arrested my imagination or so whetted my longing for faraway places" as Elobey, Annobón, and Corisco. He used the names of those far-off colonies in the Gulf of Guinea as the title of a short story that invoked a boyhood stamp album whose trophy was a stamp from those very islands. The story was about how the owner of a such a stamp album grew up to be "an unwilling visitor to one of those faraway places" as a soldier in World War II, how the dread of wartime drowned out the past, and how he longed to be back in his parents' living room, "merely dreaming of one of those places rather than actually being in one." The world conjured by stamps, the world of the imagination, was a better place.

Styron's generation came of age when the United States had a philatelist-in-chief who, as a young man, "came to think of himself as cosmopolitan, and not just because his extensive stamp collection made him a whiz at geography." As president, FDR's stamp albums weighed down his luggage. And from 1910 to 1936, Britain had a king who longed to spend three afternoons a week with his stamp collection. Ivory soap sponsored a radio program for stamp collectors, and a few colleges added courses in philately to the curriculum. Those were the

days, too, when New York City still had a stamp district, a
short walk from City Hall and the church where George
Washington began his first Inauguration Day in 1789.
But the stamp dealers who populated Nassau Street (and
advertised in magazines as seemingly unrelated as *The
New Yorker* and *Popular Mechanics*) have disappeared. In
1994, the Subway Stamp Shop hauled away 250 tons of
stamps and reinvented itself in Altoona, Pennsylvania. It
has been 280 miles from the New York subway ever since.

Stamp collecting was once so popular that whole magazines devoted to stamps rolled off the presses, week after
week or month after month, with articles that sounded
as if they should have been master's theses: "The Head of
Queen Victoria on the Penny and Two-Penny Stamps"
or "Winter Mail Service Across the Straits of Northum-
berland, From Prince Edward Island to the Mainland of
New Brunswick." Some sounded less abstruse. In 1941
a Los Angeles schoolteacher who was a well-known
philatelist moved to Holton, Kansas—population three
hundred—to take charge of a publication called *Weekly
Philatelic Gossip*. Holton was "a very strategic place" for
such a publication. Why? His explanation had the kind
of complicated precision that a stamp lover would appreciate. Holton, Kansas, stood at "the intersection point of

the diagonals of the United States, 1,700 miles from each corner—the northwest, the northeast, the southwest and the southeast."

Stamp magazines hardly had the circulation or advertising base of the *Saturday Evening Post* or *Collier's*. But like the Internet a couple of generations later, they reached the eyeballs their advertisers wanted to reach, even if they were tired eyeballs, eyeballs in need of magnifying glasses, and there were fewer and fewer of them. *Weekly Philatelic Gossip* went out of business in 1961; membership in the American Philatelic Society peaked in 1988 at nearly fifty-eight thousand. By the time Redden was selling the one-cent magenta, the society counted only thirty-two thousand members. "The ranks of hardcore collectors . . . are thinning," *The New Yorker* magazine wrote in 2015. "For the young, postage stamps can hardly compete with smart phones."

Kids don't collect stamps the way they did in the 1950s and 1960s, when Weitzman was growing up. And no wonder. Stamps don't deliver the action-adventure high of video games like *XCOM: Enemy Unknown* or *Mass Effect 3*. Stamps don't come with sci-fi suits of armor or alien pals or command of your own spaceship, and stamps don't let you rack up points for bashing what's left of the human population with a supercharged wrench.

That may be. But the why-collect-stamps question was the wrong question because the one-cent magenta is different from other stamps and has been since the experts affirmed its uniqueness toward the end of the nineteenth century.

With that affirmation came a transformation. It was no longer an ordinary stamp, a disposable element on a newspaper that was itself disposable. From the 1870s on, the one-cent magenta was prized, tucked away in closely watched storage cabinets in palaces or vaults in banks. It fit the definition for collected objects prescribed by the cultural historian Philipp Blom in 2011. Such things "are like holy relics," he wrote. "They have shed their original function and become totems, fetishes." Whoever buys an object like the one-cent magenta is not seeking status, Blom added: "Real collectors are after something else . . . The real value of a piece lies not in its auction price, but in the importance it has in the collection."

• • •

But what kind of collector is Stuart Weitzman? Surely, the one-cent magenta had an emotional pull—the boyhood story about the blank spot in his album was true—but Weitzman repeated what Redden had said about him just after the auction, that he was "not really" a stamp collector but a collector of one-of-a-kind objects. He favors Americana, but he is, above all, pragmatic. He found the one-cent magenta's rarity compelling.

"These one-of-a-kind items will always be bought for more money by people who are not collectors in their relative industries," Weitzman told me in 2016, "because we see them differently than a collector in that industry would see them." He said that was how he landed the Inverted Jenny plate block. "No one in the [stamp] industry could match what I thought was the value," he explained. Stamp collectors "saw it as a stamp, the only one." He was willing to pay more, just as he had been willing to pay more for the one-cent magenta, because he thought of the plate block "not as a stamp but as one more of those one-of-a-kind Americana items."

He asked if I'd like to see another unique item that he owned, one that "I'm really excited about." Of course, I told him.

It was a pair of shoes. They looked like a pair my mother had when I was a child, a pair I thought had been elegant, with white fabric covering the midsection. The man who saw magenta in the one-cent magenta corrected me when I ventured that the toes and heels of his pair were everyday brown. "Cognac," Weitzman said with authority, adding that the style was known in the shoe business as a "spectator pump." My mother's shoes, though, had not been autographed by the 1941 New York Yankees.

That was the season in which Joe DiMaggio had a fifty-six-game hitting streak. "He wasn't married to Marilyn yet," Weitzman explained, figuring that I would know he meant Marilyn Monroe. He probably also guessed that I would look up their marriage (it lasted all of 274 days, from January to October 1954).

In 1941, Weitzman told me, "he asked the woman he was with, 'How would you like a baseball signed by all my teammates?'"

"She went like this," Weitzman continued as he mimicked taking off one of his shoes, "and she said, 'Would they sign my shoe?'"

Twenty-seven signatures take up space, even when they are small—more than there was on one of the shoes. She had to give DiMaggio both of them. He gave them back with names that I recognized: Lefty Gomez. Phil Rizzuto. DiMaggio, who was named the most valuable player that year. Even the catcher Bill Dickey, whose nickname was "the Man Nobody Knows."

Weitzman turned over the shoes in his hands a couple

of times. Then he explained why he had them: "In spite of millions of baseballs being signed, it's the only shoe." Like the one-cent magenta, the pair was unique.

• • •

I descended so far into Stamp World that I flew to London twice to retrace Redden's steps and find out what made the one-cent magenta so special. On the second trip, I stood in the vault containing every British stamp but the one-cent magenta. "This is expected to be reference material," the Keeper of the Royal Philatelic Collection, Michael Sefi, told me. The vault is shown only to serious students of philately, which I didn't pretend to be, but it is not the only treat for someone who visits Sefi's office in St. James's Palace.

I had arrived on time, but the guard told me that Sefi was locked in. I looked alarmed, and the guard seemed to recognize the edgy expression of an American hearing a phrase that was close to *lockdown*. He smiled and explained that Sefi's room was on the courtyard where the Changing the Guard ceremony was about to begin. The regiment that would take over at Buckingham Palace would muster in that courtyard. If I hurried, I could watch the pageantry, and Sefi would step out after it ended. The New Guard played fifes and drums as they marched away. Sefi said it was better when there was a full band.

Inside, we had a long conversation about the one-cent magenta, with some thrilling show-and-tell. Sefi pulled one of George V's red albums from its shelf in the vault and carried it to a table in the bright room adjacent to the vault in which he works. He opened it to a page with the four-cent magentas from British Guiana that were issued in 1852. To me, still with the eyes of a stamp newbie, the color looked the same as the color of the one-cent magenta.

That moment was in my mind the following day, when I had lunch with Christopher Harman, the chairman of the Expert Committee at the Royal. He had a theory that the one-cent magenta had been printed on scraps of paper from earlier stamps sent to British Guiana—specifically, the margins of the sheets that originally contained the stamps from 1852 that Sefi had shown me.

This was fairly esoteric, but that did not stop us from spending nearly an hour speculating. And it didn't stop me from spending another hour speculating with another authority, David Beech, a former president of the Royal who was the curator of the British Library's philatelic collection for thirty years.

We will probably never know where the paper came from, just as we will probably never know about its cocoon phase, the time from its printing in British Guiana to its discovery by Louis Vernon Vaughan in his uncle's abandoned house. But I found myself thinking about its storied afterlife—and about what makes something collectible, valuable, and enduring.

If the one-cent magenta had not gotten out of British Guiana when it did, it wouldn't have been seen by the most influential eyes in philately.

If Edward Loines Pemberton had snapped it up when he had the chance, it wouldn't have gotten to Philippe Arnold de la Renotière von Ferrary, the collector to end all collectors, and it wouldn't have become an object far beyond the means of most philatelists.

If Edward Denny Bacon had not declared it authentic, it would have been cast off as an album weed, as a fake or a forgery.

If Arthur Hind hadn't been talked into buying it, if Small and Weinberg hadn't seen its investment potential, if du Pont hadn't shown up at the 1980 auction, the one-cent magenta would have led a less exalted life.

It has been a record-setter time after time not because it is a stamp but because it is the only one of its kind. That is what Weitzman understood. He did not care about the paper it was printed on, the celebrity factor that came with it, or the money that he spent to get it. What he wanted was the thing that no one else could have.

ACKNOWLEDGMENTS

———◆———

This book began the way I described it in the "Stamp World" chapter, with a chance encounter at a cocktail party—and then I wrote a newspaper story about the one-cent magenta. That led me to Elisabeth Scharlatt and Amy Gash at Algonquin Books of Chapel Hill—more about them later—and into Stamp World, as I came to call it.

If you are a Stamp World habitué, I know, I know, nobody uses benzene to assay stamps anymore—one accomplished philatelist showed up at my desk at the *New York Times* one day and did a demonstration of what I took to be a less volatile chemical, heptane. Besides, dunking the one-cent magenta in benzene wouldn't have yielded the information David Redden probably thought the experts at the Royal Philatelic Society needed if they were to issue the certificate he wanted. But Redden's mention of benzene captivated me, because for years my friend Tom Baker and I have chuckled at the only-in-New-York memory of the neighbor who insisted that my landlord was storing a huge barrel of benzene in the basement of the building I lived in for a couple of years when I was in my early twenties.

Tom read an early version of the manuscript and offered his usual perceptive guidance, as did several other friends, notably Barbara Guss. Robert P. Odenweller, who is as sharp-eyed about stamps as he was in the cockpits of jets, was both a source and a helper, steering me away from potential turbulence as I skimmed over Stamp World. So was David Beech, who conducted what I felt were graduate-level seminars that were as much about history and technology—to name only two subjects that we discussed—as they were about philately in general and the one-cent magenta in particular.

I'm grateful to many other philatelists and philatelic experts on both sides of the Atlantic. I appreciated the cordial welcome at the Royal Philatelic Society London and the time that the Expert Committee's chairman, Christopher G. Harman, spent in discussing theories about the committee's work and the one-cent magenta. David Skinner at the British Library also provided expertise and guidance on reference materials, as did Michael Sefi, the curator of the Royal Philatelic Collection. At the National Postal Museum in Washington, the director, Allen R. Kane, was tireless and insightful at important moments, as were Ted Wilson, the registrar in the Collections Department; and Marty Emery, the museum's manager of Internet affairs. Thomas Lera's technical knowledge was enormously helpful. Matthew Healey offered ideas early on and opened doors at the Collectors Club in New York. Robert Rose of the Philatelic Foundation was considerate and perceptive. I enjoyed my encounters with Irwin Weinberg, who died about a month after I last saw him, and Stuart Weitzman, and I was pleased to reach Virginia Baxter, Carrie Hunter, and C. Ian C. Wishart, descendants of philatelists who figured in the story of the one-cent magenta.

At the *New York Times*, Carolyn Ryan, Wendell Jamieson, and Diego Ribadeneira were wonderful, as always—encouraging, inquisitive, and, when I needed it, indulgent. I also drew on help from any number of *Times* colleagues, among them Susan Beachy, Mark Bulik, Doris Burke, Laura Craven, Alain Delaqueriere, Emma

G. Fitzsimmons, and Joan Nassivera. Thanks, too, to Warren Bodow, Wayne Bodow, Claude Giroux, Barbara Guss, Eben Price, Alison Shapiro, and Nina Shippen.

I marveled, time and again, at Elisabeth Scharlatt and Amy Gash—Elisabeth for seeing the possibilities in a story like this, Amy for seeing those possibilities through. She added a special incisiveness that's reflected on every page. I'm indebted to many others at Algonquin, among them managing editor Brunson Hoole and copy editor Matthew Somoroff. Thanks to my agent, David Black, for doing what he does once again.

And then there's the incomparable Jane, who understood from the beginning that that little smudge was important and put up with my descent into Stamp World.

NOTES

---•---

1. Stamp World

1   *a first-time author*   Mike Offit, *Nothing Personal: A Novel of Wall Street* (New York: Thomas Dunne Books, 2014).

2   *What a place for a book party*   Paul Goldberger, *The City Observed* (New York: Vintage, 1979), 227; Paul Porzelt, *The Metropolitan Club of New York* (New York: Rizzoli, 1982), 59–60; Paul R. Baker, *Stanny: The Gilded Life of Stanford White* (New York: Free Press, 1989), 142–44.

3   *one of the pianos from the movie* Casablanca   "A Star Piano's Value As Time Goes By," *New York Times*, December 14, 2012, A36, and "'Casablanca' Piano Is Sold for $602,500," *New York Times*, December 15, 2012, A20.

3   *the first book printed*   "For First Book Printed in English in New World, Let the Bidding Begin," *New York Times*, November 16, 2013, A14, and "Book of Psalms Published in 1640 Makes Record Sale at Auction," *New York Times*, Nov. 27, 2013, A20.

3   *the same copy of the Declaration of Independence*   "He's Auctioned the 1775 Declaration, Twice," *New York Times*, July 4, 2000, B2.

4   *"Get ready to freak out"*   "World's Rarest Stamp Sets Auction
         Record," *Time* online, June 18, 2014. http://time.com/2896879
         /worlds-rarest-stamp/.

5   *"a fetishistic underworld"*   Sarah Hampson, "Notes from the Phil-
         atelic Underworld: How Stamps Are Undergoing a Revival," *The
         Globe and Mail*, December 17, 2014, http://www.theglobeandmail
         .com/life/home-and-garden/design/notes-from-the-philatelic
         -underworld-how-stamps-are-undergoing-a-revival/article22118332/.

6   *"Get your mind out of the gutter"*   "The Story of the First Stamp,"
         Smithsonian online, July 19, 2013, http://www.smithsonianmag
         .com/arts-culture/the-story-of-the-first-postage-stamp-14931961/.

6   *"It is a pity"*   H.W. Fowler, *A Dictionary of Modern English Usage:
         The Classic First Edition* (Oxford: Oxford University Press, 2009).

6   *I looked in the* Oxford English Dictionary   http://www.oed.com
         /view/Entry/142410?redirectedFrom=philately#eid.

7   *He mailed himself*   Deirdre Foley Mendelssohn, "The Eccentric
         Englishman," *The New Yorker*, September 14, 2010, http://www
         .newyorker.com/books/page-turner/the-eccentric-englishman;
         http://www.wrbray.org.uk/.

7   *start pedaling*   David Leafe, "The Man Who Posted Himself,"
         (*Daily Mail*, March 19, 2012, http://www.dailymail.co.uk/news
         /article-2117448/Prankster-W-Reginald-Bray-tested-Royal-Mail
         -limits-exasperated-Hitler.html).

8   *It had not been seen in public*   Talk by Daniel A. Piazza at the Na-
         tional Postal Museum, June 7, 2015.

8   *it disappeared at a collectors' convention*   Stanley N. Bierman, *The
         World's Greatest Stamp Collectors* (Sidney, Ohio: Linn's Stamp
         News, 1980), 33.

8   *the ugliest stamp*   "Interim Stamp Uses 17 Words Just to Say 4
         Cents," *New York Times*, January 25, 1991, A18.

8   *"a shoddy-looking thing"*   Alvin F. Harlow, *Paper Chase: The Ame-
      nities of Stamp Collecting* (New York: Henry Holt and Company,
      1940), 139.

9   *"unsatisfactory to the aesthete"*   L.N. and Maurice Williams, *Rare
      Stamps* (New York: G.P. Putnam's Sons, 1967), 11.

9   *"been through the wash"*   Alex Palmer, "The Remarkable Story
      of the World's Rarest Stamp," *Smithsonian* (online), June 4, 2015,
      http://www.smithsonianmag.com/smithsonian-institution
      /remarkable-story-worlds-rarest-stamp-180955412/.

10   *a mixture of red and purple*   Author interview and email exchange
      with Frank H. Mahnke, May 2015.

10   *a shade called "Chili Pepper"*   Author interview with Ferne Mai-
      brunn, May 2015.

11   *the famous Inverted Jenny*   See George Amick, *The Inverted Jenny:
      Money, Mystery, Mania* (Sidney, Ohio: Amos Press, 1986).

12   *under his pillow*   Author interview with Robert Odenweller, Janu-
      ary 17, 2015.

12   *his picture on a stamp from Redonda*   Ralph Vigoda, "Expressing
      Himself. Where Du Pont Literally Put His Stamp on Things,"
      Philadelphia Inquirer, Feb. 15, 1996, A1.

13   *serving a thirty-year sentence*   Debbie Goldberg, "John du Pont
      Found Guilty, Mentally Ill," *Washington Post*, Feb. 26, 1997, A1.

13   *"How can I get him a pardon"*   Talk by Allen R. Kane at reception
      for Irwin Weinberg at the National Postal Museum, May 8, 2015,
      and author interview, April 6, 2016.

13   *handcuffed to his wrist*   "Irwin Weinberg Got Attached to His
      $500,000 Treasure; Then He Found He Couldn't Get Loose," *Peo-
      ple*, July 10, 1978, 43.

17   *to be bogus*   Rob Haeseler, "1 cent Magenta pretender is fake, Says
      Royal," *Linn's Stamp News*, June 21, 1999, 1.

2. Travels With David

18 *"All they told me was"* "Magna Carta Is Going on the Auction Block, Scraggly Tail and All," *New York Times*, September 25, 2007, B1.

19 *it became the most expensive* "Book of Psalms Published in 1640 Makes Record Sale at Auction," *New York Times*, Nov. 27, 2013, A20.

19 *Redden said he approached* Author interview with David N. Redden, March 22, 2016.

19 *When I told Wochok* Author interview with Taras N. Wochok, January 19, 2015.

21 *Ridley Scott's thriller* The Counselor Manohla Dargis, "Wildlife Is Tame; Not the Humans," *New York Times,* October 25, 2013, C8.

22 *invested in obscure books* Royal Philatelic Society London, press release, July 1, 2014.

22 *"We may be venerable"* "Mission Statement of the Royal Philatelic Society London," on the Society's website in 2015. The two phrases were later dropped.

23 *the Duke of York had been* David Cannadine, *George V: The Unexpected King* (London: Allen Lane-Penguin Books, 2014), 31.

23 *"it was in this hobby"* John Gore, *King George V: A Personal Memoir* (New York: Charles Scribner's Sons, 1941), 296.

23 *"is said to have been interrupted"* Monograph from Michael Sefi, "The Royal Philatelic Collection," 5.

23 *once read a paper* "The First President of the Royal Philatelic Society, London," *The London Philatelist*, December 1906, 287.

23 *"showed a most interesting and valuable display"* "Philatelic Societies' Meetings," *The London Philatelist*, December 1904, 79; Kenneth Rose, *King George V* (London: Phoenix Press, 2000), 41.

24   *"mere scraps of paper"*   Quoted in David Cannadine, "Rose's Rex,"
      London Review of Books, September 15, 1983, 4.

25   *Still, the diplomat*   Rose, *King George V*, 41.

25   *"I was that damned fool"*   "The Queen's Own: Stamps That
      Changed the World," National Postal Museum, 2004.

25   *"the greatest gathering"*   Heritage Statement—41 Devonshire Place
      West (London: Feilden + Mawson, December 2013), 13.

27   *"Doubts have more than once"*   The Postage Stamps, Envelopes,
      Wrappers, Post Cards and Telegraph Stamps of the British Colonies in
      the West Indies, Together With British Honduras and the Colonies in
      South America (London: Philatelic Society, London, 1891), 39.

27   *Sir John Wilson was well aware*   W.A. Townsend and F.G. Howe,
      The Postage Stamps and Postal History of British Guiana (London:
      Royal Philatelic Society London, 1970), 47.

28   *Inside St. James's*   Christopher Winn, *I Never Knew That About
      Royal Britain* (London: Ebury Press, 2012), 38.

29   *The stamp collection is owned personally*   Author interview with
      Michael Sefi, March 30, 2016.

30   *estimated in 2015*   Camilla Tominey, "The Queen is worth £300
      million but cash is tied up in art and . . . stamps," *Sunday Express*,
      March 8, 2015; David McClure, *Royal Legacy: How the Royal Fam-
      ily Have Made, Spent and Passed on Their Wealth* (London: Thistle
      Press, 2015).

30   *had never seen the actual one-cent*   Author interview with Michael
      Sefi, March 30, 2016.

31   *"And, I think, satisfying [Sefi's] own curiosity"*   Author interview
      with David N. Redden, June 23, 2015.

32   *"There's always something"*   Interview with Michael Sefi, June 22,
      2015.

32   *he tamped them down*   Interview with Michael Sefi, March 30, 2016.

32   *The Expert Committee's command post*   Author visit to Royal Philatelic Society London, March 12, 2015.

34   *The technology was perfected*   Author interview with David Tobin of Foster + Freeman, June 13, 2015.

36   *"It was described in Bacon as rubbed"*   Author interview with Christopher G. Harman, March 12, 2015.

36   *The mention of the rubbing*   Author interview with Matthew Healey, March 3, 2015.

38   *His hand shook*   Author interview with Peter Lister, March 12, 2015.

38   *"Here's our patient"*   This section is based on author observations on the trip to National Postal Museum on April 17, 2014, and on later conversations with Redden, Odenweller, and Thomas M. Lera.

41   *Lera, writing in a scientific journal*   Thomas M. Lera, *Winton M. Blount Postal History Symposia: Select Papers, 2010–2011* (Washington: Smithsonian Institutional Scholarly Press, 2012), 74–75.

43   *"The cunning of Wilson"*   "Master Auctioneer," *Time*, April 20, 1962, 76.

43   *Wilson turned a sale of post-Impressionist paintings*   Carol Vogel, "Theater in the Salesroom," *New York Times Book Review*, July 5, 1998, Section 7, 17.

45   *"This is like a horse race"*   Author interview with David N. Redden, June 17, 2014.

45   *But actually, it was over*   This section is based on author observations before, during, and immediately after the sale on June 17, 2014.

47   *uninspiring wording*   Holland Cotter, "On the Scene: 'The

Contemporaries,' 'Painting Now' and More," *New York Times Book Review*, June 25, 2015, BR18.

47   *Sotheby's had prequalified*   Author interview with David N. Redden, August 3, 2015.

3. 1856: Printed, Sold, and Forgotten

49   *the Post Office Mauritius stamps*   See Helen Morgan, *Blue Mauritius: The Hunt for the World's Most Valuable Stamps* (London: Atlantic Books, 2009).

49   *the Inverted Jenny stamps*   See George Amick, *The Inverted Jenny: Money, Mystery, Mania* (Sidney, Ohio: Amos Press, 1986).

49   *One of the places Columbus missed*   Daniel J. Boorstin, *The Discoverers* (New York: Random House, 1983), 653.

50   *Vespucci in 1499*   Charles B. Parmer, *West Indian Odyssey: The Complete Guide to the Islands of the Caribbean* (New York: Dodge Publishing Company, 1937), 167.

50   *A series of papal bulls*   W. Adolphe Roberts, *Lands of the Inner Sea: The West Indies and Bermuda* (New York: Coward-McCann, 1948), 159; Boorstin, 248.

51   *Guiana "hath more quantity of gold"*   Sir Walter Raleigh, *The Discoverie of the Large, Rich and Bewtiful Empire of Guiana, with a Relation of the Great and Golden Citie of Manoa (which the Spaniards call El Dorado) and the Provinces of Emeria, Arromaia, Amapaia and other Countries, with their rivers adjoining*, https://legacy.fordham.edu/halsall/mod/1595raleigh-guiana.asp.

51   *the Pilgrims weighed pointing the Mayflower*   Joshua R. Hyles, *Guiana and the Shadows of Empire: Colonial and Cultural Negotiations at the Edge of the World* (Lanham, Maryland: Lexington Books, 2013),

31. Some historians credit other early accounts with swaying the Pilgrims who favored going to Guiana. See, for example, Roland Greene Usher, *The Pilgrims and Their History* (New York: Macmillan, 1918), 47.

51 *Back in London after a huge* Paul Halsall, *Modern History Sourcebook—Sir Walter Raleigh (1554–1618): The Discovery of Guiana,* https://legacy.fordham.edu/halsall/mod/1595raleigh-guiana.asp

51 *in what they called Novo Zeelandia* James Rodway, *History of British Guiana, Volume 1* (Georgetown, Demerara: J. Thomson, 1891), 5.

51 *"there were many advantages"* Ibid., 5.

52 *Finally the British* Parmer, *West Indian Odyssey,* 168.

52 *"The museum is somewhat superior"* Roberts, *Lands of the Inner Sea,* 156.

52 *"All first-class passengers"* Evelyn Waugh, *Ninety-Two Days* (New York: Penguin Books, 1954), 20.

53 *He had already "[raced]"* James R. Kincaid, "250 Words Every Fifteen Minutes," *New York Times Book Review,* December 22, 1991, 1.

53 *"I think Saxony"* Anthony Trollope, *An Autobiography of Anthony Trollope* (New York: Dodd, Mead and Company, 1912), 43.

54 *"incarnate gale of wind"* Attributed to Wilkie Collins in Kincaid, *New York Times Book Review,* December 22, 1991, 1.

54 *"There never was a land"* Anthony Trollope, *The West Indies and the Spanish Main* (London: Chapman and Hall, 1859), 169, 170.

54 *"among the mosquitoes!"* Ibid., 181.

55 *"philatelic facts, which are usually dry"* Morgan, *Blue Mauritius: The Hunt for the World's Most Valuable Stamps,* 31–40.

55 *steamships picked up mail* James Rodway, *The Post Office in British Guiana Before 1860,* booklet published in 1890, 7.

56   *"let out the Office"*   The British Guiana: The World's Most Famous
      Stamp (Sotheby's pre-auction catalogue, 2014), 15; Townsend and
      Howe, 188.

57   *"felt exploited by the Portuguese"*   George K. Danns, *Domination
      and Power in Guyana: A Study of the Police in a Third World Context*
      (New Brunswick, N.J.: Transaction Press, 1982), 21.

57   *"Nobody expected any trouble"*   V.O. Chan, "The Riots of 1856 in
      British Guiana," *Caribbean Quarterly*, March 1970, 40.

58   *The little newspaper*   Townsend and Howe, 44.

59   *misspelled as "Patimus"*   The Stamp-Collector's Magazine, March 1,
      1870, 46.

59   *despite tussles*   The British Guiana: The World's Most Famous Stamp
      (Sotheby's pre-auction catalogue, 2014), 16.

59   *Dalton's son took over*   Townsend and Howe, 189.

60   *In a memoir*   Benjamin Penhallow Shillaber, "Experiences During
      Many Years," in *The New England Magazine*, July 1893, 619.

60   *Shillaber liked one of the* Gazette's *owners*   Ibid., 622.

61   *the* Gazette *carried no such column*   The British Guiana: The World's
      Most Famous Stamp (Sotheby's pre-auction catalogue, 2014), 23.

61   *probably ran off sheets of four*   Townsend and Howe, 48.

61   *"Mr. Wight is still alive"*   The Postage Stamps, Envelopes, Wrappers,
      Post Cards and Telegraph Stamps of the British Colonies in the West
      Indies, Together With British Honduras and the Colonies in South
      America (London: Philatelic Society, London, 1891), 39.

4. 1873: Found by a Twelve-Year-Old

63   *"The worst stamp swap"*   Viola Ilma, *Funk & Wagnalls Guide to the
      World of Stamp Collecting* (New York: Thomas Y. Crowell, 1978),
      141.

63   *grew up to be a tax collector*   The Official Gazette of British Guiana, Volume 27 (1908), 223.

63   *"was always referred to"*   Author interview with Carrie Hunter, December 14, 2015.

63   *Andrew Hunter came from a line*   Author interviews with C. Ian C. Wishart, December 10, 2015, and with Carrie Hunter, December 14, 2015.

63   *"a whole lot of old family letters"*   Quoted in Gerardine van Urk, "'World's Rarest Stamp on View," *New York Times,* May 18, 1947, Section 2, 13.

64   *"condition . . . would not be tolerated"*   L.N. and Maurice Williams, *Rare Stamps* (New York: G.P. Putnam's Sons, 1967), 11.

64   *"I was quite certain"*   Quoted in *The (Melbourne) Argus*, July 21, 1934, 7.

64   *The dealer was Alfred Smith*   Bertram Tapscott Knight Smith, *How to Collect Postage Stamps* (London: G. Bell and Sons, 1907), 157. See also *Stamp Collector*, May 25, 1903, 1.

65   *The* Timbre-Poste *would later provide*   W.A. Townsend and F.G. Howe, *The Postage Stamps and Postal History of British Guiana* (London: Royal Philatelic Society London, 1970), 46.

65   *The Persian emperor*   Mauritz Hallgren, *All About Stamps* (New York: Knopf, 1940), 17.

66   *Centuries later Charlemagne*   Daniel B. Schneider, "F.Y.I.: Special Deliverers," *New York Times,* June 3, 2001, Section 14, 2.

66   *kings and bishops*   Carl H. Scheele, *A Short History of the Mail Service* (Washington: Smithsonian Institution Press, 1970), 30; F. George Kay, *Royal Mail: The Story of the Posts in England from the Time of Edward IV to the Present Day* (London: Rockliff, 1951), 4.

66   *fashioned a monopoly*   Hallgren, *All About Stamps*, 23.

67   *A seventeenth-century entrepreneur*   "The Story of the First Postage

Stamp," *Smithsonian*, July 19, 2013, http://www.smithsonianmag
.com/arts-culture/the-story-of-the-first-postage-stamp.

67 *James E. Casey*   Wolfgang Saxon, "James E. Casey Is Dead at 95;
Started United Parcel Service," *New York Times,* June 7, 1983, B8.

67 *"Just a penny"*   Duncan Campbell-Smith, *Masters of the Post: The
Authorized History of the Royal Mail* (London: Penguin UK, 2011),
60.

68 *The credit apparently goes*   F. George Kay, *Royal Mail*, 163.

69 *Mail sent through Dockwra's system*   Ibid., 164.

70 *"unpleasant"*   Laurin Zilliacus, *Mail for the World* (New York:
John Day, 1953), 153.

71 Smithsonian *magazine's website speculated*   "The Story of the
First Postage Stamp," *Smithsonian*, July 19, 2013, http://www
.smithsonianmag.com/arts-culture/the-story-of-the-first-postage
-stamp.

71 *The philatelist David Beech*   Author interview with David Beech,
March 29, 2016.

71 *"Mr. Place, a prominent citizen"*   Zilliacus, *Mail for the World*, 157.

72 *on delivery was "an important incentive"*   Ian Jack, "The Rise and
Fall of a Great British Institution," *The Guardian*, November 22,
2011, https://www.theguardian.com/books/2011/nov/22/masters
-post-duncan-campbell-smith-review.

73 *quoted the poet Samuel Taylor Coleridge*   Samuel Taylor Coleridge,
Letters, Conversations and Recollections of S.T. Coleridge, Volume 2
(London: Edward Moxon, 1836), 114.

74 *complained that "hundreds, if not thousands"*   Quoted in Eleanor C.
Smyth, *Sir Rowland Hill: The Story of a Great Reform—As Told by
His Daughter* (London: T. Fisher Unwin, 1907), 57.

74 *detailed the ciphers*   Ibid., 58.

74 *Franking was available*   Matthew F. Glassman, *Franking Privilege:*

Historical Development and Options for Change (Washington: Congressional Research Service, April 2015), 2. See also Smyth, *Sir Rowland Hill*, 42–43.

75   *complained that "members of the favoured classes"*   Smyth, *Sir Rowland Hill*, 43.

75   *mail "refused, mis-sent or redirected"*   Ibid., 62.

76   *friends in Parliament*   Hallgren, *All About Stamps*, 51.

76   *Too foreign to the habits*   Zilliacus, *Mail for the World*, 161.

77   *As the historian F. George Kay*   Kay, *Royal Mail*, 168.

77   *"The lovely portrait"*   Ibid., 170.

80   *Mackay wrote*   James Mackay, *The Guinness Book of Stamps: Facts and Feats* (Enfield, England: Guinness Superlatives, 1982), 216.

80   *Or perhaps "timbrophily"*   Stephen Satchell and J.F.W. Auld, "Collecting and Investing in Stamps," in Satchell, ed., *Collectible Investments for the High Net Worth Investor* (Oxford: Academic Press, 2009), 215.

81   *Yahoo reported*   Vindu Goel and Joe Drape, "Yahoo Makes a Big Entrance Into Fantasy Sports Betting," *New York Times,* July 8, 2015, B1.

81   *"appeared to be a bad specimen"*   Quoted in Bertram W.H. Poole, "British Guiana 1¢ of 1856," *Mekeel's Weekly*, July 15, 1911.

82   *Vaughan "rose to the top"*   W.A. Townsend and F.G. Howe, *Postage Stamps and Postal History of British Guiana* (London: Royal Philatelic Society London, 1970), 48.

83   *The lack of an apostrophe*   "Postage Stamp Design Errors" (website), http://topicsonstamps.info/errors/britishguiana.htm.

83   *"Devoted philatelists"*   Simon Garfield, *The Error World: An Affair with Stamps* (Boston: Houghton Mifflin Harcourt, 2008), 4.

83   *"Do we collect in order to touch"*   John Bryant, "Stamp and Coin

Collecting," in M. Thomas Inge (ed.), *Handbook of American Popular Culture,* 2nd ed. (New York: Greenwood Press, 1989), 1351.

84   *"Of an evening"*   Inge (ed.), *Handbook of American Popular Culture,* xiii.

84   *Mackay claimed*   Mackay, *Guinness Book of Stamps,* author bio, inside cover.

84   *"It's an obsession"*   Author conversation with Joseph Hackmey at Royal Philatelic Society London, March 12, 2015.

84   *For $1.1 million*   "Most Expensive Newspaper Copy," World Records Academy, http://www.worldrecordacademy.com/collections /most_expensive_newspaper_copy-Romanian_newspaper_sets _world_record_80272.htm.

85   *the dentist who collected*   Michael Kimmelman, "Museums Built on the Passion to Collect . . . Anything," *New York Times,* September 4, 1998, E27.

86   *"Collecting fills a hole in a life"*   Garfield, *The Error World: An Affair with Stamps,* 2.

5. 1878: Glasgow and London

88   *"among private letters"*   Arthur D. Ferguson, "The Rarities and Early Issues of British Guiana. The Romance of Their Discovery and Rise in Value," *British Guiana Philatelic Journal,* December 1921, 4.

89   *A middle-aged London barrister*   *Who Was Who in Philately* (London: Association of British Philatelic Societies Limited), http:// www.abps.org.uk/Home/Who_Was_Who/index.xalter#H.

89   *It was the world's first*   Ibid., http://www.abps.org.uk/Home/Who _Was_Who/index.xalter#S.

89   *a large library*   Kirstyn Leuner, "Francis John Stainforth: A Biographical Sketch," (Boulder, Colorado: CU-Boulder University
Libraries Special Collections, 2014), http://libpress.colorado.edu
/stainforth/2014/12/14/francis-john-stainforth-a-biographical
-sketch/.

89   *plays and poems by women*   Stainforth, Francis John, *Catalogue of
the library of female authors of the Rev. J. Fr. Stainforth*. Collection of
the University of Colorado Boulder, http://ucblibraries.colorado.edu
/specialcollections/collections/wprp/290caption.htm.

89   *Historians of philately*   *Who Was Who in Philately*, http://www
.abps.org.uk/Home/Who_Was_Who/index.xalter#S.

90   *a church asked*   L.N. and Maurice Williams, *Rare Stamps* (New
York: G.P. Putnam's Sons, 1967), 14.

93   *"its ponderous monographs"*   Fred J. Melville, "Edward Loines
Pemberton—A Record of the Philatelic Activities of the Most Bril-
liant of the Pioneer Philatelists," *Philatelic Journal of Great Britain*,
October 1922, 176.

94   *"mastered every minute peculiarity"*   "Edward Loines Pemberton,"
The Philatelic Record, February 1879, 2.

94   *the very first stamp auction*   Melville, *Philatelic Journal of Great
Britain*, 186, 188.

94   *"many others who were his seniors"*   "In Memoriam," *The Philatelic
Record*, February 1879, 2.

94   *His* Journal *promised*   Advertisement in Edward L. Pemberton, *The
Stamp Collector's Handbook* (Dawlish: James R. Grant, and Plymouth:
Stanley Gibbons, 1874).

94   *"Ship with motto"*   Edward L. Pemberton, *The Stamp Collector's
Handbook*, 16.

95   *"it [made] one's mouth water"*   Melville, *Philatelic Journal of Great
Britain,* 179.

95   *"There are collectors"*   Interview with Ted Wilson, January 21, 2016.

96   *He wrote to Sir Edward Denny Bacon*   Quoted in Frederick A. Philbrick, "Further Notes on the Earlier Issues of British Guiana," *Philatelic Record*, July 1889, 138.

97   *Instead, according to the Williamses*   L.N. and Maurice Williams, "British Guiana's 1c Magenta," reprinted by David Feldman SA, 2014.

98   *David Redden maintains*   Author interview with David Redden, March 12, 2015.

6. 1878: The Man in the Yachting Cap

100   *"undoubtedly a love match"*   "A Crown Prince's Bride," *New York Times*, May 31, 1886, 2.

102   *Philippe Arnold de la Renotière von Ferrary*   Helen Morgan, *Blue Mauritius*, 70. The British stamp writers L.N. and Maurice Williams give his name as Philipp la Renotière von Ferrary. L.N. and Maurice Williams, *The Postage Stamp* (New York: Penguin, 1956), 58. But later the Williamses note that at one point, he dropped "von Ferrary" and wanted to be known merely as Philipp la Renotière. *The Postage Stamp*, 63.

102   *He patronized one dealer*   Alvin F. Harlow, *Paper Chase*, 210.

102   *"I would sooner buy"*   Quoted in Charles J. Phillips, "Philipp La Renotière Von Ferrary: One of the Greatest Collectors," *Stamps*, September 1932, 46.

104   *Ferrary was known to cut*   Morgan, *Blue Mauritius*, 72.

104   *"one of the few people"*   L.N. and Maurice Williams, *The Postage Stamp*, 61.

104   *"When a good stamp fell into his collection"*   Harlow, *Paper Chase*, 54.

104   *Ferrary wrote little*   The notable exception is "A Protest," a letter
      to the editor of the *Philatelic Record*, reprinted in *The Stamp News*,
      January 1882, 97.

105   *Ferrary's excuse*   Morgan, *Blue Mauritius*, 80.

105   *the artist Eugène Atget*   "The Austrian Embassy, 57 rue de Va-
      renne," J. Paul Getty Museum, http://www.getty.edu/art/collection
      /objects/172716/eugene-atget-the-austrian-embassy-57-rue-de
      -varenne-french-1905/.

106   *put bundles of cash on nails*   L.N. and Maurice Williams, *The Post-
      age Stamp*, 61.

106   *the stamp-shop clerks knew*   Morgan, *Blue Mauritius*, 80–81.

107   *a syndicated newspaper article*   "Most Valuable Bit of Paper in the
      Whole World—Although Hardly More Than an Inch Square, Its
      Owner Would Not Take $15,000 For It," *Los Angeles Herald*, Octo-
      ber 28, 1906, 7.

109   *If Ferrary was born in 1848*   See, for example, Stanley N. Bierman,
      The World's Greatest Stamp Collectors, 23. But Helen Morgan, in *Blue
      Mauritius*, maintains that he was "probably" born in 1850.

109   *the collected works*   Harlow, *Paper Chase*, 52.

109   *heard Ferrary's parents quarreling*   Stanley N. Bierman, *The World's
      Greatest Stamp Collectors*, 24.

110   *On the same page*   "The Sacrifice of a Duke," *New-York Tribune*,
      December 3, 1893, 15.

111   *The stamp writer Fred J. Melville*   Quoted in Morgan, *Blue Mauri-
      tius,* 80.

111   *"Look sharp, for Gawd's sake!"*   Quoted in L.N. and Maurice Wil-
      liams, *The Postage Stamp*, 58.

111   *Ferrary had taken up stamps*   Barth Healey, "Pastimes: Stamps,"
      New York Times, May 13, 1990, Section 1, 46.

113   *some philatelists tallied and toted*   Harlow, *Paper Chase*, 54.

113   *"a Parisian collection"*   L.N. and Maurice Williams, *The Postage
      Stamp*, 60.

113   *Ferrary played the part*   Stanley N. Bierman, *The World's Greatest
      Stamp Collectors*, 39.

114   *His will said*   Sir John Wilson, *The Royal Philatelic Collection*
      (London: Dropmore Press, 1952), 25.

114   *specifically, to the Reichspost Museum*   "The World's Greatest Rar-
      ity," *Rarities of the World 1970* (New York: Robert A. Siegel Auc-
      tion Galleries, 1970), 23.

115   *The philatelic writer Kent B. Stiles*   Quoted in "British Guiana
      Stamp of 1856 Still the 'World's Rarest,'" *Scott's Monthly Stamp
      Journal*, May 1970, 75.

117   *the Mahés—"father and son"*   Townsend and Howe, *Postage Stamps
      and Postal History of British Guiana*, 48.

118   *Redden's pre-sale catalogue*   *The British Guiana: The World's Most
      Famous Stamp* (Sotheby's pre-auction catalogue, 2014), 45.

7. 1922: The Plutocrat with the Cigar

120   *"was never publicly identified"*   Kent B. Stiles, *Stamps: An Outline of
      Philately* (New York: Harper and Brothers, 1935), 320.

121   *He put his signature*   Author interview with David N. Redden,
      March 12, 2015. Redden and his colleagues at Sotheby's failed to
      turn up any of Hind's cards before the sale of the one-cent magenta
      in 2014.

121   *The story about the second stamp*   "A Second One Cent British Gui-
      ana?" *Stamp and Cover Collectors' Review*, October 1938, 261–63.

123   *So what*   There is no way to know. The magazine's last issue was
      published in 1939, and the editors, August Dietz and August Dietz
      Jr., are long dead; August Dietz's great-grandson told me that the

magazine's files were discarded in the 1960s. August Dietz would have known that Hind liked his cigars. In the same issue, Dietz mentioned that he had visited Hind in Utica and that Hind had presented him with "a Pennsylvania 'stogie' that he tried to have me smoke." Apparently, Dietz was no more of a cigar smoker than the man with the second stamp.

123 *"He had more money than knowledge"* Sir John Wilson, *The Royal Philatelic Collection* (London: Dropmore Press, 1952), 26.

124 *He himself repeated* "Penny Stamps That Are Worth Thousands," *The Queenslander*, February 16, 1938, 40.

124 *"The difficulty in showing"* Wilson, *The Royal Philatelic Collection*, 27.

125 *described him as "headstrong"* Alvin F. Harlow, *Paper Chase*, 141.

125 *"opinionated, cynical and strong-minded"* Stanley N. Bierman, *The World's Greatest Stamp Collectors*, 145.

125 *"The unfortunate side"* Quoted in L.N. Williams, *Encyclopaedia of Rare and Famous Stamps, Volume 2* (Geneva: David Feldman, 1992), 27.

125 *the Ferrary of America* "America's Biggest Stamp Collector," *New York Times*, November 7, 1922, 27.

125 *"[A]s [Brown] had no knowledge"* L.N. and Maurice Williams, *Stamp Collecting* (New York, Penguin, 1956), 76.

126 *Hind glued many of his stamps* George H. Sloane, "Arthur Hind at the Collectors Club," *Collectors Club Philatelist*, 1923, 142.

126 *"we do not think"* "Death of Mr. Arthur Hind," *London Philatelist*, March 1933, 65.

126 *"la pièce de résistance"* Quoted in *Mauritius [auction catalogue]* (Geneva: David Feldman, 1993), 92.

127 *Even A.J. Sefi* A.J. Sefi, "Mr. Arthur Hind," *Philatelic Journal of Great Britain,* March 1933, 46–47.

127 *Sefi—a distant cousin of Michael Sefi*   Author interview with Michael Sefi, March 30, 2016.

129 *"thrifty, hard-headed"*   David H. Beetle, *Along the Oriskany* (Utica, N.Y.: Utica Observer-Dispatch, 1947), 155.

129 *not the Horatio Alger story it appeared to be*   A. J. Sefi, *Philatelic Journal of Great Britain*, 46.

129 *Hind moved to the United States*   Some accounts say that Hind arrived in 1891, though A.J. Sefi gives the date as 1890.

129 *more often a mediator*   Kevin Phillips, *William McKinley* (New York: Times Books-Henry Holt, 2003), 146.

131 *"little town with the big red-light district"*   Harold Faber, "Hudson Casts New Light on Its Red-Light Past," *New York Times*, October 21, 1994, B6.

131 *Clark Mills, New York, "a place"*   Charles J. Phillips, "Arthur Hind—Owner of the World's Highest Priced Stamp," *Stamps*, Vol. 1, No. 8, 1932, 261.

131 *a "virtual ghost town"*   Clifford Morris, *A Brief History of Clark Mills*, www.clintonchamber.org/history.cfm.

132 *Edmund Morris described*   Edmund Morris, *The Rise of Theodore Roosevelt* (New York: Random House, 1979), 240.

132 *that was soon rechristened "Arhipaca"*   Eugene E. Dziedzic and James S. Pula, *New York Mills* (Charleston, S.C.: Arcadia Publishing, 2013), 85; and "Arhipaca Opens to Public Today," *Rome Daily Sentinel*, April 19, 1930, 8.

132 *Harrison had heard*   A.J. Sefi, *Philatelic Journal of Great Britain*, 46.

132 *"Despite his great wealth"*   Stanley N. Bierman, *The World's Greatest Stamp Collectors*, 145.

133 *"didn't want a cripple in his collection"*   Harlow, *Paper Chase*, 141.

133 *echoed that idea*   Wilson, *The Royal Philatelic Collection*, 26.

133 *"repeatedly pointed out"* Stanley N. Bierman, *The World's Greatest Stamp Collectors*, 145.

133 *no more diplomatic* George H. Sloane, "Arthur Hind at the Collectors Club," *Collectors Club Philatelist*, 1923, 142.

135 *Thanksgiving Day* "Ann Leeta M'Mahon Weds Arthur Hind," *Utica Daily Press*, November 26, 1926, 3; "A. Leeta McMahon Becomes Bride of Arthur Hind," *Utica Observer-Dispatch*, November 26, 1926, 32.

135 *an affectionate nickname for the bride* "In the Matter of the Transfer Tax Proceeding in the Estate of Arthur Hind, Deceased," Surrogate's Court, Oneida County, New York, February 2, 1934, 18.

135 *The couple had been living together* Author interview with Richard L. Williams, August 14, 2014.

135 *the daughter of a harness maker* Advertisement for Leonard Gardanier, *Oswego County Gazeteer and Business Directory for 1866–67* (Oswego, New York: *The Daily Commercial Advertiser*, 1866), 99; "Leonard Gardanier," *Utica Herald-Dispatch*, March 28, 1904, 4.

136 *One listed her as an attendant* 1910 United States Census, Orange County, New York, "Middletown State Psychiatric Hospital," digital image.

136 *"She was the girl"* Author interview with Richard L. Williams, August 14, 2014.

136 *a second passport application* Passport application 593885, digital image, http://www.ancestry.com/.

136 *It was the same name she had used* SS *Cartago*, "List of United States Citizens," arriving at New Orleans, March 12, 1915, digital image, http://www.ancestry.com/.

136 *She was Mrs. Hind again* Toyo Kisen Kaisha, "Oath to Inward Passenger List," 1917, digital image, http://www.ancestry.com/.

136 *Hind bought her a strand* "A Good Philatelist, But No Jewel Buyer, Pearl Sale Indicates," *Utica Observer-Dispatch*, August 13, 1947, 3.

137 *She registered as Leeta A. Hind in 1918* SS *Brazos*, "List of United

States Citizens," arriving at San Juan, Puerto Rico, January 20, 1918, digital image, www.ancestry.com/.

137 *the SS Brazos, promoted by its owners*   Advertisement for New York & Porto Rico SS Company, *Boston Evening Transcript*, November 29, 1912, 15, http://www.ancestry.com/.

137 *she boarded the SS Carmania*   SS *Carmania*, "List of United States Citizens," arriving at New York, New York, May 31, 1919, digital image, http://www.ancestry.com/.

137 *Hind worked on his stamps*   *The British Guiana: The World's Most Famous Stamp* (Sotheby's pre-auction catalogue, 2014), 48.

137 *He turned down an offer*   "Stamp Sale Fails; Price Up $100,000," *New York Times*, June 7, 1931, 73.

138 *but he did revise his will*   Last Will and Testament of Arthur Hind, 2.

8. 1940: The Angry Widow, Macy's, and the Other Plutocrat

140 *He raised the price*   "Stamp Sale Fails; Price Up $100,000," *New York Times*, June 7, 1931, 73.

141 *"Arthur Hind was sitting in his study"*   "In the Matter of the Transfer Tax Proceeding in the Estate of Arthur Hind, Deceased," Surrogate's Court, Oneida County, New York, February 2, 1934, 1, and testimony of Ann Hind Scala, 10, 16.

142 *died on March 1*   "Arthur Hind Dies; Noted Philatelist," *New York Times*, March 2, 1933, 17.

143 *"all prominent Utica men"*   Charles J. Phillips, "Arthur Hind's Funeral," *London Philatelist*, March 1933, 66.

143 *"well-known young Utican"*   "Suit Over Hind's Estate Ended; Widow's Marriage to P.C. Scala Announced," *Utica Observer-Dispatch*, May 4, 1934, 20.

144 *disappointing a Pemberton*   "The World's Greatest Rarity," *Rarities*

of the World 1970 (New York: Robert A. Siegel Auction Galleries, 1970), 23.

144   *"had he lived a month longer"*   Kent B. Stiles, "1856 Issue Keeps Price," *New York Times*, August 7, 1938, 140.

145   *another stamp dealer, Ernest G. Jarvis*   "'Rarest Stamp' Put on Market at $37,500," *New York Times*, September 25, 1938, 58.

145   *She had steadily increased*   "$48,000 Insurance Placed on Stamp," *New York Times*, February 15, 1935, 21.

145   *"She has none of the reverence"*   "Woman Owner Not Awed by 'Terribly Homely' Penny Stamp Worth $50,000," *Olean [New York] Times-Herald*, June 6, 1940, 4.

145   *bigger and more "Barnumesque"*   Robert Hendrickson, *The Grand Emporiums* (New York: Stein and Day, 1978), 3.

146   *"That little black spot"*   "Penny Stamp Worth $50,000 to Be Displayed at the Stamp Centennial Exhibition, New York World's Fair," *Elizalde Stamp Journal*, April-May-June 1940, 12.

146   *When she finally sold it*   "Rare Stamp, Worth $50,000, Changes Hands in New York," *Boston Globe,* August 8, 1940, 3; "World's Costliest Stamp, Valued at $50,000, Sold," *New York Times*, August 8, 1940, 22.

146   *only $40,000*   "$40,000 for One Stamp," *New York Times*, August 11, 1940, 116.

146   *she pocketed $45,000*   *Rarities of the World 1970* (New York: Robert A. Siegel Auction Galleries, 1970) 23.

146   *The judge who handled the case*   "Mrs. Ann Hind Scala Granted Divorce," *Utica Daily Press*, January 16, 1946, 6.

147   *Mrs. Hind died*   "Mrs. Hind Found Dead in Her Home," *Utica Daily Press*, June 25, 1945, 2; "Mrs. Ann Hind, Sold Stamp for $50,000," *New York Times*, June 23, 1945, 13.

147   *The judge turned him down*   "Court Denies Scala Plea to Set Aside Divorce," *Utica Daily Press*, August 27, 1946, 5.

147   *Soon after the purchase*   Kent B. Stiles, "World's Rarest Stamp, a $50,000 Item, Comes Out of Hiding to Star on Television," *New York Times*, October 29, 1949, 17.

148   *the new owner recalled*   "Australian Veteran Identified as Seller of $280,000 Stamp," *New York Times*, April 2, 1970, 36.

148   *an Australian who had been*   David Lidman, "British Guiana 1c Owner Identified," *New York Times*, April 12, 1970, 150; also "A Short Account of Celanese Corporation of America," *Plastics Distributor and Fabricator*, March-April 1999, http://www.plasticsmag .com/ta.asp?aid=1801.

149   *"was not a stamp collector."*   David Lidman, "British Guiana 1c Owner Identified," *New York Times*, April 12, 1970, 150.

150   *"after seeing the destruction"*   William E. Kelly, "Former Local Man Sells Rare Stamp for $280,000," *Cumberland [Maryland] Evening Times*, April 2, 1970, 11.

151   *He left Macy's*   "Private Finbar Kenny," *New York Times,* August 2, 1942, 74.

152   *one of three inaugural events*   Christopher Gray, "Streetscapes: The 'Hybrid Pseudo-Modern' on Columbus Circle," *New York Times*, April 26, 1987, Section 8, 14.

152   *"Despair and suspense mounted"*   Stanley N. Bierman, *The World's Greatest Stamp Collectors*, 148.

153   *the first person to plead*   Martin T. Biegelman and Daniel R. Biegelman, *Foreign Corrupt Practices Act Compliance Guidebook* (Hoboken: John Wiley and Sons, 2010), 15.

153   *"a significant number of America's major corporations"*   Quoted in Biegelman and Biegelman, 14.

154   *also designing and printing stamps*   See also Stewart McBride, "The Case of the Airmailed Voter and Other Tales of the Cook Islands," *Christian Science Monitor*, March 4, 1982, 1; "Stamp Firm Stuck in Bribery Case; First Fine Posted Under New Law" (Associated Press), *Toledo [Ohio] Blade*, August 3, 1979, 25; Philip Taubman, "New York Concern Admits Rigging Pacific Vote to Keep Stamp Rights," *New York Times*, August 3, 1979, A10; Mike Koehler, "Postage Stamps, Sir Albert Henry, Flying Voters, and the FCPA," *FCPA Professor* (website), http://fcpaprofessor.com/postage-stamps-sir-albert-henry-flying-voters-and-the-fcpa/.

154   *"somewhat of a Huey Long"*   Stewart McBride, "The Case of the Airmailed Voter and Other Tales of the Cook Islands," *Christian Science Monitor*, March 4, 1982, 1.

156   *a profit of $90,000*   Richard Jewell and Vernon Harbin, *The RKO Story* (New Rochelle, N.Y.: Arlington House, 1982), 156.

156   *Bosley Crowther's review*   Bosley Crowther, "The Screen: The Saint Relaxes," *New York Times*, January 31, 1941, 15.

157   *On January 18*   Author's transcription of DVD re-release of *You Bet Your Life*, episode 50-22 and uncredited liner notes (Los Angeles: Shout! Factory, 2004).

157   *writers scribbling on an overhead projector*   Robert Dwan, *As Long As They're Laughing: Groucho Marx and You Bet Your Life* (Baltimore: Midnight Marquee Press, 2000), 84.

159   *"She did collect stamps"*   Author interview with Virginia Baxter, January 27, 2015.

159   *went on to a long career*   "Alice Backes Citron" (obituary), *Los Angeles Times*, March 27, 2007, http://www.legacy.com/obituaries/latimes/obituary.aspx?page=lifestory&pid=86973891.

9. 1970: The Wilkes-Barre Eight

160   *never went to its owners' hometown*   Author interview with Irwin Weinberg, March 19, 2016.

165   *"The rules are not working"*   Quoted in William L. Silber, *Volcker: The Triumph of Persistence* (New York: Bloomsbury Press, 2013), 74.

166   *the economy slipped*   See, for example, Paul Krugman, "Franklin Delano Obama," *New York Times*, November 10, 2008, A29.

166   *Weinberg got a glimpse*   Author interview with Irwin Weinberg, April 8, 2015; also David Gelernter, *1939: The Lost World of the Fair* (New York: Free Press, 1995).

167   *even little Lorin Maazel*   Allan Kozinn, "Lorin Maazel, an Intense and Enigmatic Conductor, Dies at 84," *New York Times*, July 14, 2014, D10.

170   *"He [was] bullish"*   Viola Ilma, *Funk & Wagnalls Guide to the World of Stamp Collecting* (New York: Thomas Y. Crowell, 1978), 137.

171   *He was so confident*   Weinberg interview, March 19, 2016.

171–72   *"Inflation and devaluation are twin specters"*   Joseph L. Lincoln, "Royalty Under Glass," *Discover* magazine, *The (Philadelphia) Sunday Bulletin*, May 30, 1976, 10.

174   *"Unique, the rarest and most valuable stamp"*   "The World's Greatest Rarity," *Rarities of the World 1970* (New York: Robert A. Siegel Auction Galleries, 1970), 71.

175   *Siegel's wife, Miriam*   Interview with Robert Rose, June 9, 2015.

176   *But it went unmentioned*   *Rarities of the World 1970*, 2–4.

176   *Small's identity was revealed*   David Lidman, "British Guiana 1c Owner Identified," *New York Times*, April 12, 1970, D31.

176   *The Waldorf was where*   "MacArthur Plaque Unveiled at Waldorf Towers, Marks His Residence There for 13 Years to 1964,"

New York Times, January 27, 1969, 16; "James A. Farley, 88, Ran Roosevelt Campaigns," *New York Times*, June 10, 1976, 1; author interview with Matt Zolbe and Meg Towner of the Waldorf, September 19, 2012.

177   *The auction had to be moved*   David Lidman, "British Guiana 1¢ Brings $280,000," *New York Times*, April 5, 1970, 122.

177   *In the crowd were notables*   Tony Hiss, "One Cent," *The New Yorker*, April 4, 1970, 34; author interview with Robert Price, April 23, 2015.

179   *Andrew Levitt had started*   Levitt, Andrew, "The United States 1851 One-Cent Blue," American Stamp Dealers Association, http://americanstampdealer.com/SubMenu%252FOne_Cent _Blue.aspx%253Fid%253D219.

179   *Weinberg looked nervous*   Hiss, *The New Yorker*, 33; author interview with Joseph L. Lincoln, April 30, 2015.

180   *The* New York Times *wrote that the Weills*   Lidman, *New York Times*, April 5, 1970, 122.

180   *"A lot of people, including Mr. Weinberg"*   Hiss, *The New Yorker*, 34; and author interview with Tony Hiss, February 25, 2015.

181   *"A lot of people questioned spending that much"*   Author interview with Ken Martin, April 30, 2015.

181   *A customer "who has a warmth for stamps"*   Lidman, *New York Times*, April 5, 1970, 122.

185   *The story was picked up*   "Irwin Weinberg Got Attached to His $500,000 Treasure; Then He Found He Couldn't Get Loose," *People*, July 10, 1978, 43.

186   *the game show "To Tell the Truth"*   Chris Rosenblum, "Businessman Reflects on Brush with World's Priciest Stamp," *Centre Daily Times* (State College, Pa.), June 21, 2014.

10. 1980: "The Man Showed Up"

187   *Weinberg cruised*   Author interview with Irwin Weinberg, April
       8, 2015.

187   *A stockbroker quoted*   Robert Metz, "Investors Try, Try Again,"
       New York Times, January 8, 1979, 61.

187–88 New York *magazine echoed*   "Better Than Blue Chips: Objects to
       Appreciate," *New York,* February 28, 1979, 80.

188   *Salomon Brothers*   H.J. Maidenberg, "Tangible Assets vs. Finan-
       cial," *New York Times*, July 16, 1979, D5.

188   *When* Stamps *magazine*   Quoted in James E. Lee, "Where Have
       All the Stamp Shops Gone?" http://www.jameslee.com/news4
       .htm.

189   *Weinberg's investors*   Author interviews with Irwin Weinberg,
       April 8, 2015, and March 19, 2016.

190   *"The queen had only twenty cottonreels"*   Author interview with
       Victor Krievins, January 20, 2015.

190   *Du Pont was thrilled*   Author interviews with Taras M. Wochok,
       January 19, 2015, and Robert P. Odenweller, January 17, 2015.

191   *The mansion itself*   Bill Ordine and Ralph Vigoda, *Fatal Match:
       Inside the Mind of Killer Millionaire John du Pont* (New York:
       Avon Books, 1998), 12.

191   *after her death*   Ibid., 120.

192   *As du Pont acknowledged*   Tom Fox, "'Nova Wrestling Coach Du
       Pont Aims at an NCAA Title," *Philadelphia Inquirer*, August 27,
       1986, A13.

192   *Villanova repudiated du Pont*   Mark Bowden and Clea Benson,
       "The Prince of Newtown Square," *Philadelphia Inquirer*, Febru-
       ary 4, 1996, 1.

192 *"a triumph that was essentially bought"* Jere Longman, Pam Belluck, and Jon Nordheimer, "A Life in Pieces: For du Pont Heir, Question Was Control," *New York Times*, February 4, 1996, 1.

192 *He was the model* Mark Bowden and Clea Benson, *Philadelphia Inquirer*, February 4, 1996, 1.

193 *Victor Krievins told me* Author interview with Victor Krievins, January 20, 2015.

193 *He built the Delaware Museum* Bill Hewitt, "A Man Possessed," *People*, February 12, 1996, 45.

194 *he called the "magenta lady."* Author interview with Victor Krievins, January 20, 2015.

194 *Warwick Paterson* Scott Paterson, "Warwick Paterson and the British Guiana 1c Magenta," *Campbell Paterson Newsletter*, 2014, 3.

194 *He provided the local police* Jere Longman, "Desperate Stand in a Dream World," *New York Times*, January 28, 1996, 1.

194 *He gave one a second job* Author interview with Robert P. Odenweller, January 17, 2015.

195 *problems like excessive drinking* Longman, Belluck, and Nordheimer, *New York Times*, February 4, 1996, 1.

195 *Du Pont took a seat* Author interview with Victor Krievins, January 20, 2015.

196 *The bidding on the one-cent magenta* Carey Winfrey, "World's Most Valuable Stamp Auctioned for a Record $850,000," *New York Times*, April 6, 1980, A1.

196 *he sent his son* Author interview with Irwin Weinberg, April 8, 2015.

197 *"more fiefdom than home"* Ordine and Vigoda, *Fatal Match*, 12.

203 *It lay in a safe-deposit box* Author interview with Robert P. Odenweller, January 17, 2015.

205   *Du Pont filed for divorce*   Longman, Belluck, and Nordheimer, *New York Times*, February 4, 1996, 1.

212   *Du Pont's eccentricities worsened*   Ordine and Vigoda, *Fatal Match*, 173.

213   *Jean could not have been his mother*   Ibid., 166.

213   *people were walking behind the walls*   Ibid., 165.

213   *"a Howard Hughes–type figure"*   Ibid., 264.

214   *The man behind the counter*   Author interview with Steve Pendergast, May 7, 2015.

11. 2014: "I Expected to See Magenta, and I Saw Magenta"

218   *"I understand you want"*   Voicemail message to author, May 21, 2015.

219   *The house that Dave Schultz*   Kris Maher, "Du Pont Estate Remade With Luxury Homes," *Wall Street Journal*, January 15, 2015, http://www.wsj.com/articles/dupont-estate-remade-with-luxury-homes-1421342284.

220   *number one customer*   Author interview with Scott R. Trepel, president of Robert A. Siegel Auction Galleries, April 28, 2015.

221   *the mystery owner*   "A Coin So Rare It Shouldn't Exist Is Out of the Vault," *New York Times*, August 13, 2013, A14.

223   *"It took me back"*   Author interview with Weitzman, May 22, 2015.

225   *an operatically complicated plot*   Summary here is based on Joseph Cowles, "The Fabulous One-Cent Magenta," http://www.thegoodartist.com/cbfc05.pdf.

227   *serial number of the*   Author interview with Ted Wilson, January 21, 2016

227   *"I was told"*   Author interview with Allen R. Kane, May 27, 2015.

231   *"We can capture a giraffe"*   Quoted in Grace Judd Banker, "Collection of Books of Stamps Is on Display," *Berkeley Daily Gazette*, March 29, 1937, 12.

231   *"[d]uring the philatelic period"*   William Styron, *The Suicide Run* (New York: Random House, 2009), 190.

232   *"came to think of himself as cosmopolitan"*   Jonathan Alter, *The Defining Moment: FDR's Hundred Days and the Triumph of Hope* (New York: Simon and Schuster, 2006), 23.

233   *the Subway Stamp Shop hauled away*   "About Our Company" on Subway Stamp Shop's website, http://www.subwaystamp.com /Aboutus.asp.

234   *"The ranks of hardcore collectors"*   Daniel Akst, "Selling a One-Cent Stamp for Millions of Dollars," *The New Yorker* (online), April 21, 2014, http://www.newyorker.com/business/currency /selling-a-one-cent-stamp-for-millions-of-dollars.

235   *"are like holy relics"*   Philipp Blom, "Collections Are Objects of Desire," *New York Times* (online), December 30, 2011, http://www .nytimes.com/roomfordebate/2011/12/29/why-we-collect-stuff /collections-are-objects-of-desire.

237   *He probably also guessed*   See, for example, "Marilyn Monroe Marries Joe DiMaggio," http://www.history.com/this-day-in-history /marilyn-monroe-marries-joe-dimaggio.

6-22-17